SECRET FILES OF THE DIOGENES CLUB

THE Secret Files OF THE DIOGENES CLUB

BY MISTER KIM NEWMAN

Secret Files of the Diogenes Club
Copyright © 2007 Kim Newman

Cover illustration and design © 2007 Lee Moyer

A MonkeyBrain Books Publication
www.monkeybrainbooks.com

The stories first appeared in the following venues:

"The Gypsies in the Wood"
in *The Fair Folk* (SFBC, 2005)

"Richard Riddle, Boy Detective in 'The Case of the French Spy'"
in *Adventure* (MonkeyBrain, 2005)

"Angel Down, Sussex"
in *Interzone* (1999)

"Clubland Heroes"
in *Retro Pulp Tales* (Subterranean Press, 2006)

"The Big Fish"
in *Interzone* (1993)

"Another Fish Story"
in *Weird Shadows Over Innsmouth* (Fedogan & Bremer, 2005)

"Cold Snap" is original to this collection.

MonkeyBrain Books
11204 Crossland Drive
Austin, TX 78726
info@monkeybrainbooks.com

ISBN: 1-932265-27-9
ISBN: 978-1-932265-27-9

Printed in the United States of America
10 9 8 7 6 5 4 3 2 1

For Pete Atkins

Thanks to the original editors of these stories:
Marvin Kaye, Chris Roberson, David Pringle, Joe R. Lansdale,
and Stephen Jones.

CONTENTS

THE GYPSIES IN THE WOOD

ACT I: THE CHILDREN OF EYE

i: "we take an interest"

"Mr. Charles Beauregard?" asked Dr. Rud, squinting through *pince-nez*.

Charles allowed he was who his *carte de visite* said he was.

"Of... the Diogenes Club?"

"Indeed."

He stood at the front door. The Criftins, the doctor's house, was large but lopsided, several buildings close together, cobbled into one by additions in different stone. At once household, clinic, and dispensary, it was an important place in the parish of Eye, if not a noteworthy landmark in the county of Herefordshire. On the map Charles had studied on the down train, Eye was a double-yolked egg: two communities, Ashton Eye and Moreton Eye, separated by a rise of trees called Hill Wood and an open space of common ground called Fair Field.

It was mid-evening, full dark and freezing. His breath frosted. Snow had settled thick in recent weeks. Under a quarter moon, the countryside was dingy white, with black scabs where the fall was melted or cleared away.

Charles leaned forward a little, slipping his face into light-spill to give the doctor a good, reassuring look at him.

Rud, unused to answering his own front door, was grumpily pitching in during the crisis. After another token glance at Charles's card, the doctor threw up his hands and stood aside.

A Royal Welsh Fusilier lounged in the hallway, giving cheek to a tweeny. The maid, who carried a heavy basin, tolerated none of his malarkey. She barged past the guard, opening the parlour door with a practiced hip-shove, and slipped inside with an equally practiced flounce, agitating the bustle-like bow of her apron-ties.

Charles stepped over the threshold.

The guard clattered upright, rifle to shoulder. Stomach in, shoulders out, eyes front, chin up. The tweeny, returning from the parlour, smirked at his tin soldier pose. The lad blushed violet. Realising Charles wore no uniform, he relaxed into an attitude of merely casual vigilance.

"I assume you are another wave of this *invasion*?" stated the doctor.

"Someone called out the army," said Charles. "Through channels, the army called out us. Which means you get me, I'm afraid."

Rud was stout and bald, hair pomaded into a laurel-curl fringe. Five

1

cultivated strands plastered across his pate, a sixth hanging awry—like a bell-pull attached to his brain. Tonight, the doctor received visitors without ceremony, collarless, in shirtsleeves and waistcoat. He ought to be accustomed to intrusions at all hours. A country practice never closed. Charles gathered that the last few days had been more than ordinarily trying.

"I did not expect a curfew, sir. We're good, honest Englishmen in Eye. And Welshmen too. Not some rebellious settlement in the Hindu Kush. Not an enemy position, to be taken, occupied and looted!"

The guard's blush was still vivid. The tweeny put her hands on her broad hips and laughed.

"Your 'natives' seem to put up a sterling defence."

"Major Chilcot has set up inspection points, prohibited entry to Hill Wood, closed the Small Man..."

"I imagine it's for your protection. Though I'll see what I can do. If anything is liable to lead to mutiny, it's shutting the pub."

"You are correct in that assumption, sir. Correct."

Charles assessed Rud as quick to bristle. He was used to being listened to. Hereabouts, he was a force with which to be reckoned. Troubles, medical and otherwise, were brought to him. If Eye was a fiefdom, the Criftins was its castle and Dr. Rud—not the vicar, Justice of the Peace or other local worthy—its Lord. The doctor didn't care to be outranked by outsiders. It was painful for him to admit that some troubles fell beyond his experience.

It would be too easy to take against the man. Charles would never entirely trust a doctor.

The bite-mark in his forearm twinged.

Pamela came to mind. His wife. His *late* wife.

She would have cautioned him against unthinking prejudice. He conceded that Rud could hardly be expected to cope. His usual run was births and deaths, boils and fevers, writing prescriptions and filling in certificates.

None of that would help now.

This sort of affair rang bells in distant places. Disturbed the web of the great spider. Prompted the deployment of someone like Mr. Charles Beauregard.

A long-case clock ticked off each second. The steady passage of time was a given, like drips of subterranean water forming a stalactite. Time was perhaps subjectively slower here than in the bustle of London—but as inevitable, unvarying, inexorable.

This business made the clock a liar. Rud did not care to think that. If time could play tricks, what *could* one trust?

The doctor escorted Charles along the hallway. Gas lights burned in glass roses, whistling slightly. Bowls of dried petals provided sweet scent to cover medical odours.

At the parlour door, the soldier renewed his effort to simulate attention. Rud showed the man Charles's card. The fusilier saluted.

"Not strictly necessary," said Charles.

"Better safe than sorry, sah!"

Rud tapped the card, turning so that he barred the door, looking up at Charles with frayed determination.

"By the bye, how precisely does membership of this institution, this *club*—with which I am unfamiliar—give you the right to interview my patient?"

"We take an interest. In matters like these."

Rud, who had probably thought his capacity for astonishment exhausted, at once caught the implication.

"Surely this case is singular? Unique?"

Charles said nothing to contradict him.

"This has happened before? How often?"

"I'm afraid I really can't say."

Rud was fully aghast. "Seldom? Once in a blue moon? Every second Thursday?"

"I really can't say."

The doctor threw up his hands. "Fine," he said, "quiz the poor lad. I've no explanation for him. Maybe you'll be able to shed light. It'll be a relief to pass on the case to someone in authority."

"Strictly, the Diogenes Club has status rather than authority."

This was too much for Rud to take aboard. Even the mandarins of the Ruling Cabal could not satisfactorily define the standing of the Diogenes Club. Outwardly, the premises in Pall Mall housed elderly, crotchety misanthropes dedicated only to being left in peace. There were, however, other layers: sections of the club busied behind locked steel doors, *taking an interest*. Gentlemanly agreements struck in Whitehall invested the Diogenes Club as an unostentatious instrument of Her Majesty's government. More often than the public knew, matters arose beyond the purview of the police, the diplomatic service, or the armed forces. Matters few institutions could afford to acknowledge even as possibilities. *Some*body had to take responsibility, even if only a job lot of semiofficial amateurs.

"Come in, come in," said Rud, opening the parlour door. "Mrs. Zeals has been feeding the patient broth."

The Criftins was low-ceilinged, with heavy beams. Charles doffed his hat to pass under the lintel.

From this moment, the business was *his* responsibility.

ii: "my mother said I never should"

The parlour had fallen into gloom. Dr. Rud turned the gas-key, bringing up light as if the play were about to begin. *Act 1, Scene 1: The parlour of the Criftins. Huddled in an armchair by the fire is…*

"Davey Harvill?"

The patient squirmed at the sound of Charles's voice, pulling up and hugging his knees, hiding his lower face. Charles put his hat on an occasional table and took off his heavy ulster, folding it over a high-backed chair.

The patient's eyes skittered, huge-pupilled.

"This gentleman is…"

Charles waved his fingers, shutting off the doctor's preamble. He did not want to present an alarming, mysterious figure.

The patient's trousers stretched tight around thin shanks, ripped in many places, cuffs high on the calf like knee-britches. He was shirtless and shoeless, a muffler wrapped around bird-thin shoulders. His calloused feet rested in a basin of dirtied water. His toenails were like thorns. Many old sores and scars made scarlet lakes and rivers on the map of his very white skin. His thatch of hair was starched with clay into the semblance of an oversized magistrate's wig; his beard matted into pelt-like chest-hair, threaded through with twigs; his moustaches hung in twisted braids, strung with bead-like pebbles.

Glimpsing himself in a glass, Rud smoothed his own stray hair-strand across his scalp.

Charles pulled a footstool close to the basin.

The patient looked like Robinson Crusoe after years on the island. Except Crusoe would have been tanned. This fellow's pallor suggested a prisoner freed from an *oubliette*. Wherever he had been marooned was away from the sun, under the earth.

An animal smell was about him.

Charles sat on the stool and took the patient's thin hands, lifting them from his knees. His fingernails were long and jagged.

"My name is Charles. May I talk with you?"

The eyes fixed on him, sharp and bright. A tiny flesh-bulb, like a drop of fresh blood, clung to the corner of the right eyelid.

"Talk, mister?"

The voice was thin and high. He spoke as if English were unfamiliar, and his native tongue lacked important consonants.

"Yes, just talk."

"Frightened, mister. Been so long."

The face was seamed. Charles would have estimated the patient's age at around his own, thirty-five.

Last week, Davey Harvill had celebrated his ninth birthday.

The patient had a child's eyes, frightened but innocent. He closed them, shutting out the world, and shrank into the chair. His nails pressed into the meat of Charles's hands.

Charles let go and stood.

The patient—Davey, he had to be called—wound a corner of the muffler in his fingers, screwing it up close to his mouth. Tears followed runnels in his cheeks.

Mrs. Zeals tried to comfort him, with coos and more broth.

"Rest," said Charles. "You're safe now. Talking can wait."

Red crescents were pressed into the heels of Charles's hands, already fading. Davey was not weak.

The patient's eyes flicked open, glittering in firelight. There was a cunning in them, now. Childlike, but dangerous.

Davey gripped Charles's arm, making him wince.

"My mother said, I never should... play with *the gypsies in the wood...* if I did, she would say, '*naughty girl to disobey!*'"

Davey let him go.

The rhyme came in a lower voice, more assured, almost mocking. Not a grown-up voice, though. A feathery chill brushed Charles's spine. It was not a boy's rhyme, but something a girl would sing. Davey smiled a secret smile, then swallowed it. He was as he had been, frightened rather than frightening.

Charles patted his shoulder.

"Has he an appetite?" he asked the housekeeper.

"Yes, sir."

"Keep feeding him."

Mrs. Zeals nodded. She was part-nurse, probably midwife too. The sort of woman never missed until she was needed, but who then meant life or death. If a Mrs. Zeals had been in the Hill Country, Charles might still be a husband and father. She radiated good sense, though this case tested the limitations of good sense as a strategy for coping.

"We shall talk again later, Davey. When you're rested."

Davey nodded, as much to himself as Charles.

"Dr. Rud, do you have a study? I should like to review the facts."

The doctor had hung back by the door, well out of reach.

"You're in charge, Mrs. Zeals," he said, stepping backwards out of the room, eyes on the patient. "Mr. Beauregard and I have matters of import to discuss. Have Jane bring up tea, a light supper, and a bottle of port."

"Yes, doctor."

Rud shot a look at the soldier. He disapproved of the invasion, but at present felt safer with an armed guard in his home.

"It's this way," he told Charles, indicating with his hands, still watching the patient. "Up the back stairs."

Charles bowed to Mrs. Zeals, smiled again at Davey, and followed the doctor.

"Extraordinary thing, wouldn't you say?" Rud gabbled.

"Certainly," Charles agreed.

"Of course, he can't be who he says he is. There's some *trick* to this."

iii: "pebble in a pond"

Rud's consulting room was on two levels, a step running across the floor raising a section like a small stage. One wall was lined with document-boxes. Locked cabinets held phials of salves, balms, cures, and patent potions. A collection of bird and small mammal skeletons, mounted under glass domes, was posed upon items—rocks, branches, green cloth representing grass—suggestive of natural habitat.

On the raised area was a desk of many drawers and recesses. Above this, a studio photograph of Dr. and Mrs. Oliver Rud was flanked by framed documents, the doctor's diploma and his wife's death certificate. Glancing at this last item, careful not to be seen to do so, Charles noted cause of death was down as *diphth.* and the signature was of another physician. He wondered if it was prominently displayed to caution the doctor against medical hubris, or to forewarn patients that miracles were not always possible.

Where was Pamela's death certificate? India?

Rud sat by the desk, indicating for Charles an adjustable chair in the lower portion of the room, obviously intended for patients. Charles sat down, suppressing a thought that straps could suddenly be fixed over his wrists, binding him at a mad surgeon's mercy. Such things, unfortunately, were within his experience. The doctor rolled up the desk-cover and opened a folder containing scrawled notes.

"Hieroglyphs," he said, showing the sheaf. "But I understand them."

A maid came in with the fare Rud had ordered. Charles took tea, while the doctor poured himself a full measure of port. A plate of precisely cut sandwiches went untouched.

"If you'll start at the beginning."

"I've been through this with Major Chilcot, and…"

Charles raised a finger.

"I know it's tiresome to rehash over and over, but this is a tale you'll retell for some years, no matter how it comes out. It'll be valuable to have its raw, original form before the facts become, as it were, *encrusted* with anecdotal frills."

Rud, vaguely offended, was realist enough to see the point.

"The yarns in circulation at the Small Man are already wild,

Mr. Beauregard. By the end of the month, it'll be full-blown myth. And heaven knows what the newspapers will make of it."

"We can take care of that."

"Can you, indeed? What useful connections to have… at any rate, the facts? Where to begin?"

"Tell me about Davey Harvill."

Rud adjusted his *pince-nez* and delved into the folder.

"An ordinary little boy. The usual childhood ailments and scrapes, none fatal. Father was well set-up for a man of his stripe. Cabinet-maker. Skilled craftsman. Made most of the furniture in this room."

"*Was* well set-up? Past tense."

"Yes, cut his arm open with a chisel and bled out before anything could be done. Two years ago. Undoubtedly an accident. Risk of the trade, I understand. By the time I was summoned, it was too late. Davey and his sisters, Sairey and Maeve, were raised by their mother, Mrs. Harvill. Admirable woman. Her children will have every chance in life. Would have had, rather. Now, it's anyone's guess. Sairey, the eldest child, is married to the local baker, Philip Riddle. She's expecting her first this spring. Maeve… well, Maeve's an unknown quantity. She is—was—two years older than her brother. A quiet, queer little girl. The sort who'd rather play by herself. Davey, or whoever this vagrant might be, says Maeve is still 'in the wood.'"

Charles sipped strong tea.

"Tell me about Davey's birthday."

"Last Wednesday. I saw him early in the morning. I was leaving Mrs. Loll. She's our local hypochondriac. Always dying, secretly fit as a horse. As I stepped out of her cottage, Davey came by, wrapped up warm, whipping a hoop. A new toy, a birthday present. Maeve trailed along behind him. 'If I don't watch him, doctor, he'll get run over by a cart,' she said. They were walking to school, in Moreton."

"Along Dark Lane?"

Rud was surprised. "You know the area?"

"I looked at the map."

"Ah, *maps*," said Rud, touching his nose. "Dark Lane is the road to Moreton *on the map*. But there's a cart-track through Hill Wood, runs up to Fair Field. From there, you can hop over a stile and be in Moreton. Not everything is on the map."

"That's an astute observation."

"Davey was rolling his hoop. There was fresh-fallen snow, but the ruts in Fair Field Track were already cut. I saw him go into the wood, his sister following, and that was it. I had other calls to make. Not something you think about, is it? Every time someone steps out of your sight, it could be the last you see of them."

"Were you the last person to see the children?"

"No. Riddle, Sairey's husband, was coming down the track the other way, with the morning's fresh-bake. He told them he had a present to give Davey later, when it was wrapped—but gave both children buns, warm from the ovens. Then, off they went. Riddle hasn't sold a bun since. In case they're cursed, if you can credit it. As we now know, Davey and Maeve didn't turn up for school."

"Why weren't they missed?"

"They were. Mrs. Grenton, the teacher, assumed the Harvills were playing truant. Giving themselves a birthday treat. Sledging on Fair Field or building a snowman. She told the class that when the miscreants presented themselves, a strapping would be their reward. Feels dreadful about it, poor woman. Blames herself. The Harvills had perfect attendance records. Weren't the truant sort. Mrs. Grenton wants me to prescribe something to make her headaches go away. Like a pebble in a pond, isn't it? The ripples. So many people wet from one splash."

Rud gulped port and refilled the measure. His hand didn't shake, but he gripped the glass-stem as if steadying his fingers.

He whistled, tunelessly. Davey's rhyme.

"*Are* there gypsies in the wood?" asked Charles.

"What? Gypsies? Oh, the rhyme. No. We only see Romanies here at Harvest Festival, when there's a fair on Fair Field. The rhyme is something Maeve sings... used to sing. One of those girls' things, a skipping song. In point of fact, I remember her mother asking her not to chant it during the fair, so as not to offend actual gypsies. I doubt the girl took any notice. The gypsies, neither, come to that. No idea where the song comes from. I doubt if Violet Harvill ever had to warn her children against playing with strangers. This isn't that sort of country."

"I've an idea the gypsies in the rhyme aren't exactly gypsies. The word's there in place of something else. Everywhere has its stories. A ghost, a dragon, a witch's ring...."

Rud thought a moment.

"The local bogey tale is *dwarves*. Kidnapping children to work in mines over the border. Blackfaced dwarves, with teeth filed to sharp points. 'Say your prayers, boyo, or the Tiny Taffs will away with you, into the deep dark earth to dig for dirty black coal.' I've heard that all my life. As you say, everywhere has its stories. Over Leintwardine way, there's a Headless Highwayman."

"All Eye lives in fear of Welsh dwarves?"

"No, even children don't—didn't—pay any attention. It came up again, of course. When Davey and Maeve went missing. There was a stupid scrap at the Small Man. It's why the Major closed the pub. English against Welsh. That's the fault-line that runs through the marches. Good-humoured mostly, but sharp-edged. We're border country, Mr. Beauregard. No one is wholly one thing or the other. Everyone has a grandparent in the other camp. But it's fierce. Come Sunday, you might hear 'love thy neighbour' from the pulpit, but we've three churches within spitting distance, each packed with folk certain the other congregations are marching in step to Hell. The Harvills call themselves English, which is why the children go to school in Moreton. The Ashton school is 'Welsh,' somehow. The school-master is Welsh, definitely."

Charles nodded.

"Of course, all Eye agrees on something now. Welsh soldiers with English officers have shut down the pub. I'm afraid the uniting factor is an assessment of the character and ancestry of Major Chilcot."

Charles considered this intelligence. He had played the Great Game among the squabbling tribes of India and Afghanistan, representing the Queen in a struggle with her Russian cousin to which neither monarch was entirely privy, exploiting and being exploited by local factions who had their own Byzantine causes and conflicts. It was strange to find a Khyber Pass in Herefordshire, a potential flashpoint for an uprising. In border countries the world over, random mischief could escalate near-forgotten enmities into riot and worse.

"When were the children missed in Ashton?"

"About five o'clock. When they didn't come in for their supper. Because it was the lad's birthday, Riddle had baked a special cake. Davey's friends came to call. Alfie Zeals, my housekeeper's son, was there. Even if brother and sister *had* played truant, they'd have been sure to be home. Presents were involved. The company waited hours. Candles burned down on the cake. Mrs. Harvill, understandably, got into a state. Riddle recounted his story of meeting the children on Fair Field Track. Alfie also goes to Moreton School and admitted Davey and Maeve hadn't been there all day. Mrs. Harvill rounded on the boy, who'd kept mum to keep his friend out of trouble. There were harsh words, tears. By then, it was dark. A party of men with lanterns formed. They came to me, in case a doctor was needed. You can imagine what everyone thought."

Charles could.

"Hill Wood isn't trackless wilderness. It's a patch between fields. You can get through it in five minutes at a stroll. Even if you get off Fair Field Track and have to wade through snow. The children couldn't be *lost* there, but mishaps might have befallen. A twisted ankle or a snapped leg, and the other too afraid to leave his or her sibling. The search party went back and forth. As the night wore on, we ventured further, to Fair Field and beyond. We should have waited till morning, when we could see tracks in the snow. By sun-up, the wood was so dotted with boot-prints that any made by the children weren't noticeable. You have to understand, we thought we'd find them at any moment. A night outside in March can be fatal for a child. Or anyone. We run to bone-freezing cold here. Frost forms on your face. Snow gets hard, like a layer of ice. Violet Harvill had to be seen to. Hysteria in a woman of her age can be serious. Some of our party had come directly from the Small Man and were not in the best state. Hamer Dando fell down and tore a tendon, which should put a crimp in his poaching for months. Came the dawn, we were no better off."

"You summoned the police?"

"We got Throttle out of bed. He's been Constable in Eye since Crimea. He lent his whistle to the search. The next day, he was too puffed to continue, so I sent for Sergeant High, from Leominster. He bicycled over, but said children run off all the time, dreaming of the South Seas, and traipse back days later, crying for mama and home cooking. I don't doubt he's right, usually. But High's reassurances sat ill with these circumstances. No boy runs away to sea when he has a birthday party to go to. Then, Davey's new whip was found in the wood, stuck into a snow bank."

"A development?"

"An unhappily suggestive one. The mother began insisting something be done, and I was inclined to support her. But what more *could* be done? We went over the ground again, stone cold sober and in broad daylight. My hands are still frozen from dismantling snowdrifts. Every hollow, every dead tree, every path. We looked. Riddle urged we call out the army. Stories went round that the children had been abducted by foreign agents. More foreign than just Welsh. I had to prescribe laudanum for Violet."

"This was all five days ago?"

Rud checked his notes. "Yes. The weekend, as you can appreciate, was a terrible time. Riddle got his way. Major Chilcot's fusiliers came over from Powys. At first, they just searched again, everywhere we'd looked before. Violet was besieged by neighbours offering to help but with no idea what to do. I doubt a single soul within five miles has had a night's uninterrupted sleep since this began."

Rud's eyes were red-rimmed.

"Then, yesterday morning," said the doctor, "Davey—or whoever he might be—came to his mother's door, and asked for his blessed cake."

Rud slapped his folder on his desk. An end to his story.

"Your patient claims to be Davey Harvill?"

"Gets upset when anyone says he can't be."

"There is evidence."

"Oh yes. Evidence. He's wearing Davey's trousers. If the army hadn't been here, he'd have been hanged for that. No ceremony, just hanged. We're a long way from the assizes."

Charles finished his tea and set down the cup and saucer.

"There's more than that," he said. "Or I wouldn't be here. Out with it, man. Don't be afraid of being laughed at."

"It's hard to credit…"

"I make a speciality of credulousness. Open-minded, we call it."

Gingerly, Rud opened the file again.

"The man downstairs. I would put his age at between thirty-five and forty. Davey is nine years old. *Ergo*, they are not the same person. But, in addition to his own scars, the patient has *Davey's*. A long, jagged mark on his calf. Done hauling over a stile, catching on a rusty nail. I treated the injury last year. The fellow has a perfect match. Davey has a growth under the right eye, like a teardrop. That's there, too."

"These couldn't be new-made."

"The scar, just maybe—though it'd have to be prepared months in advance. The teardrop is a birthmark. Impossible to contrive. It's not a family trait, so this isn't some long-lost Harvill popping up at the worst possible moment."

Upon this development, Chilcot, like all bewildered field commanders, communicated with his superiors, who cast around for some body with special responsibility for changelings.

Which would be the Diogenes Club.

"Where does he claim to have been?"

"Just 'in the wood.'"

"With the gypsies?"

"He sings that rhyme when the mood takes him, usually to end a conversation he's discomfited by. As you said, I don't think gypsies really come into it."

"You've examined him. How's his general health?"

Rud picked up a note written in shiny new ink. "What you'd expect from a tramp. Old wounds, untended but healed. Various infestations— nits, lice, the like. And malnutrition."

"No frostbite?"

Rud shook his head.

"So he's not been sleeping out of doors this past week? In the cold, cold snow?"

Rud was puzzled again. "Maybe he found a barn."

"Maybe."

"There's another… ah, anomaly," ventured the doctor. "I've not told anyone, because it makes no sense. The fellow has good teeth. But he has two missing at the front, and new enamel growing through the gums. Normal for a nine-year-old, losing milk teeth and budding adult choppers. But there is no third dentition. That's beyond freakish."

Rud slipped the paper back into the folder.

"That's Davey Harvill's file, isn't it?"

"Yes, of course… oh, I see. The patient should have a fresh folder. He is not Davey Harvill."

Rud pulled open desk drawers, searching for a folder.

"Follow your first instincts, Dr. Rud. You added notes on this patient to Davey's folder. It seemed so natural that you didn't even consider any other course. Logic dictated you proceed on an assumption you know to be impossible. So, we have reached the limits of logic."

iv: "Silas Gobbo"

In the snug of the Small Man, after breakfast, Charles read the riot act to the army. Though the reason for closing the pub was plain, it did not help Major Chilcot's case that he had billeted himself on the premises and was prone to "requisitioning" from the cellar.

"Purely medicinal," Chilcot claimed. "After a spell wandering around with icicles for fingers, a tot is a damn necessity."

Charles saw his point, but suspected it had been sharpened after a hasty gulp.

"That's reasonable, Major. But it would be politic to pay your way."

"We're here to *help* these ungrateful bounders...."

The landlord glared from behind the bar.

"Just so," said Charles.

The Major muttered but backed down.

The landlord, visibly perked, came over.

"Will the gentleman be requiring more tea?"

"No, thank you," said Charles. "Prepare a bill for myself and the Major. Keep a running tally. You have my word you will not be out of pocket. Tonight, you may reopen."

The landlord beamed.

"Between sunset and ten o'clock," insisted Chilcot.

A line appeared in the landlord's forehead.

"That's fair," said Charles.

The landlord accepted the ruling. For the moment.

The Major was another local bigwig, late in an undistinguished career. This would be the making or breaking of a younger, more ambitious officer.

While he stayed cosy in the Small Man, his men bivouacked on Fair Field under retreat-from-Moscow conditions. They were diamond-quality. Sergeant Beale, an old India hand, had rattled off a precise report of all measures taken. It wasn't through blundering on the part of the fusiliers that Maeve Harvill still hadn't turned up.

Charles left the pub and walked through Ashton Eye. Snow lay thick on roofs and in front gardens. Roads and paths were cleared, chunky drifts stained with orange mud piled at the sides. By day, the occupation was more evident. Soldiers, stamping against the cold, manned a trestle at the bottom of Fair Field Track. Chilcot, probably at Beale's prompt, had established a perimeter around Hill Wood.

At the Criftins, Charles was admitted—by a manservant, this time. He joined a small company in the hallway. A fresh fusilier stood guard at the parlour. Dr. Rud introduced Charles, vaguely as "from London," to a young couple, the woman noticeably with child, and a lady of middle years, obviously in distress.

"Philip and Sairey Riddle, and Mrs. Harvill... Violet."

He said his good mornings and shook hands.

"We've asked you to here to put the man purporting to be Davey to the test," Charles explained. "Some things are shared only among family members. Not great confidences, but trivial matters. Intelligence no one outside a home could be expected to have. Remarks made by someone to someone else when they were alone together. An impostor won't know that, no matter how carefully he prepared the fraud."

Mrs. Harvill sniffled into a kerchief. Her daughter held her shoulders.

"He is still in the parlour?" Charles asked Rud.

"Spent the night there. I've got him into a dressing gown. He's had breakfast. I had my man shave him, and make a start on his hair."

The doctor put his hand to the door.

"It is best if we hold back," said Charles. "Allow the family to meet without outsiders present."

Rud frowned.

"We'll be here, a moment away, if needs arise."

The doctor acquiesced and held the door open.

"Mam," piped a voice from inside. Charles saw Davey, in his chair, forearms and shins protruding from a dressing gown a size too small for him. Without the beard, he looked younger.

Mrs. Harvill froze and pulled back, shifting out of Davey's eyeline.

"Mam?" Almost a whine, close to tears.

Mrs. Harvill was white, hand tightly gripping her daughter's, eyes screwed shut. Her terror reminded Charles of Davey's, last night, when he felt threatened. Sairey hugged her mother, but detached herself.

"You stay here, Mam. Me and Phil'll talk with the lad. The gentlemen will look after you."

Sairey passed her mother on to Rud.

Mrs. Harvill embraced the practitioner, discomfiting him, pressing her face to his shoulder. She sobbed, silently.

Sairey, slow and graceful in her enlarged state, took her husband's arm and stepped into the parlour. Davey started out of his seat, a broad smile showing his impossible teeth-buds.

"Sairey, Phil..."

Charles closed the door.

Rud sat Mrs. Harvill on a chair and went upstairs to fetch a something to calm her. The woman composed herself. She looked at Charles, paying him attention for the first time.

"Who are you?" she asked, bluntly.

"Charles Beauregard."

"Oliver said that. I mean what are you?"

"I'm here to help."

"Where are my children? Are they safe?"

"That's what we are trying to determine, Mrs. Harvill."

The answer didn't satisfy. She looked away, ignoring him. In her pettishness, she was like Davey. Charles even thought he heard her crooning "My mother said…" under her breath. She had found a fetish object, a length of rope with a handle. She bound her hand until the fingers were bloodless, then unwound the rope and watched pink seep back.

Rud returned and gave Mrs. Harvill a glass of water into which he measured three drops from a blue bottle. She swallowed it with a grimace and he rewarded her with a sugar-lump. If her son *had* been transformed into an adult, this business had turned her—in some sense—into a child.

A muffle of conversation could be heard through the door. The temptation to eavesdrop was a fish-hook in the mind. Charles saw that the doctor felt the tug even more keenly. Only the soldier was impassive, bored with this duty but grateful to be inside in the warm.

"What *can* be keeping them?" said Mrs. Harvill.

She fiddled again with her fetish, separating the rope into strands as if undoing a child's braid. The rope was Davey's new whip, which had been found in Hill Wood.

Charles could only imagine how Violet Harvill felt.

Pamela had died, along with their newborn son, after a botched delivery. He had blamed an incompetent doctor, then malign providence, and finally himself. By accepting the commission in the Hills, he had removed his family from modern medicine. A hot, hollow grief had scooped him out. He had come to accept that he would never be the man he was before, but knew Pamela would have been fiercely disappointed if he used the loss as an excuse to surrender. She had burst into his life to challenge everything he believed. Their marriage had been a wonderful, continuous explosion. In the last hours, clinging to him—biting deep into his forearm to staunch her own screams—and knowing she would die, Pamela had talked a cascade, soothing and hectoring, loving and reprimanding, advising and ordering. In London fog, he had lost the memory for a while. An engagement to Pamela's cousin, Penelope Churchward, had been his first effort at re-forming a private world, and its embarrassing termination the spur to think again on what his wife had tried to tell him. As he found himself deeper in the affairs of the Diogenes Club, Pamela's voice came back. Every day, he would remember something of hers, something she had said or done. Sometimes, a twinge in his arm would be enough, a reminder that he had to live up to her.

Looking at Mrs. Harvill, he recalled the other loss, eclipsed by Pamela's long, bloody dying. His son, Richard Charles, twelve years dead, had lived less than an hour and opened his eyes only in death, face washed clean by the *ayah*. If he had been a girl, she would have been Pandora Sophie. Charles and Pamela had got used to calling the child "Dickie or Dora." As Pamela wished, he had served mother and child in the Indian manner, cremating them together. Most of the ashes were scattered in India, which she had loved in a way he admired but never shared. Some he had brought back to England, to placate Pamela's family. An urn rested in the vault in Kingstead Cemetery, a proper place of interment for a proper woman who would have been disowned had she spent more time at home expressing her opinions.

But what of the boy?

Losing a child is the worst thing in the world. Charles knew that, but didn't *feel* it. His son, though born, was still a part of Pamela, one loss coiled up within the other. If he ached for Dickie or Dora, it was only in the sense he sometimes felt for the other children Pamela and he would have had, the names they might have taken. The Churchwards ran to Ps and there had yet to be a Persephone, Paulus, Patricia, or Prosper.

Now he thought of the boy.

It was in him, he knew, wrapped up tight. The cold dead spot. The rage and panic. The ruthlessness.

Violet Harvill would do *anything*.

She seemed to snap out of her spell, and tied Davey's whip around her wrist, loose like a bracelet. She stood, determined.

Rud was at the parlour door.

"If you feel you're up to this, Violet…"

She said nothing but he opened the door. Sairey was laughing at something Davey had just said. The lad was smiling, an entirely different person.

"Mam," he said, seeing Mrs. Harvill.

Charles *knew* disaster was upon them. He was out of his chair and across the hall, reaching for Mrs. Harvill. She was too swift for him, sensing his grasp and ducking under it. A creak at the back of her throat grew into a keening, birdlike cry. She flew into the parlour, fingers like talons.

Her nails raked across Davey's face, carving red runnels. She got a grip on his throat.

"What've you done with them?" she demanded.

A torrent of barrack abuse poured from her mouth, words Charles would once have sworn a woman could not even know—though, at the last, Pamela had used them too. Violet Harvill's face was a mask of hate.

"What've you *done*?"

Sairey tried to shift from her chair, forgetting for a moment her unaccustomed shape. With a yelp, she sat back down, holding her belly.

Riddle and Rud seized Mrs. Harvill and pulled her away. Charles stepped in and prised the woman's fingers from Davey's throat, one by one. She continued to screech and swear.

"Get her out of the room," Charles told the doctor. "Please."

There was a struggle, but it was done.

Davey was back in his huddle, knees up against his face, eyes liquid, sing-songing.

"Naughty girl to disobey... dis-o-*bey*! Naughty girl..."

Sairey, careful now, hugged him, pressing his head to her full breast. He rocked back and forth.

Charles's collar had come undone and his cravat was loose.

He was responsible for this catastrophe.

"He'm Davey, mister," said Sairey, softly. She didn't notice she was weeping. "No doubt 'bout it. We talked 'bout what you said. Family things. When I were little, Dad do made up stories for I, stories 'bout Silas Gobbo, a little wood-carver who lives in a hollow tree in our garden and makes furniture for birds. Dad'd make tiny tables and chairs from offcuts, put 'em in the tree and take I out to the garden to show off Silas's new work. Dad told the tales over, to Davey and Maeve. Loved making little toys, did Dad. No one but Davey could've known 'bout Silas Gobbo. Not 'bout the tiny tables and chairs. Even if someone else heard the stories, they couldn't *love* Silas. Davey and Maeve do. With Dad gone, loving Silas is like loving him, remembering. Maeve used to say she wanted to marry Silas when she grew up, and be a princess."

"So you're convinced?"

"Everythin' else, from last week and from years ago, the boy still has in 'en. Mam'll never accept it. I don't know how I can credit it, but it's him."

She held her brother close. Even shaved, he seemed to be twice her age.

Charles fixed his collar.

"What does he say about Maeve?"

"She'm with Silas Gobbo. He'm moved from our tree into Hill Wood. Davey says Maeve be a princess now."

v: "filthy afternoon"

It was a dreary, depressing day. Clouds boiled over Hill Wood, threatening another snowfall. The first flakes were in circulation, bestowing tiny stinging kisses.

Charles walked down Dark Lane, towards Fair Field Track. A thin fire burned in a brazier, flames whipped by harsh, contradictory winds. The fusiliers on guard were wrapped in layers of coat and cloak. The youth who had tried to make time with Rud's tweeny was still red-cheeked, but now through the beginnings of frostbite.

Sergeant Beale, elaborately moustached and with eyebrows to match, did not feel the cold. If ordered to ship out, Beale would be equally up for an expedition through Arctic tundra or a trail across Sahara sands. Men like Major Chilcot only thought they ran the Empire; men like Beale actually did.

"Filthy afternoon, sir," commented the Sergeant.

"Looks like snow."

"Looks and feels like snow, sir. Is snow."

"Yes."

"Not good, snow. Not for the little girl."

"No."

Charles understood. If this Christmas card sprinkle turned into blizzard, any search would be off. Hope would be lost. The vanishing of Maeve Harvill would be accepted. Chilcot would pack up his soldiers and return to barracks. Charles would be recalled, to make an inconclusive report. The Small Man could open all hours of the night.

An April thaw might disclose a small, frozen corpse. Or, under the circumstances, not.

Charles looked over the trestle and into the trees.

The men of Eye and the fusiliers had both been through Hill Wood. Now, Charles—knowing he had to make sure—would have to make a third search. Of course, he wasn't just looking for the girl.

"I'll just step into the wood and have a look about, Sergeant."

"Very good, sir. We'll hold the fort."

The guard lifted the trestle so Charles could pass.

He tried to act as if he was just out for a stroll on a bracing day, but could not pull it off. Pamela nagged: It was not just a puzzle; wounded people surrounded the mystery; they deserved more than abstract thought.

Footprints were everywhere, a heavy trample marking out Fair Field Track, scattering off in dispersal patterns to all sides. Barely a square foot of virgin white remained. The black branches of some trees were iced with snow, but most were shaken clean.

Charles could recognise fifteen different types of snake native to the

Indian subcontinent, distinguishing deadly from harmless. He knew the safest covert routes into and out of the Old Jago, the worst rookery in London. He understood distinctions between spectre, apparition, phantasm, and revenant—knowledge the more remarkable for being gained firsthand rather than through dusty pedantry. But, aside from oak and elm, he could identify none of the common trees of the English countryside. Explorations of extraordinary fields had left him little time for ordinary ones.

He was missing something.

His city boots, heavily soled for cobbles, were thin and flexible. Cold seeped in at the lace-holes and seams. He couldn't feel his toes.

It was a small wood. No sooner was he out of sight of Beale than the trees thinned and he saw the khaki tents pitched on Fair Field. Davey and Maeve had been *detained* here, somehow. Everyone was convinced. Could the children have slipped out unnoticed, into Fair Field and over the stile or through a gate, disappearing into regions yet to be searched? If so, somebody should have seen them. No one had come forward.

Could they have been stolen away by passing gypsies?

In Eye, gypsies or any other strangers would be noticed. So, suspicion must range closer to home. Accusations had begun to run around. Every community had its odd ones, easy to accuse of unthinkable crimes. P.C. Throttle still said it was the Dandos, a large and unruly local clan. Accusing the Dandos had solved every other mystery in Ashton and Moreton in the last thirty years, and Throttle saw no reason to change tactics now. The fact of Davey's return had called off the witch-hunt. Even those who didn't believe Davey was who he claimed assumed he was at the bottom of the bad business.

If Davey was Davey, what had happened?

Charles went over the ground again, off the track this time, zigzagging across the small patch. He found objects trampled into muddy snow, which turned out to be broken pipes, a single man-sized glove, candle-stubs. As much rubbish was tossed here as in a London gutter. The snowfall was thickening.

Glancing up, he saw something.

Previous searches had concentrated on the ground. If Maeve had flown away, perhaps Charles *should* direct his attention upwards.

Snowflakes perished on his upturned face.

He stood before a twisted oak. A tree he could identify, even when not in leaf. An object ringed from a branch, just out of his reach. He reached up and brushed it with his fingers.

A wooden band, about eighteen inches in diameter, was loose about the branch, as if tossed onto a hook in a fairground shy. He found footholds in the trunk and climbed a yard above the ground.

He got close enough to the band to see initials burned into its inner side. *D.H.* Davey's birthday hoop.

Charles held the branch with gloved hands and let go his knee-grip on the trunk. He swung out and the branch lowered, pulled by his weight. His feet lightly touched ground, the branch bent like a bow. With one hand, he nudged the hoop, trying to work it free. The branch forked and the hoop stuck.

That was a puzzle.

The obvious trick would be to break the hoop and fix it again, around the branch. But there was no break, no fix. In which case, the toy must have been hung on the tree when it was younger, and become trapped by natural growth.

The oak was older than Davey Harvill, by many human lifetimes. It was full-grown when Napoleon was a boy. The hoop had not been hung last week, but must have been here since the Wars of the Roses.

He let go of the branch. It sprang back into place, jouncing the hoop. Snow dislodged from higher up.

The tree creaked, waving branches like a live thing.

Charles was chilled with more than cold.

About twenty feet from the ground, packed snow parted and fell away, revealing a black face. A pattern of knot-holes, rather, shaped into a face.

We see faces in everything. It is the order we attempt to put on the world—on clouds, stains on the wallpaper, eroded cliffs. Eyes, a nose, mouth. Expressions malign or benevolent.

This face seemed, to Charles, puckish.

"Good afternoon to you, Mr. Silas Gobbo," he said, touching his hat-brim.

"Who, pray, is Silas Gobbo?"

Charles turned, heart caught by the sudden, small voice.

A little girl stood among the drifts, braids escaping from a blue cap, coat neatly done up to her muffler.

His first thought was that this was Maeve!

It struck him that he wouldn't recognise her if he saw her. He had seen no picture. There were other little girls in Eye.

"Are you looking for Maeve Harvill?" he asked. "Is she your friend?"

The little girl smiled, solemnly.

"I am Maeve," she said. "I'm a princess."

He picked her up and held her as if she were his own. Inside, he melted at this miracle. He was light-headed with an instant, fast-burning elation.

"This is not how princesses should be treated, sir."

He was holding her too tight. He relaxed into a fond hug and looked down at the fresh footprints where she had been standing. Two only, as if she was set down from above, on this spot. He looked up and saw a bramble-tangle of black branches against dirty sky.

He cast around for the face he had imagined, but couldn't find it again.

Maeve's Dad would have said Silas Gobbo had rescued Maeve, returned her to her family.

It was the happy ending Charles wanted. He ran through his joy, and felt the chill again, the cold chill and the bone chill. He shifted the little girl, a delicate-boned miniature woman, and looked into her perfect, polite face.

"Princess, have you brothers and sisters?"

"David and Sarah."

"Parents? Mam and Dad."

"Father is dead. My mother is Mrs. Violet Harvill. You would do me a great service if you were to take me home. I am a tired princess."

The little bundle was warm in his arms. She kissed his cheek and snuggled close against his shoulder.

"I might sleep as you carry me."

"That's all right," he told her.

He trudged along Fair Field Track. When the guards saw him, they raised a shout.

"'E's gone and done it!"

Charles tried a modest smile. The shout was taken up, spread around. Soon, they became hurrahs.

vi: "something about the little girl"

Dr. Rud's parlour was filled with merry people, as if five Christmases had come along together and fetched up in a happy, laughing pile.

Mrs. Harvill clung to her princess, who had momentarily stopped ordering everyone as if they were servants. Philip and Sairey, stunned and overjoyed, pinched each other often, expecting to wake up. Sairey had to sit but couldn't keep in one place. She kept springing up to talk with another well-wisher, then remembering the strain on her ankles. Philip had made another cake, with Maeve's name spelled out in currants.

Rud and Major Chilcot drank port together, laughing, swapping border war stories.

People Charles had not met were present, free with hearty thanks for the hero from London.

"We combed Hill Wood and did all we could," said the Reverend Mr. Weddle, Vicar of Eye. "Too familiar, you see, with the terry-toree. Could not see the wood for the trees, though acts of prayer wore the trews from our knees. Took an outsider's eye in Ashton Eye, to endeavour to save the Princess Maeve. Hmm, mind if I set that down?"

Weddle had mentioned he was also a poet.

P.C. Throttle, of the long white beard and antique uniform, kept a close eye on the limping, scowling Hamer Dando—lest thieving fingers stray too close to the silverware. Hamer's face was stamped on half a dozen other locals of various ages and sexes, but Throttle was marking them all.

Charles's hand was shaken, again, by a huge-knuckled, blue-chinned man he understood to be the Ashton schoolmaster, Owain Gryfudd.

"Maeve's coming to the Welsh school now," he said, in dour triumph. "No more traipsing over the stile to that Episcopalian booby in Moreton. We shall see a great improvement."

Charles gathered Gryfudd captained an all-conquering rugby team, the Head-Hunters. They blacked their faces with coal before going onto the pitch. The teacher still had war paint around his collar and under his hairline, from frequent massacres of the English.

Cake was pressed upon Charles. Gryfudd clapped his back and roared off, bearing down on a frail old lady—Mrs. Grenton, of Moreton Eye school—as if charging for a match-winning try.

Whenever Mrs. Harvill saw Charles, she wept and—if Maeve wasn't in her arms—flung an embrace about him. She was giddy with joy and relief, and had been so for a full day.

Her princess was home.

As Sairey had said, she would never accept Davey as Davey. But Maeve's return ended the matter.

That, among other things, kept Charles from entering into the spirit of this celebration.

In this room, he sensed an overwhelming desire to put Davey and the mystery out of mind. Davey was upstairs, shut away from the celebration.

All's well that ends well.

But Charles knew nothing had ended. And nothing was well.

He could do no more. In all probability, his report to the Ruling Cabal would be tied with pale green ribbon and filed away forever.

He left the parlour. In the hallway, soldiers and maids sipped punch. Smiles all round.

But for Sergeant Beale.

"I suppose you'll be back to London now, sir?"

"I see no other course."

"There's something about the little girl, isn't there?"

"I fear so."

"Where *were* those kids? What happened to the boy?"

"Those, Sergeant, are the questions."

Beale nodded. He took no punch.

Charles left the Sergeant and walked to the door. A tug came at his arm. Sairey held his sleeve. The woman was bent almost double. It was nearly her time. That was all this party needed: a sudden delivery and a bouncing, happy baby.

"Phil and I'll take in Davey."

"I'm glad to hear that, Sairey. I know it won't be easy."

She snorted. "Neither one'll take him in class, not Gryfudd nor Grenton. So that's an end to his schooling. And he's a clever lad, Davey. Give him a pencil and he can draw anything to the life. Mam... she's daffy over Maeve, hasn't any left for Davey. Won't have him in the house."

Charles patted her hand, understanding.

"And what *is* it about Maeve? She calls I 'Sarah.' I've been 'Sairey' so long I forgot what my name written down in the family Bible were."

"She doesn't know Silas Gobbo."

Sairey closed her eyes and nodded.

"She frightens I," she said, so quietly no one could overhear.

Charles squeezed her fingers. He could give no reassurance.

Riddle came into the hallway, looking for his wife. He escorted her back into the warmth and light. A cheer went up. Someone began singing...

"A frog he would a wooing go...

Heigh-ho, says Rowley!

And whether his mother would let him or no..."

Other voices joined. One deep bass must be Gryffud.

"With a roly poly gammon and spinach...

Heigh-ho, says Anthony Rowley!"

Charles put on his hat and coat and left.

ACT II: UNCLE SATT'S TREASURY FOR BOYS AND GIRLS

i: "Lady of the Leprechauns"

"If that's the Gift," commented a workman, "I'd likes ter know as 'oo gave it, and when they're comin' ter fetch it back."

Kate jotted the words into a notebook, in her own shorthand. The sentiment, polished through repetition, might not be original to the speaker. She liked to record what London thought and said, even when the city thought too lightly and said too often.

"Dunno what it thinks it looks like," continued the fellow.

In shirtsleeves, cap on the back of his head, he perspired heavily.

Freezing winters and boiling summers were the order of the '90s. This June threatened the scorch of the decade. She regretted the transformation of the parasol from an object of utility into a frilly aid to flirtation. As a consequence of this social phenomenon, she didn't own such an apparatus and was just now feeling the lack—and not because she wished the attention of some dozy gentleman who paid heed only to females who flapped at him like desperate moths. Like many blessed (or cursed) with red hair, too much sun made her peel hideously. Her freckles became angry blood-dots if she took a promenade *sans* veiled hat. Such apparel invariably tangled with her large, thick spectacles.

At the South end of Regent's Park, the Gift shone, throwing off dazzles from myriad facets. Completed too late for one Jubilee, it was embarrassingly early for the next. To get shot of a White Elephant, the bankrupt company responsible made a gift of it (hence the name) to the Corporation of London. Intended as a combination of popular theatre, exhibition hall and exotic covered garden, the sprawling labyrinth had decoration enough for any three municipal eyesores. The thing looked like a crystal circus-tent whipped up by a colour-blind Sunday painter and an Italian pastry-chef.

It was inevitable that someone would eventually conceive of a use for the Gift. That visionary (buffoon?) was Mr. Satterthwaite Bulge, "Uncle Satt" to a generation of nieces and nephews, *soi-disant* Founder of Færie and Magister of Marvells (his spelling). This afternoon, she had an invitation to visit Bulge's prosperous little kingdom.

"Katharine Reed, daredevil reporter," called a voice, deep and American.

A man in a violently green checked suit cut through gawping passersby and wrung her hand. He wore an emerald bowler with shining tin buckle, an oversize crepe four-leafed clover *boutonniere*, a belt of linked discs painted like gold coins, and a russet beard fringe attached to prominent ears by wire hooks.

"Billy Quinn, *publicist*," he introduced himself, momentarily lowering his false whiskers.

She filed away the word. Was it a coinage of Quinn's? What might a publicist do? Publicise, she supposed. Make known personalities and events and products, scattering information upon the public like lumps of lava spewn from Vesuvius. She had a notion that if such a profession were to become established, her own would be greatly complicated.

"And, of course, Oi'm a leprechaun. Ye'll be familiar with *the leettle people*."

Quinn's Boston tones contorted into an approximation of Ould Oireland. Inside high-button shoes, her toes curled.

"There's not a darter of Erin that hasn't in her heart a soft spot for Seamus O'Short."

She was Dublin-born and Protestant-raised. Her father, a lecturer in Classics at Trinity College, drummed into her at an early age that *pots o' gold* and *wee fair folk* were baggages which need only trouble heathen Papists dwelling in the savage regions of dampest bog country. Whenever anyone English rabbited on about such things (usually affecting speech along the lines of Quinn's atavistic brogue), she was wont to change the subject to Home Rule.

"You're going to love this, Kate," he said, casually assuming the right to address her by a familiar name. She was grateful that he had reverted to his natural voice, though. "Here's your fairy sack."

He handed over a posset, with a drawstring. A stick protruded from its mouth, wound round with tinsel.

"That's your fairy wand. Inside, there's magic powder (sherbet) and a silver tiara (not silver). Tuppence to the generality, but *gratis* to an honoured rep of the Fourth Estate."

Rep? Representative. Now, people were *talking* in shorthand. At least, people who were Americans and *publicists* were.

Quinn led her towards the doors of the Gift.

A lady in spangled leotards and butterfly wings attracted a male coterie, bestowing handbills while bending *just so* to display her *décolletage* to its best advantage, which was considerable. The voluptuous fairy had two colleagues, also singular figures. Someone in a baggy suit of brown fur and cuirass, sporting an enormous plaster bear's head surmounted by an armoured helm. A dwarf with his face painted like a sad clown.

"Come one, come all," said Quinn. "Meet Miss Fay Twinkledust, Sir Boris de Bruin, and Jack Stump."

The trio posed *en tableau* as if for a photograph. Miss Fay and Jack Stump fixed happy grimaces on their powdered faces. Sir Boris perked up an ear through tugging on a wire. In this heat, Kate feared for the comfort and well-being of the performer trapped inside the costume.

Children flocked around, awed and wondered.

Jack Stump was perturbed by affections bestowed on him by boys and girls taller and heftier than he. Kate realised she'd seen the dwarf, dressed as a miniature mandarin, shot out of a cannon at the Tivoli Music Hall. This engagement seemed more perilous.

In the offices of the *Pall Mall Gazette*, she had done her homework and pored through a year's worth of *Uncle Satt's Treasury for Boys and Girls*. She was already acquainted with Miss Fay Twinkledust, Sir Boris de Bruin, Jack Stump, Seamus O'Short, and many others. Gloomy Goat and his cousins Grumpy (her favourite) and Grimy; Billy Boggart of Noggart's Nook; Bobbin Swiftshaft, Prince of Pixies; Wicked Witch-Queen Coelacanth. The inhabitants of Uncle Satt's Færie Aerie were beloved (or deliciously despised) by seemingly every child in the land, to the despair of parents who would rather their precious darlings practiced the pianoforte or read Euripides in the original in exactly the way they hadn't when they were children.

Kate was out of school, and near-disowned for following her disreputable Uncle Diarmid into "the scribbling trade," well before the debuts of Miss Fay *et al.*, but her younger brother and sisters were precisely of an age to fall into the clutches of Mr. Satterthwaite Bulge. Father, whose position on the *wee fair folk* was no longer tenable, lamented he was near financial ruin on Uncle Satt's account, for a mere subscription to the monthly *Treasury* did not suffice to assuage clamour for matters færie-related. There was also *Uncle Satt's Færie Aerie Annual*, purchased in triplicate to prevent unseemly battles between Humphrey, Juliet, and Susannah over whose bookshelf should have the honour of supporting the wonder volume. Furthermore, it was insisted that nursery wallpaper bear the likenesses of the færie favourites as illustrated by the artist who signed his (or her?) works "B. Loved," reckoned by connoisseurs to be the true genius of the realm which could properly be termed Uncle Satt's Færie Empire. In addition, there were china dolls and tin figures to be bought, board games to be played, pantomime theatrical events to be attended, sheet music to be performed, Noggart's Nook sugar confections to be consumed. Every penny doled out by fond parent or grandparent to well-behaved child was earmarked for the voluminous pockets of Uncle Satt.

As a consequence, Bulge could afford the Gift. On his previous record, he could probably turn the White Elephant into the wellspring of further fortunes. Pots of gold, indeed.

The Gift was not yet open to the general public, and excited queues were already forming in anticipation. No matter how emetic the Uncle Satt *oeuvre* was to the average adult, children were as lost to his Færie as the children of Hamelin were to the Pied Piper.

A little girl, no more than four, hugged Sir Boris's leg, rubbing her cheek against his fur, smiling with pure bliss.

"We don't pay these people," Quinn assured her. "We don't have to. To be honest, we would if we did but we don't. This is all gin-u-wine."

Some grown-ups were won over to the enemy or found it politic to claim so, lest they be accused of stifling the childish heart reputed to beat still in the breasts of even the hardest cynics. Many of her acquaintance, well into mature years and possessed of sterling intellects (some *not even parents*), proclaimed devotion to Uncle Satt, expressing admiration if not for the literary effulgences then for the talents of the mysterious, visionary "B. Loved." Even Bernard Shaw, whose stinging notice of *A Visit to the Fœrie Aerie* led to a splashing with glue by pixie partisans, praised the illustrations, hailing "B. Loved" a titan shackled by daisy-chains. The pictures, it had to be said, were haunting, unusual and impressive, simple in technique, yet imbued with a suggestiveness close to disturbing. Their dreamy vagueness would have passed for *avant-garde* in some salons but was paradoxically embraced (beloved, indeed) by child and adult alike. Aubrey Beardsley was still sulking because B. Loved declined to contribute to a fœrie-themed number of *The Yellow Book*, though it was bruited about that the refusal was mandated by Uncle Satt, who had the mystery painter signed to an exclusive contract. It was sometimes hinted that Bulge *was* B. Loved. Other theories had the illustrator as an asylum inmate who had sewn his own eyes shut but continued to cover paper with the images swarming inside his broken mind, a spirit medium who gave herself up to an inhabitant of another plane as she sat at the board, or a factory in Aldgate staffed by unlettered Russian immigrants overseen by a knout-wielding monk.

"Come inside," said Quinn. "Though you must first pass these Three Merry Guardians."

The publicist opened a little gate and ushered Kate into an enclosure that led to the main doors. The entrance was painted to look like the covers of a pair of magical books. Above was a red-cheeked, smiling, sparkle-eyed caricature of Uncle Satt, fat finger extended to part the pages.

Envious glares came from the many children not yet admitted to the attraction. Cutting comments were passed by parents whose offers of bribes had not impressed the Three Merry Guardians. Kate had an idea that, if his comrades were looking the other way, Jack Stump would not have been averse to slipping a half-crown into his boot and lifting a tent-corner.

"This is a Lady of the Leprechauns," said Quinn, to appease the crowds, "on a diplomatic visit to Uncle Satt. The Gift will open to one and all this very weekend. The Fœrie Aerie isn't yet ready to receive visitors."

A collective moan of disappointment rose.

Quinn shrugged at her.

Kate stepped towards the main doors. Long, hairy arms encircled her, preventing further movement. Sir Boris de Bruin shook with silent laughter.

This was very irritating!

"I had almost forgotten," said Quinn. "Before you enter, what must you do?"

She was baffled. The bear was close to taking liberties.

"What must she do, boys and girls?" Quinn asked the crowd.

"Færie name! Færie name!"

"That's right, boys and girls. The Lady of the Leprechauns must take her færie name!"

"Katharine Reed," she suggested. "Um, Kate, Katie?"

"*Nooooo*," said Quinn, milking it. "A new name. A true name. A name fit for the councils of Bobbin Swiftshaft and Billy Boggart."

"Grumpia Goatess," she ventured, quietly. She knew her face was red. The bear's bristles were scraping.

"I have the very name! Brenda Banshee!"

Kate, surprised, was horrified.

"Brenda Banshee, Brenda Banshee," chanted the children. Many of them booed.

Brenda Banshee was the sloppy maidservant in the house of Seamus O'Short, always left howling at the end of the tale. It struck Kate that the leprechaun was less than an ideal employer, given to perpetrating "hilarious pranks" on his staff, then laughing uproariously at their humiliations. In the real world, absentee landlords in Ireland were *boycotted* for less objectionable behaviour than Seamus got away with every month.

"What does Brenda Banshee do?" asked Quinn.

"She howls! She howls!"

"If you think I'm going to howl," she told Sir Boris quietly, "you're very much mistaken."

"Howl, Brenda," said Quinn, grinning. "Howl for the boys and girls."

She set her lips tight.

If Brenda Banshee was always trying to filch coins from her employer's belt o' gold, it was probably because she was an indentured servant and received no wages for her drudgery.

"I think you'd howl most prettily," whispered Sir Boris de Bruin.

It dawned on her that she knew the voice.

She looked into the bear's mouth and saw familiar eyes.

"*Charles?*"

"If I can wear this, you can howl."

She was astounded, and very conscious of the embrace in which she was trapped. Her face, she knew, was burning.

"Please howl," demanded Quinn, enjoying himself.

Kate screwed her eyes shut and howled. It sounded reedy and feeble.

Sir Boris gave her an encouraging, impertinent squeeze.

She howled enough to raise a round of applause.

"Very nice, Brenda," said Quinn. "Howl-arious. Shall we go inside?"

The book covers opened.

ii: "details, young miss"

What *did* Charles Beauregard think he was about?

She scarcely believed that an agent of the Diogenes Club would take it into his head to supplement his income by dressing up as a storybook bear in the service of Mr. Satterthwaite Bulge. She recalled John Watson's story in the *Strand* of the respectable suburban husband who earned a healthy living in disguise as a deformed beggar. Kate wondered at the ethics of publicising such a singular case; it now served as an excuse for the smugly well-off to scorn genuine unfortunates on the grounds that "they doubtless earn more than a barrister." Money would not come into this. Charles was of the stripe who does nothing for purely financial reward. Of course, he could afford his scruples. He did not toil in an underpaid calling still only marginally willing to accept those of her sex. The profession Neville St. Clair had found less lucrative than beggary was her own, journalism.

Sir Boris hung back as Quinn escorted her along a low-ceilinged tunnel hung with green-threaded muslin. Underfoot was horsehair matting, dyed dark green to approximate forest grass.

"We proceed along the Airy Path, to Noggart's Nook..."

Quinn led her to a huge tree trunk which blocked the way. The plaster creation was intricate, with grinning goblin faces worked into the bark. Their eyes glowed, courtesy of dabs of luminous paint. An elaborate mechanical robin chirruped in the branches. Quinn rapped three times on the oak. Hidden doors opened inwards.

"...and into the Realm of Bobbin Swiftshaft, Prince of the Pixies..."

Kate stepped into the tree, and down three shallow steps. Cloth trailed over her face.

"Mind how you go."

She had walked into a curtain. Extricating herself, she found she was in a vaulted space: at once cathedral, Big Top, and planetarium. The dome sparkled with constellations, arranged to form the familiar shapes of B. Loved creatures. Miss Fay, Bobbin Swiftshaft, Jack Stump, Sir Boris, Seamus, and the rest cavorted across the painted, glittering ceiling. Tinsel streamers hung, catching the light. All around was a half-sized landscape, suitable for little folk, created through tamed nature and theatrical artifice. Kate, who spent most of her life peering up at people, was here taller than the tallest tree—many were genuine dwarves cultivated in the Japanese manner, not stage fakery—and a giant beside the dwellings. The woods were fully outfitted with huts and palaces, caves and castles, stone circles and hunting lodges. Paths wound prettily through miniature woodland. Water flowed from a fountain shaped like the mouth of a big bullfrog, whose name and station escaped her. The respectable torrent poured prettily over a waterfall, agitated a pond beneath, and passed out of the realm as a stream which disappeared into a cavern. An iron grille barred the outflow, lest small persons tumble in and be swept away.

All around were strange gleams, in the air and inside objects.

"The light," she said, "it's unearthly."

Looking close, she found semiconcealed glass globes and tubes, each containing a fizzing glowworm. Some were tinted subtle ruby-red or turquoise. They shone like the eyes of ghosts.

"We're mighty proud of the lighting," said Quinn. "We use only Edison's incandescents, which burn through the wizardry of the age, *electricity*. Beneath our feet are vast dynamos, which churn to keep the Aerie illuminated. The Gift quite literally puts the Savoy in the shade."

Mr. d'Oyly-Carte's Savoy Theatre had been fully electrified for over a decade. Some metropolitan private homes were lit by Edison lamps, though the gas companies were fighting a vicious rearguard campaign against electrification, fearing the fate of the candle-makers. Despite scare stories, the uninformed no longer feared lightning-strikes from new-fangled gadgetry. They also no longer gasped in wonder at the mere use of an electrical current to spin a wheel or light a room. There was a risk that electric power would be relegated to quack medicinal devices like the galvanic weight-loss corset. In America, electrocution was used as a means of execution; in Britain, the process was most familiar from advertisements for the miracle food Bovril—allegedly produced by strapping a cow into an electric chair and throwing the switch. From H.G. Wells, the *Pall Mall Gazette*'s scientific correspondent, Kate gathered that the coming century would be an Era of Electricity. At present, the spark seemed consigned to trivial distraction; that was certainly the case here.

A bulb atop a lantern-pole hissed, flared, and popped. A tinkling rain of glass shards fell.

"Some trivial teething troubles," said Quinn.

A lanky fellow in an overall rushed to attend to the lantern. He extracted the burned-out remains, ouching as his fingers came into contact with the hot ruin. He deftly screwed in a replacement, which began at once to glow, its light rising to full brightness. Another minion was already sweeping the fragments into a pan for easy disposal.

"Unusual-looking elves," she commented.

"It takes a crew of twenty-five trained men to keep the show going," said Quinn. "When the Gift is open, they *will* be elves. Each will have their own character and place."

Uncle Satt was insistent that in Færie, as in mundane society, there was a strict order of things. If a woodsman wed a fairy princess, it was a dead cert he was a prince in disguise rather than a real peasant. The reader was expected to guess as much from a well-born character's attention to personal cleanliness. Children knew the exact forms of protocol in Uncle Satt's imaginary kingdom, baffling adults with nursery arguments about whether a knight transformed into a bear by Witch-Queen Coelacanth outranked a tiger-headed maharajah from Far Off Indee.

Charles had shambled in and was sitting on a wooden bench, head inclined so he could talk quietly with one of the worker elves. Quinn had not noticed that Sir Boris had abandoned the other Merry Guardians.

When Mr. Henry Cockayne-Cust, her editor, sent Kate to the Gift, she had considered it a rent-paying exercise, a story destined for the depths of the inside pages. Much of her work was fish-wrap before it had a chance to be read. It was a step up from "Ladies' Notes"—to which editors often tried to confine her, despite an evident lack of interest in the intricacies of fashionable feminine apparel or the supervision of servants—but not quite on a level with theatre criticism, to which she turned her pen in a pinch, which is to say when the *Gazette*'s official reviewer fell asleep during a first night.

An item ("puff piece") about the Færie Aerie seemed doomed to fall into the increasingly large purview of Quinn's profession. She lamented the colonisation of journalism by organised boosterism and the advertising trade. In some publications, people were deemed worthy of interest because of a happenstance rather than genuine achievement. The day might come when passing distraction was valued higher than matters of moment. She held it a sacred duty to resist.

If Mr. Charles Beauregard, if *the Diogenes Club*, took an interest in the Gift, an interest was worth taking. Some aspect of the endeavour not yet apparent would likely prove, in her uncle's parlance, "news-worthy."

Quinn's jibe about "daredevil" lady reporters had niggled. Now, she wondered whether there might not be a Devil here to dare.

"This, dear Brenda, is Uncle Satt."

While she was thinking, Mr. Satterthwaite Bulge had come up out of the ground.

Illustrations made Bulge a cherubic fat man, a clean-shaven Father Christmas or sober Bacchus, always drawn with gleam a-twinkle in his bright eye and smile a-twitch on his full, girlish lips. In person, Bulge was indeed stout but with no discernible expression. His face was the colour of thin milk, and so were his long-ish hair and thin-ish lips. His eyes were the faded blue of china left on a shelf which gets too much sun. He wore sober clothes of old-fashioned cut, like a provincial alderman who stretches one good suit to last a lifetime in office. Bulge seemed like an artist's blank:

a hole where a portrait would be drawn. More charitably, she thought of actors who walked through rehearsals, hitting marks and reciting lines without error, but withheld their *performance* until opening night, saving passion for paying customers.

Bulge had climbed a ladder and emerged through a trap-door, followed by another elf, a clerkish type with clips on his sleeves and a green eyeshade.

"This is Katharine Reed, of the *Pall Mall Gazette*," said Quinn.

"What's the circulation?" asked Bulge.

"Quite large, I'll wager," she said. "We're under orders not to reveal too much."

That, she knew, was feeble. In fact, she had no idea.

"I know to the precise number what the *Treasury* sells by the month. I know to the farthing what profit is to be had from the *Annual*. Details, young miss, that is the stuff of my enterprise, of *all* enterprises. Another word for *detail* is *penny*. Pennies are hard to come by. It is a lesson the *dear children* learn early."

She did not think she would ever be able to call this man "Uncle." The instant Bulge used the phrase "the *dear children*" and slid his lips into something he fondly imagined to be a smile, Kate knew his deepest, darkest secret. Mr. Satterthwaite Bulge, Uncle Satt of *Uncle Satt's Treasury for Boys and Girls*, greatly disliked children. It was an astonishing intuition. When Bulge used the word "dear," his meaning was not "beloved" but "expensive." Some parents, not least her own, might secretly agree.

"Do you consider the prime purpose of your enterprise to be educational?" she asked.

Bulge was impatient with the attempt at interview.

"That's covered in the, ah, what do you call the thing, Quinn... the *press release*. Yes, it's all covered in that. Questions, any you might ask, have already been answered. I see no purpose in repeating myself."

"She has the press release, Mr. Bulge," said Quinn.

"Good. You're doing your job. Young miss, I suggest you do yours. Why, all you have to do to manufacture an article is pen a general introduction, copy out Quinn's *release* and sign your name. Then you have your *interview with Uncle Satt* at a minimum of effort. A fine day's work, I imagine. A pretty penny earned."

The flaw, of course, was that she was not the only member of the press to receive the "release." If an article essentially identical to her own appeared in a rival paper, she would hear from Mr. Harry Cust. The editor could as devastatingly direct disapproval in person at one tiny reporter as, through editorial campaign, at an entire segment of society or tier of government. For that reason, the excellent and detailed brochure furnished by Quinn lay among spindled documents destined for use as tapers. The "press release" would serve to transfer flame from the grate to that plague of cigarettes which rendered the air in any newspaper office more noxious than the streets during the worst of a pea-soup fog.

"If I could ask a few supplementary questions, addressing matters touched upon but not explored in the release…"

"I can't be doing with this now," said Bulge. "Many things have to be seen to if the Gift is to open to the *dear children* on schedule."

"Might I talk with others involved? For instance, B. Loved remains a man of mystery. If the curtain were lifted and a few facts revealed about the artist, you could guarantee a great deal of, ah, *publicity*."

Bulge snorted. "I *have* a great deal of publicity, young miss."

"But…"

"There's no mystery about Loved. He's just a man with a paint-box."

"So, B. Loved *is* a man then, *one* man, not…"

"Talk with Quinn," Bulge insisted. "It's his job. Don't bother anyone else. None can afford breaks for idle chatter. It's all we can do to keep everyone about their work, without distractions."

Quinn, realising his employer was not making the best impression, stepped in.

"I'll be delighted to show Kate around."

"You do that, Quinn."

"She has her fairy sack."

Kate held it up.

"Tuppence lost," said Bulge. "Quinn's extravagances will be the ruin of me, young miss. I am surrounded by spendthrifts who care nought for *details*."

"Remember, sir," said Quinn, mildly, "the matter we discussed…"

Bulge snorted. "Indeed, I do. More jargon. *Public image*, indeed. Arrant mumbo jumbo and impertinence."

If Uncle Satt wrote a word published under his name, Kate would be astounded. On the strength of this acquaintance, she could hardly believe he even *read* his own periodicals.

Which begged the question of what exactly he did in his empire.

See to details? Add up pennies?

If B. Loved was a man with a paint-box, was he perhaps on the premises? If not painting murals himself, then supervising their creation. She had an intuition that the trail of the artist might be worth following.

A nearby tower toppled, at first slowly with a ripping like stiff paper being torn, and then rapidly, with an almighty crash, trailing wires that sparked and snapped, whipcracking towards the stream.

Bulge looked at Kate darkly, as if he suspected sabotage.

"You see, I am busy. These things *will* keep happening…"

Wires leaped like angry snakes. Elves kept well away from them.

"Accidents?" she asked.

"Obstacles," responded Bulge.

Bulge strode off and stared down the cables, which died and lay still. The electric lamps dimmed, leaving only cinder ghosts in the dark. Groans went up all around.

"Not again," grumbled an elf.

Someone struck a match.

Where the tower had fallen, a stretch of painted woodland was torn away, exposing bare lath. Matches flared all around and old-fashioned lanterns lit. It was less magical, but more practical.

"What is it this time, Sackham?"

"Been chewed through, Uncle," diagnosed the clerk, examining the damage. "Like before."

Bulge began issuing orders.

Kate took the opportunity to slip away. She hoped Bulge's attention to details would not extend to keeping track of her.

These things will *keep happening.*

That was interesting. That was what they called a lead.

iii: "goblins"

"Is this a common event?" she asked an idling elf.

"Not 'arf," came the reply. "If it ain't breakin' down, it's fallin' down. If it ain't burnin' up, it's messin' up."

This particular elf was staying well out of the way. Several of his comrades, under the impatient supervision of Uncle Satt, were lifting the fallen tower out of the stream. Others, mouths full of nails and hammers in their hands, effected emergency repairs.

"They says it's the *goblins*."

Kate wanted to laugh, but her chuckle died.

"No, ma'am," said the elf, "it's serious. Some 'ave seen 'em, they say, then upped and left, walkin' away from good wages. That's not a natural thing, ma'am, not with times as they are and honest labour 'ard to come by."

"But… goblins?"

"Nasty little blighters, they say. Fingernails like teeth, an' teeth like needles. Always chewin' and clawin', weakenin' things so they collapse. Usually when there's someone underneath for to be collapsed upon. The craytors get into the machinery, gum up the works. Them big dynamos grind to a 'alt with a din like the world crackin' open."

She thought about this report.

"You mean this is sabotage? Has Satterthwaite Bulge deadly rivals in the færie business? Interests set against the opening of the Gift?"

"What business is it of yours?"

The elf realised for the first time he had no idea who she was. Her relative invisibility was often an aid in her profession; many forgot she was there even as they talked to her. Now, her spell of insignificance was wearing off.

"Miss Reed is a colleague, Blenkins," came a voice.

They had been joined by a bear. His presence reassured the elf Blenkins.

"If you say so, Sir Boris," he allowed. "My 'pologies, ma'am. A bloke 'as to be careful round 'ere."

"A bloke always has to be careful around Miss Reed."

She hoped that, in the gloom, Charles could not discern the fearful burning of her cheeks. When he first strolled into her life, Kate was thirteen and determined to despise the villain set upon fetching away her idol, Pamela Churchward. Father was lecturing at London University for a year and Kate found herself absorbed into the large, complicated circle of the Churchwards. The beautiful, wise Pamela was the first woman ever to encourage Kate's ambitions. Her engagement seemed a treacherous defection, for all the bride-to-be insisted marriage would not end her independent life. Penelope, Pamela's ten-year-old cousin, said bluntly that Kate's complexion meant she would end up a governess or, at best, palmed off as wife to an untenured, adenoidal lecturer. Just then, as Kate was trying in vain not to cry, Pamela introduced her princely fiancé to her protégé.

Of course, Kate had fallen *horribly* in love with Charles. She doubted she had uttered a coherent sentence in his presence until he was a young widower. By then, courtesy of interesting, if brief, liaisons with Mr. Frank Harris, another editor, and several others, none of whom she regretted, she was what earlier decades might have branded *a fallen woman*.

Now, with Pamela gone and pernicious Penelope in retreat, she knew the thirteen-year-old nestled inside her thirty-two-year-old person remained smitten with the Man From the Diogenes Club. As a grown-up, she was more sensible than to indulge such silliness. It irritated her when he pretended to think she was still a tiny girl with rope braids down to her waist and cheeks of pillar-box red. It was, she knew, *only* pretence. Like his late wife (whom she still missed *so*), Charles Beauregard was among the select company who took Katharine Reed seriously.

"Sir Boris, you do me an injustice."

The bear-head waved from side to side.

For once, she was not the most ridiculous personage in the room.

"Still, I'm sure you intended to be a very gallant bear."

She reached up and tickled the fur around his helm. It was painted plaster and she left white scratches. She stroked his arm, which was more convincing.

Blenkins slipped away, leaving them alone.

"There's a catch at the back," Charles said, muffled. "Like a diver's helmet. If you would do me the courtesy…"

"You can't get out of this on your own?"

"As it happens, no."

She found the catch and flipped it. Charles placed his paws over his ears and rotated his head ninety degrees so the muzzle pointed sideways, then lifted the thing free. A definite musk escaped from the decapitated costume. Charles's face was blacked like Mr. G.F. Elliott, the music hall act billed as "the Chocolate-Coloured Coon." She found Elliott only marginally less unappealing than those comic turns who presented gormless, black-toothed caricatures of her own race. Charles's make-up was to prevent white skin showing through Sir Boris's mouth.

He whipped off a paw and scratched his chin.

"I've been desperate to do that for hours," he admitted.

He used his paw-glove to wipe his face. She took pity, produced a man-size handkerchief from her cuff, and set about properly cleaning off the burnt cork. He sat on a wooden toadstool and leaned forwards so she could pay close attention to the task.

"Thank you, mama," he teased.

She swatted him with the blacked kerchief.

"I could leave you looking like a Welsh miner."

He shut up and let her finish. The face of Charles Beauregard emerged. Weary, to be sure, but recognisable.

"You've shaved your cavalry whiskers," she observed.

His hand went to his neatly-trimmed moustache.

"A touch of the creeping greys, I suspect," she added, wickedly.

"Good grief, Katie," said Charles, "you're worse than Mycroft's brother!"

"I'm right, though, am I not?"

"There was a certain *tinge* of dignified white," he admitted, shyly, "which I estimated could be eliminated by judicious barbering."

"Considering your calling, I'm surprised every hair on your person hasn't been bleached. It's said to be a common side effect of stark terror."

"So I am reliably informed."

He undid strings at the back of his neck and shrugged the bear-suit loose, then stepped out of the top half of the costume. The cuirass, leather painted like steel, unlaced down the back to allow escape from straitjacket-like confines. Underneath, he wore a grimy shirt, with no collar. High-waisted but clownishly baggy furry britches stuck into heroic boots that completed the ensemble.

"The things you do for Queen and Country, Charles."

He looked momentarily sheepish.

"*Charles?*"

"I'm at present acting on my own initiative."

This was puzzling and most unlike Charles. But she knew what had brought him here. She had seized at once on the "news-worthy" aspect of the Gift.

"It's the *goblins*, isn't it?"

He flashed a humourless smile.

"Still sharp as ever, Kate? Yes, it's Blenkins's blinkin' goblins."

The hammering and tower-raising continued. The electric lights fizzled on again, then out. Then on, to burn steady. Charles instinctively stepped back, into a shadowed alcove, drawing Kate with him.

Bulge flapped a list of "to do" tasks at the elves. Mr. Sackham was presently at the receiving end of the brunt of Uncle Satt's opprobrium.

"What do you know that I don't?" she asked Charles.

"That's a big question."

She hit him on the arm. Quite hard.

"You deserved that."

"Indeed I did. My apologies, Katie. Life inside a bear costume is, I'm afraid, a strain on any temperament. When the Gift opens to the public, I should not care to let a child of my acquaintance within easy reach of anyone who was forced, as the 'show-business' slang has it, 'to wear a head.' An hour of such imprisonment transforms the most patient soul into Grendel, eager for a small, helpless person upon whom to slake his wrath."

"You have my promise that I shall write a blistering exposé of this cruel practice. The cause of the afflicted 'head-wearers' shall become as known as, in an earlier age, was that of the children employed as human chimney-brushes or, as now, those drabs sold as 'maiden tributes of modern Babylon.' A committee shall be formed and strong letters written to Members of Parliament. Fairies will chain themselves to the railings. None shall be allowed to rest in the Halls of Justice until the magic bears are free!"

"Now *you're* teasing *me*."

"I have earned that right."

"That you have, Katie."

"Now this amusing diversion is at an end, I refer you back to my initial question. What do you know that I don't?"

Charles sighed. She had sidestepped him again. She wondered if he ever regretted that she was no longer tongue-tied in his presence.

"Not much," he admitted, "and I can't talk about it here. If you would meet me outside in half an hour. I am acting on my own initiative and honestly welcome your views."

"This goblin hunt?"

"That's part of it."

"Part only?"

"Part only."

"I shall wait half an hour, no longer."

"It will take that to become presentable. I can't shamble as a demi-bear among afternoon promenaders."

"Indeed. Panic would ensue. Men with nets would be summoned. As an obvious chimera, you would be captured and confined to the conveniently nearby London Zoo. Destined to be stuffed and presented to the Natural History Museum."

"I'm so glad you understand."

He kissed her forehead, which reddened her again. She was grateful her blushes wouldn't show up under the electric lamps.

iv: "a pale green ribbon"

A full forty-five minutes later, Kate was still waiting in the park. On this pleasant afternoon, many freed from places of employment were not yet disposed to return to their homes. A gathering of shopgirls chirruped, competing for the attention of a smooth-faced youth who sported a cricket cap and a racy striped jacket. Evidently quite a wit, his flow of comments on the peculiarities of passersby kept his pretty flock in fits.

"With her colourin' and mouth," drawled the champion lad, "it's a wonder she ain't forever bein' mistook for a pillar box."

Much hilarity among the *filles des estaminets.*

"Oh Max, you are so *wicked*... you shouldn't ought to say such things..."

Kate supposed she *was* redder than usual. The condition came upon her when amused, embarrassed, or—as in this case—annoyed.

"I 'magine she's waitin' to be emptied."

"The postman's running late today," ventured the boldest of the girls.

"Bad show, what. To leave such a pert post-box unattended."

Charles emerged from the Gift at last, more typically clothed. Most would take him for a clubman fresh from a day's idleness and up for an evening's foolery.

As he approached, the girls' attention was removed entirely from Max. Their eyes followed Charles's saunter. He did such a fine job of pretending not to notice that only Kate was not fooled.

"He must have a letter that *desperately* needs postin'," said the amusing youth.

"If you will excuse me," said Charles, raising a finger.

He walked over to the group, who fluttered and gathered around

Merry Max. Charles took a firm grip on the youth's ear and dragged him to Kate. The cap fell off, revealing that his cultivated forelock was a lonely survivor on an otherwise hairless scalp.

"This fellow has something to say to you, Kate."

"Sorry," came the strangled bleat, "no 'ffence meant."

Now someone was redder than she. Max's pate was practically vermilion.

"None taken."

Charles let Max go and he fell over. When he sat up again, his congregation was flown, seeking another hero. He snatched up his cap and slunk off.

"I suppose you expect me to be grateful for your protection, Sir Boris?"

Charles shrugged. "After a day in the bear head, I had to thump *someone*. Max happened to be convenient. He was making 'short' jokes about Jack Stump earlier."

"I believe you."

He looked at her, and she was thirteen again. Then she was an annoyed grown-up woman.

"No, really. I do."

Charles glanced back at the Gift.

"So, Mr. Beauregard, what's the story? Why take an interest in Uncle Satt?"

"Bulge is incidental. The mermaid on the front of the ship. Oh, he's the one who's made the fortune. But he's not the treasure of the *Treasury*. That's the other fellow, the mysterious cove…"

"B. Loved?"

Charles tapped her forehead. "Spot on. The artist."

"What does the B stand for?"

"David."

"Beloved. From the Hebrew."

"Indeed. Davey Harvill, as was. B. Loved, as is."

The name meant nothing to her.

"Young Davey is a singular fellow. We met eight years ago, in Herefordshire. He had an unusual experience. The sort of unusual that comes under my purview."

It was fairly openly acknowledged that the Diogenes Club was a clearinghouse for the British Secret Service. Less known was its occult remit. While the Society for Psychical Research could reliably gather data on cold spots or fraudulent mediums, they were hardly equipped to cope with supernatural occurrences which constituted a threat to the natural order of things. If a spook clanked chains or formed faces in the muslin, a run-of-the-mill ghost-finder was more than qualified to provide reassurance; if it could hurt you, then the Ruling Cabal sent Charles Beauregard.

"Davey was lost in the woods and found much older than he should be. I don't mean aged by terrible experience, your 'side effects of stark terror.' He disappeared a child of nine and returned a full-grown man, as if twenty years had passed over a weekend."

"You established there was no imposture?"

"To my satisfaction."

Kate thought, tapping her teeth with a knuckle. "But not to everyone's?"

Charles spread his hands. "The lad's mother could never accept him."

She had a pang of sympathy for this boy she had never met.

"What happened after he was returned?"

"Interesting choice of words. 'Was returned?' Suggests an agency over which he had no control. Might he not have *escaped*? Davey was taken in by his older sister, Sarah Riddle. Maeve Harvill, Davey's other sister, also went into the woods. She came out like her normal self and was embraced by the mother. Sadly, Mrs. Harvill died some time afterwards. I have questions about that, but we can get to them later. Sarah, herself the mother of a young son, became sole parent to both her siblings. By then, Davey was drawing."

"The færie pictures?"

"They poured from his pencils," said Charles. "He does it all with pencils, you know. Not charcoal. The pictures became more intense, more captivating. You've seen them?"

"Who hasn't?"

"Quite. That's down to Evelyn Weddle, the Vicar of Eye. He took an interest, and brought Davey's pictures to the attention of a Glamorgan printer."

"Satterthwaite Bulge?"

"Indeed. Bulge, quite against his nature, was captivated. The pictures have strange effects, as the whole world now knows. Bulge put together the first number of his *Treasury*. It made his name."

"Who writes the copy?"

"At first, Weddle. He's the sort of the poet, alas, who rhymes 'pixie' with 'tipsy' and 'færie' with 'hurry.' Don't you hate that diphthong, by the way? It's one step away from an umlaut. What's wrong with f-a-i-r-y, I'd like to know? The vicar was so flattered to see his verses immortalised by type-setting that he cared not that his name wasn't appended. He fell by the wayside early on. Now, Bulge has many scribbling elves—though he oversees them all, and contrives to imprint his own concerns upon the work. All that business about washing your hands, respecting princes, and punishing servants. Leslie Sackham, whom you saw dancing attendance, is currently principle quill-pushing elf. They are interchangeable and rarely last more than a few months, but there's only one B. Loved."

"Is this golden-egg-laying goose chained to an easel?"

Charles shook his head. "His artistry is of a *compulsive* nature. The *Treasury* can't keep up with the flow. Even under a hugely unfair personal contract the Harvills knew no better than to accept, Davey has become very well off."

She thought of the illustrations, wondering if she would see them differently now she had some idea about their creator. They had always seemed portals into another, private world.

"What does Davey say about the time he was away?"

"He *says* little. He claims an almost complete loss of memory."

"But he draws. You think not from imagination, but from life?"

"I don't suppose he is representing a literal truth, no. But I am certain his pictures spring from the place he and his sister were taken—and I do believe they were *taken*—whether it be a literal Realm of Færie or not."

"You know the stories…"

Charles caught her meaning. "…of the little people, and babies snatched from their cribs? Changelings left in their stead? Very Irish."

"Not in the Reed household. At least, not until the rise of Uncle Satt. But, yes, those stories."

"They aren't confined to the emerald isle. Ten years ago in Sussex, a little girl named Rose Farrar was allegedly spirited away by 'angels.' That's an authenticated case. We took an interest. Rose is still listed among the missing."

"It's not just leprechauns. Someone is always accused of child abduction. Mysterious folk, outsiders, alien. Dark-complected, most like. Wicked to the bone. There are the stories of the Pied Piper and the Snow Queen. Robbers, imps and devils, Red Indians, the gypsies…"

"Funny you should mention gypsies."

"Tinkers, in Ireland. Have they ever *really* stolen babies? Why on earth would they want to? Babies are bothersome, I'm given to understand. Nonsense is usually spouted about strengthening the blood-stock of a small population, but surely you'd do better taking grown-up women for that. No, it seems to me that the interest of the stories is in the people who tell them. There is a *purpose*, a lesson. Don't go wandering off, children, for you might fall down a well. Don't talk to strangers, for they might eat you."

Afternoon had slid into evening. One set of idlers had departed, and a fresh crowd come upon the scene. This was a park, not wild woods. Nature was trimmed and tamed, hemmed in by city streets and patrolled by wardens. Treetops were black with soot.

A shout went up nearby, a governess calling her charge.

"Master Timothy! Timmy!"

Kate felt a clutch of dread. Here, in the press of people, was more danger than in all the trackless woods of England. Scattered among the bland, normal faces were blood-red, murderous hearts. She had attended enough coroners' courts to know imps and angels were superfluous in the metropolis. Caligula could pass, unnoticed, in a celluloid collar.

Master Timothy was found and smothered with tearful kisses. He didn't look grateful. Catching sight of Kate, he stuck out a fat little tongue at her.

"Beast," she commented.

Charles looked for a moment as if he was going to serve the ungracious little perisher as he had Merry Max. She laid a hand in the crook of his arm. She did not care to be complicit with another assault. Charles laid his hand on hers and tapped, understanding, amused.

"The Diogenes Club has a category for everything," he said, "no matter how outré. Maps of Atlantis—we have dozens of them, properly catalogued and folded. Hauntings, tabulated and subcategorised, with pins marked into ordnance survey charts and patterns studied by our learned consultants. Witch-Cults, ranked by the degree of unpleasantness involved in their ritual behaviour and the trouble caused in various quarters of the Empire. There's also a category for mysteries without solution. Matters we have looked into but been unable to form a conclusion upon. Like the diplomat Benjamin Bathurst, who 'walked around the horses' and vanished without trace. Or little Rose Farrar."

"The *Mary Celeste*?"

"Actually, we did fathom that. It remains under the rose for the moment. We've no pressing desire to go to war with the United States of America."

She let that pass.

"Unsolved matters constitute a large category," he continued. "Most of my reports are inconclusive. A strategy has formed for such cases. We tie a pale green ribbon around the file and shelve it in a windowless room behind a door that looks like a cupboard. The Ruling Cabal, which is to say you-know-who, disapproves of fussing with green ribbon files. As he says, 'when you are unable to eliminate the impossible, don't waste too much time worrying about it.' The ribbons are knotted tight and difficult to unpick—though, from time to time, further information comes to light. Of course, it's easier to work in the green ribbon room you think of *people* as *cases*."

"And you can't?"

"No more than you can. No, I don't mean that, Katie. You, more than anyone, are immune to that tendency. I am not. I concede that sometimes it helps to consider mysteries purely as puzzles. Pamela would nag me about it. She always thought of *people* first, last, and always."

Pamela's name did not come up often between them. It did not need to.

"So, in her memory and for fear of disappointing you, I tied the pale green ribbon loosely around Davey Harvill. I had thought the whole thing buried in Eye, a local wonder soon forgotten. However, here we are in the heart of London, before Davey's færie recreated. There are the goblins to consider. Blenkins's goblins. How did they creep into the picture?"

Kate snapped her fingers. "That's how B. Loved draws goblins, hidden as if they've crept in. You have to look twice, sometimes very closely, to see them, disguised against tree bark or peeping out of long grass. In the *Annual*, there's a plate entitled 'how many goblins are being naughty in this picture?' It shows a country market in an uproar."

"There are twenty-seven goblins in the picture. All being naughty."

"I found twenty-nine."

"Yes, well, that's a game. This is not. Workmen have been injured. Nipped as if by tiny teeth. Rats, they say. The thing is, when it's rats, parties involved usually say it isn't. *That's* when they talk about mischievous imps. No one who wants to draw in crowds of children likes to mention the tiniest rat problem. But here everyone says it's rats. Except Blenkins, and he's been told to shut up."

"...if it can hurt you..."

"I beg your pardon."

"Just something I was thinking of earlier."

There was another commotion. Kate assumed Timmy had fled his governess again, but that was not the case.

"Speak of the Devil..."

Blenkins was running through the crowds, clearly in distress.

He saw Charles and dashed over, out of breath.

"Mr. B," he said, "it's terrible what they done..."

Police whistles shrilled nearby.

"I can't credit it. 'appened so quick, sir."

Cries went up. "Fire!" and "Murder!"

"You better take us in," said Charles.

"Not the lady—beggin' your pardon, ma'am—it's too 'orrible."

"She'll be fine," said Charles, winning her all over again—though the casual assumption of the strength of her constitution in face of the truly 'orrible gave her some pause. "Come on, quick about it!"

Blenkins led them back towards the Gift.

v: "the scene of the occurrence"

There was a rumble, deep in the ground, like the awakening of an angry ogre. The doors of the Gift were thrown open, and people—some in costume—poured through. Bulge, collar burst and a bruise on his forehead, was carried out by a broken-winged fairy and a soot-grimed engineer.

Charles held Kate's arm, holding her back.

Bulge caught sight of her and glared as if she were personally to blame.

Blenkins took off his cap and covered his face with it.

Something big broke, deep inside the Gift. Cries and screams were all around.

Quinn, beard awry and hat gone, staggered into the evening light, dazed.

The elves stumbled into an encircling crowd of curious spectators. Kate realised she was in danger of belonging to this category of nuisance.

A belch of smoke escaped and rose in a black ring.

The doors clattered shut.

Breaths were held. There was a moment of quiet. No more smoke, no flames or explosions. Then, everyone began talking at once.

The police were on the scene, a troop of uniformed constables throwing up a picket around the Gift. Kate recognised Inspector Mist of Scotland Yard, a sallow man with a pendulous moustache.

Mist caught sight of Charles and Kate. He shifted his bowler to the back of his head.

"Again we meet in unusual circumstances, Inspector," said Charles.

"Unusual circumstances are an expected thing with you, Mr. Beauregard," said the policeman. "I suppose you two'll have the authority of a certain body to act as, shall we say, observers in this investigation."

Charles did not confirm or deny this, a passive sort of mendacity. She had a pang of worry. Her friend stood to lose a hard-to-define position. She had dark ideas of what form expulsion from the Diogenes Club might take.

"We're not sure any crime has been committed," she said, distracting the thoughtful Mist. "It might be some kind of accident."

"There is usually a crime somewhere, Miss Reed."

Mist might look the glum plodder, but was one of the sharpest needles in the box.

"Hullo, Quinn," said the Inspector, spotting the publicist. "Not hawking patent medicines again, are we?"

Quinn looked sheepish and shook his head.

"I'm relieved to hear it. I trust you've found respectable

employment."

The former leprechaun was pale and shaking. His green jacket was spotted with red.

Mist ordered his men to disperse only the irrelevant crowds. He told the elves not to melt into the throng just yet. Questions would have to be answered. More policemen arrived, then a clanking, hissing fire engine. Mist had the Brigade stand by.

"Let's take a look inside this pixie pavilion, shall we?"

Quinn shook his head, insistently.

Mist pulled one of the book-covers open, and stepped inside. No one from Bulge's troupe was eager to join him. Blenkins hid behind Miss Fay, whose wand was snapped and leotards laddered. Kate followed the Inspector, with Charles in her wake. In the murk of the tunnel, Mist was exasperated. He pushed the main door back open.

"Who's in charge?" he called out.

Some elves moved away from Uncle Satt, who was fiddling with his collar, trying to refasten it despite the loss of a stud.

"Mr. Bulge, if you would be so kind..."

The Inspector beckoned. Bulge advanced, regaining some of his composure.

"Thank you, sir."

Bulge entered his realm, joining the little party.

"If you would lead us to the scene of the occurrence..."

Bulge, even in the shadows, blanched visibly.

"Very well," he said, lifting a flap of black velvet. A stairwell wound into the ground. Smell hung in the air, ozone and machine oil and something else foul. Arrhythmic din boomed from below. Kate felt a touch of the quease.

Mist went first, signalling for Bulge to follow. Kate and Charles waited for them to disappear before setting foot on the wrought-iron steps.

"Into the underworld," said Charles.

"I didn't realise Noggart's Nook harboured circles of damned souls."

"Children who don't wash their hands before *and* after meals, maids who sweep dust under the carpets..."

Beneath the Gift were large, stone-walled rooms, hot and damp. Electric lamps flickered in heavily grilled alcoves.

"Good God," exclaimed Inspector Mist.

The dynamos were still in motion, though slowed and erratic. Huge cast-iron engines, set in concrete foundations, spat sparks and water-droplets as great belts kept the drums in motion. Wheels and pistons whirled and pounded, ball valves spun, and somewhere below a hungry furnace roared. The central dynamo was grinding irregularly, works impeded by a limp suit of clothes filled with loose meat.

Kate gasped and covered her mouth and nose with her hand, determined not to be overcome.

Flopping from the suit-collar was a deflated ball with a bloody smear for a face.

"Sackham," cried Bulge.

She could not recognise this rag as the clerkish elf she had seen earlier, scurrying after his master.

"What's been done to you?!" howled Bulge, with a shocking, undeniable grief.

The human tangle was twisted into the wheels of the machine, boneless legs caught in cogs. A ball valve whined to a halt and shook off its spindle. With a mighty straining and gouts of fire, the central dynamo died. Its fellows flipped over inhibitors and shut down in more orderly fashion. The lamps faded.

In the dark there was only the *stench*.

Kate felt Charles's arm around her.

ACT III: FÆRIE

i: "events have eventuated"

After a day as Sir Boris and a night at a police station, Charles needed to sleep. The situation was escalating, but he was no use in his present state. He had told Inspector Mist as much as he could and done his best to spare Kate further distress.

He was greeted at the door of his house in Cheyne Walk.

"Visitors, sir," said his man, Bairstow. "I have them in the reception room. Funereal gentlemen."

He considered himself in the hall-mirror. Unshaven, the grey that Kate—clever girl!—had deftly intuited was evident about his gills.

These visitors would not care about his appearance.

"Send in tea, Bairstow. Strong and green."

"Very good, sir."

Charles stepped into his reception room, as if he were the intruder and the others at home.

The two men were dressed like undertakers, in long black coats and gloves, crepe-brimmed hats, and smoked glasses.

"Beauregard," said the senior, Mr. Hay.

"Gentlemen," he acknowledged.

Mr. Hay took his ease in the best armchair, looking over the latest number of the *Pall Mall Gazette*, open to an article by Kate. Not a coincidence.

Mr. Effe, younger and leaner, stood by a book-case, reading spines.

Charles, not caring to be treated like a schoolboy summoned before the beak for a thrashing, slipped into a chair of his own and stretched out, fingers interlaced on his waistcoat as if settling down for a nap.

(Which would be a good idea.)

Two sets of hidden eyes fixed on him.

"Must you wear those things?" Charles asked.

Mr. Hay lowered his spectacles, disclosing very light-coloured, surprisingly humorous eyes. Mr. Effe did not follow suit. Charles amused himself by imagining a severe case of the cross-eyed squints.

At this hour in the morning, a maid would have opened the curtains. The visitors had drawn them again, which should make protective goggles superfluous. He wondered what his visitors could actually see. It was no wonder Mr. Effe had to get so close to the shelves to identify books.

"The salacious items are under lock and key in the hidden room," said Charles. "Have you read *My Nine Nights in a Harem*? I've a rare *Vermis Mysteriis*, illustrated with brass-rubbings that'd curl your hair."

"That's a giggle," snarled Mr. Effe. "Of course, you *do* have hidden rooms."

"Three. And secret passages. Don't you?"

He couldn't imagine Mr. Hay or Mr. Effe—or any of their fellows, Mr. Bee, Mr. Sea, and Mr. Dee, all the way to Mr. Eggs, Miss Why, and Mr. Zed—*having* homes, even haunted lairs. He assumed they slept in rows of coffins under the Houses of Parliament.

Mr. Effe wiped a line down a mediocre edition of *The Collected Poems of Jeffrey Aspern* and pretended to find dust on his gloved finger.

Charles knew Mrs. Hammond, his housekeeper, better than that.

"You've been acting on your own initiative," said Mr. Hay. "That's out of character for an active member of the Diogenes Club. Not that there are enough of you to make general assumptions. Sedentary bunch, as a rule."

"Did you think we wouldn't notice?" sniped Mr. Effe.

Mr. Hay raised a hand, silencing his junior.

"We're not here for recriminations."

Millie, the second-prettiest maid, brought in the tray. He approved; Lucy, the household stunner, was in reserve for special occasions. After thanking the by no means unappealing Millie, he let her escape. Mr. Effe's attempt at a charming smile had thrown a fright into the girl. Charles poured a measure of Mrs. Hammond's potent brew into a giant's teacup, but did not offer hospitality.

"Events have eventuated," said Mr. Hay. "Your Ruling Cabal was short-sighted to green-ribbon the Harvill children. You, however, were perceptive in continuing to take an interest. Even if *unsanctioned.*"

"Bad business under Regent's Park," commented Mr. Effe.

Charles expected these fellows to be up on things.

"Your assumption is that this is the same case?" asked Mr. Hay.

He swallowed tea. The Undertaking knew full well this was the same case.

"Mr. Effe, if you would do the honours," said Mr. Hay, snapping his fingers.

Mr. Effe unbuttoned his coat down the front, and reached inside.

Charles tensed, ready to defend his corner.

Mr. Effe produced a pinch of material, which he unravelled and let dangle. A pale green ribbon.

"Removed from the Harvill file," said Mr. Hay. "With the full cooperation and consultation of the Ruling Cabal."

"You're official again, pally," snapped Mr. Effe.

Charles relaxed. He would have to make explanation to the Cabal in time, but was protected now by approval from on high (rather, down below). There was a literal dark side to this. For all its stuffinesses and eccentricities, he understood the Diogenes Club: It was a comfort and shelter in a world of shadows. The Undertaking was constituted on different lines. Rivalry between the Club and the men in smoked glasses held a potential for outright conflict. It had been said of Mycroft Holmes, chairman of the Ruling Cabal, that sometimes he *was* the British Government; the troubling thing about the Undertaking was that sometimes it *wasn't*.

"We'll see your report," said Mr. Hay.

He remembered how tired he was. He closed his eyes.

When he opened them again, he was alone.

Something tickled on his face. He puffed it away, and saw that it was the ribbon.

ii: "thrones, powers, and principalities"

Kate's story dominated the front page of the *Pall Mall Gazette*. An affront to a national treasure (for so Uncle Satt was reckoned), a gruesomely mysterious death, and rumours of supernatural agency meant Harry Cust had no choice but to give her piece prominence. However, it was rewritten so ruthlessly, by Cust himself at the type-setting bench, that she felt reduced to the status of interviewee, providing raw material shaped into journalism by other hands.

She was cheered, slightly, by a telegram of approval from Uncle Diarmid, who *ought* to be reckoned a national treasure. It arrived soon after the mid-morning special was hawked in the streets, addressed not to the *Gazette* offices but to the Cheshire Cheese, the Fleet Street watering hole where Kate, and four-fifths of the journalists in London, took most meals. Uncle Diarmid always said half the trick of newspaper reporting was getting underfoot, contriving to be present at the most "news-worthy" incidents, gumming up the works to get the story.

The image conjured unpleasant memories. She had ordered chops, but wasn't sure she could face eating—though hunger pangs had struck several times through the long night and morning.

Reporters from other papers stopped by her table, offering congratulations but also soliciting unrefined nuggets of information. Anything about Satterthwaite Bulge was news. Back-files were being combed to provide follow-up pieces to fill out this afternoon and evening editions. The assumption was that the notoriously close-mouthed Inspector Mist would not oblige with further revelations about the death of Mr. Leslie Sackham in time to catch the presses.

Kate had little to add.

The story about the goblins was out, and sketches already circulated ("artists' impressions," which is to say unsubstantiated, fantastical lies) depicting malicious, oval-headed imps tormenting Mr. Sackham before tossing him to the dynamo. Most of Uncle Satt's elves had come forth with tales of goblin sightings or encounters in the dark. Blenkins was charging upwards of ten shillings a time for an anecdote. The rumour was that Scotland Yard were looking for dwarves. Jack Stump was in hiding. Kate wondered about other little people—like Master Timothy, the obnoxious child. How far could such a prankster go? Surely, nursery ill-manners did not betoken a heart black enough for murder. It made more sense to look for goblins. The sensation press had already turned up distinguished crackpots willing to expound at length about the vile habits of *genus goblinus*. Soon, there would be organised hunting parties, and rat-tail bounties offered on green, pointed ears.

Kate's chops were set before her. She had ordered them well-cooked, so that no red showed. Even so, she ate the baked potato first.

There was the problem of Mr. Sackham's obituary, which was assigned to her. The most interesting thing about the man's life was its end, already described at quite enough length. His injuries were such that it was impossible to tell whether he had been thrown (or fallen) alive into the dynamo. Indeed, the corpse was mutilated to such an extent that if the incident were encountered in a penny dreadful, the astute reader would assume Mr. Sackham not to be dead at all but that the body was a nameless tramp dressed in his clothes and sacrificed in order to facilitate a surprise in a later chapter. The second most interesting thing about Sackham was that he had penned many of the words recently published under the byline of Uncle Satt, but Cust forbade her to mention this. Exposing hypocrites was all very well, but no newspaper could afford to suggest that Satterthwaite Bulge was less than the genial "Founder of Færie and Magister of Marvells" for fear of an angry mob of children invading their offices to wreak vengeful havoc. She was reduced to padding out a paragraph on Sackham's duties at the Gift and the fact that he very nearly could legitimately call Uncle Satt his uncle; Leslie Sackham had been the son of his employer's cousin.

She finished her copy and her chops at about the same time, then gave a handy lad tuppence to rush the obit to the *Gazette* in the Strand. As Ned made his way out of the Cheese, he was entrusted with a dozen other scribblings—some on the reverse of bills, most on leaves torn from note-books—to drop off at the various newspapers on his route.

Now, she might snatch a snooze.

"Kate."

She looked up, not sure how long (or if) she had dozed in her chair.

"Charles."

He sat down.

"Scotland Yard is saying it was an accident," he said.

Kate sensed journalistic ears pricking up all around.

"That doesn't sound like Mist," she observed.

"I didn't say 'Mist,' I said 'Scotland Yard.'"

She understood. Decisions had been made in shadowed corridors.

"The Gift is declared 'unsafe' for the moment," he continued. "No grand opening this weekend, I'm afraid. There'll be investigations, by the public health and safety people and anyone else who can get his oar in. It turns out that the Corporation of London still owns the site. Uncle Satt is lessee of the ground, though he has deed and title to all structures built on and under it. There'll be undignified arguments over whose fault it all is. In the meantime, the place is under police guard. As you can imagine, Regent's Park is besieged by aspirant goblin hunters. Some have butterfly nets and elephant guns."

She looked around. The cartoonist responsible was lurking somewhere.

"I was given this," he said, producing a length of green ribbon.

"The Ruling Cabal want you to continue to take an interest?"

"They've no choice. Another body has made its desires known. There are thrones, powers, and principalities in this. For some reason beyond me, this matter is important. My remit is loose. While the police and the safety fellows are concerned with Sackham's death, I am to pull the loose ends. I have leeway as to whom I choose to involve, and I should like to choose you."

"*Again?* You'll have to put me up for membership one day."

She was teasing, but he took it seriously. "In a world of impossibilities, that should be discussed. I shall see what I can do."

Previously, when Charles involved her (or, more properly, allowed her to become involved) in the business of the Diogenes Club, she had gathered stories that would make her name if set in type but which wouldn't even pass the breed of editor willing to publish "artist's impressions," let alone Henry Cockayne-Cust. Still, she had an eternal itch to draw back the curtain. Association with Charles was interesting on other levels, if often enervating or perilous.

"If the Gift is being adequately investigated, where should we direct our attentions?"

Charles smiled.

"How would you like an audience with B. Loved?"

iii: "the Affair of the Dendrified Digit"

"So this is the house that Færie built?" said Kate.

"Bought," he corrected.

"Very nice. Pennies add up like details, indeed."

They were on a doorstep in elegant Broadley Terrace, quite near Regent's Park and a long way from Herefordshire.

"What's that smell?" asked Kate, nose wrinkling like a kitten's.

"Fresh bread," he told her.

The door was opened by a child with flour on his cheeks and a magnifying glass in his hand. The boy examined Charles's shoes and trouser-cuffs, then angled his gaze upwards. Through the lens, half his face was enlarged and distorted.

"I be a 'tective," he announced.

"What about the flour?" asked Charles.

Kate had slipped a handkerchief out of her tightly buttoned cuff, possessed of a universal feminine instinct to clean the faces of boys who were perfectly happy as they were.

The boy touched his forehead, then examined the white on his fingertips.

"I be a baker too, like my Da. I be baker by day, 'tective by night."

"Very practical," said Kate. "In my experience, detectives often neglect proper meals."

"Are you a 'tective too, mister?"

Charles looked at Kate, for a prompt.

"Sometimes," he admitted. "But don't tell anyone. Affairs of state, you know."

The boy's face distorted in awe.

"A *secret agent*.... Come in and have some of my boasters. I made them special, all by myself. Though Da helped with the oven."

Charles let Kate step into the hallway and followed, removing his hat.

A woman bustled into the hall.

"Dickie," she said, incipiently scolding, "who've you let in now?"

The woman, neat and plump, came to them. Sairey Riddle, well shy of thirty, had grey streaks. In eight years, she had filled out to resemble her late mother.

She remembered him.

"It's you," she said, face shaded. "You found *her*."

"Maeve."

"Her."

He understood the distinction.

"This is my friend, Miss Katharine Reed. Kate, this is Sairey Riddle."

"Sarah," she said, careful with the syllables now.

Dickie was clinging to his mother's skirts. Now, he looked up again at Charles.

"You be *that* 'tective. Who found Auntie when she were lost? In the olden days?"

"He means before he were... was born. It's all olden days to him.

Might as well a' been knights in armour and fire-breathing dragons."

"Yes, Dickie. I found your Aunt Maeve. One of my most difficult cases."

Dickie looked through his magnifying glass again.

"A proper *'tective*," he breathed.

"I do believe you've found a hero-worshipper," whispered Kate, not entirely satirically.

Charles was intently aware of a sudden responsibility.

"Don't mind our Dickie," said Sarah. "He's not daft and he means well."

For the first time in months, Charles felt the ache in his forearm, in the long-healed bite. It was the name, of course. By now, his son would have been almost an adult; he would have been Dickie as a child, Dick as a youth, and be on the point of demanding the full, respectful Richard.

"Are you all right?" enquired Kate, sharp as usual.

"Old wound," he said, not satisfying her.

"Have you come about the business in the park?" prompted Sarah. "We heard about poor Mr. Sackham."

"I'm afraid so. We were wondering if we might see Davey?"

Sarah bit her lower lip. He noticed a worn spot, often chewed. She glanced up at the ceiling. The shadow that had fallen over this family in Hill Wood had never been dispelled.

"It's not been one of his good days."

"I can imagine."

"We never did find out, you know, what *happened* to him. To them both."

"I know."

Sarah led them into a reception room. She left Dickie with them while she went to look in on her brother.

"Do you want to see my *clues*?" asked the boy, tugging Charles's trouser pocket.

Kate found this hilarious but stifled her giggles.

Dickie produced a cigar box and showed its contents.

"This button 'nabled me to solve the Case of the Vanishing Currant Bun. It were the fat lad from down the road. He snitched it from the tray when Da weren't looking. This playin' card, a Jack of Hearts with one corner bent off, is the key to the Scandal of the Cheatin' Governess. And this twig that looks 'zactly like a 'uman finger is a mystery whose solution no man yet knows, though I've not 'bandoned my inquiries."

Charles examined the twig, which did resemble a finger.

"What do you call the case?" he asked the boy.

"It hasn't a name yet."

"What about the Affair of the Dendrified Digit?" suggested Kate.

Dickie's eyes widened and he ran the words around his mouth.

'"What be a 'dendrified digit?'"

"A finger turned to wood."

"Very 'propriate. Are you a 'tective too, lady?"

"I'm a reporter."

"A *daredevil* reporter," Charles corrected.

Kate poked her tongue out at him while Dickie wasn't looking.

"Then you must be a 'tective's *assistant*."

Kate was struck aghast. It was Charles's turn to be amused.

Dickie reached into his box and produced a rusty nail.

"This be…"

He halted mid-sentence, swallowed, and stepped back, positioning himself so that Kate stood between the door and him.

The handle was turning.

Into the room came a little girl in blue, as perfectly dressed as a china doll on display. She had an enormous cloud of stiff blonde hair and a long, solemn, pretty face.

Beside her, Dickie looked distinctly shabby.

The girl looked at Charles and announced, "we have met before."

"It's Auntie," whispered Dickie. Charles saw the wariness the lad had around the girl; not fear, exactly, but an understanding, developed over years, that she could hurt him if she chose.

"Maeve," Charles said. "I am Mr. Beauregard."

"The man in the wood," she said. "The hero of the day. *That* day."

Kate's mouth was open. At a glance from Charles, she realised her lapse and shut it quickly. Dickie wasn't quite hiding behind Kate's skirt, but was in a position to make that retreat if needed.

Maeve wandered around the room, picking up ornaments, looking at them and putting them down in exactly the same place. She didn't look directly at Charles or Kate, but always had a reflective surface in sight to observe their faces.

Instinctively, Charles wanted to know where she was at any moment.

If Dickie were seven or eight, Maeve should be nineteen or twenty. She was exactly as she had been when he first saw her, in Hill Wood.

"I thought you'd be taller," said Kate.

The girl arched a thick eyebrow, as if she hadn't noticed Kate before.

"Might you be *Mrs.* Beauregard?"

"Katharine Reed, *Pall Mall Gazette*," she said.

"Is it *common* for ladies to represent newspapers?"

"Not at all."

"Oh, really? I rather thought it was. Most *common*."

She turned, as if dismissing a servant.

Maeve Harvill did not act like a carpenter's daughter or a baker's niece. She was a princess. Not an especially nice one.

"You'll have come to see poor David."

"Poor" David owned this house and was the support of his whole family. Charles wondered if Davey even knew that.

"About the unpleasantness in the park."

"You know about that?"

"It was in the *newspapers*," she said, tossing a glance at Kate. "Do you know Mr. Satterthwaite Bulge? He's *ghastly*."

That was the first child-thing she had said.

"Does Uncle Satt call here often?" asked Kate.

"He's not *my* uncle. He stays away unless he absolutely can't help it. Will he go to jail? I'm sure what happened to Leslie is all his fault."

"You knew the late Mr. Sackham?" Charles asked.

Maeve considered Kate and then Charles, thinking. She pressed an eyetooth to her lower lip, carefully not breaking the skin, mimicking Sarah—whom it was hard to think of as the princess's sister.

"Is this to be an *interrogation*?"

"They be 'tectives, Auntie," said Dickie.

"How exciting," she commented, as if on the point of falling asleep. "Are we to be arrested?"

She held out her arms, voluminous sleeves sliding away from bird-thin wrists.

"Do you have handcuffs in my size?"

She spied something on a small table. It was Dickie's twig-clue. She picked it up, held it alongside her own forefinger, and snapped it in half.

"Dirty thing. I can't imagine how it got in here."

Dickie didn't cry but one of his eyes gleamed with a tear-to-be.

Maeve made a fist around the twig fragments as if to crush them further, then opened her hand to show an empty palm. With a flourish she produced the twig—whole—in her other hand.

Kate clapped, slowly. Maeve smiled to herself and took a little bow.

"I be a 'tective," said Dickie, tears gone and delight stamped on his face. "Auntie Maeve be a *conjurer*."

"She should go on the halls," said Kate, unimpressed. "Mystic, Magical Maeve, the Modern Medusa."

The girl flicked the twig into a grate where no fire would burn till autumn. Neither of her hands was dirty, the neatest trick of all.

"She makes things vanish, then brings 'em back," said Dickie.

"That seems to happen quite often in this family," commented Charles.

"More things vanish than come back," said Maeve. "Has he told you about the Bun Bandit from two doors down?"

"A successful conclusion to a baffling case?"

Maeve smiled. "Sidney Silcock might not think so. He was thrashed and put on bread and water. Dickie has to keep out of the way when Sidney pays a call. A retaliatory walloping has been mentioned. There's a fellow who knows how to bide his time. I shouldn't be surprised if he waits *years*, until everyone else has forgotten what it was about. But the walloping will be *heroic*. Sidney is one to do things on an heroic scale."

"He sounds a desperate villain."

"He's desperate all right," said Maeve, smiling her secret smile again.

"Greedy Sid's sweet on 'er," said Dickie.

She glared calmly at her nephew.

Sarah came into the room, took in the scene, and nipped her lip again.

"Sarah, dear, I have been renewing a friendship. This, I am sure you realise, is Charles Beauregard, the intrepid fellow who rescued me from the *gypsies in the wood*."

"Yes, Maeve, I realise."

Sarah was not unconditionally grateful for this rescue. Sometimes she wished Charles had left well enough alone, had not lifted the princess from the snow, not carried her out of the wood.

"Davey says he'd like to see you," Sarah told Charles, quietly—like a servant in her mistress's presence. "And the lady."

"You are privileged," said Maeve. "My brother rarely likes to see me."

She was playing with a glass globe that contained a miniature woodland scene. When shook, it made a blizzard.

"Happy memories," she commented.

"Davey's upstairs, in his studio," said Sarah. "Drawing. He's better than he was earlier."

Sarah held the door open. Kate stepped into the hall, and Charles followed. Sarah looked back, at her son and her sister.

"Dickie, come help in the kitchen," she said.

Dickie stayed where he was.

"I can see he stays out of trouble while we have visitors," said Maeve. "I've been practicing new tricks."

Sarah was unsure. Dickie was resigned.

"I be all right, Ma."

Sarah nodded and closed the door on the children. A tear of blood ran down the groove of her chin, unnoticed.

"Maeve hasn't changed," said Charles as Sarah led them upstairs.

"Not since you saw her," she responded. "But she *did* change. When she were away. As much as Davey, not that anyone do listen to I. Not that Mam listened, God rest her."

From the landing, Charles looked downstairs. All was quiet.

"Come through here," said Sarah. "To the studio."

iv: "industry is a virtue"

Kate was expecting Ben Gunn—wild hair, matted beard, mad eyes. Instead, she found a presentable man, working in a room full of light. Beard he had, but neatly trimmed and free of beetles. One eye was slightly lazy, but he did not seem demented. Davey Harvill, B. Loved, sat on a stool, over paper pinned flat to a bench. His hand moved fast with a sharp pencil, filling in intricate details of a picture already sketched. To one side was a neat pile of papers, squared away like letters for posting. By his feet was a half-full wastepaper basket.

This was the neatest artists' studio she had ever seen: bare floorboards spotless, walls papered but unadorned. Uncurtained floor-to-ceiling windows admitted direct sunlight. The expected clutter was absent: no books, reference materials, divans for models, props. Davey, in shirtsleeves, had not so much as a smudge of graphite upon him. He might have been a draper's clerk doing the end-of-day accounts. It was as if the pictures were willed into being without effort, without mess. They came out of his head, whole and entire, and were transmitted to paper.

Mrs. Riddle let Kate and Charles into the room, coughed discreetly, and withdrew.

Davey looked up, nodded to Charles and smiled at Kate. His hand moved at hummingbird speed, whether his eye was upon the paper or not. Some mediums practiced automatic writing; this could be automatic drawing.

"Charles, hello," said Davey.

As far as Kate knew, the artist had not seen Charles in eight years.

"How have you been?" asked Charles.

"Very well, sir, all things considered."

He finished his drawing and, without looking, freed it from its pinnings and shifted it to the pile, neatening the corners. He unrolled paper from a scroll, deftly pinned it in place and used a penknife to cut neatly across the top. A white, empty expanse lay before him.

"Busy, of course," he said. "Industry is a virtue."

He took a pencil and, without pause, began to sketch.

Kate moved closer, to get a look at the work in progress. Most painters would have thrown her in the street for such impertinence, but Davey did not appear to mind.

Davey's pencil-point flew, in jagged, sudden strokes. A woodland appeared, populated by creatures whose eyes showed in shadows. Two small figures, hand in hand, walked in a clearing. A little boy and a girl.

Watched from the trees and the burrows.

"This is my friend Kate Reed," said Charles.

Davey smiled again, open and engaging, content in his work.

"Hello, Kate."

"Please forgive this intrusion," she ventured.

"It's no trouble. Makes a nice change."

His pencil left the children, and darted to the corners of the picture, shading areas with solid strokes that left black shadows, relieved by tiny, glittering eyes and teeth. Kate was alarmed, afraid for the safety of the boy and the girl.

"I still haven't remembered anything," said Davey. "I'm sorry, Charles. I have tried."

"That's all right, Davey."

He was back on the central figures. The children, alone in the woods, clinging together for reassurance, for safety.

"What subject is this?" she asked.

"I don't know," said Davey, looking down, seeing the picture for the first time, "the usual."

Now his eyes were on the paper, Davey stopped drawing.

"*Babes in the Wood*?" suggested Charles. "Hansel and Gretel?"

Something was wrong about the children. They did not fit either of the stories Charles had mentioned.

"Davey and Maeve," said the artist, sadly. "I know everything I draw comes from *that time*. It's as if it never ended, not really."

Charles laid a hand on the man's—the boy's—shoulder.

Davey began to work again on the children, more deliberately now.

Kate saw what was wrong. The girl was not afraid.

As Davey was doing the girl's eyes, the pencil-lead broke, scratching across her face.

"Pity," he said.

Rather than reach for an india rubber and make a minor change, he tore the paper from the block and began to make a ball of it.

"Excuse me," said Kate, taking the picture from its creator.

"It's no use," he said.

Kate spread the crumpled paper.

She saw something in it.

Charles riffled through the pile of completed illustrations. They were a sequence. The children entering the woods, taking a winding path, walking past færie dwellings without noticing, enticed ever deeper into the dark.

Kate looked back at the rejected picture.

The girl was exactly the child-woman Kate had met downstairs, Maeve. Her brother had caught the sulky, adult turn of her mouth and made her huge brush of hair seem alive. A princess, but a frightening one.

In the picture, the children were not lost. The girl was *leading* the boy into the woods.

"This is your sister," said Kate, tapping the girl's scratched face.

"Maeve," he said, not quite agreeing.

"And this is you? Davey?"

Davey hesitated. "That's not right," he said. "Let me fix it…"

He reached for his pencil, but Charles stayed his hand.

They all looked closely at the boy in the picture. He was just beginning to worry, starting to consider unthinkable things—that the girl who held his hand was, in a real sense, a stranger to him, a stranger to *everyone*, that this adventure in the woods was taking a sinister turn.

It *might* be Davey, as he was when he went into the woods eight years ago, as a nine-year-old.

But it looked more like Dickie, as he was now.

v: "Richard Riddle, Special Detective"

"If *I* were a real detective," said Auntie Maeve, "I shouldn't be content to waste my talents tracking down bun-thieves. For my quarry, I should choose more desperate criminals. Fiends who threaten the country more than they do their own trouser-buttons."

Dickie trailed down the street after his aunt.

"I should concentrate exclusively on cases which constitute a challenge, on mysteries *worth* solving. Murders, and such."

Maeve led him past the Silcock house, which gave him a pang of worry. Greedy Sid was, like the Count of Monte Cristo, capable of nurturing over long years an impulse to revenge. Behind the tall railings, bottom still smarting, the miscreant would be brooding, plotting. Dickie imagined Sidney Silcock, swollen to enormous size, become his lifelong nemesis, the Napoleon of Gluttony.

"The mystery of Leslie Sackham, for instance."

The name caught Dickie's mind.

He remembered Mr. Sackham as a bendy minion, hair floppy and cuffs ink-stained, trailing after Mr. Bulge in attitudes of contortion. A tall man, he tried always to look up to his employer, no matter what kinks that put into his neck and spine. Sometimes, Mr. Sackham told stories to children, but got them muddled and lost his audience before he reached the predictable endings. Dickie remembered one about Miss Fay Twinkledust, who put all her sparkles into a sensible investment portfolio rather than tossing them into the Silver Stream to be gobbled by the Silly Fish. Mr. Sackham had been a boring grown-up. Now he was dead, the limits of his bendiness reached inside the works of a dynamo, Dickie felt guilty for not having liked him much.

It would be fitting if he were to solve the mystery.

Everyone would be grateful. Especially if it meant the Gift could open after all. Mr. Bulge's business would be saved from the Silly Fish. Dickie understood the fortunes of the Harvill household depended in some mysterious way on the enterprises of "Uncle Satt"—though only babies and girls read that dreary *Treasury* for anything but Uncle Davey's pictures.

Maeve took his hand.

"Where are we goin'?"

"To the park, of course."

"Why?"

"To look for *clues*."

At this magic word, Dickie was seized by the *rightness* of the pursuit. Whatever else Maeve might be, she was clever. She would make a valuable detective's assistant, with her sharp eyes and odd way of looking at things. Sometimes, she frightened people. That could be useful too.

Though it was too warm out for caps, scarves, and coats, Maeve had insisted they dress properly for this sleuthing expedition. They might have to go *underground*, she said.

Dickie wore his special coat, a "reversible" which could be either a loud check or a subdued herringbone. If spotted by a suspected criminal one was "tailing," the trick was to turn the coat inside-out and so seem to be another boy entirely. He even had a matching cap. In addition, secret pockets were stuffed with the instruments of his calling. About his person, he had the magnifying glass, measuring callipers, his catapult (which he was under strict orders from Ma not to use within shot of windows), a map of the locality with secret routes pencilled in, a multipurpose penknife (with five blades, plus corkscrew, screwdriver, and bradawl), and a bottle of invisible ink. He had made up cards for himself using a potato press, in visible and invisible ink: "Richard Riddle, Special Detective." Da approved, saying he was "a regular Hawkshaw." Hawkshaw was a famous detective from the olden days.

Maeve, with a blue bonnet that matched her dress, was a touch conspicuous for "undercover" work. She walked with such confidence, however, that no one thought they were out on their own. Seeing the children—not that Aunt Maeve was *exactly* a child—in the street, people assumed there was a governess nearby, watching over them.

Dickie didn't believe in governesses. They came and went so often. Ma lamented that most found it difficult to work under a baker's wife, which proved the stupidity of the breed. He might bristle at parental decrees, especially with regards to the overrated virtues of cleanliness and tidiness, but Ma knew best—better than a governess, at any rate. Some were unaccountably prone to fits of terror. He suspected Maeve worked tricks to make governesses vanish on a regular basis, though she never brought them back again. He even wondered whether his aunt hadn't had an unseen hand in one of his greatest triumphs, the Mystery of the Cheating Governess. Despite overwhelming evidence, Miss MacAndrew had maintained to the moment of her dismissal that she had done no such thing.

In the park, children were everywhere, playing hopscotch, climbing anything that could be climbed, defending the North-West Frontier against disapproving wardens, fighting wild Red Indians with Buffalo Bill. Governesses in black bombazine flocked on the benches. Dickie imagined a cloud of general disapproval gathering above them. He pondered the possibility that they were in a secret society, pledged to make miserable the lives of all children, sworn to inflict *etiquette* and *washes* on the innocent. They dressed alike, and had the same expression—as if they'd just been made to swallow a whole lemon but ordered not to let it show.

He shouldn't be at all surprised if governesses were behind the Mystery of the Mangled Minion.

Mr. Sackham had died in the park. There were always governesses in the park. They could easily cover up for each other. In their black, they could blend in with the shadows.

He liked the theory. Hawkshaw would have found it sound.

A pretty child with gloves in the shape of rabbit-heads approached, smiling slyly. She had ribbons in her hair and sewn to her clothes. She was overdecorated, as if awarded a fresh ribbon every time she said her prayers.

"Little boy, my name is Becky d'Arbanvilliers," said the girl, who was younger than him by a year or more. "When I gwow up and Papa cwoaks, I shall be *Lady* d'Arbanvilliers. If you do something for me, I'll let you kiss my wabbits."

Maeve took the future Lady d'Arbanvilliers aside, lifted a curtain of ribbons, and whispered into her ear. Maeve was insistent but calm. The girl's face crumpled, eyes expanding. Maeve finished whispering and stood back. Becky d'Arbanvilliers looked up at her, trembling. Maeve nodded and the girl ran away, exploding into screams and floods of tears.

"Hey presto, Hawkshaw," she told Dickie. "Magic."

Becky d'Arbanvilliers fled to the coven of governesses, too hysterical to explain, but pointing in the direction where Maeve had been.

An odd thing was that two men dressed like governesses, not in long skirts but all in black with dark spectacles and curly hat-brims, were nearby. Dickie pegged them as sinister individuals. *They* paid attention to the noisy little girl.

"How cwuel," said Maeve, imitating perfectly. "To be named 'Rebecca' and yet pwevented by nature fwom pwonouncing it pwoperly."

Dickie laughed. No one else noticed that his aunt could be funny as well as frightening. It was a secret between them.

Maeve led him towards the Gift.

A barrier of trestles was set up all around the building, hung with notices warning the public not to trespass. A policeman stood by the front doors, firmly seeing away curiosity-seekers. Dickie and Maeve had visited while Uncle Davey was helping Mr. Bulge turn the Gift into the Færie Aerie, and knew other ways in and out. Special Detectives always had more information than the poor plods of the Yard.

Maeve led Dickie round to the rear of the Gift. A door there supposedly only opened from the inside, so the used-up visitors could leave to make room for fresh ones. Unless you knew it was there, you wouldn't see it. The wall was painted with a big, colour copy of one of Uncle Davey's drawings, and the door hid in a waterfall, like goblins in a puzzle.

They slipped under an unguarded trestle.

Commotion rose in the park, among governesses. Becky d'Arbanvilliers had been able to explain. Though the governess instinct was to distrust anything a child told them, *something* had upset the girl. A hunt would have to be organised.

The men dressed like governesses took an interest.

Dickie was worried for his aunt.

Maeve smiled at him.

"I shall spirit us to safety, with more magic," she announced. "Might I borrow your catapult?"

He was reluctant to hand over such a formidable weapon.

"I shall return it directly."

Dickie undid his secret pocket and produced the catapult.

Maeve examined it, twanged the rubber appreciatively, and pronounced it a fine addition to a detective's arsenal.

She made a fold in the rubber and slipped it into the crack in the falling waters that showed those who knew what to look for where the door was. She worked with her fingers for a few moments.

"This is where a conjurer chats to the audience, to take their minds off the trick being done in front of their eyes."

Dickie watched closely—he always did, but Maeve still managed tricks he could not work out.

"I say, what are you children doing?"

It was a *governess*, a skeleton in black.

"Have you seen a horrid, *horrid* little girl…? Dipped in the very essence of wickedness?"

Maeve did one of her best tricks. She put on a smile that fooled everyone but Dickie. She seemed like all the sunny girls in the world, brainless and cheerful.

"I should not like to meet a wicked little girl," she said, sounding a little like Becky d'Arbanvilliers. "No, thank you very much."

"Very wise," said the governess, fooled entirely. "Well, if you see such a creature, stay well away from her."

The woman stalked off.

Maeve shrugged and dropped the smile.

"I swear, Hawkshaw, these *people*. They're so *stupid*. They deserve... ah!"

There was a click inside the wall. Maeve pulled the catapult free and the door came open.

She handed him back the catapult and tugged him inside, into the dark.

The door shut behind them.

"This is an adventure, isn't it?"

He agreed.

vi: "intelligence reports"

Sarah Riddle, over the first shock, slumped on a hall settee, numb, and cried out.

Charles understood.

The worst thing was that this was a *familiar* anxiety.

Maeve and Dickie were missing.

"It's *her*," said Sarah. "I always knew..."

The house had been searched. Kate turned up Bitty, a maid who recalled noticing Dickie and his aunt, dressed as if to go out. That she had not actually seen them leave the house saved her position. Charles knew that even if Bitty had been there, she would not have been able to intervene. Maeve treated her family like servants; he could imagine how she treated servants.

"It's like before," said Philip Riddle, standing by his wife. "Only then it were Hill Wood. Now, it's a whole *city*."

Charles reproached himself for not considering Dickie. He had given a lot of thought to Davey and Princess Cuckoo, but rarely recalled that this household harboured one proper child. When Charles was in Eye, Dickie had not been born, was not part of the story.

Now, Charles saw where Dickie fit.

Davey had escaped *something*. Dickie would do as replacement.

"Charles," said Kate, from the top of the stairs. "Would you come up?"

He left Sarah and Philip, and joined Kate. She led him into the studio.

Davey was still drawing.

Kate showed him finished pictures in which the children ventured deeper into the woods. A smug bunny in a beribboned pinafore appeared in a clearing. The girl, more Maeve than ever, loomed over the small, terrified rabbit. In one picture, her head was inflated twice the size of her body, hair puffed like a lion's mane. She showed angry, evil eyes and a toothy, dripping shark's maw. The rabbit fled, understandably. In the next picture, Maeve was herself again, though it would be hard to forget her scary head. She was snatching the boy, Dickie, away from a clutch of old-womanish crows who sported veiled hats and reticules. Then the children came to a waterfall. Maeve used long-nailed fingers to unlock a door in the cascade—a door made of *flowing* water, not ice—to open a way into a wooded underworld.

"What does this mean, Davey?"

He drew faster than ever. Tears spotted his paper, blotching the pencilwork. His face shut tight, he rocked back and forth, crooning.

"My mother said… I never should… play with the gypsies… in the wood."

Another picture was finished and put aside.

The children were in a forested tunnel, passing a fallen tower. Goblins swarmed in the undergrowth, ears and tongues twitching, flat nostrils a-quiver.

"I know that ruin," said Kate. "It's in the Gift. We were there when it collapsed."

"And *I* know the waterfall door."

Kate began searching the studio.

"What are you looking for?" he asked her.

"A sketch-pad. Something he can carry. We have to take him to the park. All this is happening *now*. The pictures are like *intelligence reports*."

Kate opened a cupboard in the workbench and found a package of notebooks. She took several and shoved one opened under Davey's pencil, whispering to him, urging him to shift to a portable medium. After a beat of hesitation, he began again, drawing still faster, pencil scoring paper. Kate gathered the completed pictures into a sturdy artists' folder.

"Stay with him a moment," Charles told her, leaving the study.

Dickie's parents were at the foot of the stairs, looking up.

"Is this household on the telephone?" Charles asked.

"Mr. Bulge insisted," said Philip Riddle. "The apparatus is in the downstairs parlour."

"Ring up Scotland Yard and ask for Inspector Henry Mist. Tell him to meet us at the Gift."

Riddle, a solid man, didn't waste time asking for explanations. He went directly to the parlour.

Kate had Davey out of his studio and helped him downstairs. He still murmured and scribbled.

"Bad things in the woods," Kate reported. "Very bad."

Charles trusted her.

"Have you called a cab?" she asked.

"Quicker to walk."

Sarah reached out as Kate and Charles helped Davey past, pleading wordlessly. Her lip was bleeding.

"There's hope," he told her.

She accepted that as the best offer available.

On the street, he and Kate must have seemed the abductors of a lunatic. When Davey finished a picture, Kate turned the page for him.

From a window peered the fat face of a sad little boy. He alone took notice of the peculiar trio. People on the street evaded them without comment. Charles did his best to look like someone who would brook no interference.

Every pause to allow a cart or carriage primacy was a heart-blow.

The streets were uncommonly busy. People were mobile trees in these wilds, constantly shutting off and making new paths. London was more perilous than Hill Wood. Though it was a sunny afternoon and he walked on broad pavement, Charles recalled snow underfoot.

"What's in the pictures now?" he asked.

"Hard to make out. Children, goblins, woods. The boy seems all right still."

Maeve and Dickie must have taken this route, perhaps half an hour earlier. This storm had blown up in minutes.

If it weren't for Kate's leap of deduction, the absences might have gone unnoticed until teatime. Another reason to propose her for membership.

In the park, there was the expected chaos. Children, idlers, governesses, dogs. A one-man band played something from *The Mikado*.

"The crows," said Kate.

Charles saw what she meant. Some governesses gathered around a little girl, heads bobbing like birds, veiled hats like those in Davey's illustration.

"And that's the frightened bunny," he pointed out.

He remembered Maeve's temporary scary head. Davey's drawings weren't the literal truth, he hoped. They hinted at what really happened.

"Ladies," he began, "might I inquire whether you've seen two children, a girl of perhaps eleven and a slightly younger boy? You would take them for brother and sister."

The women reacted like Transylvanian peasants asked the most convenient route to Castle Dracula, with hisses and flutterings and clucks very like curses.

"That horrid, *horrid* girl…" spat one.

Even in the circumstances, he had to swallow a smirk.

"That would be the miss. You have her exactly."

The governesses continued, yielding more editorial comment but no hard news.

"Why is that man dwawing?" asked the ribboned girl.

"He's an artist," Charles told her.

"My name is Becky d'Arbanvilliers," she said proudly. "When I gwow up and Papa cwoaks, I shall be *Lady* d'Arbanvilliers."

Few prospective heirs would be as honest, he supposed. At least, out loud. In cases of suspicious death, the police were wont to remember such offhand remarks.

"Did you meet a bad girl, Becky?"

She nodded her head, solemnly.

"And where is she now?"

Becky frowned, as angry as she was puzzled.

"I *told* Miss Wodgers, but she didn't believe me. The bad girl and the nasty boy went to the waterfall in that house."

She pointed to the Gift.

"There was a girl," said the governess, whose name he presumed was Miss Rodgers. "But not the one who so upset Becky. This was a nice, polite child."

Becky looked at Charles, frustrated by her governess's gullibility.

"It was her," she insisted, stamping a tiny foot.

Davey finished one notebook and started on the next. Kate took the filled book and leafed through, then found a picture.

"*This* girl?" she asked. "And this boy."

"That's them," said Becky. "What a pwetty picture. Will the man dwaw me? I'm pwettier than the bad girl."

"Miss Rodgers," Charles prompted.

The governess looked stricken.

"Yes," she admitted. "But she *smiled* so…"

Recriminations flew around the group of governesses.

"*Will the man dwaw me?*"

Kate leafed through the folder and found a picture of the children meeting the ribboned rabbit, the one in which Maeve was not showing her scary head. She handed it over. Becky was transported with delight, terrors forgotten.

Miss Rodgers saw the picture, puzzled and disturbed.

"How did he do this? It was drawn before he set eyes on Rebecca…"

They left the governesses wondering.

From the corner of his eye, Charles glimpsed a couple in black who weren't governesses. Mr. Hay and Mr. Effe. Since this morning, he had been aware of their floating presence. The Undertaking was playing its own game and had turned up here before he did. He would worry about that later, if he got the chance. Right now, he should be inside the Gift.

By the time they found the door concealed in the waterfall design, Inspector Mist was on the scene.

"Mr. Beauregard, what is all this about?"

vii: "stage snow"

Kate knew that Charles would make a token attempt to dissuade her from continuing. The argument, a variation on a theme with which she was bored, was conducted in shorthand.

Yes, it might be dangerous.

Yes, she was a woman.

No, that wouldn't make a difference.

Settled.

Mist of the Yard was distracted by Davey's compulsive sketching.

"Is this fellow some sort of psychic medium?"

"He has a connection with this business," Charles told Mist. "This is Davey Harvill."

"The boy from Eye."

The Inspector evidently knew about the Children of Eye. Kate was not surprised. Whisper had it that Mist was high up in the Bureau of Queer Complaints, an unpublicised Scotland Yard department constituted to deal with the "spook" cases.

Mist posted constables to keep back this afternoon's crowds. Rumours circulated. The Gift was about to be opened to the public. Or razed to the ground. No one was sure. Helmeted bobbies assumed their usual attitudes, bored resignation to indicate nothing out of the ordinary taking place behind the barriers and truncheon-tapping warning that no monkey business would be tolerated. Popular phrases were recited: "move along, now" and "there's nothing to see 'ere."

Two men in black clothes augmented by very black spectacles sauntered over. At the flash of a card, they were admitted to the inner circle.

They chimed with another whisper, about funereal officials seen pottering about new-made meteor craters or the sites of unnatural vanishments. Another high-stakes player at this table, in competition or alliance with the Diogenes Club and the BQC. The poor plodders of the Society for Psychical Research must feel left out, stuck with only the least mysterious of eternal mysteries, trivial table-rappings and ghosts who did nothing but loom in sheets and say "boo!" to handy geese.

Charles made rapid introductions. "Mr. Hay and Mr. Effe, of the Undertaking. Mist you know. Katharine Reed..."

Mr. Effe bared poor teeth at her. Even without sight of his eyes, she could gauge his expression.

"Do we need the press, Beauregard?" he asked.

"*I* need *her*."

Argument was squashed. She was proud of him, again. More than proud.

"The missing boy is in there," said Mist. "And his… sister?"

"*Aunt*," corrected Charles. "Maeve. Don't be taken in by her. She's not what she seems. The boy is Richard. Dickie. He's the one in danger. We must get him out of the Gift."

"The girl too," prompted Mr. Hay.

Charles shook his head. "She's long lost," he said. "It's the boy we want, we *need*…"

"That wasn't a suggestion," said the Undertaker.

Charles and Mist exchanged a look.

"Get that door kicked in," Mist told two hefty bobbies.

They shouldered the waterfall, shaking the whole of the Gift.

"It's probably unlocked and opens outwards," Kate suggested.

The policemen stood back. The dented door swung slowly out, proving her point. Inside, it was darker than it should be. This was a bright afternoon. The ceiling of the Gift was mostly glass. It should be gloomy at worst.

White powder lay on the floor, footprints trodden in.

"Is that snow?" asked Mist.

"Stage snow," said Charles. "Remember, nothing in there is real. Which doesn't mean it's not dangerous."

"We'll need light. Willoughby, hand over your bull-lantern."

One of the bobbies unlatched a device from his belt. Mist lit the lamp. Charles took it and shone a feeble beam into the dark. Stage snow fell from a sky ceiling. It was a clever trick—reflective sparkles set into wooden walls. But Kate did not imagine the cold wind that blew from the Gift, chilling through her light blouse. She was not dressed to pay a call on the Snow Queen.

Charles ventured into the dark.

Kate helped Davey follow. He had stopped chanting out loud but his neck muscles worked as he subaudibly repeated his rhyme.

In his pictures, goblins gathered.

Mist came last, with another lamp.

Mr. Hay and Mr. Effe remained outside, in the summer sunshine.

This was not a part of Færie that Kate had seen yesterday, but Charles evidently knew his way. The walls were theatrical flats painted with convincing woodlands. Though the corridor was barely wide enough for two people side by side, scenery seemed to extend for miles. In the minimal light, the illusion was perfect. She reached out. Where she was sure snow fell through empty air, her fingers dimpled oiled canvas.

They could not be more than fifty feet inside the Gift, which she knew to cover a circle barely a hundred yards across, but it seemed miles from Regent's Park. Glancing back, she saw the Undertakers, scarecrows against an oblong of daylight. Looking forward, there was night and forest. Stars sparkled on the roof.

The passage curved, and she couldn't see the entrance any more.

Of course, the Gift was a fairground maze.

Charles, tracking clear footprints, came to a triplicate fork in the path. Three sets of prints wound into each tunnel.

"Bugger," said Mist, adding, "pardon me, miss."

She asked for light and sorted back through Davey's pictures. She was sure she had seen this. She missed it once and had to start again. Then she hit on sketches representing this juncture. On paper, Maeve led Dickie down the left-hand path. In the next picture, goblins tottered out of the trees on stilts tipped with child-sized shoes which (horribly) had disembodied feet stuffed into them. The imps made false trails down the other paths, smirking with mean delight, cackles crawling off the paper.

Kate was beginning to *hate* Davey's goblins.

Charles bent low to enter the left-hand tunnel, which went under two oaks whose upper branches tangled, as if the trees were frozen in a slapping argument. Disapproving faces twisted in the bark.

Even Kate couldn't stand up in this tunnel.

They made slow, clumsy progress. It was hard to light the way ahead. All Charles and Mist could do was cast moon-circles on the nearest surface, infernally reflecting their own faces.

The tunnel angled downwards.

She wondered if this led to the dynamo room. The interior of the Gift was on several levels. Yesterday, it had been hot here. Now snowflakes wisped on her face like ice-pricks.

"That's not likely," said Mist, looking at snowmelt in his palm.

Davey stumbled over an exposed root. Kate reached out to catch him. They fell against a barbed bramble and staggered off the path, tumbling into a chilly drift. Painted walls had given way to three-dimensional scenery, the break unnoticed. The snow must be artificially generated—ice-chips sifted from a hidden device up above—but felt unpleasantly real.

Mist and Charles played their lamps around.

Kate assumed they were in the large, central area she had visited, but in this minimal light it seemed differently shaped. Everything was larger. She was now in proportion with trees that had been miniature.

A vicious wind blew from somewhere, spattering her spectacles with snow-dots. The waterfall was frozen in serried waves, trapping bug-eyed, dunce-capped Silly Fish in a glacier grip.

Charles took off his ulster and gave it to her. She gratefully accepted.

"I never thought I'd miss my Sir Boris costume," he said.

Mist directed his lamp straight up. Its throw didn't reach any ceiling. He pointed it down, and found grass, earth, and snow—no floorboards, no paving, no matting. In the wind, trees shifted and creaked.

"Bloody good trick," said the policeman.

Davey hunched in a huddle, making tinier and tinier pictures.

There was movement in the dark. Charles turned, pointing his light at rustles. Wherever the lantern shone, all was stark and still. Outside the beam, things were evilly active. The originals of Davey's goblins, whatever they might be, were in the trees. The illustrations, satirical cartoons, were tinged with grotesque humour. Kate feared there would be nothing funny about the live models.

"*Dickie*," shouted Charles.

His echo came back, many times. Charles's breath plumed. His shout dissipated in the open night. Kate could have sworn mocking, imitative voices replaced the echo.

"There's a castle," she said, looking at Davey's latest drawings. "No, a *palace*. Maeve is leading Dickie up steps, to meet... I don't know, a prince?"

Davey was still working. His arm was in the way of a completed picture. Gently, she shifted his wrist.

In a palatial hall, Dickie was presented to a mirror, looking at himself. Only, his reflection was different. The boy in the glass had thinner eyes, pointier ears, a nastier mouth.

Davey went on to another book.

Kate showed Charles and Mist the new sequence.

"We have to find this place, quickly," said Charles. "The boy is in immediate danger."

viii: "the game is up"

Maeve had turned her ankle. Dickie's aunt did not usually act so like a girl. After helping as best he could, he left her wrapped up by the path. She kept their candle. When the mystery was solved, he could find his way back to her light. Bravely, Maeve urged him on, to follow the clues.

In the middle of the Gift, she said, was a palace.

Inside the palace was the *culprit*.

Steeled, Dickie made his way from clue to clue.

Moonbeam pools picked them out. A dagger with the very tip sheared away, a half-burned page of cipher, a cigarette end with three distinctive bands, a cameo brooch that opened to a picture of a hairy-faced little girl, an empty blue glass bottle marked with skull and crossbones, a bloodied grape-stem, a dish of butter with a sprig of parsley sunk into it, a dead canary bleached white, a worm unknown to science, a squat jade idol with its eyegems prised out, a necklace crushed to show its gems were paste, a false beard with cardboard nose attached.

Excellent clues, leading to his destination.

When he first glimpsed the palace through the trees, Dickie thought it a doll's house, much too small for him. When, at last, he found the front door, spires rose above him. It was clever, like one of Maeve's conjuring tricks.

Who *was* the culprit?

Mr. Satterthwaite Bulge (he had known the dead man best, and could have been blackmailed or have something to gain from a will)... Uncle Davey (surely not, though some said he was "touched"; he might have another person living in his head, not a nice one)... the clever gent and the Irish lady who had called this afternoon (Dickie had liked them straight off, which should not blind him to sorry possibilities)... Greedy Sid Silcock (too obvious and convenient, though he could well be in it as a minion of the true mastermind)... Miss MacAndrew (another vengeance-plotter?)... Bitty, the rosy-cheeked maid (hmmmn, something was *stirring* about her complexion)... Ma and Da (*no!*)...

He would find out.

The palace disappointed. It was a wooden façade, propped up by rough timbers. There were no rooms, just hollow space. The exterior was painted to look like stone. Inside was bare board, nailed without much care.

He could not see much. Even through his magnifying glass.

"Hello," he called.

"'lo?" came back at him, in his own voice.

Or something very like.

"You are found out."

"Out!"

The culprit was here.

But Dickie was still in the dark. He must remember to include a box of lucifers in his detective apparatus, with long tapers. Perhaps even a small lantern. Having left his candle with Maeve, so she wouldn't be lonely, he was at a disadvantage.

"The game is up," he announced, sounding braver than he felt.

"Up?"

"This palace is surrounded by *special detectives*. You are under arrest."

"Arrest?"

The culprit was an *echo*.

The dark in front of his face gathered, solidified into coherence. He made out human shape.

Dickie's hand fell on the culprit's shoulder.

"Ah hah!"

A hand gripped his own shoulder.

"Hah," came back, a gust of hot breath into his face.

He squeezed and was squeezed.

His shoulder hurt, his knees weakened. He was pushed down, as if shrinking.

The hand on his shoulder grew, fingers like hard twigs poking into him. His feet sank into earth, which swarmed around his ankles. His socks would get muddied, which would displease Ma.

Shapes moved all around.

The culprit was not alone. He had minions.

He imagined them—Greedy Sid, Miss MacAndrew, Uncle Satt, an ape, a mathematics tutor, a defrocked curate. The low folk who were part of the mystery.

"Who are you?"

"You!"

ix: "two jumps behind"

There was light ahead. A candle-flame.

Charles pointed it out.

The light moved, behind a tree, into hiding.

Charles played his lantern over the area, wobbling the beam to indicate where the others should look, then directing it elsewhere, hoping to fool the candle-holder into believing she was overlooked.

Charles was sure it was a *she*.

He handed his lantern to Kate, who took it smoothly and continued the "search."

Charles stepped off the track.

Whatever was passing itself off as snow was doing a good job. His shins were frozen as he waded. He crouched low and his bare hands sunk into the stuff.

He crept towards the tree where the light had been.

"Pretty princess," he breathed to himself, "sit tight…"

He had picked up night-skills in warmer climes, crawling over rocky hills with his face stained, dressed like an untouchable. He could cross open country under a full moon without being seen. In this dark, with so many things to hide behind, it should be easy.

But it wasn't. The going was treacherous. The snow lay lightly over brambles that could snare like barbed wire.

Within a couple of yards of the tree, he saw the guarded, flickering spill of light. He flexed his fingers into the snow, numbing his joints.

Sometimes, he had pains in his knuckles—which he had never mentioned to anyone. He stood, slowly.

He held his breath.

In a single, smooth movement, he stepped around the tree and laid a hand on...

...bark!

He summoned the others.

The candle perched in a nook, wax dribbling.

Clear little footprints radiated from a hollow in the roots. They spiralled and multiplied, haring off in all directions as if a dozen princesses had sprung into being and bolted.

Kate showed Charles a new-drawn picture of Maeve skipping away, tittering to herself.

"Have you noticed he never draws us?" he said.

"Maybe we're not in the story yet."

"We're here all right," said Mist. "Two jumps behind."

Mist supported Davey now. The lad was running out of paper. His pictures were smaller, crowded together—two or three to a page—and harder to make out.

"Let me try something," said Kate.

She laid her fingers on Davey's hand, halting his pencil. He shook, the beginnings of a fit. She took his chin and forced him to look at her.

"Davey, where's the palace?"

He was close to tears, frustrated at not being able to draw, to channel what he knew.

"Not in pictures," she said. "Words. Tell me in words."

Davey shook his head and shut his eyes. Squeaks came from the back of his throat.

"...mother said... never should..."

"Dickie's in the woods," said Kate.

"With the gypsies?"

"Yes, the naughty, naughty gypsies. That bad girl is taking Dickie to them. We can help him, but you have to help us. Please, Davey. For Dickie. These are *your* woods. You mapped them and made them. Where in the woods..."

Davey opened his eyes.

He turned, breaking Kate's hold, and waded off, snow slushing around his feet. He pressed point to paper and made three strokes, then snapped the pencil and dropped the notebook.

"This way," he said.

Davey walked with some confidence towards a stand of trees. He reached up and touched a low-hanging branch, pushing a bird's nest, sending a ripple through branch, tree and sky. He took out his penknife, opened the blade and stuck it into the backdrop. With a tearing sound, the knife parted canvas and sank to the hilt. Davey drew his knife in a straight line, across the branch and into the air. He made a corner and cut downwards, as if hacking a door into a tent. The fabric ripped, noisily.

Charles thought he could see for hundreds of yards, through the woods. Even as Davey cut his door, Charles could swear the lad stood in a real landscape.

Davey slashed the canvas, methodically.

There was a doorway in the wood.

Beyond was gloom but not dark. It looked like the quarter where backstage people worked, where Sir Boris had got dressed and prepared or took his infrequent meal and rest-breaks.

"Through here," said Dickie.

They followed. Beyond the door, it wasn't cold any more. It was close, stifling.

Dickie cut a door in an opposite wall.

"I know where you're hiding," he said, to someone beyond.

A screech filled the passage. A small person with wild hair tore between their legs, launching a punch at Davey's chest, clawing at Kate's face, sinking a shoulder into Mist's stomach.

Charles blocked her.

The screech died. The girl's face was in shadow, but could no longer be mistaken. This was not—*had never been*—Maeve Harvill. This was Princess Cuckoo, of Pixieland. Rather, of the shadow realm Davey recreated in his pictures, which Satterthwaite Bulge had named Færie and built in the real world. That was what she had wanted all along.

"Where is he?" Charles asked. "Dickie?"

The little face shut tight, lip buttoned, chin and cheeks set. This close, she seemed a genuine child. No Thuggee strangler or Scots preacher could be as iron-willed as a little girl determined not to own up.

"I know," said Davey. "It's where she took me, where I got away from."

The girl shook her head, humming furiously.

"That's an endorsement," Charles commented. "Lead on, Davey."

x: "holes"

They descended into the ground. Brickwork tunnel walls gave way to shored earth and flagstones. Kate could not believe Regent's Park was only a few feet above their heads.

She squirreled through, following Davey. Charles dragged Maeve after him. Inspector Mist held the rear.

The place smelled of muck.

They emerged in the dynamo chamber, site of the sacrifice that had kept the throngs away from the Gift so Maeve could make her private exchange. Roots thick as a man's torso burst through, spilling bricks on the floor, entwining like angry prehistoric snakes. A canvas cover over the dynamos, stained with red mud, was partially lifted. Ivy grew like a plague, twining into ironwork, twisting around stilled pistons and bent valves. The weed grip had cracked one of the great wheels.

Green sparks nestled in nooks. Fairy lights, little burning pools which needed no dynamos.

Dickie sat in front of the machine, knees together, cap straight.

"There he is," said Maeve. "No harm done. Satisfied?"

Charles shone his lantern. Emerald light-points danced in the boy's eyes. He raised a hand to shield his face.

"Princess," said the boy. "Is that you?"

They were here in time! Kate wanted to hug the errant special detective.

"Dickie," said Charles, offhandedly. "Tell me, what clue enabled you to solve the Baffling Business of the Cheating Governess?"

Dickie lowered his hand. His eyes were hard.

Ice brushed the untidy hair at the nape of Kate's neck.

"Who was the Bun Bandit?" she asked.

No answer. The lightpoints in his eyes were fixed. Seven in each. In the shape of the constellation Ursa Major.

"That's not D-Dickie," said Davey. "That's…"

"I think we know who that is," said Charles.

Kate's insides plunged. She looked at the boy. He was like Maeve, but new-made. Clean and fresh and tidy, still slightly moist. He did not yet have the knack of passing among people.

Davey whirled about the chamber, tapping roots, tearing off covers.

Maeve and the boy exchanged gazes and kept quiet.

Kate knew that Sarah Riddle would not be happy with a boy who merely *looked* like her son.

"So, it's another one," said Inspector Mist, walking around the boy.

He looked up at the policeman, unblinking, head rotating like an owl's.

"That's a good trick," Kate said.

The boy experimented with a smile of acknowledgement. It did not come off well.

Charles was with Davey, talking to him quietly, insistently.

"Think hard, Davey… this is that place, the place that was under Hill Wood…"

"Yes, I know. But this is London."

"The place where you were taken is *somewhere else*, Davey.

Somewhere that travels. Somewhere with holes that match up to holes here. I don't know how the hole was made in Eye. Perhaps it was always there. But the hole here, in the Gift, you made."

Davey nodded, to himself.

"I thought I'd got away, but I brought it with me, in my head. The drawing, the dreams. That was it, pressing on me. I cheated *them*, by their lights. I owed them."

He felt his way around now, carefully. He began humming his rhyme— his long-lost sister's rhyme—then caught himself, and was quiet, chewing his lip like a Harvill.

"A hole," he said, at last. "There's a hole. Something like a hole."

Davey took out his penknife. He shook his head and threw it away.

"Would this be any use?" suggested Inspector Mist.

The policeman pulled a giant-sized spanner from the clutches of greenery and handed it over.

Davey took the length of iron, felt its heft, and nodded.

Charles stood back. Davey took a swing, as if with an axe. The spanner clanged against exposed root. The whole chamber rung with the blow. Kate's teeth rattled. Old bark sloughed, exposing bone-yellow woodflesh. Davey struck again, and the wood parted.

There was an exhalation of foul air, and a vast inpouring of soft, insect-inhabited earth. Almost liquid, it slurried around their ankles, then grew to a tidal wave that threatened to fill the chamber. Some of the lights winked out. She found herself clinging to Charles, who held onto a dangling chain to steady his footing. Mist hopped nimbly out of the way.

The sham children paid no mind.

In the dirt, something moved. Charles deftly shifted Kate's grip to the chain and weighed in, with Davey, shovelling earth with cupped hands.

A very dirty little boy was disclosed, spitting leaves.

Charles whispered in his ear.

"Jack of Hearts, with one corner bent off," Dickie shouted.

Davey hugged his nephew, who was a bit embarrassed.

The dirty boy looked at his clean mirror image. Dickie had a spasm of fear, but got over it.

"You'd better leave," Charles told the impostor.

The failed changeling stood, lifted his shoulders at the girl in a well-I-*tried* shrug, and stepped close to the fissure in the wall. The gap seemed too narrow. As the faux Dickie neared the hole, he seemed to fold thinner, and be sucked beyond, into deeper, frothing darkness. The stench settled, but remained fungoid and corpse-filthy.

Everyone looked at Maeve.

"So, Princess Cuckoo," said Charles, hands on hips, "what's to be done with you?"

She regarded him, blankly.

xi: "you might not know what you get back"

The place was changing. The roots withdrew. The crack in the wall narrowed, as if healing. A machine-oil tang cut through the peaty smell.

"The holes are closing," said Davey.

Charles considered the Princess. It had been important that there be *two* cuckoos, Prince and Princess. Davey's escape from the realm beyond the holes had stalled some design. If Dickie had been successfully supplanted, it would have started again, rumbling inexorably towards its end. Charles did not even want to guess what had just been thwarted. Plans laid in a contingent world were now abandoned—which should be enough for the Ruling Cabal.

That unknown place rubbed against thinning, permeable walls. Davey's drawings were not the first signs that barriers could be breached. Everywhere, he once said, has its stories. Many places also had their holes, natural or special-made. It was difficult, but travellers could pass through veils that separated there from here and here from there.

This girl-shaped person was one such.

"Princess, if I may call you that…"

She nodded. Her face was thinner now, cheekbones more apparent, pupils oval, skin a touch green in the lamplight.

"…outside the Gift are two men dressed in black."

She knew the Undertaking.

"They would like me to hand you over to them. You are a *specimen* of great interest. As you once had *plans* for us, they have plans for you. Which you might not care for."

"It doesn't matter," she said.

"You say that now. You're disappointed, of course. Your life for the past eight years—and I can imagine it has been utterly strange—was geared up to this moment. And it's proven a bust."

"No need to rub it in, Mr. Detective."

"I am just trying to make you realise this might not be the *worst* moment of your sojourn here."

The girl spat out a bitter little laugh.

She *was* like a child. Perhaps they all were. That childishness was evident in all the impressions that came through the holes, dressed up and painted in and cut about by Davey Harvill and Uncle Satt and Leslie Sackham and George MacDonald and Arthur Rackham and many, many others. They were the *little* people, small in their wonderments, prone to spasms of sunlit joy and long rainy afternoon sulks.

"Mr. Hay and Mr. Effe might tire of asking questions. It can be boring, not getting answers. In the end, the Undertaking might just *cut you up* in the name of science. To find wings folded inside your shoulder-bones, then spread them on a board and pin you like a butterfly. There's a secret museum for creatures like you. It's possible you'd be under glass for a long time."

A thrill passed through her. A horror.

That was something to be proud of. He had terrified the Medusa.

"What do you want?" she said, quietly.

"His sister," he said, nodding at Davey.

She thought it over.

"There's a balance. She can't be here if I am. Not for long. You saw, with Dickie. Things bend."

"You're not going to *let her go*?" said Kate.

Charles sympathised with Kate's outrage. Mist, as well. This girl was responsible for at least one murder. Sackham, obviously—to keep the Gift shut, so her business could proceed. Almost certainly, she had contrived the death of Violet Harvill, who could not be fooled forever. (Did Davey know that? How could he not?) Charles was certain the Princess would answer for her failure to the powers she served or represented.

"It is for the best," he told Kate.

Mist gave him the nod. Good man.

"I should warn you," said the Princess, "you might not know what you get back. Time passes differently."

He understood. If thirty years fly past in a three days, what might not transpire in eight years?

The Princess stood by the fissure, which pulsed—almost like a mouth.

She looked at them all.

"Good-bye, Hawkshaw," she said. "The Dickie who was almost is less fun."

Dickie frowned. Kate had most of the dirt off his face.

"Auntie," he said. "I know you didn't mean it."

The Princess seemed sad but said nothing. Suddenly boneless and flimsy, she slid into the slit as if it were a post-box and she a letter. Long seconds passed. The fissure bulged and creaked. An arm flopped out.

Davey took hold of the hand and pulled.

Charles grabbed Davey's waist and hauled. Mist and Kate lent their strength. Even so, it was hard going. Davey's grip slipped on oily skin. Charles's forearm ached, as he felt the old bite.

A shoulder and head, coated with mud, emerged. Eyes opened in the mask of filth. Bright, alive eyes.

Then, in a long tangle, a whole body slithered out. She drew breath, as if just born, and gave vent to a cry. Noise filled the dynamo chamber.

"Let's take the quickest way out," Charles said.

Kate went ahead with the lanterns. The three men carried the limp, adult length of the rescued girl between them. Dickie, magnifying glass held up, followed.

When they banged out of the waterfall door, Mist ordered a constable to fetch water from the horse-trough in Regent's Crescent. The newfound girl lay on the ground, head in Davey's lap. A drapery wound around her, plastered to her body like a toga, but her bare, gnarled feet stuck out.

Kate held Dickie back.

Mr. Hay and Mr. Effe exchanged dark glances, unreadable. When Charles looked again, they were gone. A worry for another day.

Philip and Sarah Riddle got past the cordon and bustled around, too relieved at the return of Dickie to ask after the new arrival. They took their son, scolding and embracing him.

Mist had his men round up buckets of water, and had to stop P.C. Willoughby from dashing one in the woman's face.

"Looks like she's been buried alive, sir," said the constable.

"It's not so bad," said Dickie, bravely.

Charles requisitioned a flannel from a stray governess, soaked it, and cleaned the face of the woman who had come back.

A beautiful blank appeared with the first wash. She was exactly like the Princess. Then a few lines became apparent, and a white streak in her hair.

"Maeve," said Davey.

The woman looked up, recognising her brother.

Charles would have taken her for a well-preserved forty or a hard-lived thirty. He stood back, and looked at the family reunion.

"How long's it been?" she said.

"Not but a moment," said Davey.

She closed her eyes and smiled, safe.

Charles found that Kate was holding his elbow, face against his sleeve. He suspected a manoeuvre to conceal tears. A pricking in his eyes suggested discreet dabbing might be in order to repair his own composure.

A crowd began to assemble. There was still interest in the Gift. It occurred to Charles that it might even be safe to open the place, though Mist would have to write up the Sackham case carefully for the BQC files.

Maeve rolled in Davey's grasp and flung her arms around his neck.

Sarah Riddle noticed her sister, recognised her at once. She gasped, in wonder. Her husband, puzzled at first, caught on and began to dance a jig.

Charles slipped his own arm around Kate's waist. Her hands were hooked into his coat. They had been through a great deal together. Again. Pamela had been right about Katharine Reed; she was an extraordinarily promising girl. No, that was then. Now, she was an extraordinarily delivering woman.

He lifted her face from his arm and set her spectacles straight.

"What should a fairy tale have?" he asked.

Kate sniffed. "A happy ending," she ventured.

He kissed her nose, which set her crying again.

She arched up on tip-toes and kissed him on the lips, which should not have been the surprise it was.

Mist gave a nod to Willoughby.

The constable raised big hands to his belt, thumb tapping the handle of his truncheon.

"Move along, now," he told the gathering crowds. "There's nothing to see 'ere."

Richard Riddle, Boy Detective in "The Case Of The French Spy"

I: "wmjhu-ojbhu dajjq jh qrs prbhufs"

"Gosh, Dick," said Violet, "an ammonite!"

A chunk of rock, bigger than any of them could have lifted, had broken from the soft cliff and fallen on the shingle. Violet, on her knees, brushed grit and grime from the stone.

They were on the beach below Ware Cleeve, looking for clues.

This was not strictly a fossil hunting expedition, but Dick knew Violet was mad about terrible lizards—which was what "dinosaur" meant in Greek, she had explained. On a recent visit to London, Violet had been taken to the prehistoric monster exhibit in Crystal Palace Park. She could not have been more excited if the life-size statues turned out to be live specimens. Palaeontology was like being a detective, she enthused: working back from clues to the truth, examining a pile of bones and guessing what kind of body once wrapped around them.

Dick conceded her point. But the dinosaurs died a long, long time ago. No culprit's collar would be felt. A pity. It would be a good mystery to solve. The Case of the Vanishing Lizards. No, The Mystery of the Disappearing Dinosaurs. No, The Adventure of the Absent Ammonites.

"Coo," said Ernest. "Was this a *monster*?"

Ernest liked monsters. Anything with big teeth counted.

"Not really," Violet admitted. "It was a cephalopod. That means 'head-foot.'"

"It was a head with only a foot?" Ernest liked the idea. "Did it hop up behind enemies, and sink its fangs into their bleeding necks?"

"It was more like a big shrimp. Or a squid with a shell."

"Squid are fairly monstrous, Ernest," said Dick. "Some grow giant and crush ships with their tentacles."

Ernest made experimental crushing motions with his hands, providing squelching noises with his mouth.

Violet ran her fingers over the ammonite's segments.

"Ammon was the ram-headed God of Ancient Egypt."

Dick saw Ernest imagining that—an evil God butting unbelievers to death.

"These are called 'ammonites' because the many-chambered spiral looks like the horn of a ram. You know, like the big one in Mr. Crossan's field."

Ernest went quiet. He liked fanged monsters, giant squid, and evil Gods, but had a problem with *animals*. Once, the children were forced to go a long way round to avoid Mr. Crossan's field. Ernest had come up with many tactical reasons for the detour, and Dick and Violet pretended to be persuaded by his argument that they needed to throw pursuers off their track.

The three children were about together all the time this summer. Dick was down from London, staying with Uncle Davey and Aunt Maeve. Both were a bit dotty. Uncle Davey used to paint fairyland scenes for children's books, but was retired from that and drawing only to please himself. Last year, Violet showed up at Seaview Chase unannounced, having learned it was David Harvill's house. She liked his illustrations, but genuinely liked the pictures in his studio even more.

Violet had taken an interest in Dick's detective work. She had showed him around Lyme Regis, and the surrounding beaches and countryside. She wasn't like a proper girl, so it was all right being friends with her. Normally, Dick couldn't admit to having a girl as a friend. In summer, it was different. Ernest was Violet's cousin, two years younger than her and Dick. Ernest's father was in Africa fighting Boers, so Ernest was with Violet's parents for the school holidays.

They were the Richard Riddle Detective Agency. Their goal: to find mysteries, then solve them. Thus far, they had handled the Matter of the Mysterious Maidservant (meeting the Butcher's Boy, though she was supposed to have a sweetheart at sea), the Curious Affair of the Derelict Dinghy (Alderman Hooke was lying asleep in it, empty beer bottles rolling around his feet) and the Puzzle of the Purloined Pasties (still an open case, though suspicion inevitably fell upon Tarquin "Tiger" Bristow).

Ernest had reasoned out his place in the firm. When Dick pointed the finger of guilt at the villain, Ernest would thump the miscreant about the head until the official police arrived. Violet, Ernest said, could make tea and listen to Dick explain his chain of deduction. Ernest, Violet commented acidly, was a dependable strong-arm man… unless the criminal owned a sheep, or threatened to make him eat parsnips, or (as was depressingly likely) turned out to be "Tiger" Bristow (the Bismarck of Bullies) and returned Ernest's head-thumping with interest. Then, Dick had to negotiate a peace, like between Americans and Red Indians, to avoid bloodshed. When Violet broke off the Reservation, people got scalped.

It was a sunny August afternoon, but strong salt wind blew off the sea. Violet had tied back her hair to keep it out of her face. Dick looked up at Ware Cleeve: It was thickly wooded, roots poking out of the cliff-face like the fingers of buried men. The Tower of Orris Priory rose above the treetops like a periscope.

Clues led to Orris Priory. Dick suspected smugglers. Or spies.

Granny Ball, who kept the pasty-stall near the Cobb, had warned the detectives to stay away from the shingle under the Cleeve. It was a haunt of "sea-ghosts." The angry souls of shipwrecked sailors, half-fish folk from sunken cities, and other monsters of the deep (Ernest liked this bit) were given to creeping onto the beach, clawing away at the stone, crumbling it piece by piece. One day, the Cleeve would collapse.

Violet wanted to know why the sea-ghosts would do such a thing. The landslide would only make another cliff, further inland. Granny winked and said "never you mind, lass" in a highly unsatisfactory manner.

Before her craze for terrible lizards, Violet had been passionate about myths and legends (it was why she liked Uncle Davey's pictures). She said myths were expressions of common truth, dressed up to make a point. The shingle beach was dangerous, because rocks fell on it. People in the long ago must have been hit on the head and killed, so the sea-ghost story was invented to keep children away from danger. It was like a "beware the dog" sign (Ernest didn't like this bit), but out of date—as if you had an old, non-fierce hound but put up a "beware of dangerous dog" sign.

Being on the shingle wasn't really dangerous. The cliffs wouldn't fall and the sea-ghosts wouldn't come.

Dick liked Violet's reasoning, but saw better.

"No, Vile, it's been *kept up*, this story. Granny and other folk round here tell the tale to keep us away because *someone* doesn't want us seeing what they're about."

"Smugglers," said Ernest.

Dick nodded. "Or spies. Not enough clues to be certain. But, mark my word, there's wrong-doing afoot on the shingle. And it's our job to root it out."

It was too blowy to go out in Violet's little boat, the S.S. *Pterodactyl*, so they had come on foot.

And found the ammonite.

Since the fossil wasn't about to hop to life and attack, Ernest lost interest and wandered off, down by the water. He was looking for monster tracks, the tentacle-trails of a giant squid most likely.

"This might be the largest ammonite ever found here," said Violet. "If it's a new species, I get to name it."

Dick wondered how to get the fossil to Violet's house. It would be a tricky endeavour.

"You, children, what are you about?"

Men had appeared onto the beach without Dick noticing. If they had come from either direction along the shore, he should have seen them.

"You shouldn't be here. Come away from that evil thing, at once, *now*."

The speaker was an old man with white hair, *pince-nez* on a black ribbon, an expression like someone who's just bit into a cooking apple by mistake, and a white collar like a clergyman's. He wore an old-fashioned coat with a thick, raised collar, cut away from tight britches and heavy boots.

Dick recognised the Reverend Mr. Sellwood, of Orris Priory.

With him were two bare-armed fellows in leather jerkins and corduroy trousers. Whereas Sellwood carried a stick, they toted sledge-hammers, like the ones convicts use on Dartmoor.

"Foul excrescence of the Devil," said Sellwood, pointing his stick at Violet's ammonite. "Brother Fose, Brother Fessel, do the Lord's work."

Fose and Fessel raised their hammers.

Violet leaned over, as if protecting a pet lamb from slaughtermen.

"Out of the way, foolish girl."

"It's *mine*," she said.

"It's nobody's, and no good to anybody. It must be smashed. God would wish it…"

"But this find is important. To *science*."

Sellwood looked as if that bite of cooker was in his throat, making his eyes water.

"Science! Bah, stuff and nonsense! Devil's charm, my girl, that's what this is!"

"It was alive, millions of millions of years ago."

"The Earth is less than six thousand years old, child, as you would know if you read your scriptures."

Violet, angry, stood up to argue. "But that's not true. There's *proof*. This is…"

Fose and Fessel took their opportunity, and brought the hammers down. The fossil split. Sharp chips flew. Violet—appalled, hands in tiny fists, mouth open—didn't notice her shin bleeding.

"You *can't*…"

"These so-called proofs, stone bones and long-dead dragons," said Sellwood, "are the Devil's trickeries."

The Brethren smashed the ammonite to shards and powder.

"This was put here to fool weak minds," lectured the Reverend. "It is the Church Militant's sacred work to destroy such obscenities, lest more be tempted to blasphemy. This is not science, this is sacrilege."

"It was mine," Violet said quietly.

"I have saved you from error. You should thank me."

Ernest came over to see what the noise was about. Sellwood bestowed a smile on the lad that afforded a glimpse of terrifying teeth.

Teeth on monsters were fine with Ernest; teeth like Sellwood's would give him nightmares.

"A job well done," said the Reverend. "Let us look further. More infernal things may have sprung up."

Brother Fose leered at Violet and patted her on the head, which made her flinch. Brother Fessel looked stern disapproval at this familiarity. They followed Sellwood, swinging hammers, scouting for something to break to bits. Dick had an idea they'd rather be pounding on something that squealed and bled than something so long dead it had turned to stone.

Violet wasn't crying. But she was hating.

More than before, Dick was convinced Sellwood was behind some vile endeavour. He had the look of a smuggler, or a spy.

Richard Riddle, Boy Detective, would bring the villain to book.

II: "Qrs Ndps ja qrs Dggjhbqs Dhhbrbfdqjm"

Uncle Davey had let Dick set up the office of the Richard Riddle Detective Agency in a small room under the eaves. A gable window led to a small balcony that looked like a ship's crow's-nest. Seaview Chase was a large, complicated house on Black Ven, a jagged rise above Lyme Bay, an ideal vantage point for surveying the town and the sea.

Dick had installed his equipment—a microscope, boxes and folders, reference books, his collection of clues and trophies. Violet had donated some small fossils and her hammers and trowels. Ernest wanted space on the wall for the head of their first murderer: He had an idea that when a murderer was hanged, the police gave the head as a souvenir to the detective who caught him.

The evening after the fossil-smashing incident, Dick sat in the office and opened a new file and wrote "Qrs Ndps ja qrs Dggjhbqs Dhhbrbfdqjm" on a fresh sheet of paper. It was the R.R.D.A. Special Cipher for "The Case of the Ammonite Annihilator."

After breakfast the next day, the follow-up investigation began. Dick went into the airy studio on the first floor and asked Uncle Davey what he knew about Sellwood.

"Grim-visage?" said Uncle Davey, pulling a face. "Dresses as if it were fifty years ago? Of him, I know, to be frank, not much. He once called with a presentation copy of some verminous volume, printed at his own expense. I think he wanted me to find a proper publisher. Put on a scary smile to ingratiate. Maeve didn't like him. He hasn't been back. Book's around somewhere, probably. Must chuck it one day. It'll be in one of those piles."

He stabbed a paintbrush towards the stacks which grew against one wall and went back to painting—a ship at sea, only there were eyes in the sea if you looked close enough, and faces in the clouds and the folds of sail-cloth. Uncle Davey liked hiding things.

When Violet and Ernest arrived, they set to searching book-piles.

It took a long time. Violet kept getting interested in irrelevant findings. Mostly titles about pixies and fairies and curses.

Sellwood's book had migrated to near the bottom of an especially towering pile. Extracting it brought about a bad tumble which alerted Aunt Maeve, who rushed in assuming the whole of Black Ven was giving way and the house would soon be crashing into Lyme Bay. Uncle Davey cheerfully kicked the spill of volumes into a corner and said he'd sort them out one day, then noticed a wave suitable for hiding an eye in and forgot about the children. Aunt Maeve went off to get warm milk with drops of something from Cook.

In the office, the detectives pored over their find for clues.

"'*Omphalos Diabolicus, or: The Hoax of 'Pre-History,*'" intoned Dick, "'by the Reverend Daniel Sturdevant Sellwood, published 1897, Orris Press, Dorset.' Uncle Davey said he paid for the printing, so I deduce that he is the sole proprietor of this phantom publisher. Ah-hah, the pages have not been cut after the first chapter, so I further deduce that it must be deadly dull stuff."

He tossed the book to Violet, who got to work with a long knife, slitting the leaves as if they were the author's throat. Then she flicked through pages, pausing only to report relevant facts. One of her talents was gutting books, discovering the few useful pages like a prospector panning gold-dust out of river-dirt.

Daniel Sellwood wasn't a proper clergyman any more. He had been booted out of the Church of England after shouting that the Bishop should burn Mr. Darwin along with his published works. Now, Sellwood had his own sect, the Church Militant—but most of his congregation were paid servants. Sellwood came from a wealthy Dorset family, rich from trade and shipping, and had been packed off to parson school because an older brother, George, was supposed to inherit the fortune—only the brother was lost at sea, along with his wife Rebecca and little daughter Ruth, and Daniel's expectations increased. The sinking of the *Sophy Briggs* was a famous maritime mystery like the *Mary Celeste* and Captain Nemo: Thirty years ago, the pride of the Orris-Sellwood Line went down in calm seas, with all hands lost. Sellwood skipped over the loss in a sentence, then spent pages talking up the "divine revelation" which convinced him to found a church rather than keep up the business.

According to Violet, a lot of folk around Lyme resented being thrown out of work when Sellwood dismantled his shipping concern and dedicated the family fortune to preaching anti-Darwinism.

"What's an omphalo-thing?" asked Ernest.

"The title means 'the Devil's Belly-Button,'" said Violet, which made Ernest giggle. "He's put Greek and Latin words together, which is poor

Classics. Apart from his stupid ideas, he's a *terrible* writer. Listen... 'all the multitudinarious flora and fauna of divine creation constitute veritable evidence of the proof of the pellucid and undiluted accuracy of the Word of God Almighty Unchallenged as set down in the shining, burning, shimmering sentences, chapters and, indeed, books of the Old and New Testaments, hereinafter known to all righteous and right-thinking men as the Holy Bible of Glorious God.' It's as if he's saying, 'this is the true truthiest truest truth of truthdom ever told truly by truth-trusters.'"

"How do the belly-buttons come into it?" asked Dick.

"Adam and Eve were supposed to have been created with navels, though—since they weren't born like other people—they oughtn't to have them."

This was over Ernest's head but Dick knew how babies came and that his navel was a knot, where a cord had been cut and tied.

"To Sellwood's way of thinking, just as Adam and Eve were created to *seem* as if they had normal parents, the Earth was created as if it had a prehistory, with geological and fossil evidence in place to make the planet appear much older than it says in the Bible."

"That's silly," said Ernest.

"Don't tell me, tell Sellwood," said Violet. "He's a silly, stupid man. He doesn't want to know the truth, or anyone else to either, so he breaks fossils and shouts down lecturers. His theory isn't even original. A man named Gosse wrote a book with the same idea, though Gosse claimed *God* buried fossils to fool people while Sellwood says it was the Devil."

Violet was quite annoyed.

"I think it's an excuse to go round bullying people," said Dick. "A cover for his real, sinister purpose."

"If you ask me, what he does is sinister enough by itself."

"Nobody did ask you," said Ernest, which he always said when someone was unwise enough to preface a statement with "if you ask me." Violet stuck her tongue out at him.

Dick was thinking.

"It's likely that the Sellwood family were smugglers," he said.

Violet agreed. "Smugglers had to have ships, and pretend to be respectable merchants. In the old days, they were all at it. You know the poem..."

Violet stood up, put a hand on her chest, and recited, dramatically.

"'If you wake at midnight, and hear a horse's feet,
Don't go drawing back the blind, or looking in the street.
Them that ask no questions isn't told a lie,
Watch the wall, my darling, while the gentlemen go by.
Five and twenty ponies, trotting through the dark,
Brandy for the parson, 'baccy for the clerk;

Laces for a lady, letters for a spy,

And watch the wall, my darling, while the gentlemen go by.'"

She waited for applause, which didn't come. But her recitation was useful. Dick had been thinking in terms of spies *or* smugglers, but the poem reminded him that the breeds were interdependent. It struck him that Sellwood might be a smuggler of spies, or a spy for smugglers.

"I'll wager 'Tiger' Bristow is in this, too," he said, snapping his fingers.

Ernest shivered, audibly.

"Is it spying or smuggling?" he asked.

"It's both," Dick replied.

Violet sat down again, and chewed on a long, stray strand of her hair.

"Tell Dick about the French Spy," suggested Ernest.

Dick was intrigued.

"That was a long time ago, a hundred years," she said. "It's a local legend, not evidence."

"You yourself say legends always shroud some truth," declared Dick. "We must consider *all* the facts, even rumours of facts, before forming a conclusion."

Violet shrugged.

"It is about Sellwood's *house*, I suppose…"

Dick was astonished. "And you didn't think it was relevant! Sometimes, I'm astonished by your lack of perspicacity!"

Violet looked incipiently upset at his tone, and Dick wondered if he wasn't going too far. He needed her in the Agency, but she could be maddening at times. Like a real girl.

"Out with it, Vile," he barked.

Violet crossed her arms and kept quiet.

"I apologise for my tactlessness," said Dick. "But this is vitally important. We might be able to put that ammonite-abuser out of business, with immeasurable benefit to *science*."

Violet melted. "Very well. I heard this from Alderman Hooke's father…"

Before her palaeontology craze, Violet fancied herself a collector of folklore. She had gone around asking old people to tell stories or sing songs or remember why things were called what they were called. She was going to write them all up in a book of local legends and had wanted Uncle Davey to draw the pictures. She was still working on her book, but it was about Dinosaurs in Dorset now.

"I didn't make much of it, because it wasn't much of a legend. Just a scrap of history."

"With a spy," prompted Ernest. "A spy who came out of the sea!"

Violet nodded. "That's more or less it. When England was at war with

France, everyone thought Napoleon..."

"Boney!" put in Ernest, making fang-fingers at the corners of his mouth.

"Yes, Boney... everyone thought he was going to invade, like William the Conqueror. Along the coast people watched the seas. Signal-fires were prepared, like with the Spanish Armada. Most thought it likely the French would strike at Dover, but round here they tapped the sides of their noses..."

Violet imitated an old person tapping her long nose.

"...and said the last army to invade Britain had landed at Lyme, and the next would too. The last army was Monmouth's, during his rebellion. He landed at the Cobb and marched up to Sedgmoor, where he was defeated. There are *lots* of legends about the Duke of Monmouth..."

Dick made a get-to-the-point gesture.

"Any rate, near the end of the 18th Century, a man named Jacob Orris formed a vigilance patrol to keep watch on the beaches. Orris's daughter married a sea-captain called Lud Sellwood; they begat drowned George and old Devil's Belly-Button. Come to think, Orris's patrol was like Sellwood's Church Militant—an excuse to shout at folk and break things. Orris started a campaign to get 'French beans' renamed 'Free-from-Tyranny beans,' and had his men attack grocer's stalls when no one agreed with him. Orris was expecting a fleet to heave to in Lyme Bay and land an army, but knew spies would be put ashore first to scout around. One night, during a terrible storm, Orris caught a spy flung up on the shingle."

"And...?"

"That's it, really. I expect they hit him with hammers and killed him, but if anyone really knows, they aren't saying."

Dick was disappointed.

"Tell him how it was a *special* spy," said Ernest.

Dick was intrigued again. Especially since Violet obviously didn't want to say more.

"He was a sea-ghost," announced Ernest.

"Old Hooke said the spy had *walked* across the channel," admitted Violet. "On the bottom of the sea, in a special diving suit. He was a Frenchman, but—and you have to remember stories get twisted over the years—he had gills *sewn* into his neck so he could breathe underwater. As far as anyone knew round here, all Corsicans were like that. They said it was probably Boney's cousin."

"And they killed him?"

Violet shrugged. "I expect so."

"And kept him *pickled*," said Ernest.

"Now that *isn't* true. One version of this story is that Orris had the dead spy stuffed, then hidden away. But the family would have found the thing and thrown it out by now. And we'd know whether it was a man or, as Granny Ball says, a trained seal. Stories are like limpets on rocks. They stick on and get thicker until you can't see what was there in the first place."

Dick whistled.

"I don't see how this can have anything to do with what Sellwood is about now," said Violet. "This may not have happened, and if it did, it was a hundred years ago. Sellwood wasn't even born then. His parents were still children."

"My dear Vile, a century-old mystery is still a mystery. And crime can seep into a family like water in the foundations, passed down from father to son…"

"Father to *daughter* to son, in this case."

"I haven't forgotten that. This mystery goes deep. It's all about the past. And haven't you said that a century is just a heartbeat in the long life of the planet?"

She was coming round, he saw.

"We have to get into Orris Priory," said Dick.

III: "Ba bq wdp sdpy qj abho, bq wjtfoh'q is *rboosh*"

"Why are we on the shingle?" asked Ernest. "The Priory is up there, on top of the Cleeve."

Dick had been waiting for the question. Deductions impressed more if he didn't just come out with cleverness, but waited for a prompt.

"Remember yesterday? Sellwood seemed to turn up suddenly, with Fose and Fessel. If they'd been walking on the beach, we'd have seen them ages before they arrived. But we didn't. Therefore, there must be a secret way. A smugglers' tunnel."

Violet found some pieces of the fossil. She looked towards the cliff.

"We were facing out to sea, and they came from behind," she said.

She tossed her ammonite shard, which rebounded off the soft rock-face.

The cliff was too crumbly for caves that might conceal a tunnel. The children began looking closely, hoping for a hidden door.

After a half hour, Ernest complained that he was hungry.

After an hour, Violet complained that she was fed up with rocks.

Dick stuck to it. "If it was easy to find, it wouldn't be *hidden*," he kept saying.

Ernest began to make helpful suggestions which didn't help but needed to be argued with.

"*Maybee* they came up under the sea and swam ashore?"

"They weren't wet and we would have seen them," countered Dick.

"*Maybee* they've got invisible diving suits that don't show wetness?"

"Those haven't been invented yet."

"*Maybee* they've invented them but kept it quiet?"

"It's not likely…"

"But not *impossible*, and you always say that 'when you've eliminated the impossible…'"

"Actually, Ernest, it *is* impossible!"

"Prove it."

"The only way to prove something impossible is to devote your entire life to trying to achieve it, and the lives of everyone to infinity throughout eternity, then *not* succeed…"

"Well, get started…"

"…and that's *impractical*!"

Dick knew he was shouting, but when Ernest got into one of these *maybee* moods—which he called his "clever spells"—everyone got a headache, and usually wound up giving in and agreeing with something they knew to be absurd just to make Ernest shut up. After that, he would be hard to live with for the rest of the day, puffed up like a toad with a smugness that Violet labelled "very unattractive," which prompted him to snipe that he didn't want to attract anyone like her, and her to counter that he would change his mind in a few years, and him to… well, it was a cycle Dick had lived through too often.

Then Violet found a hinge. Two, in fact.

Dick got out his magnifying glass and examined the hinges. Recently oiled, he noted. Where there were hinges, there must be a door. Hidden.

"Where's the handle?" asked Ernest.

"Inside," said Violet.

"What's the use of a door it only opens from one side?"

"It'd keep out detectives, like us," suggested Violet.

"There was no open door when Sellwood was here. It closed behind him. He'd want to open it again, rather than go home the long way."

"He had two big strong men with hammers," said Violet, "and we've got you and Ernest."

Dick tried to be patient.

He stuck his fingers into a crack in the rock, and worked down, hoping to get purchase enough to pull the probable door open.

"Careful," said Violet.

"*Maybee*…"

"Shut up, Ernest," said Dick.

He found his hand stuck, but pulled free, scraping his knuckles.

There was an outcrop by the sticking point, at about the height where you'd put a door-handle.

"Ah-hah," said Dick, seizing and turning the rock.

A click, and a section of the cliff pulled open. It was surprisingly light, a thin layer of stone fixed to a wooden frame.

A section of rock fell off the door.

"You've broken it now," said Ernest.

It was dark inside. From his coat-of-many-hidden-pockets, Dick produced three candlestubs with metal holders and a box of matches. For his next birthday, he hoped to get one of the new battery-powered electrical lanterns—until then, these would remain R.R.D.A. standard issue.

Getting the candles lit was a performance. The draught kept puffing out match-flames before the wicks caught. Violet took over and mumsily arranged everything, then handed out the candles, showing Ernest how to hold his so wax didn't drip on his fingers.

"Metal's hot," said Ernest.

"Perhaps we should leave you here as lookout," said Dick. "You can warn us in case any *dogs* come along."

The metal apparently wasn't *too* hot, since Ernest now wanted to continue. He insisted on being first into the dark, in case there were monsters.

Once they were inside, the door swung shut.

They were in a space carved out of the rock and shored up with timber. Empty barrels piled nearby. A row of fossil-smashing hammers arranged where Violet could spit at them. Smooth steps led upwards, with the rusted remains of rings set into the walls either side.

"'Brandy for the parson, 'baccy for the clerk,'" said Violet.

"Indubitably," responded Dick. "This is clear evidence of smuggling."

"What do people smuggle these days?" asked Violet. "Brandy and tobacco might have been expensive when we were at war with France and ships were slow, but that was ages ago."

Dick was caught out. He knew there was still contraband, but hadn't looked into its nature.

"Jewels, probably," he guessed. "And there's always spying."

Ernest considered the rings in the wall.

"I bet prisoners were chained here," he said, "until they turned to skellytones!"

"More likely people hold the rings while climbing the slippery stairs," suggested Violet, "especially if they're carrying heavy cases of… jewels and spy-letters."

Ernest was disappointed.

"But they *could* be used for prisoners."

Ernest cheered up.

"If I was a prisoner, I could 'scape," he said. He put his hand in a ring, which was much too big for him and for any grown-up too. Then he pulled and the ring came out of the wall.

Ernest tried to put it back.

Dick was tense, expecting tons of rock to fall on them.

No collapse happened.

"Be careful touching things," he warned his friends. "We were lucky that time, but there might be deadly traps."

He led the way up.

IV: "dh *jtifbsqqs*"

The steps weren't steep, but went up a long way. The tunnel had been hewn out of rock. New timbers, already bowed and near cracking, showed where the passage had been shored after falls.

"We must be under the Priory," Dick said.

They came to the top of the stairs, and a basement-looking room. Wooden crates were stacked.

"Cover your light," said Dick.

Ernest yelped as he burned his hand.

"Carefully," Dick added.

Ernest whimpered a bit.

"What do you suppose is in these?" asked Violet. "Contraband?"

"Instruments of evil?" prompted Ernest.

Dick held his candle close to a crate. The slats were spaced an inch or so apart. Inside were copies of *Omphalos Diabolicus*.

"Isn't the point of smuggling to bring in things people *want*?" asked Violet. "I can't imagine an illicit market for unreadable tracts."

"There could be coded spy messages in the books," Dick suggested hopefully.

"Even spies trained to resist torture in the dungeons of the Tsar wouldn't be able to read through these to get any message," said Violet. "My *deduction* is that these are here because Sellwood can't get anybody to buy his boring old book."

"*Maybee* he should change his name to Sellwords."

Dick had the tiniest spasm of impatience. Here they were, in the lair of an undoubted villain, having penetrated secret defences, and all they could do was make dubiously sarky remarks about his name.

"We should scout further," he said. "Come on."

He opened a door and found a gloomy passageway. The lack of windows suggested they were still underground. The walls were panelled, wood warped and stained by persistent damp.

The next room along had no door and was full of rubble. Dick thought the ceiling had fallen in, but Violet saw at once that the detritus was broken-up fossils.

"Ammonites," she said, "also brachiopods, nautiloids, crinoids, plagiostoma, coroniceras, gryphaea *and* calcirhynchia."

She held up what looked like an ordinary stone.

"This could be the knee-bone of a *scelidosaurus*. One was discovered in Charmouth, in Liassic cliffs just like these. The first near-complete dinosaur fossil to come to light. This might have been another find as important. Sellwood is a vandal and a wrecker. He should be hit on the head with his own hammers."

Dick patted Violet on the back, hoping she would cheer up.

"It's only a knee," said Ernest. "Nothing interesting about knees."

"Some dinosaurs had *brains* in their knees. Extra brains to do the thinking for their legs. Imagine if you had brains in your knees."

Ernest was impressed.

"If *I'd* found this, I wouldn't have broken it," said Violet. "I would have *named* it. *Biolettosaurus*, Violet's Lizard."

"Let's try the next room," said Dick. "There might still be useful fragments."

Reluctantly, Violet left the room of broken stone bones.

Next was a thick wooden door, with iron bands across it, and three heavy bolts. Though the bolts were oiled, it was a strain to pull them—Dick and Violet both struggled. The top and bottom bolts shifted, but the middle one wouldn't move.

"Let me try," said Ernest. "Please."

They did, and he didn't get anywhere.

Violet dipped back into the fossil room and came back with a chunk they used as a hammer. The third bolt shot open.

The banging and clanging sounded fearfully loud in the enclosed space.

They listened, but no one came. *Maybee*, Dick thought—recognising the Ernestism—Sellwood was up in his Tower, scanning the horizon for spy-signals, and his Brethren were taking afternoon naps.

The children stepped through the doorway, and the door swung slowly and heavily shut behind them.

This room was different again.

The floor and walls were solid slabs which looked as if they'd been in place a long time. The atmosphere was dank, slightly mouldy. A stone trough, like you see in stables, ran along one wall, fed by an old-fashioned pump. Dick cupped water in his hand and tasted it. There was a nasty, coppery sting, and he spat.

"It's a *dungeon*," said Ernest.

Violet held up her candle.

A winch-apparatus, with handles like a threshing machine, was fixed to the floor at the far side of the room, thick chain wrapped around the drum.

"Careful," said Violet, gripping Dick's arm.

Dick looked at his feet. He stood on the edge of a circular hole, like a well. It was a dozen feet across, and uncovered.

"There should be a cap on this," announced Dick. "To prevent accidents."

"I doubt if Sellwood cares much about accidents befalling intruders."

"You're probably right, Vile. The man's a complete rotter."

Chains extended from the winch unto a solid iron ring in the ceiling and then down into the Hole.

"This is an *oubliette*," said Violet. "It's from the French. You capture your *prisonnier* and *jeté* him into the Hole, then *oublié* them—forget them."

Ernest, nervously, kept well away from the edge. He had been warned about falling into wells once, which meant that ever since he was afraid of them.

Violet tossed her rock-chunk into the pool of dark, and counted. After three counts—thirty feet—there was a thump. Stone on stone.

"No splash," she said.

Up from the depths came another sound, a gurgling groan—something alive but unidentifiable. The noise lodged in Dick's heart like a fish-hook of ice. A chill played up his spine.

The cry had come from a throat, but hardly a human one.

Ernest dropped his candle, which rolled to the lip of the pit and fell in, flame guttering.

Round, green eyes shone up, fire dancing in the fish-flat pupils.

Something grey-green, weighted with old chains, writhed at the bottom of the Hole.

Ernest's candle went out.

Violet's grip on Dick's arm hurt now.

"What's *that*?" she gasped.

The groan took on an imploring, almost pathetic tone, tinged with cunning and bottomless wrath.

Dick shrugged off his shiver. He had a moment of pure joy, the *click* of sudden understanding that often occurs at the climax of a case, when clues fit in the mind like jigsaw pieces and the solution is plain and simple.

"That, my dear Vile, is your French spy!"

V: *"Obdijfbntp Gdmbqbgs"*

"Someone's coming," said Ernest.

Footfalls in the passageway!

"Hide," said Dick.

The only place—aside from the Hole—was under the water-trough. Dick and Violet pinched out their candles and crammed in, pulling Ernest after them.

"They'll see the door's not bolted," said Ernest.

Violet clamped her hand over her cousin's mouth.

In the enclosed space, their breathing seemed horribly loud.

Dick worried. Ernest was right.

Maybee the people in the passage weren't coming to *this* room. *Maybee* they'd already walked past, on their way to smash fossils or get a copy of Sellwood's book.

The footsteps stopped outside the door.

Maybee this person didn't know it was usually bolted. *Maybee* this dungeon was so rarely visited they'd *oublié* whether it had been bolted shut after the last time.

Maybee…

"Fessel, Fose, Milder, Maulder," barked a voice.

The Reverend Mr. Daniel Sturdevant Sellwood, calling his brethren.

"And who's been opening *my* door," breathed Violet.

It took Dick long seconds to recognise the storybook quotation.

"Who was last here?" shouted Sellwood. "This is inexcusable. With the Devil, one does not take such risks."

"En cain't git ouwt of thic Hole," replied someone.

"Brother Milder, it has the wiles of an arch-fiend. That is why only *I* can be trusted to put it to the question. Who last brought the slops?"

There was some argument.

Maybee they'd be all right. Sellwood was so concerned with stopping an escape that he hadn't thought anyone might break *in*.

One of the Brethren tentatively spoke up, and received a clout round the ear.

Dick wondered why anyone would *want* to be in Sellwood's Church Militant.

"Stand guard," Sellwood ordered. "Let me see what disaster is so narrowly averted."

The door was pushed open. Sellwood set a lantern on a perch. The children pressed further back into shrinking shadow. Dick's ankle bent the wrong way. He bit down on the pain.

He saw Sellwood's shoes—with old-fashioned buckles and gaiters— walk past the trough, towards the Hole. He stopped, just by Dick's face.

There was a pumping, coughing sound.

Sellwood filled a beaker.

He poured the water into the Hole.

Violet counted silently, again. After three, the water splashed on the French spy. It cried out, with despair and yearning.

"Drink deep, spawn of Satan!"

The creature howled, then gargled again. Dick realised it wasn't making animal grunts but *speaking*. Unknown words which he suspected were not French.

The thing had been here for over a hundred years!

"Fose, Milder, in here, now. I will resume the inquisition."

Brethren clumped in. Dick saw heavy boots.

The two bruisers walked around the room, keeping well away from the Hole. Dick eased out a little to get a better view. He risked a more comfortable, convenient position. Sellwood had no reason to suspect he was spied upon.

Brother Fose and Brother Milder worked the winch.

The chains tightened over the Hole, then wound onto the winch-drum.

The thing in the *oubliette* cursed. Dick was sure "*f'tagn*" was a swear-word. As it was hauled upwards, the creature struggled, hissing and croaking.

Violet held Dick's hand, pulling, keeping him from showing himself.

A head showed over the mouth of the Hole, three times the size of a man's and with no neck, just a pulpy frill of puffed-up gill-slits. Saucer-sized fish-eyes held the light, pupils contracting. Dick was sure the creature, face at floor-level, saw past the boots of its captors straight into his face. It had a fixed maw, with enough jagged teeth to please Ernest.

"Up," ordered Sellwood. "Let's see all of the demon."

The Brethren winched again, and the thing hung like Captain Kidd on Execution Dock. It was manlike, but with a stub of fishtail protruding beneath two rows of dorsal spines. Its hands and feet were webbed, with nastily curved yellow nail-barbs. Where water had splashed, its skin was rainbow-scaled, beautiful even. Elsewhere, its hide was grey and taut, cracked, flaking or mossy, with rusty weals where the chains chafed.

Dick saw that the thing was missing several finger-barbs. Its back and front were striped across with long-healed and new-made scars. It had been whipping boy in this house since the days when Boney was a warrior way-aye-aye.

He imagined Jacob Orris trying to get Napoleon's secrets out of the "spy." Had old Orris held up charts and asked the man-fish to tap a claw on hidden harbours where the invasion fleet was gathered?

Ernest was mumbling "sea-ghost" over and over, not frightened but awed. Violet hissed at him to hush.

Dick was sure they'd be caught, but Sellwood was fascinated by the creature. He poked his face close to his captive's, smiling smugly. A cheek muscle twitched around his fixed sneer. The man-fish looked as if it would like to spit in Sellwood's face but couldn't afford the water.

"So, *Diabolicus Maritime*, is it today that you confess? I have been patient. We merely seek a statement we all know to be true, which will end this sham once and for all."

The fish-eyes were glassy and flat, but moved to fix on Sellwood.

"You are a *deception*, my infernal guest, a lure, a living trick, a lie made flesh, a creature of the Prince of Liars. Own that Satan is your maker, imp! Confess your evil purpose!"

Sellwood touched fingertips to the creature's scarred chest, scraping dry flesh. Scales fluttered away, falling like dead moths. Dick saw Sellwood's fingers flex, the tips biting.

"The bones weren't enough, were they? Those so-called 'fossils,' the buried lies that lead to blasphemy and disbelief. No, the Devil had a second deceit in reserve, to pile upon the Great Untruth of 'Pre-History.' No mere dead dragon, but a live specimen, one of those fabled 'missing links' in the fairy tale of 'evolution.' By your very existence, you bear false witness, testify that the world is older than it has been proved over and over again to be, preach against creation, tear down mankind, to drag us from the realm of the angels into the festering salt-depths of Hell. The City of the Damned lies under the Earth, but you prove to my satisfaction that it extends also under the sea!"

The man-fish had no ears, but Dick was certain it could hear Sellwood. Moreover, it *understood*, followed his argument.

"So, own up," snapped the Reverend. "One word, and the deception is at an end. You are not part of God's Creation, but a sea-serpent, a monstrous forgery!"

The creature's lipless mouth curved. It barked, through its mouth. Its gills rippled, showing scarlet inside.

Sellwood was furious.

Dick, strangely, was excited. The prisoner was *laughing* at its captor, the laughter of a patient, abiding being.

Why was it still alive? Could it be killed? Surely, Orris or Sellwood or some keeper in between had tried to execute the monster?

In those eyes was a promise to the parson. *I will live when you are gone.*

"Drop it," snapped Sellwood.

Fose and Milder let go the winch, and—with a cry—the "French spy" was swallowed by its Hole.

Sellwood and his men left the room, taking the lantern.

Dick began breathing properly again. Violet let Ernest squirm a little, though she still held him under the trough.

Then came a truly terrifying sound, worse even than the laughter of the fish-demon.

Bolts being drawn. Three of them.

They were trapped!

VI: "wsff imjturq-tk bh M'fysr"

Now was the time to keep calm.

Dick knew Violet would be all right, if only because she had to think about Ernest.

For obvious reasons, the children had not told anyone where they were going, but they would be missed at tea-time. Uncle Davey and Aunt Maeve could easily overlook a skipped meal—both of them were liable to get so interested in something that they wouldn't notice the house catching fire—but Cook kept track. And Mr. and Mrs. Borrodale were sticklers for being in by five o'clock with hands washed and presentable.

It must be past five now.

Of course, any search party wouldn't get around to the Priory for days, maybe weeks. They'd look on the beaches first, and in the woods.

Eventually, his uncle and aunt would find the folder marked "Qrs Ndps ja qrs Dggjhbqs Dhhbrbfdqjm." Aunt Maeve, good at puzzles, had taught him how to cipher in the first place. She would eventually break the code and read Dick's notes, and want to talk with Sellwood. By then, it would probably be too late.

They gave the Brethren time enough to get beyond earshot before creeping out from under the trough. They unbent with much creaking and muffled moaning. Violet lit her candle.

Dick paced around the cell, keeping away from the Hole.

"I'm thirsty," said Ernest.

"Easily treated," said Violet.

She found the beaker and pumped water into it. Ernest drank, made a face, and asked for more. Violet worked the pump again.

Water splashed over the brimful beaker, into the trough.

A noise came out of the Hole.

The children froze into mannequins. The noise came again.

"Wah wah… *wah wah*…"

There was a pleading tone to it.

"Wah wah…"

"'Water,'" said Dick, snapping his fingers. "It's saying 'water.'"

"Wah wah," agreed the creature. "Uh, wah wah."

"'Water. Yes, water.'"

"Gosh, Dick, you *are* clever," said Violet.

"Wat war," said the creature, insisting. "Gi' mee wat war, i' oo eese…"

"'Water,'" said Dick, "'Give me—'"

"'—water, if you please,'" completed Violet, who caught on swiftly. "Very polite for a sea-ghost. Well brought-up in Atlantis or Lyonesse or

R'lyeh, I imagine."

"Where?" asked Dick.

"Sunken cities of old, where mer-people are supposed to live."

More leftovers from Violet's myths and legends craze. Interesting, but not very helpful.

Ernest had walked to the edge of the Hole.

"This isn't a soppy mer-person," said Ernest. "This is a Monster of the Deep!"

He emptied the beaker into the dark.

A sigh of undoubted gratitude rose from the depths.

"Wat war goo', tanks. Eese, gi' mee moh."

Ernest poured another beakerful. At this rate, they might as well be using an eye-dropper.

Dick saw the solution.

"Vile, help me shift the trough," he said.

They pulled one end away from the wall. It was heavy, but the bolts were old and rusted and the break came easily.

"Careful not to move the other end too much. We need it under the pump."

Violet saw where this was going. Angled down away from the wall, the trough turned into a sluice. It didn't quite stretch all the way to the *oubliette*, but pulling up a loose stone put a notch into the rim which served as a spout.

"Wat war eese," said the creature, mildly.

Dick nodded to Violet. She worked the pump.

Water splashed into the trough and flowed down, streaming through the notch and pouring into the pit.

The creature gurgled with joy.

Only now did Dick wonder whether watering it was a good idea. It might not be a French spy or even a maritime demon, but it was definitely one of Granny Ball's sea-ghosts. If Dick had been treated as it had been, he would not be well-disposed towards land-people.

But the water kept flowing.

Violet's arm got tired, and she let up for a moment.

"I' oo eese," insisted the creature, with a reproachful, nannyish tone. "Moh wat war."

Violet kept pumping.

Dick took the candle and walked to the edge of the Hole. Ernest sat there, legs dangling over the edge, fingers playing in the cool cascade.

The boys looked down.

Where water fell, the man-fish was changed—vivid greens and reds and purples and oranges glistened. Its spines and frills and gills and webs were sleek. Even its eyes shone more brightly.

It turned, mouth open under the spray, letting water wash around it, wrenching against its chains.

"Water makes the Monster strong," said Ernest.

The creature looked up at them. The edges of its mouth curved into something like a smile. There was cunning there, and a bottomless well of malice, but also an exultation. Dick understood: When it was wet, the thing felt as he did when he saw through a mystery.

It took a grip on one of its manacles and squeezed, cracking the old iron and casting it away.

"Can I stop now?" asked Violet. "My arm's out of puff."

"I think so."

The creature nodded, a human gesture awkward on the gilled, neckless being.

It stood up unshackled, and stretched as if waking after a long sleep in an awkward position. The chains dangled freely. A clear, thick, milky-veined fluid seeped from the weals on its chest. The man-fish carefully smoothed this secretion like an ointment.

There were pools of water around its feet. It got down on its knees—did it have spare brains in them?—and sucked the pools dry. Then it raised its head and let water dribble through its gills and down over its chest and back.

"Tanks," it said.

Now it wasn't parched, its speech was easier to understand.

It took hold of the dangling chains, and tugged, testing them.

Watering the thing in the Hole was all very well, but Dick wasn't sure how he'd feel if it were up here with them. If he were the creature, he would be very annoyed. He ought to be grateful to the children, but what did anyone know about the feelings of sea-ghosts? Violet had told them the legend of the genie in the bottle: At first, he swore to bestow untold riches upon the man who set him free, but after thousands of years burned to make his rescuer suffer horribly for waiting so long.

It was too late to think about that.

Slick and wet, the man-fish moved faster than anything its size should. No sooner had it grasped the chains than it had climbed them, deft as a sailor on the rigging, quick as a lizard on the flat or a salmon in the swim.

It held on, hanging just under the ring in the ceiling, head swivelling around, eyes taking in the room.

Dick and Ernest were backed against the door, taking Violet with them.

She was less spooked than the boys.

"*Bonjour, Monsieur le Fantôme de la Mer,*" she said, slowly and clearly in the manner approved by her tutor, M. Duroc. "*Je m'appelle Violette Borrodale… permettez-moi de presente a vous mon petit cousin*

Ernest… et Rishard Riddle, le detective juvenile celebré."

This seemed to puzzle the sea-ghost.

"Vile, I don't think it's really French," whispered Dick.

Violet shrugged.

The creature let go and leaped, landing frog-like, knees stuck out and shoulders hunched, inches away from them. This close, it stank of the sea.

Dick saw their reflections in its huge eyes.

Its mouth opened. He saw row upon row of sharklike teeth, all pointed and shining. It might not have had a proper meal in a century.

"Scuze mee," it said, extending a hand, folding its frill-connected fingers up but pointing with a single barb.

The wet thorn touched Richard's cheek.

Then it eased the children aside, and considered the bolted door.

"Huff… puff… blow," it said, hammering with fish-fists. The door came off its hinges and the bolts wrenched out of their sockets. The broken door crashed against the opposite wall of the passage.

"How do you know the Three Little Pigs?" asked Violet.

"Gur' nam 'Ooth," it said, "ree' to mee…"

"A girl read to him," Dick explained.

So not all his captors had been tormentors. Who was 'Ooth? Ruth? Someone called Ruth fit into the story. The little girl lost with the *Sophy Briggs*. Sellwood's niece.

The sea-ghost looked at Violet. Dick deduced all little girls must look alike to it. If you've seen one pinafore, you've seen them all.

"'Ooth," it said, with something like fondness. "'Ooth kin' to mee. Ree' mee story-boos. *Liss in Wonlan… Tripella Liplik Pik… Taes o Eh Ah Po…*"

"What happened to Ruth?" Violet asked.

"Sellwoo' ki' 'Ooth, an' hi' bro tah Joh-jee," said the creature, cold anger in its voice. "Tey wan let mee go sea, let mee go hom. Sellwoo' mak shi' wreck, tak ever ting, tak mee."

Dick understood. And was not surprised.

This was the nature of Sellwood's villainy. Charges of smuggling and espionage remained unproven, but he was guilty of the worst crime of all—murder!

People were coming now, alerted by the noise.

The sea-ghost stepped into the passage, holding up a hand—fingers spread and webs unfurled—to indicate that the children should stay behind.

They kept in the dark, where they couldn't see what was happening in the passage.

The man-fish leaped, and landed on someone.

Cries of terror and triumph! An unpleasant, wet crunching... followed by unmistakable chewing.

More people came on the scene.

"The craytur's out o' thic Hole," shrieked someone.

A very loud bang! A firework stink.

The man-fish staggered back past the doorway, red blossoming on its shoulder. It had more red stuff around its mouth, and scraps of cloth caught in its teeth.

It roared rage and threw itself at whoever had shot it.

Something detached from something else and rolled past the doorway, leaving a trail of sticky splashes.

Violet kept her hand over Ernest's eyes, though he tried to pick at her fingers.

"Spawn of Satan, you show your true colours at last!"

It was Sellwood.

"Milder, Fessel, take him down."

The Brethren grunted. The doorway was filled with struggling bodies, driving the children back into the cell. They pressed flat against the wet, cold walls.

Brother Milder and Brother Fessel held the creature's arms and wrestled it back, towards the Hole.

Sellwood appeared, hefting one of his fossil-breaking hammers.

He thumped the sea-ghost's breastbone with all his might, and it fell, sprawling on the flagstones. Milder and Fessel shifted their weight to pin him down.

Still, no one noticed the children.

The creature's shoulder wound closed like a sea-anemone. The bruise in the middle of its chest faded at once. It looked hate up at the Reverend.

Sellwood stood over the wriggling man-fish. He weighed his hammer.

"You're devilish hard to kill, demon! But how would you like your skull pounded to paste? It might take a considerable while to recover, eh?"

He raised the hammer above his head.

"You there," said Violet, voice clear and shrill and loud, "stop!"

Sellwood swivelled to look.

"This is an important scientific discovery, and must not be harmed. Why, it is practically a living dinosaur."

Violet stood between Sellwood and the pinned man-fish. Dick was by her side, arm linked with hers. Ernest was in front of them, fists up like a pugilist.

"Don't you hurt my friend the Monster," said Ernest.

Sellwood's red rage showed.

"You see," he yelled, "how the foulness spreads! How the lies take hold! You see!"

Something snapped inside Milder. He rolled off the creature, limbs loose, neck flopping.

The sea-ghost stood up, a two-handed grip on the last of Sellwood's Brethren, Fessel.

"Help," he gasped. "Children, help…"

Dick had a pang of guilt.

Then Fessel was falling into the *oubliette*. He rattled against chains, and landed with a final-sounding crash.

The sea-ghost stepped around the children and took away Sellwood's hammer, which it threw across the room. It clanged against the far wall.

"I am not afraid of you," announced the Reverend.

The creature tucked Sellwood under its arm. The Reverend was too surprised to protest.

"Shouldn' a' ki' 'Ooth a' Joh-jee, Sellwoo'. Shouldn' a' ki'."

"How do you know?" Sellwood was indignant, but didn't deny the crime.

"Sea tol' mee, sea tel' mee all ting."

"I serve a greater purpose," shouted Sellwood.

The sea-ghost carried the Reverend out of the room. The children followed.

The man-fish strode down the passage, towards the book-room. Two dead men—Maulder and Fose—lay about.

"Their heads are gone," exclaimed Ernest, with a glee Dick found a little disturbing. At least Ernest wasn't picking up one of the heads for the office wall.

Sellwood thumped the creature's back. Its old whip-stripes and poker-brands were healing.

Dick, Violet, and Ernest followed the escapee and its former gaoler.

In the book-room, Sellwood looked with hurried regret at the crates of unsold volumes and struggled less. The sea-ghost found the steps leading down and seemed to contract its body to squeeze into the tunnel. Sellwood was dragged bloody against the rock ceiling.

"Come on, detectives," said Dick, "after them!"

VII: *"Dhqrmjkjp Bnqryjp Ibjffsqqd"*

They came out under Ware Cleeve. Waves scraped shingle in an eternal rhythm. It was twilight, and chilly. Well past tea-time.

The man-fish, burden limp, tasted the sea in the air.

"Tanks," it said to the children, "tanks very' mu'."

It walked into the waves. As sea soaked through his coat, Sellwood was shocked conscious and began to struggle again, shouting and cursing and praying.

The sea-ghost was waist-deep in its element.

It turned to wave at the children. Sellwood got free, madly striking *away* from the shore, not towards dry land. The creature leaped completely out of the water, dark rainbows rippling on its flanks, and landed heavily on Sellwood, claws hooking into meat, pressing the Reverend under the waves.

They saw the swimming shape, darting impossibly fast, zigzagging out into the bay. Finned feet showed above the water for an instant and the man-fish—the sea-ghost, the French spy, the living fossil, the snare of Satan, the Monster of the Deep—was gone for good, dragging the Reverend Mr. Daniel Sturdevant Sellwood with him.

"...to Davey Jones's locker," said Ernest.

Dick realised Violet was holding his hand, and tactfully got his fingers free.

Their shoes were covered with other people's blood.

"*Anthropos Icthyos Biolletta*," said Violet. "Violet's Man-Fish, a whole new *phylum*."

"I pronounce this case closed," said Dick.

"Can I borrow your matches?" asked Violet. "I'll just nip back up the tunnel and set fire to Sellwood's books. If the Priory burns down, we won't have to answer questions about dead people."

Dick handed over the box.

He agreed with Violet. This was one of those stories for which the world was not yet ready. Writing it up, he would use a double cipher.

"Besides," said Violet, "some books deserve to be burned."

While Violet was gone, Dick and Ernest passed time skipping stones on the waves. Rooting for ammunition, they found an ammonite, not quite as big and nice as the one that was smashed, but sure to delight Violet and much easier to carry home.

ANGEL DOWN, SUSSEX

I: "too late in the year, surely, for wasps"

The Reverend Mr. Bartholomew Haskins, rector of Angel Down, paused by the open gate of Angel Field. His boots sank a little into the frost-crusted mud. Ice water trickled in his veins. He was momentarily unable to move. From somewhere close by came the unmistakable, horrid buzz of a cloud of insects.

It was too late in the year, surely, for wasps. But his ears were attuned to such sounds. Since childhood, he'd been struck with a horror of insects. Jane, his sister, had died in infancy of an allergic reaction to wasp stings. It was thought likely that he might share her acute sensitivity to their venom, but the reason for his persistent fear—as for so much else in his life—was that it was his stick, poked into a pulpy nest, which had stirred the insects to fury. As a boy, he had prayed to Jane for forgiveness as often as he prayed to Our Lord. As a man, he laboured still under the burden of a guilt beyond assuaging.

"Bart," prompted Sam Farrar, the farmer, "what is it?"

"Nothing," he lied.

At the far end of Angel Field was a copse, four elms growing so close together by a shallow pond their roots and branches were knotted. A flock of sheep were kept here. As Sam hauled his gate shut behind them, Haskins noticed the sheep forming a clump, as if eager to gather around their owner. There were white humps in the rest of the field, nearer the copse. They didn't move. Wasps did swarm over them.

Hideous, dreadful creatures.

Haskins forced himself to venture into Angel Field, following the farmer. He kept his arms stiffly by his side and walked straight-legged, wary of exciting a stray monster into sudden, furious hostility.

"Never seen anything like this, Bart," said Sam. "In fifty year on the land."

The farmer waded through his flock and knelt by one of the humps, waving the wasps away with a casual, ungloved hand. The scene swam before Haskins's eyes. A filthy insect crawled on Sam's hand and Haskins's stomach knotted with panic.

He overcame his dread with a supreme effort and joined his friend. The hump was a dead sheep. Sam picked up the animal's woolly head and turned its face to the sunlight.

The animal had been savagely mutilated. Its skull was exposed on one side. The upper lip, cheek, and one side of the nose were torn away as if

107

by shrapnel.

"I think it's been done with acid."

"Should you be touching it, then?"

"Good point."

Sam dropped the beast's head. The seams in his face deepened as he frowned.

"The others are the same. Strange swirls etched into their hides. Look."

There were rune-like patches on the dead sheep. They might have been left by a weapon or branding iron. The skin and flesh were stripped off or eaten away.

"My Dad'd never keep beasts in Angel Field. Not after the trouble with my Aunt Rose. That was in '72, afore I was born. You know that story, of course. Was kept from me for a long time. This is where it happened."

The wasps had come back. Haskins couldn't think.

"Always been something off about Angel Field. Were standing stones here once, like at Stonehenge but smaller. After Rose, Grandad had 'em all pulled down and smashed to bits. There was a fuss and a protest, but it's Farrar land. Nothing busybodies from Up London could do about it."

Grassy depressions, in a circle, showed where the stones had stood for thousands of years. The dead sheep were within the area that had once been bounded by the ring.

It seemed to Haskins that the insects were all inside the circle too, gathering. Not just wasps, but flies, bees, hornets, ants, beetles. Wings sawed the air, so swiftly they blurred. Mouth-parts stitched, stingers dripped, feelers whipped, legs scissored. A chitinous cacophony.

Bartholomew Haskins was terrified, and ashamed of his fear. Soon, Sam would notice. But at the moment, the farmer was too puzzled and annoyed by what had befallen his sheep.

"I tell you, Bart, I don't know whether to call the vet or the constable."

"This isn't natural," Haskins said. "Someone did this."

"Hard to picture, Bart. But I think you're right."

Sam stood up and looked away, at his surviving sheep. None bore any unusual mark, or seemed ailing. But they were spooked. It was in their infrequent bleating. If even the sheep felt it, there must be something here.

Haskins looked about, gauging the positions of the missing stones. The dead sheep were arranged in a smaller circle within the larger, spaced nearly evenly. And at the centre was another bundle, humped differently.

"What's this, Sam?"

The farmer came over.

"Not one of mine," he said.

The bundle was under a hide of some sort. Insects clung to it like a ghastly shroud. They moved, as if the thing were alive. Haskins struggled to keep his gorge down.

The hide undulated and a great cloud of wasps rose into the air in a spiral. Haskins swallowed a scream.

"It's moving."

The hide flipped back at the edge and a small hand groped out.

"Good God," Sam swore.

Haskins knelt down and tore away the hide. It proved to be a tartan blanket, crusted with mud and glittering with shed bug scales.

Large, shining eyes caught the sun like a cat's. The creature gave out a keening shriek that scraped nerves. There was something of the insect in the screech, and something human. For a moment, Haskins thought he was hearing Jane again, in her dying agony.

The creature was a muddy child. A little girl, of perhaps eight. She was curled up like a buried mummy, and brown all over, clothes as much as her face and limbs. Her feet were bare, and her hair was drawn back with a silvery ribbon.

She blinked in the light, still screeching.

Haskins patted the girl, trying to soothe her. She hissed at him, showing bright, sharp, white teeth. He didn't recognise her, but there was something familiar in her face, in the set of her eyes and the shape of her mouth.

She hesitated, like a snake about to strike, then clung to him, sharp fingers latched onto his coat, face pressed to his chest. Her screech was muffled, but continued.

Haskins looked over the girl's shoulder at Sam Farrar. He was bewildered and agoggle. In his face, Haskins saw an echo of the girl's features, even her astonished expression.

It couldn't be…

…but it was. Missing for over fifty years and returned exactly as she had been when taken.

This was Rose Farrar.

II: "beyond the veil"

"There is one who would speak with you, Catriona Kaye," intoned Mademoiselle Astarte. "One who has passed beyond the veil, one who cares for you very much."

Catriona nodded curtly. The medium's lacquered fingers bit deeply into her hand. She could smell peppermint on the woman's breath, and gin.

Mademoiselle Astarte wore a black dress, shimmering with beaded fringes. A tiara of peacock feathers gave her the look of an Aztec priestess.

A rope of pearls hung flat against her chest and dangled to her navel. As table-rappers went, she was the bee's roller-skates.

She shook her head slightly, eyes shut in concentration. Catriona's hand really hurt now.

"A soldier," the medium breathed.

The Great War had been done with for seven years. It was a fair bet that anyone of Catriona's age—she was a century baby, born 1900—consulting a woman in Mademoiselle Astarte's profession would be interested in a soldier. Almost everyone had lost a soldier—a sweetheart, a brother, even a father.

She nodded, noncommittally.

"Yes, a soldier," the medium confirmed. A lone tear ran neatly through her mascara.

There were others in the room. Mademoiselle didn't have her clients sit about a table. She arranged them on stiff-backed chairs in a rough semicircle and wandered theatrically among them, seizing with both hands the person to whom the spirit or spirits who spoke through her wished to address themselves.

Everyone was attentive. The medium put on a good show.

Mademoiselle Astarte's mother, a barrel-shaped lady draped in what might once have been a peculiarly ugly set of mid-Victorian curtains, let her fingers play over the keys of an upright piano, tinkling notes at random. It was supposed to suggest the music of the spheres, and put the spirits at ease. Catriona was sure the woman was playing "Knocked 'Em in the Old Kent Road" very slowly.

Smoke filtered into the room. Not scented like incense, but pleasantly woody. It seemed to come from nowhere. The electric lamps were dimmed with Chinese scarves. A grey haze gathered over the carpet, rising like a tide.

"His passing was sudden," the medium continued. "But not painful. A shock. He hardly knew what had happened to him, was unaware of his condition."

Also calculated: no upsetting details—choking on gas while gutted on barbed wire, mind smashed by months of bombardment and shot as a coward—and a subtle explanation for why it had taken years for the spirit to come through.

There was a fresh light. It seemed sourceless, but the smoke glowed from within as it gathered into a spiral. A prominent china manufacturer gasped, while his wife's face was wrung with a mix of envy and joy—they had lost a son at Passchendaele.

A figure was forming. A man in uniform, olive drab bleached grey. The cap was distinct, but the face was a blur. Any rank insignia were unreadable.

Catriona's hands were almost bloodless. She had to steel herself to keep from yelping. Mademoiselle Astarte yanked her out of her chair and held tight.

The figure wavered in the smoke.

"He wants you to know…"

"…that he cares for me very much?"

"Yes. Indeed. It is so."

Mademoiselle Astarte's rates were fixed. Five pounds for a session. Those whose loved ones "made contact" were invariably stirred enough to double or triple the fee. The departed never seemed overly keen on communicating with those left behind who happened to be short of money.

Catriona peered at the wavering smoke soldier.

"There's something I don't understand," she said.

"Yes, child…"

Mademoiselle Astarte could only be a year or two older than her.

"My soldier. Edwin."

"Yes. Edwin. That is the name. I hear it clearly."

A smile twitched on Catriona's lips.

"Edwin… isn't… actually *dead.*"

The medium froze. Her nails dug into Catriona's bare arms. Her face was a study in silent fury. Catriona detached Mademoiselle Astarte's hands from her person and stood back.

"The music is to cover the noise of the projection equipment, isn't it?"

Mademoiselle's mother banged the keyboard without interruption. Catriona looked up at the ceiling. The chandelier was an arrangement of mirror pendants clustered around a pinhole aperture.

"There's another one of you in the room upstairs. Cranking the projector. Your father, I would guess. It's remarkable how much more reliable your connection with the spirit world has become since his release from Pentonville."

She poked her hand into the smoke and wiggled her fingers. Greatcoat buttons were projected onto her hand. The sepia tint was a nice touch.

"You bitch," Mademoiselle Astarte spat, like a fishwife.

The others in the circle were shocked.

"I really must protest," began the china manufacturer. His bewildered wife shook her head, still desperate to believe.

"I'm afraid this woman has been rooking you," Catriona announced. "She is a clever theatrical performer, and a rather nasty specimen of that unlovely species, the confidence trickster."

The medium's hands leaped like hawks. Catriona caught her wrists and held the dagger-nails away from her face. Her fringes writhed like the fronds of an angry jellyfish.

"You are a disgrace, Mademoiselle," she said, coldly. "And your sham is blown. You would do well to return to the music-halls, where your prestidigitation does no harm."

She withdrew tactfully from the room. A commotion erupted within, as sitters clamoured for their money back, and Mademoiselle and her mother tried in vain to calm them. The china manufacturer, extremely irate, mentioned the name of a famous firm of solicitors.

In the hallway, Catriona found her good cloth coat and slipped it on over a moderately fringed white dress. It was daringly cut just above the knee, barely covering the rolled tops of her silk stockings. She fixed a cloche hat over her bobbed brown hair, catching sight of her slightly too satisfied little face in the hall mirror. She still had freckles, which made the carefully placed beauty mark a superfluous black dot. Her mouth was nice, though, just the shape for a rich red Cupid's bow. She blew a triumphant kiss at herself, and stepped out onto Phene Street.

Her cold anger was subsiding. Charlatanry always infuriated her, especially when combined with cupidity. The field of psychical research would never be taken seriously while the flim-flam merchants were in business, fleecing the grieving and the gullible.

Edwin Winthrop awaited her outside, the Bentley idling at the kerb like a green and brass land-yacht. He sat at the wheel, white scarf flung over his shoulder, a large check cap over his patent-leather hair, warmed not by a voluminous car coat but by a leather flying jacket. The ends of his moustache were almost unnoticeably waxed, and he grinned to see her, satisfied that she had done well at the séance. Her soldier was seven years out of uniform, but still obscurely in the service of his country.

"Hop in, Catty-Kit," he said. "You'll want to make a swift get-away, I suspect. Doubtless, the doers of dastardly deeds will have their fur standing on end by now, and be looking to exact a cowardly revenge upon your pretty little person."

A heavy plant-pot fell from the skies and exploded on the pavement a foot away from her white pumps. It spread shrapnel of well-watered dirt and waxy aspidistra leaves. She glanced up at the town house, noticing the irate old man in an open window, and vaulted into the passenger seat.

"Very neatly done, Cat," Edwin complimented her.

The car swept away, roaring like a jungle beast. Fearful curses followed. She blushed to hear such language. Edwin sounded the bulb-horn in reply.

She leaned close and kissed his chilled cheek.

"How's the spirit world, my angel?" she asked.

"How would I know?" he shrugged.

"I have it on very good authority that you've taken up residence there."

"Not yet, old thing. The Hun couldn't get shot of me on the ground or in the air during the late unpleasantness, and seven stripes of foul fellow have missed their chance since the cessation. Edwin Winthrop, Esquire, of Somerset and Bloomsbury, is pretty much determined to stick about on this physical plane for the foreseeable. After all, it's so deuced interesting a sphere. With you about, one wouldn't wish to say farewell to the corporeal just yet."

They drove through Chelsea, towards St. James's Park. It was a bright English autumn day, with red leaves in the street and a cleansing nip in the air.

"What do you make of this?"

One hand on the wheel, he produced a paper from inside his jacket. It was a telegram.

"It's from the Old Man," he explained.

The message was terse, three words. Angel Down Sussex.

"Is it an event or a place?" she asked.

Edwin laughed, even teeth shining.

"A bit of both, Catty-Kit. A bit of both."

III: "in the Strangers Room"

Strictly speaking, the gentle sex were not permitted within the portals of the Diogenes Club. When this was first brought to Winthrop's attention, he had declared his beloved associate to be not a woman but a minx and therefore not subject to the regulation. The Old Man, never unduly deferential to hoary tradition, accepted this and Catriona Kaye was now admitted without question to the Strangers Room. As she breezed into the discreet building in Pall Mall and sat herself daintily down like a deceptively well-behaved schoolgirl, Winthrop derived petty satisfaction from the contained explosions of fury that emanated from behind several raised numbers of *The Times*. He realised that the Old Man shared this tiny pleasure.

Though he had served with the Somerset Light Infantry and the Royal Flying Corps during the Great War, Edwin Winthrop had always been primarily responsible to the Diogenes Club, least known and most eccentric instrument of the British Government. If anything, peace had meant an increase in his activities on their behalf. The Old Man—Charles Beauregard, Chairman of the Club's Ruling Cabal—had formed a section to look into certain matters no other official body could be seen to take seriously. Winthrop was the leading agent of that special section, and Catriona Kaye, highly unofficially, his most useful aide. Her interest in psychical research, a subject upon which she had written several books, dovetailed usefully with the section's remit, to deal with the apparently inexplicable.

The Old Man joined them in the Strangers Room, signalled an attendant to bring brandy, and sat himself down on an upholstered sofa. At seventy-two, his luxurious hair and clipped moustache were snow white but his face was marvellously unlined and his eyes still bright. Beauregard had served with the Diogenes Club for over forty years, since the days when the much-missed Mycroft Holmes chaired the Cabal and the Empire was ceaselessly harried by foreign agents after naval plans.

Beauregard complimented Catriona on her complexion; she smiled and showed her dimple. There was a satirical undercurrent to this exchange, as if all present had to pretend always to be considerably less clever than they were, but were also compelled to communicate on a higher level their genuine acuities. This meant sometimes seeming to take the roles of windy old uncle and winsome young flirt.

"You're our authority on the supernatural, Catriona," said the Old Man, enunciating all four syllables of the name. "Does Angel Down mean anything to you?"

"I know of the story," she replied. "It was a nine-day wonder, like the *Mary Celeste* or the Angel of Mons. There's a quite bad Victorian book on the affair, Mrs. Twemlow's *The Girl Who Went With the Angels*."

"Yes, our little vanished Rosie Farrar."

Until today, Winthrop had never heard of Angel Down, Sussex.

"There was a wave of 'angelic visitations' in the vicinity of Angel Down in the 1870s," Catriona continued, showing off rather fetchingly. "Flying chariots made of stars harnessed together, whooshing through the treetops, leaving burned circles in fields where they touched ground. Dr. Martin Hesselius, the distinguished specialist in supernatural affairs, was consulted by the Farrar family and put the business down to a plague of fire elementals. More recently, in an article, Dr. Silence, another important researcher in the field, has invoked the Canadian wendigo or wind-walker as an explanation. But in the popular imagination, the visitors have always been angels, though not perhaps the breed we are familiar with from the Bible and Mr. Milton. The place name suggests that this rash of events was not unprecedented in the area. Mrs. Twemlow unearthed medieval references to miraculous sightings. The visitations revolved around a neolithic circle."

"And what about the little girl?" Winthrop asked.

"This Rosie Farrar, daughter of a farmer, claimed to have talked with the occupants of these chariots of fire. They were cherubs, she said, about her height, clad in silvery-grey raiment, with large black eyes and no noses to speak of. She was quite a prodigy. One day, she went into Angel Field, where the stones stood, and was transported up into the sky, in the presence of witnesses, and spirited away in a fiery wheel."

"Never to be seen again?" Winthrop ventured.

"Until yesterday," the Old Man answered. "Rose has come back. Or, rather, a child looking exactly as Rose did fifty years ago has come back. In Angel Field."

"She'd be an old woman by now," Winthrop said.

"Providing time passes as we understand it in the Realm of the Angels," said Catriona.

"And where exactly might that be, Cat?"

She poked her tongue out at him, just as the attendant, a fierce-looking ghurka, returned with their brandy. He betrayed no opinion, but she was slightly cowed. Serve her right.

"The local rector made the report. One Bartholomew Haskins. He called the Lord Lieutenant, and the matter was passed on to the Diogenes Club. Now, I'm entrusting it to you."

"What does this girl have to say for herself?" Catriona asked. "Does she actually claim to be Rosie Farrar?"

"She hasn't said anything yet. Photographs exist of the real Rose, and our girl is said to resemble them uncannily."

"Uncannily, eh?" said Winthrop.

"Just so."

"I should think this'll make for a jolly weekend away from town," Winthrop told the Old Man. "Angel Down is near enough to Falmer Field for me to combine an investigation with a couple of sorties in *Katie*."

Winthrop had kept up his flying since the War, maintaining his own aeroplane, a modified Camel fighter named *Katie*. She was getting to be a bit of an antique paraded next to the latest line in gleaming metal monoplanes, but he trusted her as much as he did Catriona or the Bentley. He knew the kite's moods and foibles, and could depend on her in a pinch. If she could come through the best efforts of the late Baron von Richthofen's Flying Circus, she could survive any peace-time scrape. If he were to tangle with "chariots of stars," he might have need of the faithful *Katie*.

Catriona was thoughtful. As ever, she saw this less as a jaunt than he did. He needed her to balance him. She had a strong sense of what was significant, and kept him from haring off on wild streaks when he needed to be exercising the old brain-box.

"Has this miraculous reappearance been made public?"

The Old Man's brows knit. "I'm afraid so. The Brighton *Argus* carried the story this morning, and the afternoon editions of all the dailies have it, in various lights. Haskins knows enough to keep the child away from the press for the moment. But all manner of people are likely to take an interest. You know who I mean. It would be highly convenient if you could come up with some unsensational explanation that will settle the matter before it goes any further."

Winthrop understood. It was almost certain this business was a misunderstanding or a hoax. If so, it was best it were blown up at once. And, if not, it was sadly best that it be thought so.

"I'll see what I can do, Beauregard."

"Good man. Now, you children run off and play. And don't come back until you know what little Rosie is up to."

IV: "a demure little thing"

With Sam Farrar queerly reluctant to take his miraculously returned aunt into his house, Haskins had to put the little girl up at the rectory. He wondered, chiding himself for a lack of charity, whether Sam's hesitation was down to the question of the stake in Farrar Farm, if any, to which Rose might be entitled. It was also true that for Sam and Ellen to be presented in late middle age with a child they might be expected to raise as their own would be an upheaval in their settled lives.

The girl had said nothing yet, but sat quietly in an oversized chair in his study, huddled inside one of Haskins's old dressing gowns. Mrs. Cully, his housekeeper, had got the poor child out of her filthy clothes and given her a bath. She had wanted to throw away the ruined garments, but Haskins insisted they be kept for expert examination. Much would hinge on those dirty rags. If it could be proven that they were of more recent provenance than 1872, then this was not Rose Farrar.

Haskins sat at his desk, unable to think of his sermon. His glance was continually drawn to the girl. Now she had stopped keening, she seemed a demure little thing. She sat with one leg tucked up under her and the other a-dangle, showing a dainty, uncallused foot. With her face clean and her hair scrubbed—she insisted on having her silver ribbon back—she could have been any well-brought-up child waiting for a story before being packed off to bed.

Telegrams had arrived all morning. And the telephone on his desk had rung more often than in the last six months. He was to expect a pair of investigators from London. Representatives from Lord Northcliffe's *Mail* and Lord Beaverbrook's *Express* had made competing overtures to secure the "rights" to the story. Many others had shown an interest, from charitable bodies concerned with the welfare of "a unique orphan" to commercial firms who wished "the miracle girl" to endorse their soap or tonic. Haskins understood that the girl must be shielded from such public scrutiny, at least until the investigators had assessed her case.

One telegram in particular stirred Haskins. A distinguished person offered Rose any service it was within his power to perform. Haskins had replied swiftly, inviting the author-knight to Angel Down. If anyone could get to the bottom of the matter, it would be the literary lion whose sharpness of mind was reputed to be on a par with that of the detective he had made famous and who had worked so tirelessly in his later years to demonstrate the possibility of the miraculous here on Earth.

The girl seemed unaware of Haskins's fascination with her. She was a Victorian parent's idea of perfection—pretty as a picture, quiet as a mouse, poised as a waxwork. Haskins wondered about the resemblance to Sam Farrar. It had seemed so strong in the first light of discovery but was now hard to see.

He got up from his desk, abandoning his much-begun and little-developed sermon, and knelt before the child. He took her small hands, feeling bird-like bones and fragile warmth. This was a real girl, not an apparition. She had been vigorously bathed and spent the night in the guest bedroom. Ghosts did not leave dirty bathwater or crumpled sheets. She had consumed some soup last night and half an apple for breakfast.

Her eyes fixed his and he wanted to ask her questions.

Since she had stopped making her peculiar noise, she had uttered no sound. She seemed to understand what was said to her but was disinclined to answer. She did not even respond to attempted communication via rudimentary sign language or Mrs. Cully's baby-talk.

"Rose?" he asked.

There was no flicker in her eyes.

Sam had produced pictures, yellowed poses of the Farrar children from the dawn of photography. One among a frozen gaggle of girls resembled exactly this child. Sam reluctantly confirmed the child in the portrait as his vanished Aunt Rose, the Little Girl Who Went With the Angels.

"What happened to you, Rose?"

According to the stories, she had been swept up to the Heavens in a column of starlight.

Haskins heard a buzzing. There was a wasp in the room!

He held the girl's hands too tightly. Her face contorted in pain. He let go and made an attempt to soothe her, to prevent the return of her screeches.

Her mouth opened, but nothing came out.

The wasp was still here. Haskins was horribly aware of it. His collar was damp and his stomach shifted.

There was more than one.

The buzzing grew louder. Haskins stood up and looked about for the evil black-and-yellow specks.

He looked again at Rose, suddenly afraid for her. The girl's face shifted and she was his sister, Jane.

It was like an injection of wasp venom to the heart.

Her mouth was a round aperture, black inside. The wasp shrill was coming from her.

Haskins was terrified, dragged back to his boyhood, stripped of adult dignities and achievements, confronted with his long-dead victim.

He remembered vividly the worst thing he had ever done. The stick sinking into the nest. His cruel laughter as the cloud swarmed from the sundered ovoid and took flight, whipped away by strong wind.

Jane stood on the chair, dressing gown a heavy monk's robe. She still wore her silver ribbon. She wasn't *exactly* Jane. There was some Rose in her eyes. And a great deal of darkness, of something else.

She reached out to him as if for a cuddle. He fell to his knees, this time in prayer. He tried to close his eyes.

The girl's mouth was huge, a gaping circle. Black apparatus emerged, a needle-tipped proboscis rimmed with whipping feelers. It was an insectile appendage, intricate and hostile, parts grinding together with wicked purpose.

Her eyes were black poached eggs overflowing their sockets, a million facets glinting.

The proboscis touched his throat. A barb of ice pierced his skin. Shock stopped his heart and stilled his lungs, leaving his mind to flutter on for eternal seconds.

V: "a funny turn"

Angel Down Rectory was a nice little cottage close by the church, rather like the home Catriona had grown up in. Her kindly father was a clergyman in Somerset, in the village where Edwin's distant father had owned the Manor House without really being Lord of the Manor.

Colonel Winthrop had been literally distant for most of his later life, stationed in India or the Far East after some scandal which was never spoken of in the village. An alienist might put that down as the root of a streak of slyness, of manipulative ruthlessness, that fitted his son for the murkier aspects of his business. Recognising this dark face, fed with blood in the trenches and the skies, as being as much a part of Edwin's personality as his humour, generosity, and belief in her, Catriona did her best to shine her light upon it, to keep him fixed on a human scale. The Reverend Kaye mildly disapproved of her spook-chasing and changed the subject whenever anyone asked about his daughter's marriage plans, but was otherwise as stalwart, loyal, and loving a parent as she could wish.

They had found the village with ease, homing in on a steeple visible from a considerable distance across the downs. For such a small place, Angel Down was blessed with a large and impressive church, which was in itself suggestive. If a site can boast an ancient stone circle and a long-established Christian church, it is liable to have been a centre of unusual spiritual activity for quite some time.

There was something wrong. She knew it at once. She made no claim to psychic powers, but had learned to be sensitive. She could almost always distinguish between an authentic spectre and a fool in a bedsheet, no matter how much fog and shadow were about. It was a question of reading the tiniest signs, often on an unconscious level.

"Careful, dearest," she told Edwin, as they got out of the car.

He looked at her quizzically. She couldn't explain her unsettling feeling, but he had been with her in enough bizarre situations to accept her shrug of doubt as a trustworthy sign of danger ahead. He thrust a hand into his coat pocket, taking hold of the revolver he carried when about the business of the Diogenes Club.

She heard something. A sound like an insect, but then again not. It was not within her experience.

Edwin rapped on the door with his knuckles.

A round pink woman let them in. Upon receipt of Edwin's card, the housekeeper—Mrs. Cully—told them they were expected and that she would tell the rector of their arrival.

The narrow hallway was likeably cluttered. A stand was overburdened with coats and hats, boots lined up for inspection nearby, umbrellas and sticks ready for selection. A long-case clock ticked slow, steady seconds.

There was no evidence of eccentricity.

Mrs. Cully returned, pink gone to grey. Catriona was immediately alert, nerves singing like wires. The woman couldn't speak, but nodded behind her, to the rector's study.

With his revolver, Edwin pushed open the door.

Catriona saw a black-faced man lying on the carpet, eyes staring. His hands were white.

Edwin stepped into the room and Catriona followed. They both knelt by the prone man. He had a shock of red-grey hair and wore a clerical collar, taut as a noose around his swollen throat.

The Reverend Mr. Haskins—for this could be none other—was freshly dead. Still warm, he had no pulse, heartbeat, or breath. His face was swollen and coal-coloured. His mouth and eyes were fixed open. Even his tongue was black and stiff. Droplets of blood clung to his hard, overripe cheeks.

"Snakebite?" she asked, shuddering.

"Could be, Cat," he said, standing up.

She was momentarily troubled. Did she hear the soft slither of a dire reptile winding across the carpet? She was not fond of the beasts. A criminal mandarin-sorcerer had once tried to murder Edwin with a black mamba delivered in a Harrod's hamper. She had been unfortunate enough to be sharing a punt with him when the scheme came to hissing light. She had cause to remember that snakes can swim.

"And who have we here?" he asked.

She stood. Edwin had found the girl, sat calmly in an armchair, wearing a man's large dressing gown, leafing through a picture book of wild flowers. The supposed Rose Farrar was a tiny thing, too sharp-featured to be considered pretty but with a striking, triangular face and huge, curious eyes. Her expression was familiar to Catriona. She had seen it on shell-shocked soldiers coming home from a war that would always be fought in their minds.

She wanted to warn Edwin against touching the girl. But that would have been ridiculous.

"Little miss, what happened?" he asked.

The girl looked up from her book. For a moment, she seemed like a shrunken adult. The real Rosie would be almost sixty, Catriona remembered.

"He had a funny turn," the child said.

That much was obvious.

"Do you have a name, child?" he asked.

"Yes," she said, disinclined to reveal more.

"And what might it be?" Catriona asked.

The little girl turned to look at her, for the first time, and said, "Catriona."

It was a tiny shock.

"I am Catriona," Catriona said. "And this is Edwin. You are...?"

She held up her book. On the page was a picture of a wild rose, delicate green watercolour leaves with incarnadine petal splashes.

"Rose," the girl said.

This was considerably more serious than a hoax. A man was dead. No longer just a puzzle to be unpicked and forgotten, this was a mystery to be solved.

A panicked cough from the doorway drew their attention. It was Mrs. Cully, eyes fixed on the ceiling, away from the corpse.

"There's another come visiting," she said.

Catriona knew they must have been racing newspapermen to get here. There would be reporters all over the village, and soon—when this latest development was out—front-page headlines in all the papers.

"Is it someone from the press?" Edwin asked.

The woman shook her head. A big, elderly man gently stepped around her and into the room. He had a large, bushy moustache and kindly eyes. She knew him at once.

"Sir Arthur," said Edwin, "welcome to Angel Down. I wish the circumstances of our meeting had been different."

VI: "venomous lightning"

Winthrop shifted his revolver to his left hand, so he could extend his right arm and shake hands with Sir Arthur Conan Doyle. The author was in his mid-sixties, but his grip was firm. He was an outdoor-looking man, more Watson than Holmes.

"You have me at a disadvantage, sir."

"I am Edwin Winthrop, of the Diogenes Club."

"Oh," said Sir Arthur, momentously, "*them.*"

"Yes, indeed. Water under the bridge, and all that."

Sir Arthur rumbled. He had clearly not forgotten that the Diogenes Club had once taken such a dim view of his mentioning their name in two pieces placed in the *Strand* magazine that considerable pressure had been brought to ensure the suppression of further such narratives. While the consulting detective was always slyly pleased that his feats be publicised, his civil servant brother—Beauregard's predecessor—preferred to hide his considerable light under a bushel. Sir Arthur had never revealed the exact nature of the Club and Mycroft's position within it, but he had drawn attention to a man and an institution who would far rather their names were unknown to the general public. No real lasting harm was done, though the leagues who followed Sherlock Holmes were tragically deprived of thrilling accounts of several memorable occasions upon which he had acted as an instrument of his older brother and his country.

"And this is Miss Catriona Kaye," Winthrop continued.

"I know who she is."

The sentence was like a slap, but Catriona did not flinch at it.

"This woman," Sir Arthur said, "has made it her business to harass those few unselfish souls who can offer humanity the solace it so badly needs. I've had a full account of her unwarranted attack this morning on Mademoiselle Astarte of Chelsea."

Winthrop remembered that Sir Arthur was a committed, not to say credulous, Spiritualist.

"Sir Arthur," said Catriona, fixing his steely gaze, "Mademoiselle Astarte is a cruel hoaxer and an extortionist. She does your cause—nay, *our* cause—no credit whatsoever. I too seek only light in the darkness. I should have thought, given your well-known association with the most brilliant deductive mind of the age, you would see my activities as a necessary adjunct to your own."

She had him there. Sir Arthur was uncomfortable, but too honest a man not to admit Catriona was right. In recent years, he had been several times duped by the extraordinary claims of hoaxers. There was that business with the fairies. He looked around the room, avoiding Catriona's sharp eyes. He saw the body of Mr. Haskins. And the girl curled up in the chair.

"Good Lord," he exclaimed.

"This is exactly the scene we found," Winthrop said.

"I heard a noise earlier, as we arrived," Catriona revealed. "Something like an insect."

"It seems as if a whole hive of bees has stung him."

Sir Arthur had trained as a doctor, Winthrop remembered.

"Could it have been poison?" he asked.

"If so, someone's tidied up," Sir Arthur said, confidently turning the swollen head from side to side. "No cup or glass with spilled liquid. No half-eaten cake. No dart stuck in the flesh. The face and chest are swollen but not the hands or, I'll wager, the feet. I'd say whatever struck him did so through this wound here, in the throat."

A florin-sized red hole showed in the greasy black skin.

"It is as if he were struck by venomous lightning."

Sir Arthur found an orange blanket in a basket by the sofa and spread it over the dead man. The twisted shape was even more ghastly when shrouded.

"The girl says he had a 'funny turn,'" Winthrop said.

For the first time, Sir Arthur considered the child.

"Is this Rose? Has she spoken?"

The girl said nothing. She was interested in her book again. At her age, she could hardly be expected to be much concerned with grown-up things.

If she was the age she seemed.

Sir Arthur went over to the chair and examined the girl. His hands, steady as a rock when patting down a gruesome corpse, trembled as they neared her hair. He touched fingertips to the silver ribbon that held back her curls, and drew them away as if shocked.

"Child, child," he said, tears in his eyes, "what wonders have you seen? What hope can you give us?"

This was not the dispassionate, scientific interrogation Winthrop had planned. He was touched by the old man's naked emotion. Sir Arthur had lost a son in the War, and thereafter turned to Spiritualism for comfort. He betrayed a palpable need for confirmation of his beliefs. Like the detective he had made famous, he needed evidence.

The possible Rose was like a child queen regarding an aged and loyal knight with imperious disdain. Sir Arthur literally knelt at her feet, looking up to her.

"Do you know about the Little People?" she asked.

VII: "a gift from faerie"

Catriona had been given to understand that Rose did not speak, but she was becoming quite chatty. Sir Arthur quizzed her about "the Little People," who were beginning to sound more like fairies than cherubs. She wondered if Rose were not one of those children who cut her personality to suit the adult or adults she was with, mischievous with one uncle, modest with the next. The girl was constantly clever, she felt, but otherwise completely mercurial.

It was only a few years since the name of Sir Arthur Conan Doyle, a watchword for good sense to most of Great Britain, had been devalued by the affair of the Cottingley Fairies. Two little girls, not much older than this child, had not only claimed to be in regular communion with the wee folk but produced photographs of them—subsequently shown to be amateur forgeries—which Sir Arthur rashly endorsed as genuine, even to the extent of writing *The Coming of the Fairies*, an inspirational book about the case. Though the hoax had been exploded a dozen times, Sir Arthur stubbornly refused to disbelieve. Catriona sensed the old man's *need* for faith, his devout wish for the magical to penetrate his world and declare itself irrefutably.

"I went away with them," the girl told them. "The Little People. I was in their home in the sky. It's inside of a cloud, and like a hollow tree, with criss-cross roots and branches. We could all fly there, or float. There was no up or down. They played with me for ever such a long time. And gave me my ribbon."

She turned her head, showing the ribbon in her hair. Catriona had noticed it before.

"Rose, may I see your ribbon?" Sir Arthur asked.

Catriona wasn't comfortable with this. Surely something should be done for poor Mr. Haskins before the girl was exhaustively interviewed.

Rose took the ribbon out of her hair solemnly and offered it to Sir Arthur.

"Extraordinary," he said, running it through his fingers. He offered it to Catriona.

She hesitated a moment and accepted the thing.

It was not any fabric she knew. Predominantly silvery, it was imprinted with green shapes, like runes or diagrams. Though warm to the touch, it might be a new type of processed metal. She crumpled the ribbon into a ball, then opened her fist. The thing sprang back into its original shape without a crease.

"You're bleeding," Edwin said.

The edges were sharp as pampas grass. Without feeling it, she had shallowly grazed herself.

"May I have it again now?" Rose asked.

Catriona returned the ribbon, which the girl carefully wound into her hair. She did not knot it, but *shaped* it, into a coil which held back her curls.

"A gift from faerie," Sir Arthur mused.

Catriona wasn't sure. Her hand was began to sting. She took a hankie from her reticule and stemmed the trickle of blood from the scratch.

"Rose, my dear," said Sir Arthur. "It is now 1925. What year was it when you went away, to play with the Little People? Was it a long time ago? As long ago, ahem, as 1872?"

The girl didn't answer. Her face darkened, as if she were suddenly afraid or unable to do a complicated sum in mental arithmetic.

"Let's play a game?" Edwin suggested, genially. "What's this?"

He held up a pencil from the rector's desk.

"Pencil," Rose said, delighted.

"Quite right. And this?"

The letter-opener.

"A thin knife."

"Very good, Rose. And this?"

He picked the telephone receiver up from its cradle.

"Telly Phone," the girl said.

Edwin set the receiver down and nodded in muted triumph.

"Alexander Graham Bell," he said, almost sadly. "1876."

"She's been back two days, man," Sir Arthur said, annoyed. He turned to the girl and tried to smile reassuringly. "Did the rector tell you about the telephone? Did you hear it make a ring-ring noise, see him talk to friends a long way away with it?"

Rose was guarded now. She knew she had been caught out.

If this was a hoax, it was not a simple one. That ribbon was outside nature. And Haskins had died by means unknown.

"Why don't you use that instrument to summon the police?" said Sir Arthur, nodding at the telephone.

"Call the police?" Edwin said. "Tut-tut, what would Mr. Holmes say? This matter displays unusual features which the worthy Sussex constabulary will not be best equipped to deal with."

"This man should at least have a doctor look at him."

"He has had one, Sir Arthur. You."

The author-knight was not happy. And neither was she.

VIII: "a changeling"

Winthrop was satisfied that this girl was not the real Rose, and that an imposture was being planned—perhaps as part of a scheme to dupe the farmer, Sam Farrar, out of his property. The Reverend Mr. Haskins must have stumbled onto the trick and been done nastily to death. From the look of the rector's throat, something like a poison-tipped spear had been used on him. It remained for the girl to be persuaded to identify the conspirators who had tutored her in imposture. She was too young to be guilty by herself.

"Now, missy, let's talk about this game you've been playing," he said. "The dress-up-and-pretend game. Who taught it to you?"

The girl's face was shut. He thought she might try crying. But she was too tough for that. She was like any adult criminal, exposed and sullen, refusing to cooperate, unaffected by remorse.

"It's not that simple, Edwin," Catriona said. "The ribbon."

Winthrop had thought of that. Lightweight metallicised fabrics were being used in aircraft manufacture these days, and that scrap might well be an offcut. It was a strange touch, though.

"There's something else. Look at her."

He did. She had an ordinary face. There was something about the eyes, though. A violet highlight.

"There are Little People," she said. "There are, there are. They are bald, and have eyes like saucers, and no noses. They played with me. For a long time. And they have friends here, on the ground. Undertakers with smoked glasses."

"What is your name?"

"Rose," she said, firmly.

Was she trying to get back to the story she had been taught? Or had she been hypnotised into believing what she was saying?

Suddenly, he saw what Catriona meant.

The girl's face had changed, not just its expression but its shape. Her nose was rounder, her chin less sharp, her cheekbones gone. Her mouth had been thin, showing sharp teeth; now she had classic bee-stung lips, like Catriona's. Her curls were tighter, like little corkscrews.

He stood back from her, worried by what he had seen. He glanced at the rector's body, covered with its orange blanket. It was not possible, surely, that this child…

…this angel?

"What is it, man? What is it?"

Sir Arthur was agitated, impatient at being left out. He must feel it humiliating not to have spotted the clue. Of course, he had come into it later and not seen the girl as she was when Winthrop and Catriona had arrived. It seemed now that her face had always been changing, subtly.

"Consider her face," Winthrop said.

"Yes."

"It changes."

The violet highlights were green now.

Sir Arthur gasped.

The girl looked older, twelve or thirteen. Her feet and ankles showed under the dressing gown. Her shoulders filled the garment out more. Her face was thinner again, eyes almost almond.

"This is not the girl who was taken away," Sir Arthur said. "She is one of *them*, a Changeling."

For the first time, Winthrop rather agreed with him.

"There are bad fairies," Sir Arthur said. "Who steal away children and leave one of their own in the crib."

Winthrop knew the folktales. He wasn't satisfied of their literal truth, but he realised in a flash that this girl might be an instance of whatever phenomenon gave rise to the stories in the first place.

You didn't have to believe in fairies to know the world was stranger than imagined.

"Who are you, Rose?" Catriona asked, gently.

She knelt before the girl, as Sir Arthur had done, looking up into her shifting face.

Winthrop couldn't help but notice that the girl's body had become more womanly inside the dressing gown. Her hair straightened and grew longer. Her eyebrows were thinner and arched.

"Rose?"

Catriona reached out.

The girl's face screwed up and she hissed, viciously. She opened her mouth, wider than she should have been able to. Her incisors were needle-fangs. She hissed again, flicking a long, fork-tipped tongue.

A spray of venom scattered at Catriona's face.

IX: "cruel cunning"

The shock was so great she almost froze, but Catriona flung her hand in front of her eyes. The girl's sizzling spit stung the back of her hand. She wiped it instinctively on the carpet, scraping her skin raw. She had an idea the stuff was deadly.

The girl was out of her chair and towering above her now, shoulders and hips swaying, no longer entirely human. Her skin was greenish, scaled. Her eyes were red-green, with triangular pupils. Catriona thought she might even have nictitating membranes.

Catriona remembered the slither of the mamba.

She was frozen with utter panic, and a tiny voice inside nagged her for being weak.

Edwin seized the letter opener—the thin knife—from the desk and stabbed at the snake girl.

A black-thorned green hand took his wrist and bent it backwards. He dropped his weapon. Her hissing face closed in on his throat.

Catriona's panic snapped. She stuck her foot between the girl's ankles and scythed her legs out from under her.

They all fell in a tangle.

Rose broke free of them, leaving the dressing gown in a muddle on the floor.

She stood naked by Sir Arthur, body scaled and shimmering, as beautiful as horrid. She was striped in many shades of green, brown, yellow, red, and black. She had the beginnings of a tail. Her hair was flat against her neck and shoulders, flaring like a cobra's hood. Her nose and ears were slits, frilled inside with red cilia.

Catriona and Edwin tried to get up, but were in each other's way.

Rose smiled, fangs poking out of her mouth, and laid her talons on Sir Arthur's lapels. She crooned to him, a sibilant susurrus of fascination. In the movements of her hips and shoulders and the arch of her eyes, there was a cruel cunning that was beyond human. This was a creature that killed for the pleasure of it, and was glad of an audience.

Sir Arthur was backed against a mantelpiece. His hand reached out, and found a plain crucifix mounted between two candlesticks. The Reverend Mr. Haskins had evidently not been very High Church, for there were few other obvious signs of his profession in the room.

Rose's black-red lips neared Sir Arthur's face, to administer a killing kiss. Her fork-tipped tongue darted out and slithered between his eyes and across his cheek, leaving a shining streak.

Sir Arthur took the cross and interposed it between his face and hers. He pressed it to her forehead.

Rose reacted as if a drop of molten lead had been applied. She screeched inhumanly and turned away, crouching into a ball. The scales on her legs and back sizzled and disappeared, like butter pats on a hot griddle. Her body shrank again, with a cracking of bones.

"Oh my stars," said someone from the doorway.

Two men, strangers, stood in the hall, amazed at the scene. The one who spoke was a prosperous-looking man, face seamed and clothes practical. Behind him was the silhouette of someone large, soft, and practically hairless.

Rose looked up at the newcomers. Her eyes were round again, and full of puzzlement rather than malice. Catriona had a sense that the monster was forgotten.

The girl snatched up the dressing gown and slipped into it, modestly closing it over her body. Then she hurled herself at a window, and crashed through the panes into the gathering dusk outside.

She hit the ground running and was off, away over the fields.

"I knew that weren't Aunt Rose," said the newcomer.

X: "Anti-Christine"

"The Great Beast is among you," announced the fat bald man, referring to himself rather than the departed Rose.

Sir Arthur still clung to the cross that had seen off the Rose creature.

"Of all things, I thought of *Dracula*," he said, wondering at his survival. "Bram Stoker's novel."

Winthrop was familiar with the book.

"The cross had exactly the effect on that creature as upon the vampires in *Dracula*."

"Ugh," said the bald man, "what a horrid thing. Put it away, Sir Arthur."

Farrar had noticed the rector's body, and was sunk into a couch with his head in his hands. This was too weird for most people. The honest farmer would have to leave these matters for the experts in the uncanny.

The man who had arrived with Farrar wore a once-expensive coat. The astrakhan collar was a little ragged and his pinstripe trousers shiny at the knees. A great deal of this fellow's time was spent on his knees, for one reason or other. His face was fleshy, great lips hanging loose. Even his hands were plump, slug-white flippers. His great dome shone and his eyes glinted with unhealthy fire.

Winthrop recognised the controversial figure of Aleister Crowley, self-styled "wickedest man in England." Quite apart from his well-known advocacy of black magic, sexual promiscuity, and drug use, the brewery heir—perhaps from a spirit of ingrained contrariness—had blotted his copybook in loudly advocating the Kaiser's cause during the War. In his younger days, he was reckoned a daring mountaineer, but his vices had transformed him into a flabby remnant who looked as though he would find a steep staircase an insurmountable obstacle.

"Aren't you supposed to be skulking in Paris?" Winthrop asked.

"Evidently, sir, you have the advantage of me," Crowley admitted.

"Edwin Winthrop, of the Diogenes Club."

The black magician smiled, almost genuinely.

"Charles Beauregard's bright little boy. I have heard of you, and of your exploits among the shadows. And this charming *fille de l'occasion* must be Miss Catriona Kaye, celebrated exposer of charlatans. I believe you know that dreadful poseur A.E. Waite. Is it not well past time you showed him up for the faker he is, dear lady?"

Crowley loomed over Catriona. Winthrop remembered with alarm that he was famous for bestowing "the serpent's kiss," a mouth-to-mouth greeting reckoned dangerous to the receiving party. He contented himself with kissing her knuckles, like a gourmand licking the skin off a well-roasted chicken leg.

"And Sir Arthur Conan Doyle, whose fine yarns have given me and indeed all England such pleasure. This is a most distinguished company."

Sir Arthur, who could hardly fail to know who Crowley was, looked at his crucifix, perhaps imagining it might have an efficacy against the Great Beast.

If so, Crowley read his mind. "That bauble holds no terror for a magus of my exalted standing, Sir Arthur. It symbolises an era which is dead and gone, but rotting all around us. I have written to Mr. Trotsky in Moscow, offering to place my services at his disposal if he would charge me with the responsibility of eradicating Christianity from the planet."

"And has he written back?" Catriona asked, archly.

"Actually, no."

"*Quelle surprise!*"

Crowley flapped his sausage-fingers at her.

"Naughty, naughty. Such cynicism in one so young. You would make a fine Scarlet Woman, my dear. You have all the proper attributes."

"My sins are scarlet enough already, Mr. Crowley," Catriona replied. "And, to put it somewhat bluntly, I doubt from your general appearance that you would be up to matching them these days."

The magus looked like a hurt little boy. For an instant, Winthrop had a flash of the power this man had over his followers. He was such an obvious buffoon one might feel him so pathetic that to contradict his constant declamations of his own genius would be cruel. He had seriously harmed many people, and sponged unmercifully off many others. The Waite he had mentioned was, like the poet Yeats, another supposed initiate of a mystic order, with whom he had been conducting an ill-tempered feud over the decades.

"The time for the Scarlet Woman is ended," Crowley continued, back in flight. "Her purpose was always to birth the perfect being, and now that has been superseded. I hurried here on the boat train when news reached me that *she* had appeared on Earth. She who will truly bring to an end the stifling, milk-and-water age of the cloddish carpenter."

"I find your tone objectionable, man," Sir Arthur said. "A clergyman is dead."

"A modest achievement, I admit, but a good start."

"The fellow's mad," Sir Arthur blustered. "Quite cuckoo."

Winthrop tended to agree but wanted to hear Crowley out.

He nodded towards the smashed window. "What do you think she is,

Crowley? The creature you saw attacking us?"

"I suppose Anti-Christ is too masculine a term. We shall have to get used to calling her the Anti-Christine."

Catriona, perhaps unwisely, giggled. She was rewarded with a lightning-look from the magus.

"She was brought to us by demons, in the centre of a circle of ancient sacrifice, enlivened by blood offerings. I have been working for many years to prepare the Earth for her coming, and to open the way for her appearance upon the great stage of magickal history. She has begun her reign. She has many faces. She is the get of the Whore of Babylon and the Goat of Mendes. She will cut a swathe through human society, mark my words. I shall be her tutor in sublime wickedness. There will be blood-letting and licence."

"For such a committed foe of Christianity, you talk a lot of Bible phrases," Winthrop said. "Your parents were Plymouth Brethren, were they not?"

"I sprang whole from the earth of Warwickshire. Is it not strange that such a small county could sire both of England's greatest poets?"

Everyone looked at him in utter amazement.

"Shakespeare was the other," he explained. "You know, the *Hamlet* fellow."

Sir Arthur was impatient and Catriona amused, but Winthrop was alert. This man could still be dangerous.

"'The Great God Pan,'" Catriona said.

Crowley beamed, assuming she was describing him.

"It's a short story," she said. "By Arthur Machen. That's where he's getting all this nonsense. He's casting Rose in the role of the anti-heroine of that fiction."

"Truths are revealed to us in fictions," Crowley said. "Sir Arthur, who has so skilfully blended the real and the imagined throughout his career, will agree. And so would Mr. Stoker, whom you mentioned. There are many, indeed, who believe your employers, Mr. Winthrop, are but the inventions of this literary knight."

Sir Arthur grumbled.

"At any rate, since the object of my quest is no longer here, I shall depart. It has been an unalloyed pleasure to meet you at such an exhilarating juncture."

Crowley gave a grunting little bow, and withdrew.

XI: "a living looking-glass"

"Well," said Catriona, hardly needing to elaborate on the syllable.

"He's an experience, and no mistake," Edwin admitted.

Having been yanked from horror into comedy, she was light-headed. It seemed absurd now, but she had been near death when the Rose Thing was closing on her throat.

"I see it," said Sir Arthur, suddenly.

He lifted the blanket from the rector's head and pointed to the ghastly wound with the crucifix. Despite everything else, Sir Arthur was pleased with himself, and amazed.

"I've made a *deduction*," he announced. "I've written too often of them, but never until now truly understood. It's like little wheels in your head, coming into alignment. Truly, a marvellous thing."

Sam Farrar looked up from his hands. He was glumly drained of all emotion, a common fellow unable to keep up with the high-flown characters, human and otherwise, who had descended into his life.

"The creature we saw had extended eye-teeth," Sir Arthur lectured. "Like a snake's fangs. Perhaps they were what put me in mind of Bram Stoker's vampires. Yet this wound, in the unfortunate Reverend Mr. Haskins's throat, suggests a single stabbing implement. It is larger, rounder, more of a gouge than a bite. The thing we saw would have left two small puckered holes. Haskins was attacked by something different."

"Or something differently shaped," Edwin suggested.

"Yes, indeed. We have seen how the Changeling can alter her form. Evidently, she has a large repertoire."

Catriona tried to imagine what might have made the wound.

"It looks like an insect bite, Sir Arthur," she said, shuddering, "made by… good lord… a *gigantic mosquito*."

"Bart hated insects," Farrar put in, blankly. "Had a bad experience years ago. Never did get the whole story of it. If a wasp came in the room, he was froze up with fear."

An idea began to shape in her mind.

The Reverend Mr. Haskins hated insects. And she had a horror of snakes. Earlier, she had thought Rose was the sort of child who presented herself to suit who she was with. That had been a real insight.

"She's who we think she is," she said.

Sir Arthur shook his head, not catching her drift.

"She is who we want her to be, or what we're afraid she is," she continued. "Sir Arthur wished to think her a friend to the fairies, and so she seemed to be. Edwin, for you it would be most convenient if she were a fraud; when you thought that most strongly, she made the slip about the telephone. The Reverend Mr. Haskins was in terror of insects, and she became one; I am not best partial to crawling reptiles, and so she took the form of a snake woman. Every little thing, she reacts to. When I asked her what her name was, she quoted mine back to me. Sir Arthur, you thought of a scene in a novel, and she played it out. She's like a living looking-glass, taking whatever we think of her and becoming exactly that thing."

Sir Arthur nodded, convinced at once. She was not a little flattered to detect admiration in his eyes. She had made a deduction too.

Edwin was more concerned.

"We've got to stop Crowley," he said.

"*Crowley?*" she questioned.

"If he gets hold of her, she'll become what *he* thinks she is. And he thinks she's the end the world."

XII: "the altar of sex magick"

There was only one place the Anti-Christine could have flown to: Angel Field, where once had stood a stone circle. Crowley knew Farrar Farm, since he had called there first, assuming the divine creature would be in the care of her supposed nephew. But Angel Field was a mystery, and there were no streetlights out here in the wilds of Sussex to guide the way.

Before departing, penniless, for England, he had telegraphed several of his few remaining disciples, beseeching funds and the loan of a car and driver. He was an international fugitive, driven from his Abbey of Thelema in Sicily at the express order of the odious Mussolini, and reduced to grubbing a living in Paris, with the aid of a former Scarlet Woman who was willing to sell her body on the streets to keep the magus in something approaching comfort.

He had left these damp, dreary islands for ever, he had hoped. He was no longer welcome in magical circles in London, brought low by the conspirings of lesser men who failed stubbornly to appreciate his genius.

No chauffeured car awaited him at Victoria, so he had hired one, trusting his manner and force of personality to convince one Alfred Jenkinsop, Esq., that he was good for the fee once the new age had dawned. As it happened, he expected the concept of money to be wiped away with all the other detritus of the dead past.

He found Jenkinsop in his car, outside Farrar Farm, reading *The Sporting Life* by torchlight. The fellow perked up to see him, and stuck his head out of the window.

"Have you seen a female pass this way?" Crowley asked.

Jenkinsop was remarkably obtuse on the point. It took him some moments to remember that he had, in fact, happened to see a girl, clad only in a dressing gown, running down the road from the rectory and onto the farm.

"Which way did she go?"

Jenkinsop shrugged. Crowley made a mental note to erase his somewhat comical name from the record of this evening when he came to write the official history of how the Anti-Christine was brought to London as a protegé of the Great Beast.

"Come, man," he said, "follow me."

The driver showed no willingness to get out of the car.

"It's a cold night, guv," he said, as if that explained all.

Crowley left him to "the pink 'un," and trudged through Farrar's open front gate. His once-expensive shoes sank in mud and he felt icy moisture seep in through their somewhat strained seams. Nothing to one who had survived the treacherous glacial slopes of Chogo-Ri, but still a damned nuisance.

If Farrar's vandal of a grandfather hadn't smashed the stones, it would have been easier to find Angel Field. It was a cloudless night, but the moon was just a shining rind. He could make out the shapes of hedgerows, but little more.

He had an alarming encounter with a startled cow.

"Mistress Perfection," he called out.

Only mooing came back.

Finally, he discerned a fire in the night and made his way towards it. He knew his feet stood upon the sod of Angel Field. For the Anti-Christine was at the centre of the light, surrounded by her impish acolytes.

They were attendant demons, Crowley knew. Naked, hairless, and without genitals. They had smooth, grey, dwarf bodies and large black insect eyes. Some held peculiar implements with lights at their extremities. They all turned, with one fluid movement, to look at him.

She was magnificent. Having shed her snakeskin, she had become the essence of voluptuous harlotry, masses of electric gorgon-hair confined by a shining circlet of silver, robe gaping open immodestly over her gently swelling belly, wicked green eyes darting like flames. Her teeth were still sharp. She looked from side to side, smile twisted off-centre.

This was the rapturous creature who would degrade the world.

Crowley worshipped her.

The occasion of their meeting called for a ceremony. The imps gathered around him, heads bobbing about his waist-height. Some extended spindle-fingered hands, tipped with sucker-like appendages, and touched him.

He unloosed his belt and dropped his trousers and drawers. He knelt, knees well-spaced, and touched his forehead to the cold, wet ground.

One of the imps took its implement and inserted it into Crowley's rectum. He bit a mouthful of grassy sod as the implement expanded inside him.

Crowley's body was the altar of sex magick.

The commingling of pain and pleasure was not new to him. This was quite consistent with the theory and practice of magick he had devised over many years of unparalleled scholarship. As the metallic probe pulsed inside him like living flesh, he was thrust forward into his new golden dawn.

The imp's implement was withdrawn.

Hands took Crowley's head and lifted it from the dirt. The Anti-Christine looked at him with loathing and love. Their mouths opened, and they pounced. Crowley trapped her lower lip between his teeth and bit until his mouth was full of her blood. He broke the serpent's kiss, and she returned in kind, nipping and nibbling at his nose and dewlaps.

Her lips were rouged with her own blood, and marked with his teeth. *Oh joy!*

"Infernal epitome," he addressed her, "we must get you quickly to London, where you can spread your leathery wings, open your scaled legs, and begin to exert a real influence. We shall start with a few seductions, of men and women naturally, petty and great persons, reprobates and saints. Each shall spread your glorious taint, which will flash through society like a new tonic."

She looked pleased by the prospect.

"There will be fire and pestilence," he continued. "Duels and murders and many, many suicides. Piccadilly Circus will burn like Nero's Rome. Pall Mall will fall to the barbarians. The Thames will run red and brown with the blood and ordure of the King and his courtiers. We shall dig up the mouldy skeletons of Victoria and Albert and revivify them with demon spells, to set them copulating like mindless mink in Horseguard's Parade. St. Paul's shall be turned into a brothel of Italianate vileness, and Westminster Abbey made an adjunct to the London Zoological Gardens, turned over to obscene apes who will defecate and fornicate where the foolishly pious once sat. The London *Times* will publish blasphemies and pornography, illustrated only by the greatest artists of the age. The Lord Mayor's head will be used as a ball in the Association Football Cup Final. Cocaine, heroin, and the services of child prostitutes will be advertised in posters plastered to the sides of all omnibuses. Willie Blasted Yeats shall be burned in effigy in place of Saint Guy Fawkes on every November 5th, and all the other usurpers of the Golden Dawn laid low in their own filth. All governments, all moralities, all churches, will collapse. The City will burn, must burn. Only we Secret Chiefs will retain our authority. You shall beget many children, homunculi. It will be a magnificent age, extending for a thousand times a thousand years."

In her shining, darting eyes, he saw it was all true. He buttoned up his trousers and spirited her away to where Jenkinsop waited with the car, unwitting herald of welcome apocalypse.

XIII: "the fire-wheel"

Winthrop held *Katie*'s stick back, flying at an angle, nose into the wind, so the dark, shadowed quilt of Sussex filled his view. The dawnlight just pricked at the East, flashing off ponds and streams. Night-flying was tricky in a country dotted with telegraph poles and tall trees, but at least there wasn't some Fokker stalking him. He tried to keep the Camel level with the tiny light funnels that were the headlamps of what must be Crowley's car.

They had got to Farrar Farm just after Crowley's departure, with Rose or Christine or whatever the girl chose to be called. Winthrop had set Catriona and Sir Arthur on their tail in the Bentley, and borrowed Sir Arthur's surprisingly sprightly runabout to make his way to the airfield at Falmer, where his aeroplane was hangared. It was like the War again, rousing a tired ground staff to get him into the air within minutes of his strapping on helmet and boots.

He had assumed few automobiles would be on the roads of Sussex at this hour of the morning, but had homed in on a couple of trundling milk trucks before picking up the two vehicles he assumed were Crowley's car and his own Bentley. He trusted Catriona at the wheel, though Sir Arthur had seemed as startled at the prospect of being driven by a woman as he had when confronted by the girl's monstrous snake-shape. When Winthrop had last seen them, Sir Arthur was still clutching his crucifix and Catriona was tucking stray hair under her sweet little hat.

He wished he had time to savour the thrill of being in the air again. He also regretted not storing ammunition and even a couple of bombs with *Katie*. Her twin machine-guns were still in working order, synchronised to fire through the prop blades, but he had nothing to fire out of them. His revolver was under his jacket, but would be almost useless: It was hard to give accurate fire while flying one-handed, with one's gun-arm flapping about in sixty-mile-an-hour airwash.

Suddenly, the sun rose. In the West.

A blast of daylight fell on one side of Winthrop's face. He felt a tingle as if he were being sunburned. For a moment, the air currents were all wrong, and he nearly lost control of *Katie*.

The landscape below was bleached by light. The two cars were quite distinct on the road. They were travelling between harvested wheat-fields. There were circles and triangles etched into the stubble, shapes that reminded Winthrop of those on Rose's silver ribbon.

Winthrop looked at the new sun.

It was a wheel of fire, travelling in parallel with *Katie*. He pushed the stick forward and climbed up into the sky, and the fire-shape climbed with him. Then it whizzed underneath the Camel and came up on his right side.

He looped up, back and below, feeling the tug of gravity in his head and the safety harness cutting into his shoulders. It would take a demon from hell to outfly a Sopwith Camel in anger, as the fire-wheel recognised instantly by shooting off like a Guy Fawkes rocket, whooshing up in a train of sparks.

Katie was now flying even, and sparks fell fizzing all around. Winthrop was afraid they were incendiaries of unknown design, but they passed *through* his fuselage and wings, dispersing across the fields.

His eyes were blotched with light-bursts. It was dark again and the fire-wheel gone. Winthrop recalled the stories of the signs in the sky at the time of Rose Farrar's disappearance. He assumed he had just had personal experience of them. He would make sure they went into the report.

Proper dawn was upon them.

A long straight stretch of road extended ahead of Crowley's car. They were nearing the outskirts of the city. Crowley's driver must be a good man, or possessed of magical skills, since the Bentley was lagging behind.

He knew he had to pull a reckless stunt.

Throttling *Katie* generously, he swooped low over the car and headed off to the left, getting as far ahead of Crowley as possible, then swung round in a tight semicircle, getting his nose in alignment with the oncoming vehicle. He would only get one pass at this run.

He took her down, praying the road had been maintained recently.

Katie's wheels touched ground, lifted off for a moment, and touched ground again.

Through the whirling prop, Winthrop saw Crowley's car. They were on a collision course.

The car would be built more sturdily than the canvas and wood plane. But *Katie* had whirling twin blades in her nose, all the better to scythe through the car's bonnet and windshield, and severely inconvenience anyone in the front seat.

Crowley might think himself untouchable. But he wouldn't be doing his own driving.

Winthrop hoped a rational man was behind the wheel of Crowley's car.

The distance between the two speeding vehicles narrowed.

Winthrop was oddly relaxed, as always in combat. A certain fatalism possessed him. If it was the final prang, so be it. He whistled under his breath.

It had been a good life. He was grateful to have known Cat, and the Old Man. He had done his bit, and a bit more besides. And he was with *Katie* at the last.

Crowley's car swerved, plunging through a hedgerow. Winthrop whooped in triumph, exultant to be alive. He cut the motors and upturned the flaps. Wind tore at the wings as *Katie* slowed.

Another car was up ahead.

The Bentley.

XIV: "'I believe…'"

Catriona pressed down on the foot-brake with all her strength. She was not encouraged by Sir Arthur's loud prayer. The aeroplane loomed large in the windshield, prop blades slowing but still deadly. She couldn't remember whether they were wood or metal, but guessed it wouldn't make much difference.

The Bentley and the Camel came to a halt, one screeching and the other purring, within a yard of each other. She recommenced breathing and unclenched her stomach. That was not an experience she would care to repeat.

Somewhat shaken, she and Sir Arthur climbed out of the car. Edwin was already on the ground, pulling off his flying helmet. He had his revolver.

"Come on, you fellows," he said. "The enemy's downed."

She helped Sir Arthur along the road. The car they had been pursuing had jumped the verge and crashed into a hedge. Crowley was extricating himself from the front seat with some difficulty. A stunned driver sat in the long grass, thrown clear of his car, shaking his head.

The rear door of the car was kicked open and a female fury exploded from it.

Rose was in mostly human shape, but Catriona could tell from her blazing snake-eyes she had been filled with Crowley's cracked fancies. She was transformed into a species of demonic Zuleika Dobson, set to enslave and conquer and destroy London and then the world. As the dawnlight shone in the Anti-Christine's frizzy halo of hair, Catriona believed that this creature was capable of fulfilling Crowley's mad prophecies. She was a young woman now, still recognisably the child she had been, but with a cast of feature that suggested monumental cruelty and desperate vice. Her hands were tipped with claw-nails.

Her inky eyes radiated something. Hypnotic black swirls wound in her pupils. She was humming, almost subaudibly, radiating malicious female energy. Sir Arthur gasped. And Edwin skidded to a halt. The revolver fell from his hand.

Catriona was appalled. Even these men, whom she respected, were struck by Rose. Then, she was fascinated. It was alien to her, but she saw what magnificence this creature represented. This was not madness, but…

No, she decided. It was madness.

"You are powerless to stop her," Crowley yelled. "Bow down and worship her filthiness!"

Catriona fixed Rose's eyes with her own.

She took Sir Arthur's hand and reached out for Edwin's. He hesitated, eyes on Rose's body, then clutched. Catriona held these men fast.

It was Sir Arthur who gave her the idea. And, perhaps, another distinguished author-knight, J.M. Barrie.

"Do you believe in fairies?" she asked.

Crowley looked aghast.

Sir Arthur and Edwin understood.

With all her heart, she imagined benevolence, worshipped purity, conceived of goodness, was enchanted by kindly magic. As a child, she had loved indiscriminately, finding transcendent wonders in sparkling dew on spun webs, in fallen leaves become galleons on still ponds.

"*I* believe in fairies," she declared.

She recognised her kinship with the kindly knight. She was a sceptic about many things, but there was real magic. She could catch it in her hand and shape it.

The English countryside opened up for her.

She truly believed.

Rose was transfixed. She dwindled inside her dressing gown, became a girl again. Dragonfly wings sprouted from her back, and delicate feelers extended from her eyebrows. She hovered a few inches above the grass. Flowers wound around her brow. She shone with clean light.

Sir Arthur was tearful with joy, transported by the sight. Edwin squeezed her hand.

Spring flowers sprouted in the autumn hedgerow.

Crowley was bewildered.

"No," he said, "you are scarlet, not watercolour."

He was cracked and had lost.

"Come here," Catriona said, to the girl.

Rose, eight years old again and human, skipped across the road and flew into her arms, hugging her innocently. Catriona passed her on to Sir Arthur, who swept her up and held her fiercely to him.

"I think your new age has been postponed," Edwin told Crowley.

"Curse you," Crowley swore, shaking his fist like the melodrama villain he wished he was.

"You're going to pay for the car, sir," said the driver. "Within the hour."

Crowley was cowed. He looked like a big baby in daylight. His bald head was smudged and his trousers were badly ripped and stained.

There were new people on the scene. She supposed it was inevitable.

You couldn't land a biplane and crash a car without attracting attention.

Two men stood on the other side of the road. Catriona didn't know where they could have come from. She had heard no vehicle and there were no dwellings in sight.

Rose twisted in Sir Arthur's hug to look at the men.

Catriona remembered what the girl had said about the friends of the Little People. Undertakers in smoked glasses.

The two men were the same height, tall even without their black top hats. They wore black frock coats, black trousers, black cravats, black gloves. Even black spats and black-tinted glasses that seemed too large for human eyes. Their faces were ghost-white, with thin lips.

"They've come for me," Rose said. "I must go away with them."

Gently, Sir Arthur set her down. She kissed him, then kissed Catriona and Edwin, even Crowley.

"Don't worry about me," she said, sounding grown-up, and went to the undertakers. They each took one of her hands and walked her down the road, towards a shimmering light. For a while, the three figures were silhouetted. Then they were gone, and so was the light.

Edwin turned to look at Catriona, and shrugged.

XV: "the vicinity of the inexplicable"

The Old Man nodded sagely when Winthrop concluded his narrative. He did not seem surprised by even the most unusual details.

"I know the Undertaking," Beauregard said. "All in black, with hidden eyes. They appear often in the vicinity of the inexplicable. Like the Little Grey People."

They were back in the Strangers Room.

"I suppose we should worry about Rose," Winthrop mused, "but she told us not to. Considering that she seems to be whatever we think she is, she might have meant that it would be helpful if we thought of her as safe and well since she would then, in fact, be so. It was Cat who saw through it all, and hit upon the answer."

Catriona was thoughtful.

"'I don't know, Edwin," she said. "I don't think we saw a quarter of the real picture. The Little Grey People, the fire-wheel in the skies, the Changeling, the undertakers. All this has been going on for a long time, since well before the original Rose was taken away. We were caught between the interpretations put on the phenomena in the last few days by Sir Arthur and Crowley, fairies and the Anti-Christine. In the last century, it was angels and demons. Who knows what light future researchers will shine upon the business?"

Winthrop sipped his excellent brandy.

"I shouldn't bother yourself too much about that, old thing. We stand at the dawn of a new era. Not the apocalypse Crowley was prattling about, but an age of scientific enlightenment. Mysteries will be penetrated by rational inquiry. We shall no longer need to whip up fairy tales to cope with the fantastical. Mark my words, Catty-Kit. The next time anything like this happens, we shall get to the bottom of it without panic or hysteria."

CLUBLAND HEROES

Catriona Kaye would always remember the first time she looked up and saw one of them. In her case, it was the woman—the Aviatrix—swooping from a cloudless sky. An unhooded hawk, the Aviatrix was tracking quarry through holiday crowds who were beneath her.

Like the 20th Century, Catriona was nineteen years old. On an unseasonably warm Spring Bank Holiday, she had motored down to Brighton in a charabanc with a rowdy group of nurses and their quieter patients. Most of the party were about her own age, but the girls, in flapping white uniforms, seemed a different species from the haunted-eyed men, all veterans of the Great War. In theory, she was researching an article for the *Girls' Paper* on angelic latter-day Florence Nightingales aiding the recovery of shell-shocked officers. The commission had devolved into an outing to the seaside. The mostly tiny nurses, strong in the upper arm as wrestlers, got behind wheelchairs and pushed mind-shattered men along the promenade like babies in perambulators. They even held races, which made Catriona fear for fellows who had come through the War whole in limb but might here take a nasty spill.

Between the piers, she observed human behaviour. Fellows in striped suits and straw boaters loitered, eyeing each passing ankle, calling out cheerful impertinences. She had already fended off several propositions, and would have been more flattered had supposedly heartbroken suitors not instantly recovered to press their attentions on the next girl to twirl a parasol. Old ladies occupied deck chairs, snoozing or staring out to sea. Families shared fish and chips. Boys built sand-castles and conducted sieges with tin soldiers. Hardier types in bathing costume dared the still-freezing sea and, through wracks of shivers, proclaimed their dips most invigorating. By the West Pier, a knot of children gathered around a tall thin striped box, looking up with mouths open as Punch and Judy went through their eternal ritual of bloody farce. A cheer rose from the audience as the crocodile clamped long jaws around the policeman's wooden helmet.

A news-vendor sang "Have You Seen Him?," promoting the *Daily Herald*'s competition. Among the teeming crowds at the resort supposedly lurked that master of concealment, Lobby Ludd, whose silhouette was printed on the front page (in Fleet Street, Catriona had learned the expression "slow news day") and on circulation-boosting posters. Keen-eyed readers brandished *Heralds* and barked "you are Mr. Lobby Ludd and I claim my five pounds" at bewildered local characters, sometimes tugging genuine whiskers in an attempt to unmask the elusive gent. She had witnessed several scuffles, with indignant non-Ludds battered by rolled-up newspapers, and one genuine fist-fight.

Floss, who could have boxed for Lancashire, trundled Captain Duell up to the guardrail and locked the brake on his wheelchair.

"I've got to spend a penny. Mind the cabbage, would you, love?"

At first, Catriona had been shocked to hear nurses say such things, but she'd soon seen they were ferociously devoted to their gentlemen. When a Member of Parliament touring the convalescent hospital refused to visit the shell-shock ward on the grounds that the patients there were all shamming cowards, Floss had rolled up her mutton-chop sleeve and personally punched his head for him. Captain Duell, twice sole survivor of his battalion, had served twenty-eight months in the trenches.

Floss tripped off in search of a convenience.

Catriona looked into the Captain's watery eyes. He was in a near-permanent dream-state. He didn't flinch at loud noises—those cases were left behind at the Royal Vic, since Brighton on a Bank Holiday wasn't where they'd be at their most comfortable—or stutter to the point of incomprehensibilty. He just seemed used up, forever on the point of falling asleep or starting awake, head hung loose on his neck, lolling forwards. Always tired, never resting. She couldn't imagine what he'd seen.

A middle-aged woman carrying a *Herald* stared at Captain Duell, comparing his face to the front page silhouette. Catriona tensed, sure the Captain was about to be harangued as a probable Lobby Ludd, but the woman thought better of it and passed by, looking for another suspect character.

Catriona shrugged a smile at Captain Duell, forgetting momentarily that he had little idea she was there. Then, she saw something *spark* in his eyes. She knew better than to believe in miracle cures, but had learned that every tiny interaction with the world outside their minds was a triumphant step.

The Captain looked upwards, eyes rising. He lifted his head, detaching his chin from his breast.

"Yes," said Catriona, "look at me."

His gaze passed up over her face. She tried to encourage him with a smile, but he didn't focus on her. She was puzzled as Captain Duell looked up higher, above her head, into the sky.

The crowds hushed. She had a *frisson*, almost of fear, and twisted away from the man in the wheelchair, following his eyeline. All along the sea-front faces were turned upwards. Fingers pointed. Breaths were held. Then, thunderous applause rolled over the sea. A cheer went up.

A woman flew out of the skies, towards the prom.

Catriona had, of course, heard about the Aviatrix.

Since her stunning debut, the *Girls' Paper* had three times pictured Lady Lucinda Tregellis-d'Aulney—"Lalla" to her friends and an Angel of

Terror to her foes—on the cover. Shortly after the armistice, distracted from her initial aerial experiments over Dartmoor, the Aviatrix had swooped upon an escaped murderer, bearing the terrified felon up into the sky and dropping him back in Prince Town Jail.

The principles of Lady Lucinda's winged flight had been explained in learned articles which Catriona understood only vaguely. She had imagined a classical angel—though she knew a human with functional bird-wings ought to have a sternum like a yacht's centreboard to anchor the necessary muscles. The Aviatrix's wings, hardly visible unless sunlight caught them just so, were more like a butterfly's than a bird's. Complex matter seeped from spiracles along her backbone, like ectoplasm from a medium, unfolding into sail-like structures at once extraordinarily strong and supernaturally fine. Extruded through vents in her white leather flying jacket, the wings lasted a few hours. Shed, they liquesced like cobweb, melting to silvery scum. But while Lalla had wings, she could fly.

Like everyone, Catriona was awestruck.

She knew from her father, a country parson, that this was an age of miracles foreseen only by M. Verne and Mr. Wells. In his lifetime, the world had accepted the telephone, the Maxim gun, recorded sound, the motor-car, the aeroplane, motion pictures, raised hemlines, world war. But those were things, concepts, reproducible. The Aviatrix was a person, an embodied marvel, a heroine literally above ordinary humanity.

Captain Duell tried to speak. Catriona was concerned for him; how could she explain that he wasn't "seeing things?" Everyone else also saw the woman in the sky. She wasn't an angel come for him.

The Aviatrix hovered, wings beating every few seconds, a rainbow shimmer of facets in sunlight. She was barely twenty feet above the sea, ankles primly together, arms casually folded. With a *whoosh*, she swam through the air, like a phantasmal manta ray. She flew over the beach, up towards the prom.

All at once, Catriona actually saw the woman with the wings. Lady Lucinda wore white jodhpurs and riding boots, matching her slightly baggy jacket. An abbreviated yellow leather flying helmet freed waves of pale gold hair that swirled about her shoulders, while tinted goggles concealed her eyes and a long white scarf trailed behind her. A button-down holster hung from her belt, heavy with a service revolver. As insignia on the breast of her jacket and caste-mark on her helmet forehead, she wore the d'Aulney coat of arms—birds and castles.

Catriona realised the Aviatrix was looking through the crowds, checking each upturned face. She was searching for someone. Since doing so well with the jail-breaker, she had specialised in tracking down escaped or wanted felons, like a Wild West bounty hunter—though no d'Aulney would ever stoop to seeking payment for doing his or her duty. Her late brother Aulney Tregellis-d'Aulney, vanquished over No Man's Land by Hans von Hellhund (the so-called "Demon Ace"), had never claimed a penny of his RFC pay.

The outfit showed little of the woman inside—bee-stung red lips and a blot of artificial beauty mark. It struck Catriona that Lady Lucinda painted her face like an actress, so as to give the best effect from a distance. Up close, her mouth would be an exaggerated scarlet bow.

Now the wings hung like a kite, and the Aviatrix held out her arms for balance, gliding on an air current. She seemed to walk on a glass promenade above the general run of humanity, considering then rejecting each.

Catriona recalled that Lady Lucinda had announced that she would hunt down and bring in an international revolutionary known as the Crocodile. The anarchist was behind a series of dynamite outrages on the Continent and reportedly intent upon bringing his stripe of violent upheaval to England.

A chill crept through her. A bomb on the sea-front, timed to go off at the height of a Bank Holiday, would be devastating, resulting in enormous loss of life. With the War so fresh in mind, it was scarcely conceivable that such horrors should resume, and on the mainland. And yet she knew better. Humanity's capacity for beastliness was undimmed even after the mass slaughter of the trenches.

The Aviatrix passed overhead. Catriona had the illusion she could reach up and touch the heels of her boots, though the woman was a good ten feet beyond her grasp. Captain Duell rose from his chair, back creaking, uniform wrinkled around his waist from so long in a sitting position. He was still trying to speak. Floss was back, an arm around the patient, cooing to him, supporting him.

Everyone else—Catriona included—looked to the Aviatrix. At last, Lady Lucinda stopped, as if a gem had caught her eye in a tray of coals. She stood still, above the entrance to the West pier, and looked down at the Punch and Judy theatre. Her scarf streamed like a banner. She slipped her goggles up onto her forehead, disclosing long-lashed blue-grey eyes.

The puppet play continued, but the young audience was hushed, staring at the new arrival, who put a finger to her lips, entreating them to keep the secret a moment longer. The policeman puppet seemed to turn to look up too, truncheon in its arms. A slit opened in the front of the theatre, the puppeteer's eyes shining through.

The Aviatrix smiled and made fists against her chest, crossing her wrists in a pose of concentration, then beat her wings. A hummingbird gust bore down and ripped away the striped fabric of the theatre, revealing a bearded fellow holding up the policeman and covering his face with the crocodile. The stall fell, struts twisting around the puppeteer's legs. Hung inside the stall were the familiar figures of Punch and Judy, their dog and baby. A string of sausages turned out, upon examination, to be linked sticks of dynamite.

The Crocodile waved his crocodile hand, as if warding off the harpy who fell viciously upon him.

Claw-tipped gloves slashed across the anarchist's arm, tearing the puppet off his hand, and hooked into his face, digging deep. A slapstick blood spray spattered the audience.

"You are Mr. Lobby Ludd," said the Aviatrix. "And I claim my five pounds."

Catriona felt more than she could cope with – awe, terror, love, disgust. She fainted, unnoticed. When Floss revived her with smelling salts, the show was over, the Crocodile in police custody, the heroine fluttered away. Relieved holidaymakers, only now sensing the peril averted, redoubled their efforts to enjoy their day away from normal life.

In the mêlée, someone had stolen her purse.

Eight years and many singular experiences later, Catriona Kaye had learned to accept that she shared a world with women who flew. Indeed, by comparison, the Aviatrix was almost a routine marvel. After all, Lady Lucinda was a public figure, while her own adventuring usually involved matters which tended to be kept from the newspapers or recorded only as buried, inconclusive items at the foot of the column on an obscure inside page.

In the Bloomsbury flat she shared with Edwin, she sat up in bed, swathed in a sumo-size kimono, fiddling with a Chinese puzzle box. Souvenir of a gruesome bit of business she thought of as The Malign Magics of the Murder Mandarin of Mayfair, the box had defeated her fingers for fourteen months. It held the preserved forefinger of a centuries-dead courtesan-sorceress whose sharpened nail-talon had several times altered the course of history. Or maybe the rattling, lightweight treasure inside the box was a very old twig.

Catriona was no longer primarily a journalist, an *observer*—though she had published books about bogus spiritualists and genuine hauntings. Through her complicated association with Edwin Winthrop of the Diogenes Club, she was a *participant* in a secret life conducted busily just beyond the perceptions of the man or woman in the street. She was still alive and sane; if she thought about it, she was rather pleased with herself for that— such a happy, if provisional, outcome seemed so unlikely for a person in her line.

She slid lacquered panels back and forth, rattling the box, discovering new configurations with each click. The fiddling was at least educational, expanding her knowledge of Chinese characters.

"Still no joy?"

Edwin came into the small bedroom, with a tray of tea, toast, and Catriona's mother's marmalade. He wore a cardinal-scarlet, floor-length dressing gown that might have done for a ball-gown, over last night's dress shirt with the collar popped and the tie undone. There had been talk of disowning and a cessation of parental relations when she elected to share accommodation with a man to whom she was not married, but it hadn't lasted.

This was a decade of change.

"It's always three moves away."

Edwin kissed her cheek, took away the puzzle box and poured her a cup of tea, ritually tipping in just the splash of milk she liked.

This morning, he was being especially considerate. He had been out at his club—always *the* Club—last night. She gathered he had not slept.

"You're going to ask me to do something?"

"A brilliant deduction, Catty-Kit," he said, sitting on the bed, legs stretched over the coverlet, pillows propped behind his back. His hair smelled of tobacco; the inner rooms of the Diogenes Club were a perpetual fug, thicker even than the pea-soupers which still afflicted London.

"And it's going to be wretched?"

Edwin rattled the puzzle box next to his ear. He subscribed to the old twig theory. He had also suggested solving the puzzle with an Alexandrine sword-stroke, but she knew he was only teasing.

"It's just a tiny little murder," he admitted.

"That's extreme," she said, nibbling a corner of toast. "Couldn't you just have whoever it is crippled?"

"Not murder as in *committing*, murder as in *investigating*…"

"You may not have heard, ducks, but there's an excellent service for that. Those fellows in the bell-shaped helmets, the ones who always know the time and have those dear little whistles. They don't take kindly to lady journalists getting under their size-eleven boots, or so I've read in the *Police Gazette*."

Edwin shrugged, noncommittally.

"Good fellows the 'peelers,' even out in the trackless *terra incognita* that is Heathrow, Surrey. A fine yeoman constabulary excellently qualified for locating missing bicycles, rescuing cats from trees, and cuffing apple-scrumpers around the earhole. Maybe just a bit baffled by Murder Most Foul, though. The penetrating intellect and discreet tact of Miss Catriona Kaye would be much appreciated in certain circles."

He marmaladed more toast and chewed it over.

"If Mr. Charles Beauregard of the Ruling Cabal of the Diogenes Club wants me to do something," she said, "he could always ask me himself."

Edwin paused midmouthful. He always looked naughty boyish when his superior and mentor was involved.

"Better yet, Charles could nominate me for membership, you could second me, and we wouldn't have to go round the houses every time the least-publically-acknowledged of the Kingdom's intelligence and investigative agencies has a task uniquely suited to my abilities."

Edwin scoffed.

"That *would* be murder. A woman member of the Diogenes Club! The ravens would flee the Tower of London. Sir Henry Merrivale would bust a corset. Anarchy in the streets. England would fall."

"Serve it right. This is 1927. We've got the vote. And the Married Women's Property Act."

This was an old scab, picked at whenever they got bored. The last thing she wanted was to be a member of Edwin's club, but it was still an annoyance that she put herself so frequently at the disposal of an institution that would only allow her into a select few rooms of their cavernous premises in Pall Mall, refusing her admittance to the rest of the place on the spurious grounds of her sex. As it happens, she had seen everything anyway—with the connivance of Charles and Edwin, and disguised as a post-boy, while thwarting the efforts of Ivan Dragomiloff, the *soi-disant* "ethical assassin," and saving the somewhat over-capacious hide of that bloody-minded old reactionary Sir Henry.

"'Sides, *independence* is what makes you an asset," said Edwin, touching her nose. "We trust your objectivity. Diogenes isn't entirely free from the compromises, rivalries, and politickings that shackle all servants of the crown. Sometimes, only a free agent will do."

"You aren't making this trip to the country any more attractive."

Edwin smiled, a line of white beneath his clipped moustache. He made adorably sad eyes, like Buster Keaton.

"And that's not going to work either, beast."

He was tickling. Which wasn't fair.

"The problem has features of uncommon interest."

He shifted a facet of the box. It would be just like him to solve the thing without even trying, after she'd spent months on it.

"You mean, it's embarrassing *and* dangerous."

"Not at all. It's probably very ordinary, run of the mill, and even, as murders go, tedious. But there's an *aspect* that stands out. Almost certainly an irrelevance, but it needs mulling over. It's something with which the locals have not a hope in Hades of coping. Only you, Catty-Kit, can bring to bear the tact and cunning needed. Hark, what's that? Britannia, calling the finest of her daughters to do her duty…"

She swallowed the last of the toast.

"Aren't you curious?"

He was maddeningly right.

"So, is it a dagger of ice, melted away in an open wound? A beheaded corpse in a room locked from the inside, with the head missing? The venomous bite of a worm unknown to science?"

"None of the above, old thing. Plain blunt instrument, applied to the back of the noggin with undue force. Probably a length of lead pipe. Or a fireplace poker. Mr. Peeter Blame, our luckless householder, apparently surprises a burglar in the course of felonious filching, gets badly bashed on the bonce, then left to die on the kitchen floor. Usual portable valuables missing. Cash, watch, minor jewelry. String of housebreakings in the vicinity. Official description of the fellow sought to help the police with their enquiries almost certainly runs to a striped jersey, crepe-soled shoes, a black domino mask, a beret, and a big black bag marked 'SWAG.'"

She was being led by the nose. He was daring her to spot what was wrong with this picture.

"Peter Blame?"

"*Peeter*. Pee, double-e, ter. If you ask me, that's an invitation to unlawful killing by itself. The late, lamented had an endearing habit of bringing suit against newspapers who misspelled his name."

"Was he mentioned much in the 'papers?"

"In the legal notices, which contributed to the problem, really. He had the habit of bringing suit against people for all sorts of things. A stickler for the letter, rather than the spirit, of the law."

She knew what he meant.

"So, Mr. Peeter Blame, of the Extraneous E, was one of those busybodies who enjoys dragging all and sundry into court?" she deduced. "Thus scattering motives for murder throughout the countryside in which he lived. Heathrow, you said. I assume he's also been known to, ah, strongly criticise the constabulary currently charged with investigating his demise?"

Edwin barked a laugh.

"They didn't hold an inquest, Catty-Kit. They threw a party. With streamers and funny hats. I'm making that up, but you get my drift. An area of the law in which Mr. Battered Blame took especial interest was the licensing of establishments that serve alcoholic beverages."

"Ouch."

"Indeed. Last January, he was successful in ensuring the dismissal of several policemen and the disbarring of a Justice of the Peace on the grounds that they not only allowed the Coat and Dividers, the local pub, to stay open after regular hours but were photographed drinking there."

"Photographed?"

"Another of Blame's hobbies. Flash photography. Neat bit of trickery, done through a mullioned window. All the faces clear and the clock over the bar in perfect focus. Pints in mid-pull, merry coppers in mid-draught, JP rendering the 'sober as a judge' saying inapplicable. Twenty minutes past midnight. On January the first."

"New Year's Eve? Are you *sure* killing Mr. Blame was strictly against the law?"

"'Fraid so. Even the smallest, and smallest-*minded*, of His Majesty's subjects deserves full restitution when knocked off by skull-cracking crooks."

Catriona pulled her kimono tighter. She saw the trap closing.

"I'll concede being a killjoy and a bounder isn't grounds for justifiable homicide," she said. "But there's an elephant in the room, something colossal you've omitted mention of. The Diogenes Club doesn't concern itself with page seven stuff, no matter how flagrant the misapplication of local justice. Charles is only concerned with matters momentous. It takes a serious threat to the nation to get him out of his armchair. Even then, he's only *excited* by a serious threat to our plane of existence. So? Perfidious foreigners or supernatural spookery?"

"Maybe both, maybe neither."

She was close to teasing it out of him.

"I give up. What's the feature of uncommon interest?"

Edwin's eyes shone.

"The *address*. The Hollyhocks, Heathrow, Surrey. Mr. Blame has... had... unusual neighbours. His property abutted the Drome."

"Ah." Catriona saw it. "The Splendid Six."

"Those are the fellows. And lady. Mustn't forget the lovely Lalla Tregellis-d'Aulney."

Catriona considered the situation.

"When an ordinary everyday unsolved murder is committed *right next door* to the greatest sleuths and saviours in the land, it's a tad awkward."

"Rather."

"So it had better get itself jolly well solved."

"Indeed."

"Quickly and quietly."

"On the nose, admirable girl."

She thought about it.

"But you want *me* to look into it? You're staying out yourself, along with the whole Club?"

"Matter of jurisdiction. Diogenes prefers the shadows, you know. And the Splendid Six... well, they're great ones for the spotlight. We've got by so far on staying out of each other's way. Best all round, really. But Captain Rattray put in a personal telephone call to Charles, on his private line..."

"Captain *Dennis* Rattray. Blackfist?"

"Yes, Blackfist. He asked our opinion. Not something he does often. Rather, not something he's done ever before. The thing is that the Splendid

Six are all very well when you want the Eastern Empire saved from a Diabolical Mastermind or need a Royal Princess rescued from the inbred descendants of a lost legion of Roman soldiers maintaining a fiefdom in a hidden Welsh valley, but they aren't who you want to turn loose on a mundane robbery-murder. It'd be like using a team of Derby winners to pull the milk-cart."

"But I'm a suitable dray-horse? Very flattering."

"You have to appreciate our quandary. We can't go charging in mob-handed and take over from the police."

"What you mean is that Charles doesn't like the Club being called in like a tradesman to tidy up a mess on the doorstep of a crew of glory-hogs who won't sully themselves with it. Blackfist didn't ask for your help, he told you to take out the rubbish and lock the gate behind you. So, to get out of the who-can-spit-further contest, you're palming this off on me—because I'm 'independent.' Well, I'm not really allowed to poke into murders. I know there's this craze for amateur detectives, but they're usually so well-connected that the police bite their lips and pretend to appreciate the 'help.' I don't have an ancient title, a chair in advanced cleverness at an Oxbridge college, or an obliging nephew in Scotland Yard. I don't think my press card will get much respect. I'm not even eccentric."

Edwin took out a sealed envelope and pressed it into her hand.

"Don't think of yourself as 'amateur,' think of yourself as 'unsalaried.' This will give you all the official status you need. Guaranteed to make any bobby in the land doff his helmet and snap a salute. And, indeed, bite their lips."

She examined the seal.

"Good grief. That's…"

"Yes, and he addressed it personally. Look."

She turned over the envelope and saw her name, written in a most distinguished scrawl. It was misspelled: Catrina Kay.

"You feel like saluting yourself, don't you?" Edwin teased.

Actually, she felt hollow and terrified. Being noticed from on high was deeply discomfiting.

But she had no choice.

"And here, oh my best beloved, is a train ticket."

Rattling out of Paddington Station, Catriona had a compartment to herself. Having purchased the current number of *British Pluck* from the magazine stall, she read up on the latest exploits of the Splendid Six, individually and as a side.

Teddy Trimingham, the Blue Streak, had successfully smashed his own land-speed record, in a bullet-shaped multipurpose vehicle of his own design, the Racing Swift. Lord Piltdown, the All-Rounder, had just attained his century of centuries in an exhibition match at the Oval, then celebrated by shinning up Nelson's Column and bellowing in triumph from atop the Admiral's stone hat, terrifying the pigeons. The Aviatrix had snatched a fleeing poisoner (and his Eurasian mistress) from a ship at sea just before the absconding pair reached the safety of international waters, and bore the miscreants back to Scotland Yard. And the Six had foiled the Clockwork Cagliostro's grand scheme to seize Edinburgh Castle with wind-up tin soldiers, smashing his ingenious army into scrap metal and springs. Nothing unusual, there.

Since that Bank Holiday in Brighton, she had got used to the Splendid Six and their like. She knew there had always been such unusual individuals, cheerfully eager to turn their talents to the cause of the helpless. Just as there had always been darker fellows, only marginally less gifted, who served only their own interests or flew the Jolly Roger. For every Aviatrix or Clever Dick, there was a Spring-Heel'd Jack or a Wicked William; Edwin had once theorised that the stalemate between these unique persons, clubland heroes and villains, meant that the rest of the world could get on with whatever they were doing relatively unimpaired. Some great battles of Good and Evil turned out to be little more than squabbles: The Aviatrix's continuing campaign to bring Hans von Hellhund to international justice had more to do with her brother's defeat than the Demon Ace's minor postwar smuggling activities.

Sometimes, though, the rest of the world's business *was* impaired by the doings of superior individuals. Throughout last year's General Strike, the Splendids had been staunch in helping to keep "essential services" running. Something about press photographs of the Blue Streak working as a volunteer driver (joking about the snail's pace of a London omnibus) struck her as comical yet disturbing, while she had very definite feelings about Lady Lalla Tregellis-d'Aulney hovering over union meetings and taking a note of who spoke out the loudest. Catriona's own sympathies had not entirely been with the government in that time of national crisis— she had rowed with Edwin throughout, and he had shown the unexpected decency not to crow at her grief when the strike failed. Many a mine-worker or factory girl, raised on *British Pluck* or the *Girls' Paper*, looked up in awe and admiration, but moderated their opinion when the Six flew what socialist commentators were quick to label their "true colours." Trimingham didn't call himself the "Red Streak," did he? Zooming heroically through certain areas of the country, a Splendid was as liable to be the target of a tossed half-brick as the prompt of a hearty cheer.

At the back of *Pluck* was a helpful article about the Drome. A plot of scrubby flatland had first been turned into a proving ground for Trimingham's pioneering contraptions, where he could whizz and whoosh and go bang well away from the prying eyes of foreign spies or rival inventors. (Peeter "I'll see you in court" Blame must have enjoyed living next door to that racket!) The Splendid Six first convened when the Good Fellows Four put out the call for new recruits to battle the plague hordes of the Rat Rabbi, Norwegicus Cohen, and the Celestial Schemer, Dien Ch'ing. At the successful conclusion of that exploit, the Drome became the Head Quarters of the Six, home to their famed Museum of Mystery. There, surrounded by souvenirs a good deal more impressive than a puzzle box, the Six sat around King Arthur's original table, each in their appointed place. The round table was recovered from the Shadow Realm of Perfidious Albion during an adventure that had run in *British Pluck* for six consecutive numbers under the title "Against the Nights of the Underground Fable." From the article, she deduced that at meetings the original GFF had the Aviatrix serve the tea, and put the brown-skinned Chandra Nguyen Seth, the Mystic Maharajah, on a stool in the draughty corner.

A fold-out map of the Drome kept her busy turning the magazine upside-down to examine details. The village of Heathrow (and its railway station) was shown, but there was no indication as to which of the adjacent properties had belonged to the late Peeter Blame.

As he saw her off, Edwin had given a final friendly suggestion.

"If you can get this settled without even involving the Splendid Sausages, that would probably be for the best."

That would suit her perfectly.

However, she had muttered "some hope."

She considered the portraits dotted in misty ovals around the map: bright eyes (inevitably blue with silver-grey flecks), forthright chins set against underhandedness, devil-may-care half-smiles eager for adventure, stalwart knotted brows ready for any intellectual challenge, gleaming teeth suitable for biting into a fresh red English apple, dashing signatures (and one thumb-print).

The Splendid Six were heroes. And they terrified her.

It was fortunate there was little reason for anyone to visit Heathrow. The station was tiny and dilapidated: boards missing from the platform, sign hanging askew. She alone alighted, taking care to avoid jets of steam aimed at ankle-height. The engine came to the boil again and the hissing, clanking train trundled off, picking up speed in anticipation of more interesting stops further down the line.

An old man emerged from a hut. He tripped over someone's left luggage, which had literally taken root. The two suitcases were furred over with moss, weeds sprouting from cracks in the leather.

"You the missy from up Lunnon?"

The toothless apparition wore a battered station-master's cap on the back of his head. He had a white fringe around his collapsed face, thinning hair up top, sparse beard under his chin. He walked bow-legged with the aid of a stick. A single medal hung from his loose blue tunic.

"I'm Catriona Kaye," she said.

"Come about the killin'?"

He gurned something that might have been a smile, making a puckered black hole of his mouth.

"Yes. I suppose so."

"I'm 'Arbottle."

"Pleased to meet you, Mr. Harbottle."

"*Sergeant* 'Arbottle," he insisted.

He snatched off his cap and looked at it with disgust.

"Wrong 'at. Sorry."

Sergeant Harbottle dashed into the hut and came out wearing a policeman's helmet that must have been issued in Victoria's reign. Or perhaps William and Mary's. The chin-strap hung loose under his wattles.

"I'm Station-Master, Post-Master, Captain of Militia, and Police Sergeant. Do the milk-round, too."

"Very public-spirited."

"No one else would take the jobs. Not since New Year's Eve."

Catriona understood.

"That might change now."

There wasn't much point coming at this case from the angle of motive.

"Sergeant, please understand I'm here only to offer you assistance. I have full confidence in your ability to bring this unpleasant matter to a neat conclusion."

"Eh?"

"I'm sure you'll bag the culprit."

"Never had one of those round here before. Culp-whatchamacallits. But you're right, missy. Once I put my mind to something, it gets done."

"Should we begin by visiting the scene of the crime?"

Harbottle went cross-eyed.

"'E's been taken away. What with the warm weather, it was best. I'm sure you understand, missy. Deaders gives off a bit of a pong."

"So I understand."

"What for you be wantin' to nose round where a deader's been, then?"

"Clues, Sergeant. Every sleuth needs clues."

"I've never 'ad a clue."

"That, I'll be bound, will change also."

Harbottle's face set in a crumpled version of a determined look. Catriona wondered if she wouldn't be best off on her own.

Then again, she wasn't "up Lunnon" now.

"Lead the way," she invited.

Harbottle produced a collapsible bone-shaker bicycle from his shed and unfolded it into a shape to delight a Parisian surrealist. He apologised that there was no room for two and told her she'd have to keep up, then began pedaling down a muddy lane away from the station.

She had to drag her feet to let him stay level with her. His conveyance wobbled alarmingly from side to side and his legs were too long, forcing his knees out as he pushed on the pedals. If it hadn't been for the modest slope of the lane, adding gravity to motive power, she feared Harbottle would have made even slower progress. She didn't like to think about his return journey.

A jolly rustic, sat outside the Coat and Dividers, shouted "get off and milk it."

Harbottle spat a stream of brown juice and invective at the fellow, who lifted his pint in salute. Catriona checked the nurse's watch pinned to her blouse. Opening time wasn't for an hour.

"The last sergeant," muttered Harbottle. "Billy Beamish."

She looked back at the celebrating ex-copper. He toasted her too, and showed every indication of having toasted any passerby, human or animal, for the last two days.

"Grieving hard, I see."

"Oh, not him. Billy Beamish hated Pee-ee-eeter Blame worse than poison. Lost his job, see. Lot of them lost their jobs. For drinkin' after hours. Not me, though. I'm temperance."

The Coat and Dividers was in the fork of a Y-junction. A triangle of green with a tree and some small cottages made up the rest of Heathrow. Untended geese muddled about. It was rather pleasant, if dusty.

Harbottle pedaled past a mile-post, then hopped off the bike with a creaking of bones and spokes. From here on, the gradient was against him. He made better time pushing the thing.

"Here's the Hollyhocks."

The cottage was set in its own grounds, very neat and tidy, with regimented rows of petunias and roses. The white filigree gate was set in an arched bower threaded through with pretty red and purple flowers, its picturesque aspect marred somewhat by a superfluity of engraved boards with black warnings: "No Hawkers or Circulars," "Trespassers Will Be Prosecuted to the Full Extent of the Law," "Uninvited Callers Unwelcome," "Keep Off the Grass," "It is Impermissible to Operate a Motorised Conveyance in This Thoroughfare," and "Vagrancy and

Mendicancy Are Criminal Offences—The Police *Will* Be Called!" Each board was signed "P. Blame, Esq."

The gate was open. And so was the cottage's door.

"There's someone inside," said Catriona.

"I told you, 'e's been taken away on account of the potential whiff…"

"Not the owner," she said. "Have you ever heard about the murderer returning to the scene of the crime?"

"Why'd 'e want to do a fool thing like that?"

"Hard to fathom, the criminal mind. Even for sleuths such as we."

She opened her purse.

"What's that there?" asked Harbottle, eyes bulging.

"It's a ladylike little automatic."

"It's a pop-pop gun is what it is. A concealed weapon!"

"It's not concealed. I'm showing it to you."

He thought about that.

She ventured into the garden of the Hollyhocks and stepped up to the doorway.

"Knock knock," she said, rapping the open door with the barrel of her ladylike little automatic.

"Who's there?" came a squeak.

"That's what I should be asking," she said.

Little sharp eyes showed in the gloom inside the cottage, one much larger than the other.

"What wight have you to quiz me, madame?"

"I'm with the police," she said.

A little boy stepped into the light. He wore his oiled-down hair centre-parted, and was dressed in grey shorts and a matching blazer. His gaze was resolute, but his chin a touch underdeveloped. The child held up a magnifying glass the size of a large lollipop, which was why one of his watery blue eyes seemed four times the size of the other, emphasising the steely grey flecks.

"You're late," he said. "The clues are getting cold."

There was a sticky black-red splash on the rug. The boy held his glass over it, and peered at the mess.

"Blood, bwains, bits of bone," he said. "Nothing intewesting."

Catriona stood out of the way as the boy detective poked about, examining things through his glass. The study where the body had been found was a mess. From the neatness of the garden and the rest of the cottage, it was an easy deduction that the room had been thoroughly ransacked by the murderer. Or else an earlier clue-hunt from one of the too many sleuths on this case.

"Here, a file has been wemoved."

The boy solemnly pointed at a gap in the bookshelves, as obvious as a missing front tooth in a broad smile, between "Oct–Dec '26" and "Apr–Jun '27."

"January to March of this year," he proclaimed.

"Amazing," commented Catriona, drily.

"It's simple, weally," he responded, pleased. "A perspicacious person can tell from the files either side which is missing."

Harbottle scratched his head in admiration.

The boy beamed a wide, not-very-pleasant smile.

This, she knew, was Master Richard Cleaver, "Clever Dick," the brightest eleven-year-old lad in the land. He had taken a double first in Chemistry and Oriental Languages from Oxford last year. Independently wealthy from the patent of a new, more efficient type of paperclip he had twisted out of one of his mother's hairpins when he was seven, he divided his time between solving mysteries that baffled the police and adventuring with the rest of the Splendid Six.

She should have brought the Chinese puzzle box. Clever Dick could probably open it in seconds.

"This isn't the first murder I've solved," he announced, somewhat prematurely. "If it weren't for my bwain-power, the Andover Axeman would never have been hanged. Last Whitsun half-holiday, I wecovered the Cwown Jewels. They'd been stolen by Iwish oiks. Served them wight when they got shot."

She reminded herself not to laugh at the child.

His bumps of intellect might be swollen to incredible proportions, but those of humour and humility had withered away entirely.

"I proved Nanny Nuggins was a Bolshevik spy. Stalin sent her to Sibewia for failing to kidnap me."

She deduced that Stalin had never met Master Richard.

"You must have got on well with Mr. Blame," she ventured. "You had a lot in common. An interest in the law."

Clever Dick made a face.

"Ugh! No fear. That common fellow kept saying I ought to be in school. He alleged there were laws about where childwen should be."

Catriona was beginning to sympathise with the unlamented departed.

Clever Dick sorted through strews of papers on the desk.

"I think you'd better leave those alone," she said, mildly.

"I don't think that and you can't make me."

He patted his hands on the papers to prove it, pawing around the desk.

"See. I'm *not* leaving these clues alone. And there's nothing you can do about it. I can identify seventy-eight different types of type-witer letter.

I can hold my bweath for four and a half minutes. I have a medal from Scotland Yard."

"So have I," she said. "But it's not done to brag, is it?"

Clever Dick whirled around and looked at her for the first time, applying all his reputed intellect. He was genuinely puzzled by what she'd said, and didn't like the sensation.

"Whyever not? If you've earned something, it's yours. Why shouldn't you bwag?"

"Nobody likes a smart-arse," she suggested, mildly.

The boy waved it away.

"Nonsense. You are a silly person. And a girl, besides. I didn't know they let girls in the police. Or old smelly men without teeth."

Harbottle grunted. "'Ere, you mind your manners, Sonny-Jim-me-Lad."

The brainiest boy in Britain stuck out his tongue at them.

Catriona looked at the papers on the desk. Correspondence with lawyers, courts, newspapers. Blame kept copies of all his letters.

"Those are my clues," said Clever Dick. "You find your own!"

This was becoming tiresome.

"I'm ever so much cleverer than you. I can deduce masses of things about you. You live in a house in Bloomsbury but were bwought up in Somerset or Dorset. You had marmalade on toast for bweakfast with a man who has a moustache."

"It's a flat."

"I *meant* flat when I said house!"

"Somerset."

"I knew it. Your type-witer has a faulty shift-key. You don't spend much money on clothes. That purse was a gift fwom someone Canadian. You have a two-inch scar just above your knee. It's no use pwessing your skirt down. I've seen the wolled tops of your stockings."

She deduced that in a few years' time, Clever Dick was not going to be popular with the ladies.

"You were wecently nearly killed by a Chinaman. (So was I, so there!) You have no bwothers or sisters. And you lied about being a police girl. No, you didn't. You were twying to be clever when you said you were 'with the police' because this fathead is a policeman and you *are* with him. It's no use twying to be clever, because I'll always outfox you. Do you play chess? I can beat anyone, without looking at the board. You're married but you won't wear a wing."

"I'm not."

"Yes, you are. Your husband is the bweakfast fellow."

She wasn't about to explain her domestic arrangements to an eleven-year-old.

Sweetly, she said "I don't believe you can really hold your breath for four and a half minutes."

"Can so."

"Prove it."

He huffed in a breath, expanding his cheeks and screwing his eyes shut, then began to nod off the seconds.

She looked cursorily around the room, but thought she'd learned all she could for the moment. Later, she would have to spend hours going through all the papers and files, mulling over and rejecting dozens of leads. It was the sort of investigative work the Splendid Six never had to deal with, any more than they cooked their own supper or cleaned their own guns.

Clever Dick's face went red, then distinctly blue. He continued nodding.

She pressed a finger to her lips for quiet and shooed Harbottle out of the room and cottage, following him on tip-toes.

She heard a certain straining behind her, but thought little of it.

Outside, she found a shining reception committee.

Three more of the Splendid Six were crowded into the tiny cottage garden. Blackfist, the All-Rounder, and the Aviatrix. The space wasn't quite suitable for such *big* persons, though only the tall, wide, shambling Lord Piltdown was really much larger than the ordinary.

When her feet were on the ground, Lady Lucinda—Catriona was slightly shocked to realise—was *tiny*, at least a handspan shorter than her own five foot two. From that first sight, she had reckoned the Aviatrix a full fathom of Amazon glory. Without wings, the woman was a petite, long-faced debutante whose jodhpurs wrinkled over thin legs.

Captain Rattray, Blackfist, was a smiling, casual fellow with patent-leather hair and arrow-collar features. On a thin gold chain around his neck hung the famous Fang of Night, the purple-black gemstone he had plucked from the forehead of a prehuman cyclopaean idol discovered in a cavern temple under the Andes. The story was that when the Captain made a fist around the jewel, his body became granite-impervious to harm and his blows landed with the force of a wrecking-ball. Unconsciously, or perhaps not, he fingered his magical knuckle-duster all the time. The fingertips of his left hand were stained black, as if qualities of the gem were seeping into his skin.

He stuck out his free hand to shake hers.

"Miss Kaye, welcome to Heathrow. I'm in the way of being Dennis Rattray."

She shook his hand. He had a firm but not crushing grip.

"Blackfist, don't ch'know? Silly cognomen, hung on me by the yeller press, but have to live with it. This lively filly is Lalla d'Aulney..."

Catriona nodded at the woman, who gave a token curtsey like a little girl presented to disreputable foreign Royalty.

"And dear old Pongo Piltdown. Don't be alarmed by his fizzog and the massive shoulders business. He's the compleat gent."

Lord Piltdown extended a yard-long arm and took her hand with supple, thick, complex fingers. His immaculate cuff slid back over a thickly-furred wrist. He bent low and kissed her knuckles with his wide, rubber-lipped mouth.

The All-Rounder had been found frozen in a glacier under the Yorkshire estate of an aristocratic family whose son and heir had just been lost in the Boer War. The bereaved parents raised "Pongo" as their own, sending him to Uppingham, where he gained his nickname by captaining the rugby and cricket sides, proving himself nigh-unvanquishable at the bat and nigh-unstoppable as a bowler. He was also the author of several slim volumes of privately published poetry, favouring as subjects courtly love, English country sports (he was a Master of Fox Hounds), and the superiority of tradition over shallow modernity. His views on the proper place of women made Sir Henry Merrivale seem like Dame Ethel Smyth.

Lord Piltdown gave her back her hand, which was slightly moist. His beetle-browed face was marked by a distinct blush, and he screwed a monocle into one of his eyes.

"Pongo likes you," said Lady Lucinda, looking at her sideways. "Watch out, or you'll be showered with rhymes."

The All-Rounder covered his face with his enormous hands, peeking out shyly between banana-fingers. His perfectly tailored tuxedo would have served her as a survival tent. Two-thirds of his body was barrel torso, supported by bent, spindly legs that gave the impression of powerful, coiled springs. She noted he wore stout, polished leather gloves on his feet.

"It's a shame you should visit in such unhappy circumstances," said Blackfist. "This is an idyllic spot, sheltered in the bosom of Mama England. It's almost sacred to us, untainted by the bloodier businesses for which we are best known. I don't mind telling you it strikes home, such a common-or-garden crime right smack next door. We shall not rest until our good neighbour has been avenged."

Harbottle tugged what little forelock he could find.

"A burglar did it, sir," he said. "We'll feel his collar soon."

From inside the cottage came a spluttering explosion. Catriona checked her watch. Nearly five minutes. Clever Dick had broken his record.

The boy came into the garden. His comrades broke out in identical, indulgent, tolerant smiles. Blackfist patted Clever Dick on the head, mussing his hair.

"We sent our best and brightest to lend a hand," he said.

"Thank you very much," she responded.

"I found a big fat clue," announced Clever Dick. "A missing file."

"Very significant, I'm sure," said the Aviatrix.

"It could be," Catriona admitted.

"The beginning of the year is missing," said the boy. "Wemember what happened then? After the New Year's Eve lock-in at the Coat and Dividers? Old Blamey made a gang of enemies. I'd venture one or more took bloody wevenge on him."

"That's a theory," she said.

Captain Rattray's smile grew. "We've found young Master Richard's theories often have a funny way of hitting the nail right smack on the jolly old head."

"It'll be that Beamish," said Lady Lucinda. "You can tell he's a wrong 'un."

"Frightful rotter," said Blackfist, "drunk as a lord—no offence, Pongo—from noon til Maundy Thursday, and spouting off all manner of resentment against the deceased. That's a throbbing eyesore of a motive."

As he spoke, Rattray grasped the Fang of Night. His hand turned black-purple instantly, skin taking on a rough, gritty texture. A flush of colour appeared at his neck and swarmed up around his jawline, extending vein-tendrils across his cheek, stiffening around his lips and eyes. Inside his Norfolk jacket, the upper left quarter of his body became swollen and lumpy.

"Give the fellow a good grilling and he'll crack, spill the beans."

Blackfist's speech became slurred. He apprehended the change and let go of his jewel. The effect rolled back and he smoothed his face, dabbing spittle from his mouth with his breast-pocket hankie.

"Sorry about that," he said. "No call for the Auld Blackie here."

"When are you arresting Beamish?" demanded the Aviatrix.

Four of the Six looked at Catriona, expectantly, intently. Even Harbottle joined in.

She had never felt smaller, and mentally cursed Edwin for sending her here. He must have known what she'd be contending with. These people were accustomed to purported master crooks who usurped the BBC's airwaves to issue proud boasts about the authorship of atrocities as yet uncommitted, helpfully outlining their wicked plans in good time for them to be thwarted. The Splendid Six specialised in crimes that were vastly complicated but easily solved.

"I'm not strictly supposed to make an arrest. That's Sergeant Harbottle's duty. I'm here to advise him."

"I'll have Beamish in jug before tea-time," said Harbottle.

"I wouldn't advise that."

"Really, I think you should consider it, Miss Gayle," said the Aviatrix.

"The fellow has practically been bragging about it. Sitting there drunk and celebrating."

"It's 'Miss Kaye,' Lady Lucinda. Before we arrest anyone, we'll need to establish some things. My reading of the situation is that at first everyone assumed Mr. Blame was killed during a burglary, robber or robbers unknown being the culprits. Now, general opinion seems to have swung around to indict someone with a grudge against the victim."

"Items were stolen to make it look like a burglawy," said Clever Dick. "It's an old, old twick."

"Absolutely."

"The Mountmain Gang only stole the Cwown Jewels as a distwaction. The weal point of their waid on the Tower of London was to assassinate the Sergeant-at-Arms who shot Aoife Mountmain during the Iwish Civil War. I was the only one who wealised."

"It's the copper-bottomed truth, Miss Kaye," said Blackfist. "We were all haring off after the orb and sceptre, while brainbox Dickie saw the veritable answer to the mystery. Made us all feel proper clods and no mistake. Still, turned out all right in the end. There are two nations who'll be glad never to hear from the Mountmains again."

"See, I'm clever and you're stupid. Now, awwest Beamish."

Catriona's back was literally against a wall, covered in ivy. Through the window, she saw the untidy desk, the missing file.

"It's a mistake to harp on the solution of your last case when dealing with this one," she said. "If a murderer can fake a burglary to conceal his identity, could he not also fake a ransacking for the same reason? If ex-Sergeant Beamish or any of the others who lost their livelihoods after the New Year's party were guilty, why would they take away the file covering their grudge against Mr. Blame?"

"To hide their motive, twitty girl."

"But it doesn't hide their motive. The missing file *points directly at it*. Why not take away a file covering something else, say the nuisance suit that led to the bankruptcy of the local newspaper? And point the finger of guilt at *someone else*? In fact, that's what I think has been done. The missing file isn't evidence against Beamish, it's evidence *for* him."

She saw Clever Dick follow her reasoning. His face started to go red, as if he were holding his breath again. He got bad-tempered, which she took as an admission that he, junior genius, was forced to agree with her, a girl.

"But the missing file, which contains nothing of value, also rules out the unknown burglar theory."

"Ah-ha," said Clever Dick, trying to trump her again, "but what if it didn't just contain papers but also something *pwecious*, something *concealed...*"

"Then why take the whole file? If it were a golden penknife or the deed to an oil-well or something, the burglar would just have taken it, rather than be burdened with a lot of irrelevant letters of complaint and dry-as-dust writs. No, the missing file is just a distraction..."

"You're rather good at this, aren't you?" said Blackfist, admiring.

Lord Piltdown nodded, bristly chin squashing his four-in-hand cravatte, and—without bending over—fingered the lawn, raising little earthy divots.

"I don't like to blow my own trumpet," she said.

"So 'oo should I arrest?" demanded Harbottle.

Everyone looked at her again. Lady Lucinda lit a cigarette and sucked on a long white holder, pluming smoke through her nostrils. Clever Dick held up his magnifying glass and big-eyed at her.

"I'm not quite ready to stick my neck out yet," she admitted.

There was evident disappointment.

"She's got no idea," said Clever Dick.

Catriona had to admit, though not out loud, that the brat wasn't far off the mark. She'd shot down two theories and it wasn't yet time for lunch, but had no suitable replacement.

Maybe it was natural causes?

Or suicide?

Or one of those fiendish suicides supposed to look like murder so an innocent was hanged and which, therefore, are acts of attempted homicide as much as self-slaughter?

That was ridiculous—the sort of thing she'd expect Clever Dick to suggest.

Her head was beginning to ache.

At last, she was alone in the cottage. Harbottle had tottered off on his bike to the Coat and Dividers for his lunch, while the Splendids had got bored with watching her mundane sleuthing and gone back to the Drome. Sifting through wastepaper baskets, opening drawers, and the like were all pursuits far less exciting than following a trail of burning corpses left in the wake of the Witch-Queen of Northumberland or skirmishing with the terror lizards of Maple White Land.

Catriona sat in a chair with a wonky wheel at the small desk in Peeter Blame's study, wriggling a little in the dead man's seat, trying to think herself back into the crime. One surprisingly useful thing Harbottle had done—prompted, he admitted, by a suggestion from ex-Sergeant Beamish—was to employ the victim's own photographic apparatus to take flashlight snaps of the scene of the crime before the "deader" was taken away. Prints rush-developed by a local photographical society, of which the deceased had been a member until he found cause to sue the chairman and committee, now lay before her on the blotter. Though the desk was shoved up against a window—the *moderne* arches and watch-tower of the Drome were visible beyond the forsythia at the end of the back garden— the study was gloomy even in early afternoon. She snapped on a green-shaded reading lamp to examine the snaps.

Blame lay in a huddle, a spatter from his caved-in head on the rug, his chair—the one in which she was sitting—overturned. From the proximity of body to chair, she assumed he had been at his desk when attacked. The thought made her swivel round (the wonky wheel complained) to look at the low doorway through which the murderer must have entered. She had an intuition-flash of a dark, strong shape stepping quickly across the room, blunt instrument raised but arcing down, colliding with Blame's cheek...

A close-up showed a wound where she'd imagined the blow landing.

...and lifting him out of his chair, which caught in his legs and fell with him. She didn't go as far as to tip the chair over, but she looked and judged where the assaulted man would have fallen. There was a stain on the wall and a star-crack in the plaster where his head must have struck. The bloody rug was beneath it, smooth now but wrinkled in the photographs.

One blow had not been enough. The killer had applied the bludgeon many more times, concentrating on the side and top of the head. A panicky burglar, making sure not to leave a witness? A grudge-holding local, exterminating an enemy? That old fail-safe, the escaped homicidal lunatic? She could rule out the last—no reported escapees in the vicinity. Or did it come down to the Splendids? One of their many archenemies, frustrated at their untouchability, taking out his or her wrath on their nearest neighbour? Could Blame himself have been the minion of a master villain like Dien Ch'ing or the Clockwork Cagliostro, crushed out of hand for hesitating to follow an order or learning too much of some appalling terror plot? It was tempting to write Edwin's "tiny little murder" into a more satisfying, momentous storyline, to unmask Blame and his attacker as secret players in the great game of clubland heroes and diabolical masterminds. Then, there might at least be the illusion of a point to it.

There was a small fireplace, complete with poker and andirons, all present and correct. A cursory glance around showed other easily-accessible blunt instruments, in their place. The inference was that the murderer brought his own cricket bat or monkey wrench or whatever and had taken it away with him.

She looked back at the photographs.

Under the blood, Peeter Blame looked a sad old man, all dignity torn away. He wouldn't be suing anyone any more. It was difficult to consider the victim as the mean-spirited curmudgeon all accounts made him out to be. The neatness of his garden and the trivial comforts of his cottage made him less a caricature, more pitiable than odious.

She found a droplet of water in her eye and blotted it with her hankie.

A siren sounded, loud enough to rattle teeth and shake every small object in the room. Then, from the Drome, she saw a cloud of white smoke as a large steel shutter opened, lifting a section of lawn to give egress from an underground hangar. A vehicle shot out of the dark, belching flame and crunching gravel. From a perch high above, the Aviatrix—fully winged—launched herself into the air and followed the flapping pennants of the Racing Swift, her scarf streaming behind her.

The Splendid Six were off adventuring.

Perhaps a personal call from the Prime Minister or an even more exalted personage, and a deadly threat to every man, woman, and child in Britain? A human fiend, almost certainly foreign, working some vast, subtle, nigh-unbelievable plot? Again.

In any case, the Blue Streak's latest wonder-wheels whooshed down the lane past the Hollyhocks—Catriona saw the All-Rounder clinging to the roof, huge teeth bared as the rushing wind slipped into his mouth and blew back his lips—and took a sharp turn, spattering pebbles against Mr. Blame's collection of homemade signs ("It is Impermissible to Operate a Motorised Conveyance in This Thoroughfare"), and tearing for the London Road.

It took long seconds for the noise to die down. Even then, Catriona could still feel it in her inner-ear.

No better course of action occurred to her than to examine Blame's remaining files. It would have to be done eventually, and she was in any case stuck.

The first box-file covered the last three months of 1916. It was full to bulging, papers tied into packets and tamped down by a metal spring. A puff of dust suggested that the box hadn't been disturbed in a while. She sampled some of the packets—several contained back-and-forth between Blame (Commander Blame, RN, he signed himself) and the Admiralty. She gathered that after having a ship sunk under him at Jutland, he had cooled his heels ashore while agitating for a new command only to be "retired" on the grounds of an unspecified, much-contested injury sustained in action. Blame's letters, then hand-written (and hand-written *twice* if these were copies) foamed with indignation and barely veiled accusations of dereliction of duty on the part of those bodies who kept him from active service in the nation's hour of direst need. He also had a bee in his bonnet about a particular type of propellor-screw in wide use which he alleged was susceptible to fail under certain conditions and should thus be withdrawn before further disastrous reversals affected the course of the war. There were many, many articles—laboriously transcribed by hand, rather than clipped—on this subject, and an exchange of heated debate in the public forum of the *Times* letters column. The minutiae of stress-points and knot-rates defeated her.

Still, she could add Admiral Viscount Jellicoe and most of the Royal Navy, plus the letter column editor of the *Times*, to the list of suspects. Blame had begun his retirement hobby of bringing suit by naming them all in a massive, still-unresolved private prosecution on the grounds of "high treason."

The next two dozen boxes—four to a year—were more of the same, with a gradual shift as Blame turned his attentions from national to local issues. Mixed in with suits against bird-watchers, a gypsy tribe, the Kaiser (!), and the holder of the patent on a "faster" photographic plate which Blame claimed to have invented first were more innocuous items. Letters of welcome from societies concerned with local history, gardening, photography, and the welfare of naval veterans—which gave her the picture of an active, frustrated man casting around for a cause, for some form of companionship. With sadness, she found each of these involvements terminated in quarrel and, inevitably, a flurry of lawsuits. At first, he had acted through a London firm of solicitors, then local lawyers—of course, he had ended up suing them too. Finding few professionals willing to bring suit against colleagues, Blame had become an amateur enthusiast, representing himself on the rare occasions his complaints made it before the bench, whereupon they were almost invariably if reluctantly upheld.

She was amazed to find Blame even successfully brought an action for breach of promise against one Maggie McKay Brittles, a barmaid at the Coat and Dividers. An addendum listed every expense he had been put to in his pursuit of a lass thirty years his junior. Maggie's arm, muscled from pulling pints and cuffing drunks, could certainly have wielded a mean blunt instrument.

Peeter Blame's chair was not comfortable. Catriona's back ached and she had only progressed as far as 1922. It was evening outside. Midges buzzed in the pre-sunset summer haze.

A noise alerted her to the return of the Splendid Six.

The Racing Swift almost idled on its passage back to the Drome, probably at a mere 100 m.p.h. A foghorn that might be sounded in Dover and heard in Calais honked as the car passed the cottage.

Everything rattled again. She choked on the dust her investigations had put into the air.

With renewed determination, she opened the first of the 1923 files. Still more of the same. Blame succeeded in proving that the members of a ramblers' association on a walking tour of the district were technically subject to the laws concerning tramps and beggars, and got them jailed until their holiday time was up and they had to go back to office jobs in Bradford. By now, much of her empathy was washed away. She reimagined the crime as if she were stalking into the study with a length of lead-pipe in her hand and venom in her heart.

The first connection of metal and bone was so satisfying!

The second 1923 file felt different.

It was nothing obvious—though a rough comparison made by balancing each box on her palm as if she were a human set of scales showed that the second box was much lighter than the first. In mid-1922, Blame had purchased a type-writer—the receipt was in the box, along with a writ against the vendor for "price-gouging"—and had switched from making two copies of all documents by hand to using carbon-paper and a flimsy second sheet. She could even see him learning to type—at first, his more impassioned passages (Marked by Use of Capital Initials and Triple Exclamation Points!!!) tended to rip through to the flimsy, which must render the top-copy a stencil. That partially explained the change in weight and bulk.

She tapped her front teeth with a pencil and looked at the type-writer, its case off, on the desk. The letters were worn away from the E, S, and T keys.

On the lawn of the Drome, the Splendids—in cricketing or croquet whites—were served supper by a deferential staff whose livery included Splendid Six armbands. Occasionally, a braying laugh—Trimingham's—could be heard. Between courses, there was a great deal of champagne flute clinking.

Catriona hadn't eaten since an apple on the train. Harbottle had said he'd bring a sandwich back for her, but had never returned.

She stood up and stuck her fingers into the small of her back.

She thought about foraging in the dead man's larder, but that didn't seem right. After being exposed to his personality for hours, she assumed he'd reach out from beyond the grave and sue her for pilfering. He'd probably also sue her for not identifying his murderer in double-quick time, usurping the powers of the police without real legal standing, and sitting in his bloody chair.

As a compromise, she decided to make herself tea.

The cottage kitchen was a walk-in cupboard with a sink and a stove, and cupboards that locked. She suspected Blame had duplicated the cramped set-up of some ship on which he had served. A hairpin served to pick the locks, which revealed single items of crockery—one cup, one saucer, one plate, one bowl, etc.—and tins of tea, powdered milk, cocoa, sugar, and so on. No major clues, though there was something heartbreaking about a man who only had one teacup, and disturbing also since she was about to make use of it.

She got a fire going in the stove and set a kettle on it.

The cup was clean, but best to wash it anyway. That done, she decided to do the same for the teapot, which was a little dusty.

Dust!

The second 1923 file had produced no dust-puff when opened.

She went back, but it was impossible to check. There was moderate dust in both opened 1923 boxes, disturbed by her thorough search. She lifted the lid of the third 1923 file carefully, as if a live grenade nestled below. No dust-puff. The fourth file, the same. The desk was crowded now with opened boxes. She took a random 1926 file, and didn't get a puff.

Of course, the recent files—in more common use—would have less dust than the older ones, whose business was settled. But that didn't explain what she could swear was a sudden change. It's not as if dust became extinct or radically changed quality at the beginning of April, 1923.

Dust gone. And the boxes lighter. That 1926 file was practically empty when compared with the stuffed earlier boxes. Blame certainly hadn't moderated his habits; if anything, he'd become a more enthusiastic litigant as the years wore on.

She chewed her lip.

A whistle shrilled in the kitchen. The kettle boiling.

She had finished her tea and her search through the files, and was sunk in a deep dark thought pattern, when a rap came on the window.

She jumped, startled.

Black knuckles pressed against the pane. A white smile gleamed through the glass.

"I say, uh, Miss Kaye, it's Dennis... Captain Rattray, um, Blackfist, don't ch'know... we were wonderin' if you'd care to join us at the Drome for a bit of a feed. Strawberries and cream, what. Hungry work, this sleuthin', I'll be bound."

It took some work to calm down. She smoothed her hair and her skirt, and constructed a smile.

"That would be most pleasant, Captain," she responded, her voice brittle and fakey inside her head. "I'll just have to wash my hands."

"We're terribly informal, I don't mind saying. No need to stand on the old ceremonials."

"Dusty," she said, showing her hands.

Whyever had she done that! The answer was in the dust!

Blackfist smiled and nodded. He was clutching his gem. His whole hand glistened like a bitumen cactus studded with flint-chips.

She passed through into the kitchen, ran the tap over her fingers, dried herself off, and stepped out into the garden.

"Lovely evenin', isn't it? So bally peaceful."

The Captain smelled the breeze and looked at his ease.

"I say, bit of a scrape this afternoon, don't ch'know. Frightful business in the fens. Viking skeleton fellers with axes like, well, like big axes. Some sort of a geas, according to Mystic Mary. Know what a geas is?"

"Yes."

"Cor," he breathed admiration. "I didn't."

It was a warm evening, but she felt a touch of chill in the air. Autumn coming. She feared for the petunias and roses of the Hollyhocks when the frosts came. There was no gardener to see them through the next cold snap.

Blackfist offered her his arm and led her down the garden path, towards a small gate—once wired shut but recently opened by a few judicious snips, she noticed—that led onto the Drome.

At the white filigree table (oblong, not Arthurian) on the lawn, Catriona found herself seated between Chandra N. Seth, the Mystic Maharajah, and Teddy Trimingham, the Blue Streak.

Seth had piercing blue eyes in a carved teak, fearsomely bearded face, and his large, bulbous turban bore a sapphire to match. He reputedly possessed amazing mesmeric and mentalist abilities and had taught Houdini some of the most dangerous fakir tricks, but he also had a high-pitched voice and a strange way of adding "hmmm" to every sentence that would disqualify him from the talkies. Trimingham was squiffy on champagne and kept "accidentally" brushing her thigh as he described the various crashes he had survived. A matinee idol in photographs, his face close-up was shiny and oddly textured, except for goggle-shapes around his eyes. He was proud of the number of times he had caught fire and put out the flames by going faster.

Though Blackfist still blathered about being terribly informal, Lord Piltdown had dressed for dinner in a tropical white tuxedo with a sunflower in the lapel and a white silk hat that perched steadily on his heavy brow-ridge, and Lady Lucinda had exchanged her flying gear for a backless silver cocktail number that cost more than a house in Chelsea. When the Aviatrix turned, Catriona saw the double-row of spiracles outlining her spine, dribbling liquescing traces of wing-matter. The goo was discreetly dabbed away by one of the maids with a towel.

Clever Dick had chocolate all over his face and was explaining how he had known at once the afternoon's phantom horde weren't proper Vikings because they had horns on their helmets.

"Any fool knows it's a fallacy that Viking helms were horned."

"New one on me," said Captain Rattray. "Bless."

Catriona drank good champagne in moderation and scoffed strawberries like someone who had missed dinner. An afternoon in the small and dusty study, not to mention the small and dusty mind, of Mr. Peeter Blame made for a shocking contrast with an evening among the Splendids. She imagined the camps eyeing at each other across the forsythia; rather, she imagined Mr. Blame glaring fury at the Drome and these fantastical creatures barely noticing him. At first. Their world took little account of Peeter Blames, and barely acknowledged Catriona Kayes. She was their guest now because she was seen as the creature—a step above a servant—of Charles Beauregard, who carried some weight in heroic circles even if he stayed out of the public eye.

"I'm surpwised the Diogenes Club has *girls*!"

She thought Clever Dick might have snuck some champers. Or maybe his brain boiled over on chocolate alone.

"I think they would be too," she said.

"Girls," repeated Clever Dick, eyes wide, sneer eager.

Catriona noticed the Aviatrix's mouth pinching tight as if she were restraining herself from slicing a silver salver across Britain's boy brainbox as if topping a breakfast egg. For the first time, she felt a disturbing kinship with the flying woman. Then she remembered the Crocodile's blood raining down on children's faces and the taloned gloves; this rose had thorns.

"How… hmmm… is your most excellent investigation… hmmm… coming?"

She spread her empty hands.

"As I thought… hmmmm… I shall concentrate my third eye… hmmm… and seek answer on the psychic plane."

"She's orff again," belched Trimingham. "Bloody Mystic Mary."

Seth pressed fingertips to his forehead, shut his conventional eyes, and hummed to himself. His gem glowed eerily.

"It's a twick," said Clever Dick, smugly. "A little 'lectric bulb. It's not *weal* magic. Not like Wattway's Fang of Night. That's pwoper magic. The darkie does it all with *twicks*!"

It occurred to Catriona that she had come across Chandra N. Seth before, under another name, when she was chasing fraudulent mediums.

"It doesn't matter if it's a trick," said Lalla. "What matters is if it works."

"Girls *and* darkies. We shouldn't have them. We could go back to being the Good Fellows Four."

"Of whom… hmmm… you were not… hmmm… one."

"Ho, she's awake now," burbled Trimingham.

"The matter is clouded… hmmm… but truth will emerge, as trueness always does and… hmmm… justice will prevail."

The Mystic Maharajah laid a hand on Catriona's and looked deep into her eyes. Clever Dick was wrong about one thing: He wasn't non-Caucasian, but a dyed white man whose name used to be Sid Ramsbottom. His vocal mannerisms were the same, though. Mystic Sid had been on the halls as Woozo the Wizzard.

She laughed the wrong way and champagne got in her nose.

"Sorry," she said.

Seth let go of her hand, and seemed direly offended.

The All-Rounder picked up a bowl-sized teacup, little finger perfectly extended, and raised about a gallon to his mouth, which he sucked down in a long, noisy draught. He dabbed his lips with a napkin and excused himself from the table, bowing formally to Catriona and Lady Lucinda, then bounded across the lawn, raising divots at each clutch, followed by a footman who replaced the sods and smoothed them over by hand.

"Pongo puts in an hour in the nets every night," said Trimingham. "Never know when the MCC will call."

As dark gathered, lamps automatically came on, shining columns rising around the Drome, criss-crossing the lawn, playing like searchlights across the grounds.

"One of mine, you know," said Trimingham. "Inventions."

Every few seconds a roving lighthouse beam shone on the Hollyhocks, bleaching the cottage white.

"We have light all night," said Captain Rattray.

"No darkness... hmmm... need apply."

She could imagine.

"So," said Edwin, springing from his chair as she was admitted into the Strangers Room of the Diogenes Club, "who dun it?"

"Ha ha," said Catriona. "Who didn't?"

Charles Beauregard was also present, which meant that here at least she was taken seriously. In the end, if there weren't such a horrid business at the bottom of it, her trip to Heathrow would have been ridiculous.

"Catriona, would you care for a light lunch?" offered Charles. "Then, we'll debrief."

"I'm fine, thank you Charles."

She had spent the night at the Coat and Dividers, eaten a proper country breakfast prepared by Maggie Brittles (who, surprisingly, was the first person she had met who even tried to seem sorry that Peeter Blame was dead), bade Harbottle a fond farewell (though overnight he'd forgotten who she was), and taken the train up to town.

"Then, if you'd care to oblige, we'll have your report."

She sat in an armchair, allowing the men to return to theirs. As always with Charles in the room, Edwin was boyish, eager to please the house-captain but also concerned with demonstrating his own brand of 20th Century sharpness.

"Do I need to tell you anything? You must already know."

At her tart tone, Charles's face fell.

"And I can't *prove* anything. You must know that too. Someone told me last night that... hmmm, justice will prevail..."

"Chandra Nguyen Ramsbottom, that's him exactly!" exclaimed Edwin. "Mimickry, another of your talents!"

"Well, justice *won't* prevail, will it? In this case, it *can't*."

"Please be assured, Catriona, that you have not been used, that there was a real purpose to what we have asked you to do."

Despite herself, she believed Charles.

"As for proof, well… if I thought there was proof to be had, I'd have sent Edwin. No offence, young fellow, but it's what you're good at and if it's not there you're at a loss. Catriona, I wanted you to look into the murder of Peeter Blame because of your capacity for *feeling*…."

"I beg your pardon."

"Nobody could *like* the deceased, I understand, but that doesn't mean he shouldn't be *felt* for. What happened to him was not permissible. Do you understand?"

She was beginning to.

"So, which of 'em was it?" asked Edwin, flashing a grin. "My ten bob is on that Pongo fellow. Long reach, plenty of cricket bats in his kit, super-human strength…"

"In a small room, he'd have done more damage, I think," she said. "See, I can cope with evidence and proofs too. And it took more delicate fingers to go through Mr. Blame's files and extract all the relevant documents. That said, I wouldn't rule Lord Piltdown out. My *feeling*, since you set so much stock in it, Charles, is that it was Rattray or Trimingham in the study with the blunt instrument, and Lady Lucinda or—and I really mean this—Clever Brat handled the file-filleting to get the Splendids off the hook."

"So you think they *all* did it?"

"If all six can be roped in on a spur-of-the-moment thing, yes."

Charles steepled his fingers and considered the case.

"To sum up," he began, "what's missing from the files?"

"All documentation in connection with lawsuits Blame was trying to bring against the Splendid Six, collectively or as individuals. My feeling—that word again—is that there were dozens of them. Just sitting in his cottage for a day, I saw a dozen different ways in which an ordinary person would be infuriated by having clubland heroes as next-door neighbours, and Peeter Blame was far touchier than the average."

"You've ruled out any link between him and their recorded enemies? That Clockwork fellow or the Demon Ace?"

"Edwin, I thought of that. No, this had nothing to do with defending the realm or warding off villains vile. It was about roses shrivelled by passing cars and bright lights shone into the cottage at all hours of the night and people flying overhead heedless of who crawled below and grumbled. It was about the *noise*, and the *view*, and the *commotion*, and the *flaunting*, and the *obnoxiousness*. And frustration, because Blame could sue and sue all he liked, but no court in the land was going to haul in a hero of the age of marvels. Every complaint he lodged would have been quietly quashed. He managed to get rid of a local Justice of the Peace, remember. He must have thought that a victory which would clear the way for a new local bench to sympathise with his complaints. That's how bloody stupid he was; he really thought that getting a JP sacked wouldn't set the county judiciary against him forever. He believed all that stuff about impartial justice that we're supposed to uphold. My guess is that, frustrated in his usual avenue of action, he took to complaining in person, over the hedge, at every opportunity, nagging, whining, moaning..."

Charles nodded.

"And one of them snapped," he concluded. "Went over, maybe to make a gesture of peace, found Blame resolute, not properly respectful of a national hero. So our Splendid killed him, in a moment. The others clubbed together, tidied up, and walked away..."

"And called *you* to get it dealt with."

His face darkened. "Yes, Catriona. They called me."

"That's what annoys you, isn't it? That's why you'll have them for this. Not for the murder—after all, this is 1927, everyone we know has killed someone or something—but for treating the Diogenes Club like a window-washing service."

"I say, Catty-Kit, that's going a bit far..."

"I hope I'm better than that, Catriona."

"I hope you are too."

Charles rose. Above the fireplace hung a portrait of a corpulent man with gimlet eyes, in immaculate Victorian morning dress. One of the Club's founders, and literally a huge figure in the secret world. Charles looked up to him, and thought.

"I'm sorry," she said. "But this business is all about getting angry. Blame was angry, permanently. His murderer lost his rag for a moment. Now it's me and you. This is what appals me the most, the *contempt*. To them, Blame wasn't even worth using their abilities. No black fist or mystic energies or invented contraption, just a plain old common or garden cosh, as used by the dimmest thug. I admit if it were otherwise, we'd have them bang to rights. But it wasn't calculated. Peeter Blame wasn't really murdered, he was *swatted*—like a midge."

Charles turned.

"This, Catriona, is what I will promise. The Drome will fall. A wrong done to the least of the King's subjects is still a wrong, no matter how eminent the wrong-doer might be. The Splendid Six will be removed from the game."

"And the game goes on?"

"Of course. But while I have anything to say about it, rules will be observed."

Charles Beauregard turned again, and looked into the empty, cold fireplace.

Edwin held her arm and escorted her out of the Strangers Room.

It happened over months. She perceived the fingers of Charles Beauregard pulling loose ends. Sometimes, she suspected he merely stayed his hand, suspending services that would otherwise step in to protect the Splendids from themselves.

Trimingham suffered a serious smash-up on the proving grounds, and his insurers finally cavilled at the loss, repudiating his daredevilry as a compulsive, nigh-suicidal mania for taking unnecessary risks, which drove his inventing businesses into insolvency. Lady Lucinda, turning thirty, was struck by a debilitating ailment which led to a permanent loss of her power of flight (she could still grow wings but they wouldn't lift her). Clever Dick's investment portfolio went down in flames with the Wall Street Crash and he became a recluse, suffering a serious case of teenage facial eruptions which led unkind souls to rename him "Spotted Dick." Lord Piltdown, searching for his Northern roots, simply disappeared on a fjord, leaving behind an elegant but empty suit and shaggy footprints that gave out on glacial ice. The MCC missed him dreadfully and she couldn't help but wonder if the Neolithic Nobleman hadn't been the only true innocent among the Splendids. Captain Rattray made an unwise marriage to a mercenary Tiller girl and, fifteen days later, was the first of the Splendids actually to be hauled into court (Peeter Blame, you are avenged!). His divorce action drew mildly mocking, then outright critical, press comment, as more and more lurid detail spilled out in the dock. Noel Coward penned a witty, nasty revue sketch that made Blackfist impossible to take seriously, especially when the whole truth came out about the long-term physical alterations wrought upon his body by the Fang of Night. Chandra Seth announced to the world that he would perform a fabulous feat of endurance, buried in a glass coffin on the banks of the Thames for a month, but had to be rescued after three days when panicky humming alarmed passersby. In the wake of this fiasco, five women showed up alleging that they were deserted wives of the Mystic Maharajah, who had lived under a bewildering number of names. The line-up and thus the name fluctuated: the Splendid Five, then Three, then it was all off.

The Splendids were eclipsed in popular imagination by the dramatic and headline-hogging reappearance of a dark defender (the original Doctor Shade!) once thought dead. *British Pluck* suspended its serial exploits of the Six, and began to run stories of Shade, who worked alone and struck by night, travelling from his secret lair in Big Ben by autogyro to combat the enemies of decency. Catriona wondered what the point was of having a secret lair but letting everyone know the address?

"Happy now?" asked Edwin, tossing her a folded *Herald*.

They were in the flat, warmed by a nice coal fire as the first January of a new decade brought snow to the city. The puzzle box was on a mantelpiece, undisturbed for some months. There were new matters mysterious, requiring the attention of the Diogenes Club. And Catriona had been freshly accorded the privileged status of Lady Member, prompting a serious blood pressure condition for Sir Henry Merrivale. He was not mollified by the fact that she was obliged by oath not to own up to her status for at least fifty years after her death.

She looked at a foot-of-the-column note in the paper.

"The Heathrow Drome has been reclaimed by HM Government," said Edwin, "set aside for purposes of military aviation."

"That'll gobble up the Hollyhocks as well."

"They'd never have got an airfield sited with Blame next door to file suit against the scheme."

"True."

Though no longer eminent, the Splendid Six were all free. No one had ever answered in court for the murder of Peeter Blame.

"Catty-Kit, you've pursued this hawklike. Were they that bad"

"They were worse, Edwin. That's what I feel."

He put his arms around her.

"And that's why we value you."

"For having feelings you know you ought to have but can't stretch to?"

"That's a fairly merciless way of putting it."

"But no argument from you."

Charles and Edwin were clubland heroes too, veterans of wars that didn't make it to the history books. They quietly refused the offered knighthoods and would never murder anyone who happened across their way, but they worked in the same arena as the Splendid Six and Doctor Shade, coping with the worst of the world, mulling over intelligence which would cause anarchic panic if it became public knowledge. They had to contain in their minds a big picture, the sweep of an ongoing saga of adventure.

Which was why they needed her. To ground them in the importance of the mundanities, to speak for those in whose name the great struggles were undertaken. Charles understood that deeply—she had been surprised to learn that she was not the first Lady Member associated with the Diogenes Club—and Edwin superficially, though he would grow into a proper understanding.

Without her, they might be monsters too.

THE BIG FISH

The Bay City cops were rousting enemy aliens. As I drove through the nasty coast town, uniforms hauled an old couple out of a grocery store. The Taraki family's neighbours huddled in thin rain, howling asthmatically for bloody revenge. Pearl Harbor had struck a lot of people that way. With the Tarakis on the bus for Manzanar, neighbours descended on the store like bedraggled vultures. Produce vanished instantly, then destruction started. Caught at a sleepy stop light, I got a good look. The Tarakis had lived over the store; now, their furniture was thrown out of the second-storey window. Fine china shattered on the sidewalk, spilling white chips like teeth into the gutter. It was inspirational, the forces of democracy rallying round to protect the United States from vicious oriental grocers, fiendishly intent on selling eggplant to a hapless civilian population.

Meanwhile my appointment was with a gent who kept three pictures on his mantelpiece, grouped in a triangle around a statue of the Virgin Mary. At the apex was his white-haired mama, to the left Charles Luciano, and to the right, Benito Mussolini. The Tarakis, American-born and registered Democrats, were headed to a dustbowl concentration camp for the duration, while Gianni Pastore, Sicilian-born and highly unregistered *capo* of the Family Business, would spend his war in a marble-fronted mansion paid for by nickels and dimes dropped on the numbers game, into slot machines, or exchanged for the favours of nice girls from the old country. I'd seen his mansion before and so far been able to resist the temptation to bean one of his twelve muse statues with a bourbon bottle.

Money can buy you love but can't even put down a deposit on good taste.

The palace was up in the hills, a little way down the boulevard from Tyrone Power. But now, Pastore was hanging his mink-banded fedora in a Bay City beachfront motel complex, which was a real estate agent's term for a bunch of horrible shacks shoved together for the convenience of people who like sand on their carpets.

I always take a lungful of fresh air before entering a confined space with someone in Pastore's business, so I parked the Chrysler a few blocks from the Seaview Inn and walked the rest of the way, sucking on a Camel to keep warm in the wet. They say it doesn't rain in Southern California, but they also say the U.S. Navy could never be taken by surprise. This February, three months into a war the rest of the world had been fighting since 1936 or 1939 depending on whether you were Chinese or Polish, it was raining almost constantly, varying between a light fall of misty drizzle in the dreary daytimes to spectacular storms, complete with DeMille lighting effects, in our fear-filled nights. Those trusty Boy Scouts scanning the horizons for Jap subs and Nazi U-boats were filling up influenza wards, and manufacturers of raincoats and umbrellas who'd not yet converted their plants to defense production were making a killing. I didn't mind the rain. At least rainwater is clean, unlike most other things in Bay City.

A small boy with a wooden gun leaped out of a bush and sprayed me with sound effects, interrupting his onomatopoeic chirruping with a shout of "die you slant-eyed Jap!" I clutched my heart, staggered back, and he finished me off with a quick burst. I died for the Emperor and tipped the kid a dime to go away. If this went on long enough, maybe little Johnny would get a chance to march off and do real killing, then maybe come home in a box or with the shakes or a taste for blood. Meanwhile, especially since someone spotted a Jap submarine off Santa Barbara, California was gearing up for the War Effort. Aside from interning grocers, our best brains were writing songs like "To Be Specific, It's Our Pacific," "So Long Momma, I'm Off to Yokahama," "We're Gonna Slap the Jap Right Off the Map," and "When Those Little Yellow Bellies Meet the Cohens and the Kellys." Zanuck had donated his string of Argentine polo ponies to West Point and got himself measured for a comic opera Colonel's uniform so he could join the Signal Corps and defeat the Axis by posing for publicity photographs.

I'd tried to join up two days after Pearl Harbor but they kicked me back onto the streets. Too many concussions. Apparently, I get hit on the head too often and have a tendency to black out. When they came to mention it, they were right.

The Seaview Inn was shuttered, one of the first casualties of war. It had its own jetty, and by it were a few canvas-covered motor launches shifting with the waves. In late afternoon gloom, I saw the silhouette of the *Montecito*, anchored strategically outside the three-mile limit. That was one good thing about the Japanese; on the downside, they might have sunk most of the U.S. fleet, but on the up, they'd put Laird Brunette's gambling ship out of business. Nobody was enthusiastic about losing their shirt-buttons on a rigged roulette wheel if they imagined they were going to be torpedoed any moment. I'd have thought that would add an extra thrill to the whole gay, delirious business of giving Brunette money, but I'm just a poor, twenty-five-dollars-a-day detective.

The Seaview Inn was supposed to be a stopping-off point on the way to the *Monty* and now its trade was stopped off. The main building was sculpted out of dusty ice cream and looked like a three-storey radiogram with wave-scallop friezes. I pushed through double doors and entered the lobby. The floor was decorated with a mosaic in which Neptune, looking like an angry Santa Claus in a swimsuit, was sticking it to a sea-nymph who shared a hairdresser with Hedy Lamarr. The nymph was naked except for some strategic shells. It was very artistic.

There was nobody at the desk and thumping the bell didn't improve matters. Water ran down the outside of the green-tinted windows. There were a few steady drips somewhere. I lit up another Camel and went exploring. The office was locked and the desk register didn't have any entries after December 7, 1941. My raincoat dripped and began to dry out, sticking my jacket and shirt to my shoulders. I shrugged, trying to get some air into my clothes. I noticed Neptune's face quivering. A thin layer of water had pooled over the mosaic and various anemone-like fronds attached to the sea god were apparently getting excited. Looking at the nymph, I could understand that. Actually, I realised, only the hair was from Hedy. The face and the body were strictly Janey Wilde.

I go to the movies a lot but I'd missed most of Janey's credits: *She-Strangler of Shanghai*, *Tarzan and the Tiger Girl*, *Perils of Jungle Jillian*. I'd seen her in the newspapers though, often in unnervingly close proximity with Pastore or Brunette. She'd started as an Olympic swimmer, picking up medals in Berlin, then followed Weissmuller and Crabbe to Hollywood. She would never get an Academy Award but her legs were in a lot of cheesecake stills publicising no particular movie. Air-brushed and made-up like a good-looking corpse, she was a fine commercial for sex. In person she was as bubbly as domestic champagne, though now running to flat. Things were slow in the detecting business, since people were more worried about imminent invasion than missing daughters or misplaced love letters. So when Janey Wilde called on me in my office in the Cahuenga Building and asked me to look up one of her ill-chosen men friends, I checked the pile of old envelopes I use as a desk diary and informed her that I was available to make inquiries into the current whereabouts of a certain big fish.

Wherever Laird Brunette was, he wasn't here. I was beginning to figure Gianni Pastore, the gambler's partner, wasn't here either. Which meant I'd wasted an afternoon. Outside it rained harder, driving against the walls with a drumlike tattoo. Either there were hailstones mixed in with the water or the Jap air force was hurling fistfuls of pebbles at Bay City to demoralise the population. I don't know why they bothered. All Hirohito had to do was slip a thick envelope to the Bay City cops and the city's finest would hand over the whole community to the Japanese Empire with a ribbon around it and a bow on top.

There were more puddles in the lobby, little streams running from one to the other. I was reminded of the episode of *The Perils of Jungle Jillian* I had seen while tailing a child molester to a Saturday matinee. At the end, Janey Wilde had been caught by the Panther Princess and trapped in a room which slowly filled with water. That room had been a lot smaller than the lobby of the Seaview Inn and the water had come in a lot faster.

Behind the desk were framed photographs of pretty people in pretty clothes having a pretty time. Pastore was there, and Brunette, grinning like tiger cats, mingling with showfolk: Xavier Cugat, Janey Wilde, Charles Coburn. Janice Marsh, the pop-eyed beauty rumoured to have replaced Jungle Jillian in Brunette's affections, was well represented in artistic poses.

On the phone, Pastore had promised faithfully to be here. He hadn't wanted to bother with a small-timer like me but Janey Wilde's name opened a door. I had a feeling Papa Pastore was relieved to be shaken down about Brunette, as if he wanted to talk about something. He must be busy because there were several wars on. The big one overseas and a few little ones at home. Maxie Rothko, bar owner and junior partner in the *Monty*, had been found drifting in the seaweed around the Santa Monica pier without much of a head to speak of. And Phil Isinglass, man-about-town lawyer and Brunette frontman, had turned up in the storm drains, lungs full of sandy mud. Disappearing was the latest craze in Brunette's organisation. That didn't sound good for Janey Wilde, though Pastore had talked about the Laird as if he knew Brunette was alive. But now Papa wasn't around. I was getting annoyed with someone it wasn't sensible to be annoyed with.

Pastore wouldn't be in any of the beach shacks, but there should be an apartment for his convenience in the main building. I decided to explore further. Jungle Jillian would expect no less. She'd hired me for five days in advance, a good thing since I'm unduly reliant on eating and drinking and other expensive diversions of the monied and idle.

The corridor that led past the office ended in a walk-up staircase. As soon as I put my size nines on the first step, it squelched. I realised something was more than usually wrong. The steps were a quiet little waterfall, seeping rather than cascading. It wasn't just water, there was unpleasant, slimy stuff mixed in. Someone had left the bath running. My first thought was that Pastore had been distracted by a bullet. I was wrong. In the long run, he might have been happier if I'd been right.

I climbed the soggy stairs and found the apartment door unlocked but shut. Bracing myself, I pushed the door in. It encountered resistance but then sliced open, allowing a gush of water to shoot around my ankles, soaking my dark blue socks. Along with water was a three-weeks-dead-in-the-water-with-rotten-fish smell that wrapped around me like a blanket. Holding my breath, I stepped into the room. The waterfall flowed faster now. I heard a faucet running. A radio played, with funny little gurgles mixed in. A crooner was doing his best with "Life is Just a Bowl of Cherries," but he sounded as if he were drowned full fathom five. I followed the music and found the bathroom.

Pastore was face down in the overflowing tub, the song coming from under him. He wore a silk lounging robe that had been pulled away from his back, his wrists tied behind him with the robe's cord. In the end he'd been drowned. But before that hands had been laid on him, either in anger or with cold, professional skill. I'm not a coroner, so I couldn't tell how long the Family Man had been in the water. The radio still playing and the water still running suggested Gianni had met his end recently, but the stench felt older than sin.

I have a bad habit of finding bodies in Bay City and the most profit-minded police force in the country have a bad habit of trying to make connections between me and a wide variety of deceased persons. The obvious solution in this case was to make a friendly phone call, absent-mindedly forgetting to mention my name while giving the flatfeet directions to the late Mr. Pastore. Who knows, I might accidentally talk to someone honest.

That is exactly what I would have done if, just then, the man with the gun hadn't come through the door....

I had Janey Wilde to blame. She'd arrived without an appointment, having picked me on a recommendation. Oddly, Laird Brunette had once said something not entirely uncomplimentary about me. We'd met. We hadn't seriously tried to kill each other in a while. That was as good a basis for a relationship as any.

Out of her sarong, Jungle Jillian favoured sharp shoulders and a veiled pillbox. The kiddies at the matinee had liked her fine, especially when she was wrestling stuffed snakes, and dutiful Daddies took no exception to her either, especially when she was tied down and her sarong rode up a few inches. Her lips were four red grapes plumped together. When she crossed her legs you saw swimmer's smooth muscle under her hose.

"He's very sweet, really," she explained, meaning Mr. Brunette never killed anyone within ten miles of her without apologising afterwards, "not at all like they say in those dreadful scandal sheets."

The gambler had been strange recently, especially since the war shut him down. Actually the *Montecito* had been out of commission for nearly a year, supposedly for a refit although as far as Janey Wilde knew no workmen had been sent out to the ship. At about the time Brunette suspended his crooked wheels, he came down with a common California complaint, a dose of crackpot religion. He'd been tangentially mixed up a few years ago with a psychic racket run by a bird named Amthor, but had apparently shifted from the mostly harmless bunco cults onto the hard stuff. Spiritualism, orgiastic rites, chanting, incense, the whole deal.

Janey blamed this sudden interest in matters occult on Janice Marsh, who had coincidentally made her name as the Panther Princess in *The Perils of Jungle Jillian*, a role which required her to torture Janey Wilde at least once every chapter. My employer didn't mention that her own career had hardly soared between *Jungle Jillian* and *She-Strangler of Shanghai*, while the erstwhile Panther Princess had gone from Republic to Metro and was being built up as an exotic in the Dietrich–Garbo vein. Say what you like about Janice Marsh's *Nefertiti*, she still looked like Peter Lorre to me. And according to Janey, the star had more peculiar tastes than a seafood buffet.

Brunette had apparently joined a series of fringe organisations and become quite involved, to the extent of neglecting his business and thereby irking his long-time partner, Gianni Pastore. Perhaps that was why person or persons unknown had decided the Laird wouldn't mind if his associates died one by one. I couldn't figure it out. The cults I'd come across mostly stayed in business by selling sex, drugs, power, or reassurance to rich, stupid people. The Laird hardly fell into the category. He was too big a fish for that particular bowl.

The man with the gun was English, with a Ronald Colman accent and a white aviator's scarf. He was not alone. The quiet, truck-sized bruiser I made as a fed went through my wallet while the dapper foreigner kept his automatic pointed casually at my middle.

"Peeper," the fed snarled, showing the photostat of my license and my supposedly impressive deputy's badge.

"Interesting," said the Britisher, slipping his gun into the pocket of his camel coat. Immaculate, he must have been umbrella-protected between car and building because there wasn't a spot of rain on him. "I'm Winthrop. Edwin Winthrop."

We shook hands. His other companion, the interesting one, was going through the deceased's papers. She looked up, smiled with sharp white teeth, and got back to work.

"This is Mademoiselle Dieudonné."

"Geneviève," she said. She pronounced it "Zhe-ne-vyev," suggesting Paris, France. She was wearing something white with silver in it and had quantities of pale blonde hair.

"And the gentleman from your Federal Bureau of Investigation is Finlay."

The fed grunted. He looked as if he'd been brought to life by Willis H. O'Brien.

"You are interested in a Mr. Brunette," Winthrop said. It was not a question, so there was no point in answering him. "So are we."

"Call in a Russian and we could be the Allies," I said.

Winthrop laughed. He was sharp. "True. I am here at the request of my government and working with the full co-operation of yours."

One of the small detective-type details I noticed was that no one even suggested that informing the police about Gianni Pastore was a good idea.

"Have you ever heard of a place called Innsmouth, Massachusetts?"

It didn't mean anything to me and I said so.

"Count yourself lucky. Special Agent Finlay's associates were called upon to dynamite certain unsafe structures in the sea off Innsmouth back in the twenties. It was a bad business."

Geneviève said something sharp in French that sounded like swearing. She held up a photograph of Brunette dancing cheek to cheek with Janice Marsh.

"Do you know the lady?" Winthrop asked.

"Only in the movies. Some go for her in a big way but I think she looks like Mr. Moto."

"Very true. Does the Esoteric Order of Dagon mean anything to you?"

"Sounds like a Church-of-the-Month alternate. Otherwise, no."

"Captain Obed Marsh?"

"Uh-uh."

"The Deep Ones?"

"Are they those coloured singers?"

"What about Cthulhu, Y'ha-nthlei, R'lyeh?"

"*Gesundheit.*"

Winthrop grinned, sharp moustache pointing. "No, not easy to say at all. Hard to fit into human mouths, you know."

"He's just a bedroom creeper," Finlay said, "he don't know nothing."

"His grammar could be better. Doesn't J. Edgar pay for elocution lessons?"

Finlay's big hands opened and closed as if he were rather there were a throat in them.

"Gené?" Winthrop said.

The woman looked up, red tongue absently flicking across her red lips, and thought a moment. She said something in a foreign language that I did understand.

"There's no need to kill him," she said in French. *Thank you very much*, I thought.

Winthrop shrugged and said "fine by me." Finlay looked disappointed.

"You're free to go," the Britisher told me. "We shall take care of everything. I see no point in your continuing your current line of inquiry. Send in a chit to this address," he handed me a card, "and you'll be reimbursed for your expenses so far. Don't worry. We'll carry on until this is seen through. By the way, you might care not to discuss with anyone what you've seen here or anything I may have said. There's a War on, you know. Loose lips sink ships."

I had a few clever answers but I swallowed them and left. Anyone who thought there was no need to kill me was all right in my book, and I wasn't using my razored tongue on them. As I walked to the Chrysler, several ostentatiously unofficial cars cruised past me, headed for the Seaview Inn.

It was getting dark and lightning was striking down out at sea. A flash lit up the *Montecito* and I counted five seconds before the thunder boomed. I had the feeling there was something out there beyond the three-mile limit besides the floating former casino, and that it was angry.

I slipped into the Chrysler and drove away from Bay City, feeling better the further inland I got.

I take *Black Mask*. It's a long time since Hammett and the fellow who wrote the Ted Carmady stories were in it, but you occasionally get a good Cornell Woolrich or Erle Stanley Gardner. Back at my office, I saw the newsboy had been by and dropped off the *Times* and next month's pulp. But there'd been a mix-up. Instead of the *Mask*, there was something inside the folded newspaper called *Weird Tales*. On the cover, a man was being attacked by two green demons and a stereotype vampire with a widow's peak. "'Hell on Earth,' a Novelette of Satan in a Tuxedo by Robert Bloch" was blazed above the title. Also promised were "A new Lovecraft series, 'Herbert West—Re-Animator' and 'The Rat Master' by Greye la Spina." All for fifteen cents, kids. If I were a different type of detective, the brand who said *nom de* something and waxed a moustache whenever he found a mutilated corpse, I might have thought the substitution an omen.

In my office, I've always had five filing cabinets, three empty. I also had two bottles, only one empty. In a few hours, the situation would have changed by one bottle.

I found a glass without too much dust and wiped it with my clean handkerchief. I poured myself a generous slug and hit the back of my throat with it.

The radio didn't work but I could hear Glenn Miller from somewhere. I found my glass empty and dealt with that. Sitting behind my desk, I looked at the patterns in rain on the window. If I craned I could see traffic on Hollywood Boulevard. People who didn't spend their working days finding bodies in bathtubs were going home not to spend their evenings emptying a bottle.

After a day, I'd had some excitement but I hadn't done much for Janey Wilde. I was no nearer being able to explain the absence of Mr. Brunette from his usual haunts than I had been when she left my office, leaving behind a tantalising whiff of *essence de chine*.

She'd given me some literature pertaining to Brunette's cult involvement. Now, the third slug warming me up inside, I looked over it, waiting for inspiration to strike. Interesting echoes came up in relation to Winthrop's shopping list of subjects of peculiar interest. I had no luck with the alphabet soup syllables he'd spat at me, mainly because "Cthulhu" sounds more like a cough than a word. But the Esoteric Order of Dagon was a group Brunette had joined, and Innsmouth, Massachusetts, was the East Coast town where the organisation was registered. The Esoteric Order had a temple on the beach front in Venice, and its mumbo-jumbo hand-outs promised "ancient and intriguing rites to probe the mysteries of the Deep." Slipped in with the recruitment bills was a studio biography of Janice Marsh, which helpfully revealed the movie star's place of birth as Innsmouth, Massachusetts, and that she could trace her family back to Captain Obed Marsh, the famous early 19th Century explorer of whom I'd never heard. Obviously Winthrop, Geneviève, and the FBI were well ahead of me in making connections. And I didn't really know who the Englishman and the French girl were.

I wondered if I wouldn't have been better off reading *Weird Tales*. I liked the sound of Satan in a Tuxedo. It wasn't Ted Carmady with an automatic and a dame, but it would do. There was a lot more thunder and lightning and I finished the bottle. I suppose I could have gone home to sleep but the chair was no more uncomfortable than my Murphy bed.

The empty bottle rolled and I settled down, tie loose, to forget the cares of the day.

Thanks to the War, Pastore only made Page 3 of the *Times*. Apparently the noted gambler-entrepreneur had been shot to death. If that was true, it had happened after I'd left. Then, he'd only been tortured and drowned. Police Chief John Wax dished out his usual "over by Christmas" quote about the investigation. There was no mention of the FBI, or of our allies, John Bull in a tux and Mademoiselle la Guillotine. In prison, you get papers with neat oblongs cut out to remove articles the censor feels provocative. They don't make any difference: All newspapers have invisible oblongs. Pastore's sterling work with underprivileged kids was mentioned but someone forgot to write about the junk he sold them when they grew into underprivileged adults. The obit photograph found him with Janey Wilde and Janice Marsh at the premiere of a George Raft movie. The phantom Jap sub off Santa Barbara got more column inches. General John L. DeWitt, head of the Western Defense Command, called for more troops to guard the coastline, prophesying "death and destruction are likely to come at any moment." Everyone in California was looking out to sea.

After my regular morning conference with Mr. Huggins and Mr. Young, I placed a call to Janey Wilde's Malibu residence. Most screen idols are either at the studio or asleep if you telephone before ten o'clock in the morning, but Janey, with weeks to go before shooting started on *Bowery to Bataan*, was at home and awake, having done her thirty lengths. Unlike almost everyone else in the industry, she thought a swimming pool was for swimming in rather than lounging beside.

She remembered instantly who I was and asked for news. I gave her a *precis*.

"I've been politely asked to refrain from further investigations," I explained. "By some heavy hitters."

"So you're quitting?"

I should have said yes, but "Miss Wilde, only you can require me to quit. I thought you should know how the federal government feels."

There was a pause.

"There's something I didn't tell you," she told me. It was an expression common among my clients. "Something important."

I let dead air hang on the line.

"It's not so much Laird that I'm concerned about. It's that he has Franklin."

"Franklin?"

"The baby," she said. "Our baby. My baby."

"Laird Brunette has disappeared, taking a baby with him?"

"Yes."

"Kidnapping is a crime. You might consider calling the cops."

"A lot of things are crimes. Laird has done many of them and never spent a day in prison."

That was true, which was why this development was strange. Kidnapping, whether personal or for profit, is the riskiest of crimes. As a rule, it's the province only of the stupidest criminals. Laird Brunette was not a stupid criminal.

"I can't afford bad publicity. Not when I'm so near to the roles I need."

Bowery to Bataan was going to put her among the screen immortals.

"Franklin is supposed to be Esther's boy. In a few years, I'll adopt him legally. Esther is my house-keeper. It'll work out. But I must have him back."

"Laird is the father. He will have some rights."

"He said he wasn't interested. He... um, moved on... to Janice Marsh while I was... before Franklin was born."

"He's had a sudden attack of fatherhood and you're not convinced?"

"I'm worried to distraction. It's not Laird, it's her. Janice Marsh wants my baby for something vile. I want you to get Franklin back."

"As I mentioned, kidnapping is a crime."

"If there's a danger to the child, surely..."

"Do you have any proof that there is danger?"

"Well, no."

"Have Laird Brunette or Janice Marsh ever given you reason to believe they have ill will for the baby?"

"Not exactly."

I considered things.

"I'll continue with the job you hired me for, but you understand that's all I can do. If I find Brunette, I'll pass your worries on. Then it's between the two of you."

She thanked me in a flood and I got off the phone feeling I'd taken a couple of strides further into the La Brea tar pits and could feel sucking stickiness well above my knees.

I should have stayed out of the rain and concentrated on chess problems but I had another four days' worth of Jungle Jillian's retainer in my pocket and an address for the Esoteric Order of Dagon in a clipping from a lunatic scientific journal. So I drove out to Venice, reminding myself all the way that my wipers needed fixing.

Venice, California, is a fascinating idea that didn't work. Someone named Abbot Kinney had the notion of artificially creating a city like Venice, Italy, with canals and architecture. The canals mostly ran dry and the architecture never really caught on in a town where, in the twenties, Gloria Swanson's bathroom was considered an aesthetic triumph. All that was left was the beach and piles of rotting fish. Venice, Italy, is the Plague Capital of Europe, so Venice, California, got one thing right.

The Esoteric Order was up the coast from Muscle Beach, housed in a discreet yacht club building with its own small marina. From the exterior, I guessed the cult business had seen better days. Seaweed had tracked up the beach, swarmed around the jetty, and was licking the lower edges of the front wall. Everything had gone green: wood, plaster, copper ornaments. And it smelled like Pastore's bathroom, only worse. This kind of place made you wonder why the Japs were so keen on invading.

I looked at myself in the mirror and rolled my eyes. I tried to get that slap-happy, let-me-give-you-all-my-worldly-goods, gimme-some-mysteries-of-the-orient look I imagined typical of a communicant at one of these bughouse congregations. After I'd stopped laughing, I remembered the marks on Pastore and tried to take detecting seriously. Taking in my unshaven, slept-upright-in-his-clothes, two-bottles-a-day lost soul look, I congratulated myself on my foresight in spending fifteen years developing the ideal cover for a job like this.

To get in the building, I had to go down to the marina and come at it from the beach-side. There were green pillars of what looked like fungus-eaten cardboard either side of the impressive front door, which held a stained glass picture in shades of green and blue of a man with the head of a squid in a natty monk's number, waving his eyes for the artist. Dagon, I happened to know, was half-man, half-fish, and God of the Philistines. In this town, I guess a Philistine God blended in well. It's a great country: if you're half-fish, pay most of your taxes, eat babies, and aren't Japanese, you have a wonderful future.

I rapped on the squid's head but nothing happened. I looked the squid in several of his eyes and felt squirmy inside. Somehow, up close, cephalopod-face didn't look that silly.

I pushed the door and found myself in a temple's waiting room. It was what I'd expected: subdued lighting, old but bad paintings, a few semipornographic statuettes, a strong smell of last night's incense to cover up the fish stink. It had as much religious atmosphere as a two-dollar bordello.

"Yoo-hoo," I said, "Dagon calling…"

My voice sounded less funny echoed back at me.

I prowled, sniffing for clues. I tried saying *nom de* something and twiddling a nonexistent moustache but nothing came to me. Perhaps I ought to switch to a meerschaum of cocaine and a deerstalker, or maybe a monocle and an interest in incunabula.

Where you'd expect a portrait of George Washington or Jean Harlow's Mother, the Order had hung up an impressively ugly picture of "Our Founder." Capt. Obed Marsh, dressed up like Admiral Butler, stood on the shore of a Polynesian paradise, his good ship painted with no sense of perspective on the horizon as if it were about three feet tall. The Capt., surrounded by adoring if funny-faced native tomatoes, looked about as unhappy as Errol Flynn at a Girl Scout meeting. The painter had taken a lot of trouble with the native nudes. One of the dusky lovelies had hips that would make Lombard green and a face that put me in mind of Janice Marsh. She was probably the Panther Princess's great-great-great grandmother. In the background, just in front of the ship, was something like a squid emerging from the sea. Fumble-fingers with a brush had tripped up again. It looked as if the tentacle-waving creature were about twice the size of Obed's clipper. The most upsetting detail was a robed and masked figure standing on the deck with a baby's ankle in each fist. He had apparently just wrenched the child apart like a wishbone and was emptying blood into the squid's eyes.

"Excuse me," gargled a voice, "can I help you?"

I turned around and got a noseful of the stooped and ancient Guardian of the Cult. His robe matched the ones worn by squid-features on the door and baby-ripper in the portrait. He kept his face shadowed, his voice sounded about as good as the radio in Pastore's bath, and his breath smelled worse than Pastore after a week and a half of putrefaction.

"Good morning," I said, letting a bird flutter in the higher ranges of my voice, "my name is, er…"

I put together the first things that came to mind.

"My name is Herbert West Lovecraft. Uh, H.W. Lovecraft the Third. I'm simply fascinated by matters Ancient and Esoteric, don't ch'know."

"Don't ch'know" I picked up from the fellow with the monocle and the old books.

"You wouldn't happen to have an entry blank, would you? Or any incunabula?"

"Incunabula?" He wheezed.

"Books. Old books. Print books, published before 1500 *anno domini*, old sport." See, I have a dictionary too.

"Books…"

The man was a monotonous conversationalist. He also moved like Laughton in *The Hunchback of Notre Dame* and the front of his robe, where the squidhead was embroidered, was wet with what I was disgusted to deduce was drool.

"Old books. Arcane mysteries, don't ch'know. Anything cyclopaean and doom-haunted is just up my old alley."

"The *Necronomicon*?" He pronounced it with great respect, and great difficulty.

"Sounds just the ticket."

Quasimodo shook his head under his hood and it lolled. I glimpsed greenish skin and large, moist eyes.

"I was recommended to come here by an old pal," I said. "Spiffing fellow. Laird Brunette. Ever hear of him?"

I'd pushed the wrong button. Quasi straightened out and grew about two feet. Those moist eyes flashed like razors.

"You'll have to see the Cap'n's Daughter."

I didn't like the sound of that and stepped backwards, towards the door. Quasi laid a hand on my shoulder and held it fast. He was wearing mittens and I felt he had too many fingers inside them. His grip was like a gila monster's jaw.

"That will be fine," I said, dropping the flutter.

As if arranged, curtains parted, and I was shoved through a door. Cracking my head on the low lintel, I could see why Quasi spent most of his time hunched over. I had to bend at the neck and knees to go down the corridor. The exterior might be rotten old wood but the heart of the place was solid stone. The walls were damp, bare, and covered in suggestive carvings that gave primitive art a bad name. You'd have thought I'd be getting used to the smell by now, but nothing doing. I nearly gagged.

Quasi pushed me through another door. I was in a meeting room no larger than Union Station, with a stage, rows of comfortable armchairs, and lots more squid-person statues. The centrepiece was very like the mosaic at the Seaview Inn, only the nymph had less shells and Neptune more tentacles.

Quasi vanished, slamming the door behind him. I strolled over to the stage and looked at a huge book perched on a straining lectern. The fellow with the monocle would have salivated, because this looked a lot older than 1500. It wasn't a Bible and didn't smell healthy. It was open to an illustration of something with tentacles and slime, facing a page written in several deservedly dead languages.

"The *Necronomicon*," said a throaty female voice, "of the mad Arab, Abdul Al-Hazred."

"Mad, huh?" I turned to the speaker. "Is he not getting his royalties?"

I recognised Janice Marsh straight away. The Panther Princess wore a turban and green silk lounging pajamas, with a floor-length housecoat that cost more than I make in a year. She had on jade earrings, a pearl cluster pendant, and a ruby-eyed silver squid brooch. The lighting made her face look green and her round eyes shone. She still looked like Peter Lorre, but maybe if Lorre put his face on a body like Janice Marsh's, he'd be up for sex goddess roles too. Her silk thighs purred against each other as she walked down the temple aisle.

"Mr. Lovecraft, isn't it?"

"Call me H.W. Everyone does."

"Have I heard of you?"

"I doubt it."

She was close now. A tall girl, she could look me in the eye. I had the feeling the eye-jewel in her turban was looking me in the brain. She let her fingers fall on the tentacle picture for a moment, allowed them to play around like a fun-loving spider, then removed them to my upper arm, delicately tugging me away from the book. I wasn't unhappy about that. Maybe I'm allergic to incunabula or perhaps an undiscovered prejudice against tentacled creatures, but I didn't like being near the *Necronomicon* one bit. Certainly the experience didn't compare with being near Janice Marsh.

"You're the Cap'n's Daughter?" I said.

"It's an honorific title. Obed Marsh was my ancestor. In the Esoteric Order, there is always a Cap'n's Daughter. Right now, I am she."

"What exactly is this Dagon business about?"

She smiled, showing a row of little pearls. "It's an alternative form of worship. It's not a racket, honestly."

"I never said it was."

She shrugged.

"Many people get the wrong idea."

Outside, the wind was rising, driving rain against the Temple. The sound effects were weird, like sickening whales calling out in the Bay.

"You were asking about Laird? Did Miss Wilde send you?"

It was my turn to shrug.

"Janey is what they call a sore loser, Mr. Lovecraft. It comes from taking all those bronze medals. Never the gold."

"I don't think she wants him back," I said, "just to know where he is. He seems to have disappeared."

"He's often out of town on business. He likes to be mysterious. I'm sure you understand."

My eyes kept going to the squid-face brooch. As Janice Marsh breathed, it rose and fell and rubies winked at me.

"It's Polynesian," she said, tapping the brooch. "The Cap'n brought it back with him to Innsmouth."

"Ah yes, your home town."

"It's just a place by the sea. Like Los Angeles."

I decided to go fishing, and hooked up some of the bait Winthrop had given me. "Were you there when J. Edgar Hoover staged his fireworks display in the twenties?"

"Yes, I was a child. Something to do with rum-runners, I think. That was during Prohibition."

"Good years for the Laird."

"I suppose so. He's legitimate these days."

"Yes. Although if he were as Scotch as he likes to pretend he is, you can be sure he'd have been deported by now."

Janice Marsh's eyes were sea-green. Round or not, they were fascinating. "Let me put your mind at rest, Mr. Lovecraft or whatever your name is," she said, "the Esoteric Order of Dagon was never a front for boot-legging. In fact it has never been a front for anything. It is not a racket for duping rich widows out of inheritances. It is not an excuse for motion picture executives to gain carnal knowledge of teenage drug addicts. It is exactly what it claims to be, a church."

"Father, Son, and Holy Squid, eh?"

"I did not say we were a Christian church."

Janice Marsh had been creeping up on me and was close enough to bite. Her active hands went to the back of my neck and angled my head down like an adjustable lamp. She put her lips on mine and squashed her face into me. I tasted lipstick, salt, and caviar. Her fingers writhed up into my hair and pushed my hat off. She shut her eyes. After an hour or two of suffering in the line of duty, I put my hands on her hips and detached her body from mine. I had a fish taste in my mouth.

"That was interesting," I said.

"An experiment," she replied. "Your name has such a ring to it. Love... craft. It suggests expertise in a certain direction."

"Disappointed?"

She smiled. I wondered if she had several rows of teeth, like a shark.

"Anything but."

"So do I get an invite to the back-row during your next Dagon hoe-down?"

She was businesslike again. "I think you'd better report back to Janey. Tell her I'll have Laird call her when he's in town and put her mind at rest. She should pay you off. What with the War, it's a waste of manpower to have you spend your time looking for someone who isn't missing when you could be defending Lockheed from Fifth Columnists."

"What about Franklin?"

"Franklin the President?"

"Franklin the baby."

Her round eyes tried to widen. She was playing this scene innocent. The Panther Princess had been the same when telling the white hunter that Jungle Jillian had left the Tomb of the Jaguar hours ago.

"Miss Wilde seems to think Laird has borrowed a child of hers that she carelessly left in his care. She'd like Franklin back."

"Janey hasn't got a baby. She can't have babies. It's why she's such a psycho-neurotic case. Her analyst is getting rich on her bewildering fantasies. She can't tell reality from the movies. She once accused me of human sacrifice."

"Sounds like a square rap."

"That was in a film, Mr. Lovecraft. Cardboard knives and catsup blood."

Usually at this stage in an investigation, I call my friend Bernie at the District Attorney's office and put out a few fishing lines. This time, he phoned me. When I got into my office, I had the feeling my telephone had been ringing for a long time.

"Don't make waves," Bernie said.

"Pardon," I snapped back, with my usual lightning-fast wit.

"Just don't. It's too cold to go for a swim this time of year."

"Even in a bathtub."

"Especially in a bathtub."

"Does Mr. District Attorney send his regards?"

Bernie laughed. I had been an investigator with the DA's office a few years back, but we'd been forced to part company.

"Forget him. I have some more impressive names on my list."

"Let me guess. Howard Hughes?"

"Close."

"General Stillwell?"

"Getting warmer. Try Mayor Fletcher Bowron, Governor Culbert Olson, and State Attorney General Earl Warren. Oh, and Wax, of course."

I whistled. "All interested in little me. Who'd 'a thunk it?"

"Look, I don't know much about this myself. They just gave me a message to pass on. In the building, they apparently think of me as your keeper."

"Do a British gentleman, a French lady, and a fed the size of Mount Rushmore have anything to do with this?"

"I'll take the money I've won so far and you can pass that question on to the next sucker."

"Fine, Bernie. Tell me, just how popular am I?"

"Tojo rates worse than you, and maybe Judas Iscariot."

"Feels comfy. Any idea where Laird Brunette is these days?"

I heard a pause and some rumbling. Bernie was making sure his office was empty of all ears. I imagined him bringing the receiver up close and dropping his voice to a whisper.

"No one's seen him in three months. Confidentially, I don't miss him at all. But there are others…" Bernie coughed, a door opened, and he started talking normally or louder. "…of course, honey, I'll be home in time for Jack Benny."

"See you later, sweetheart," I said, "your dinner is in the sink and I'm off to Tijuana with a professional pool player."

"Love you," he said, and hung up.

I'd picked up a coating of green slime on the soles of my shoes. I tried scraping them off on the edge of the desk and then used yesterday's *Times* to get the stuff off the desk. The gloop looked damned esoteric to me.

I poured myself a shot from the bottle I had picked up across the street and washed the taste of Janice Marsh off my teeth.

I thought of Polynesia in the early 19th Century and of those fish-eyed native girls clustering around Capt. Marsh. Somehow, tentacles kept getting in the way of my thoughts. In theory, the Capt. should have been an ideal subject for a Dorothy Lamour movie, perhaps with Janice Marsh in the role of her great-great-great and Jon Hall or Ray Milland as girl-chasing Obed. But I was picking up Bela Lugosi vibrations from the set-up. I couldn't help but think of bisected babies.

So far none of this running around had got me any closer to the Laird and his heir. In my mind, I drew up a list of Brunette's known associates. Then, I mentally crossed off all the ones who were dead. That brought me up short. When people in Brunette's business die, nobody really takes much notice except maybe to join in a few drunken choruses of "Ding-Dong, the Wicked Witch is Dead" before remembering there are plenty of other Wicked Witches in the sea. I'm just like everybody else: I don't keep a score of dead gambler-entrepreneurs. But, thinking of it, there'd been an awful lot recently, up to and including Gianni Pastore. Apart from Rothko and Isinglass, there'd been at least three other closed casket funerals in the profession. Obviously you couldn't blame that on the Japs. I wondered how many of the casualties had met their ends in bathtubs. The whole thing kept coming back to water. I decided I hated the stuff and swore not to let my bourbon get polluted with it.

Back out in the rain, I started hitting the bars. Brunette had a lot of friends. Maybe someone would know something.

By early evening, I'd propped up a succession of bars and leaned on a succession of losers. The only thing I'd come up with was the blatantly obvious information that everyone in town was scared. Most were wet, but all were scared.

Everyone was scared of two or three things at once. The Japs were high on everyone's list. You'd be surprised to discover the number of shaky citizens who'd turned overnight from chisellers who'd barely recognise the flag into true red, white, and blue patriots prepared to shed their last drop of alcoholic blood for their country. Everywhere you went, someone sounded off against Hirohito, Tojo, the Mikado, *kabuki*, and *origami*. The current rash of accidental deaths in the Pastore–Brunette circle were a much less popular subject for discussion and tended to turn loudmouths into closemouths at the drop of a question.

"Something fishy," everyone said, before changing the subject.

I was beginning to wonder whether Janey Wilde wouldn't have done better spending her money on a radio commercial asking the Laird to give her a call. Then I found Curtis the Croupier in Maxie's. He usually wore the full soup and fish, as if borrowed from Astaire. Now he'd exchanged his carnation, starched shirtfront, and pop-up top hat for an outfit in olive drab with bars on the shoulder and a cap under one epaulette.

"Heard the bugle call, Curtis?" I asked, pushing through a crowd of patriotic admirers who had been buying the soldier boy drinks.

Curtis grinned before he recognised me, then produced a supercilious sneer. We'd met before, on the *Montecito*. There was a rumour going around that during Prohibition he'd once got involved in an honest card game, but if pressed he'd energetically refute it.

"Hey cheapie," he said.

I bought myself a drink but didn't offer him one. He had three or four lined up.

"This racket must pay," I said. "How much did the uniform cost? You rent it from Paramount?"

The croupier was offended. "It's real," he said. "I've enlisted. I hope to be sent overseas."

"Yeah, we ought to parachute you into Tokyo to introduce loaded dice and rickety roulette wheels."

"You're cynical, cheapie." He tossed back a drink.

"No, just a realist. How come you quit the *Monty*?"

"Poking around in the Laird's business?"

I raised my shoulders and dropped them again.

"Gambling has fallen off recently, along with leading figures in the industry. The original owner of this place, for instance. I bet paying for wreaths has thinned your bankroll."

Curtis took two more drinks, quickly, and called for more. When I'd come in, there'd been a couple of chippies climbing into his hip pockets. Now he was on his own with me. He didn't appreciate the change of scenery and I can't say I blamed him.

"Look cheapie," he said, his voice suddenly low, "for your own good, just drop it. There are more important things now."

"Like democracy?"

"You can call it that."

"How far overseas do you want to be sent, Curtis?"

He looked at the door as if expecting five guys with tommy guns to come out of the rain for him. Then he gripped the bar to stop his hands shaking.

"As far as I can get, cheapie. The Philippines, Europe, Australia. I don't care."

"Going to war is a hell of a way to escape."

"Isn't it just? But wouldn't Papa Gianni have been safer on Wake Island than in the tub?"

"You heard the bathtime story, then?"

Curtis nodded and took another gulp. The juke box played "Doodly-Acky-Sacky, Want Some Seafood, Mama" and it was scary. Nonsense, but scary.

"They all die in water. That's what I've heard. Sometimes, on the *Monty*, Laird would go up on deck and just look at the sea for hours. He was crazy, since he took up with that Marsh popsicle."

"The Panther Princess?"

"You saw that one? Yeah, Janice Marsh. Pretty girl if you like clams. Laird claimed there was a sunken town in the bay. He used a lot of weird words, darkie bop or something. Jitterbug stuff. Cthul-whatever, Yog-Gimme-a-Break. He said things were going to come out of the water and sweep over the land, and he didn't mean U-boats."

Curtis was uncomfortable in his uniform. There were dark patches where the rain had soaked. He'd been drinking like W.C. Fields on a bender but he wasn't getting tight. Whatever was troubling him was too much even for Jack Daniel's.

I thought of the Laird of the *Monty*. And I thought of the painting of Capt. Marsh's clipper, with that out-of-proportion squid surfacing near it.

"He's on the boat, isn't he?"

Curtis didn't say anything.

"Alone," I thought aloud. "He's out there alone."

I pushed my hat to the back of my head and tried to shake booze out of my mind. It was crazy. Nobody bobs up and down in the water with a sign round their neck saying "Hey Tojo, Torpedo Me!" The *Monty* was a floating target.

"No," Curtis said, grabbing my arm, jarring drink out of my glass.

"He's not out there?"

He shook his head.

"No, cheapie. He's not out there alone."

All the water taxis were in dock, securely moored and covered until the storms settled. I'd never find a boatman to take me out to the *Montecito* tonight. Why, everyone knew the waters were infested with Japanese subs. But I knew someone who wouldn't care any more whether or not his boats were being treated properly. He was even past bothering if they were borrowed without his permission.

The Seaview Inn was still deserted, although there were police notices warning people away from the scene of the crime. It was dark, cold, and wet, and nobody bothered me as I broke into the boathouse to find a ring of keys.

I took my pick of the taxis moored to the Seaview's jetty and gassed her up for a short voyage. I also got my .38 Colt Super Match out from the glove compartment of the Chrysler and slung it under my armpit. During all this, I got a thorough soaking and picked up the beginnings of influenza. I hoped Jungle Jillian would appreciate the effort.

The sea was swelling under the launch and making a lot of noise. I was grateful for the noise when it came to shooting the padlock off the mooring chain, but the swell soon had my stomach sloshing about in my lower abdomen. I am not an especially competent seaman.

The *Monty* was out there on the horizon, still visible whenever the lightning lanced. It was hardly difficult to keep the small boat aimed at the bigger one.

Getting out on the water makes you feel small. Especially when the lights of Bay City are just a scatter in the dark behind you. I got the impression of large things moving just beyond my field of perception. The chill soaked through my clothes. My hat was a felt sponge, dripping down my neck. As the launch cut towards the *Monty*, rain and spray needled my face. I saw my hands white and bath-wrinkled on the wheel and wished I'd brought a bottle. Come to that, I wished I was at home in bed with a mug of cocoa and Claudette Colbert. Some things in life don't turn out the way you plan.

Three miles out, I felt the law change in my stomach. Gambling was legal and I emptied my belly over the side into the water. I stared at the remains of my toasted cheese sandwich as they floated off. I thought I saw the moon reflected greenly in the depths, but there was no moon that night.

I killed the engine and let waves wash the taxi against the side of the *Monty*. The small boat scraped along the hull of the gambling ship and I caught hold of a weed-furred rope ladder as it passed. I tethered the taxi and took a deep breath.

The ship sat low in the water, as if its lower cabins were flooded. Too much seaweed climbed up towards the decks. It'd never reopen for business, even if the War were over tomorrow.

I climbed the ladder, fighting the water-weight in my clothes, and heaved myself up on deck. It was good to have something more solid than a tiny boat under me, but the deck pitched like an airplane wing. I grabbed a rail and hoped my internal organs would arrange themselves back into their familiar grouping.

"Brunette," I shouted, my voice lost in the wind.

There was nothing. I'd have to go belowdecks.

A sheet flying flags of all nations had come loose, and was whipped around with the storm. Japan, Italy, and Germany were still tactlessly represented, along with several European states that weren't really nations any more. The deck was covered in familiar slime.

I made my way around towards the ballroom doors. They'd blown in and rain splattered against the polished wood floors. I got inside and pulled the .38. It felt better in my hand than digging into my ribs.

Lightning struck nearby and I got a flash image of the abandoned ballroom, orchestra stands at one end painted with the name of a disbanded combo.

The casino was one deck down. It should be dark but I saw a glow under a walkway door. I pushed through and cautiously descended. It wasn't wet here but it was cold. The fish smell was strong.

"Brunette," I shouted again.

I imagined something heavy shuffling nearby and slipped a few steps, banging my hip and arm against a bolted-down table. I kept hold of my gun, but only through superhuman strength.

The ship wasn't deserted. That much was obvious.

I could hear music. It wasn't Cab Calloway or Benny Goodman. There was a Hawaiian guitar in there but mainly it was a crazy choir of keening voices. I wasn't convinced the performers were human and wondered whether Brunette was working up some kind of act with singing seals. I couldn't make out the words, but the familiar hawk-and-spit syllables of "Cthulhu" cropped up a couple of times.

I wanted to get out and go back to nasty Bay City and forget all about this. But Jungle Jillian was counting on me.

I made my way along the passage, working towards the music. A hand fell on my shoulder and my heart banged against the backsides of my eyeballs.

A twisted face stared at me out of the gloom, thickly bearded, crater-cheeked. Laird Brunette was made up as Ben Gunn, skin shrunk onto his skull, eyes large as hen's eggs.

His hand went over my mouth.

"Do Not Disturb," he said, voice high and cracked.

This wasn't the suave criminal I knew, the man with tartan cummerbunds and patent leather hair. This was some other Brunette, in the grips of a tough bout with dope or madness.

"The Deep Ones," he said.

He let me go and I backed away.

"It is the time of the Surfacing."

My case was over. I knew where the Laird was. All I had to do was tell Janey Wilde and give her her refund.

"There's very little time."

The music was louder. I heard a great number of bodies shuffling around in the casino. They couldn't have been very agile, because they kept clumping into things and each other.

"They must be stopped. Dynamite, depth charges, torpedoes…"

"Who?" I asked. "The Japs?"

"The Deep Ones. The Dwellers in the Sister City."

He had lost me.

A nasty thought occurred to me. As a detective, I can't avoid making deductions. There were obviously a lot of people aboard the *Monty*, but mine was the only small boat in evidence. How had everyone else got out here? Surely they couldn't have swam?

"It's a war," Brunette ranted, "us and them. It's always been a war."

I made a decision. I'd get the Laird off his boat and turn him over to Jungle Jillian. She could sort things out with the Panther Princess and her Esoteric Order. In his current state, Brunette would hand over any baby if you gave him a blanket.

I took Brunette's thin wrist and tugged him towards the staircase. But a hatch clanged down and I knew we were stuck.

A door opened and perfume drifted through the fish stink.

"Mr. Lovecraft, wasn't it?" a silk-scaled voice said.

Janice Marsh was wearing pendant squid earrings and a lady-sized gun. And nothing else.

That wasn't quite as nice as it sounds. The Panther Princess had no nipples, no navel, and no pubic hair. She was lightly scaled between the legs and her wet skin shone like a shark's. I imagined that if you stroked her, your palm would come away bloody. She was wearing neither the turban she'd affected earlier nor the dark wig of her pictures. Her head was completely bald, skull swelling unnaturally. She didn't even have her eyebrows pencilled in.

"You evidently can't take good advice."

As mermaids go, she was scarier than cute. In the crook of her left arm, she held a bundle from which a white baby face peered with unblinking eyes. Franklin looked more like Janice Marsh than his parents.

"A pity, really," said a tiny ventriloquist voice through Franklin's mouth, "but there are always complications."

Brunette gibbered with fear, chewing his beard and huddling against me.

Janice Marsh set Franklin down and he sat up, an adult struggling with a baby's body.

"The Cap'n has come back," she explained.

"Every generation must have a Cap'n," said the thing in Franklin's mind. Dribble got in the way and he wiped his angel-mouth with a fold of swaddle.

Janice Marsh clucked and pulled Laird away from me, stroking his face.

"Poor dear," she said, flicking his chin with a long tongue. "He got out of his depth."

She put her hands either side of Brunette's head, pressing the butt of her gun into his cheek.

"He was talking about a Sister City," I prompted.

She twisted the gambler's head around and dropped him on the floor. His tongue poked out and his eyes showed only white.

"Of course," the baby said. "The Cap'n founded two settlements. One beyond Devil Reef, off Massachusetts. And one here, under the sands of the Bay."

We both had guns. I'd let her kill Brunette without trying to shoot her. It was the detective's fatal flaw, curiosity. Besides, the Laird was dead inside his head long before Janice snapped his neck.

"You can still join us," she said, hips working like a snake in time to the chanting. "There are raptures in the deeps."

"Sister," I said, "you're not my type."

Her nostrils flared in anger and slits opened in her neck, flashing liverish red lines in her white skin.

Her gun was pointed at me, safety off. Her long nails were lacquered green.

I thought I could shoot her before she shot me. But I didn't. Something about a naked woman, no matter how strange, prevents you from killing them. Her whole body was moving with the music. I'd been wrong. Despite everything, she was beautiful.

I put my gun down and waited for her to murder me. It never happened.

I don't really know the order things worked out. But first there was lightning, then, an instant later, thunder.

Light filled the passageway, hurting my eyes. Then, a rumble of noise which grew in a crescendo. The chanting was drowned.

Through the thunder cut a screech. It was a baby's cry. Franklin's eyes were screwed up and he was shrieking. I had a sense of the Cap'n drowning in the baby's mind, his purchase on the purloined body relaxing as the child cried out.

The floor beneath me shook and buckled and I heard a great straining of abused metal. A belch of hot wind surrounded me. A hole appeared. Janice Marsh moved fast and I think she fired her gun, but whether at me on purpose or at random in reflex I couldn't say. Her body sliced towards me and I ducked.

There was another explosion, not of thunder, and thick smoke billowed through a rupture in the floor. I was on the floor, hugging the tilting deck. Franklin slid towards me and bumped, screaming, into my head. A half ton of water fell on us and I knew the ship was breached. My guess was that the Japs had just saved my life with a torpedo. I was waist deep in saltwater. Janice Marsh darted away in a sinuous fish motion.

Then there were heavy bodies around me, pushing me against a bulkhead. In the darkness, I was scraped by something heavy, cold-skinned and foul-smelling. There were barks and cries, some of which might have come from human throats.

Fires went out and hissed as the water rose. I had Franklin in my hands and tried to hold him above water. I remembered the peril of Jungle Jillian again and found my head floating against the hard ceiling.

The Cap'n cursed in vivid 18th Century language, Franklin's little body squirming in my grasp. A toothless mouth tried to get a biter's grip on my chin but slipped off. My feet slid and I was off-balance, pulling the baby briefly underwater. I saw his startled eyes through a wobbling film. When I pulled him out again, the Cap'n was gone and Franklin was screaming on his own. Taking a double gulp of air, I plunged under the water and struggled towards the nearest door, a hand closed over the baby's face to keep water out of his mouth and nose.

The *Montecito* was going down fast enough to suggest there were plenty of holes in it. I had to make it a priority to find one. I jammed my knee at a door and it flew open. I was poured, along with several hundred gallons of water, into a large room full of stored gambling equipment. Red and white chips floated like confetti.

I got my footing and waded towards a ladder. Something large reared out of the water and shambled at me, screeching like a seabird. I didn't get a good look at it. Which was a mercy. Heavy arms lashed me, flopping boneless against my face. With my free hand, I pushed back at the thing, fingers slipping against cold slime. Whatever it was was in a panic and squashed through the door.

There was another explosion and everything shook. Water splashed upwards and I fell over. I got upright and managed to get a one-handed grip on the ladder. Franklin was still struggling and bawling, which I took to be a good sign. Somewhere near, there was a lot of shouting.

I dragged us up rung by rung and slammed my head against a hatch. If it had been battened, I'd have smashed my skull and spilled my brains. It flipped upwards and a push of water from below shoved us through the hole like a ping-pong ball in a fountain.

The *Monty* was on fire and there were things in the water around it. I heard the drone of airplane engines and glimpsed nearby launches. Gunfire fought with the wind. It was a full-scale attack. I made it to the deck-rail and saw a boat fifty feet away. Men in yellow slickers angled tommy guns down and sprayed the water with bullets.

The gunfire whipped up the sea into a foam. Kicking things died in the water. Someone brought up his gun and fired at me. I pushed myself aside, arching my body over Franklin, and bullets spanged against the deck.

My borrowed taxi must have been dragged under by the bulk of the ship.

There were definitely lights in the sea. And the sky. Over the city, in the distance, I saw firecracker bursts. Something exploded a hundred yards away and a tower of water rose, bursting like a puffball. A depth charge.

The deck was angled down and water was creeping up at us. I held on to a rope webbing, wondering whether the gambling ship still had any lifeboats. Franklin spluttered and bawled.

A white body slid by, heading for the water. I instinctively grabbed at it. Hands took hold of me and I was looking into Janice Marsh's face. Her eyes blinked, membranes coming round from the sides, and she kissed me again. Her long tongue probed my mouth like an eel, then withdrew. She stood up, one leg bent so she was still vertical on the sloping deck. She drew air into her lungs—if she had lungs—and expelled it through her gills with a musical cry. She was slim and white in the darkness, water running off her body. Someone fired in her direction and she dived into the waves, knifing through the surface and disappearing towards the submarine lights. Bullets rippled the spot where she'd gone under.

I let go of the ropes and kicked at the deck, pushing myself away from the sinking ship. I held Franklin above the water and splashed with my legs and elbows. The *Monty* was dragging a lot of things under with it, and

I fought against the pull so I wouldn't be one of them. My shoulders ached and my clothes got in the way, but I kicked against the current.

The ship went down screaming, a chorus of bending steel and dying creatures. I had to make for a launch and hope not to be shot. I was lucky. Someone got a polehook into my jacket and landed us like fish. I lay on the deck, water running out of my clothes, swallowing as much air as I could breathe.

I heard Franklin yelling. His lungs were still in working order.

Someone big in a voluminous slicker, a sou'wester tied to his head, knelt by me and slapped me in the face.

"Peeper," he said.

"They're calling it the Great Los Angeles Air Raid," Winthrop told me as he poured a mug of British tea. "Some time last night a panic started, and everyone in Bay City shot at the sky for hours."

"The Japs?" I said, taking a mouthful of welcome hot liquid.

"In theory. Actually, I doubt it. It'll be recorded as a fiasco, a lot of jumpy characters with guns. While it was all going on, we engaged the enemy and emerged victorious."

He was still dressed up for an embassy ball and didn't look as if he'd been on deck all evening. Geneviève Dieudonné wore a fisherman's sweater and fatigue pants, her hair up in a scarf. She was looking at a lot of sounding equipment and noting down readings.

"You're not fighting the Japs, are you?"

Winthrop pursed his lips. "An older war, my friend. We can't be distracted. After last night's action, our Deep Ones won't poke their scaly noses out for a while. Now I can do something to lick Hitler."

"What really happened?"

"There was something dangerous in the sea, under Mr. Brunette's boat. We have destroyed it and routed the… uh, the hostile forces. They wanted the boat as a surface station. That's why Mr. Brunette's associates were eliminated."

Geneviève gave a report in French, so fast that I couldn't follow.

"Total destruction," Winthrop explained, "a dreadful setback for them. It'll put them in their place for years. Forever would be too much to hope for, but a few years will help."

I lay back on the bunk, feeling my wounds. Already choking on phlegm, I would be lucky to escape pneumonia.

"And the little fellow is a decided dividend."

Finlay glumly poked around, suggesting another dose of depth charges. He was cradling a mercifully sleep-struck Franklin, but didn't look terribly maternal.

"He seems quite unaffected by it all."

"His name is Franklin," I told Winthrop. "On the boat, he was…"

"Not himself? I'm familiar with the condition. It's a filthy business, you understand."

"He'll be all right," Geneviève put in.

I wasn't sure whether the rest of the slicker crew were feds or servicemen and I wasn't sure whether I wanted to know. I could tell a Clandestine Operation when I landed in the middle of one.

"Who knows about this?" I asked. "Hoover? Roosevelt?"

Winthrop didn't answer.

"Someone must know," I said.

"Yes," the Englishman said, "someone must. But this is a war the public would never believe exists. In the Bureau, Finlay's outfit are known as 'the Unnameables,' never mentioned by the press, never honoured or censured by the government, victories and defeats never recorded in the official history."

The launch shifted with the waves, and I hugged myself, hoping for some warmth to creep over me. Finlay had promised to break out a bottle later, but that made me resolve to stick to tea as a point of honour. I hated to fulfil his expectations.

"And America is a young country," Winthrop explained. "In Europe, we've known things a lot longer."

On shore, I'd have to tell Janey Wilde about Brunette and hand over Franklin. Some flack at Metro would be thinking of an excuse for the Panther Princess's disappearance. Everything else—the depth charges, the sea battle, the sinking ship—would be swallowed up by the War.

All that would be left would be tales. Weird tales.

ANOTHER FISH STORY

In the summer of 1968, while walking across America, he came across the skeleton fossil of something aquatic. All around, even in the apparent emptiness, were signs of the life that had passed this way. Million-year-old seashells were strewn across the empty heart of California, along with flattened bullet casings from the ragged edge of the Wild West and occasional sticks of weathered furniture. The sturdier pieces were pioneer jetsam, dumped by exhausted covered wagons during a long dry desert stretch on the road to El Dorado. The more recent items had been thrown off overloaded trucks in the '30s, by Okies rattling towards orange groves and federal work programs.

He squatted over the bones. The sands parted, disclosing the whole of the creature. The scuttle-shaped skull was all saucer-sized eye-sockets and triangular, saw-toothed jaw. The long body was like something fished out of an ash-can by a cartoon cat—fans of rib-spindles tapering to a flat tail. What looked like arm-bones fixed to the dorsal spine by complex plates that were evolving towards becoming shoulders. Stranded when the seas receded from the Mojave, the thing had lain ever closer to the surface, waiting to be revealed by sand-riffling winds. Uncovered as he was walking to it, the fossil—exposed to the thin, dry air—was quickly resolving into sand and scraps.

Finally, only an arm remained. Short and stubby like an alligator leg, it had distinct, barb-tipped fingers. It pointed like a sign-post, to the West, to the Pacific, to the city-stain seeping out from the original blot of *El Pueblo de Nuestra Senora de la Reyna de los Angeles de Rio Porciunculo*. He expected these route-marks. He'd been following them since he first crawled out of a muddy river in England. This one scratched at him.

Even in the desert, he could smell river-mud, taste foul water, feel the tidal pull.

For a moment, he was under waters. Cars, upside-down above him, descended gently like dead, settling sharks. People floated like broken dolls just under the shimmering, sunlit ceiling-surface. An enormous pressure squeezed in on him, jamming thumbs against his open eyes, forcing liquid salt into mouth and nose. A tubular serpent, the size of a streamlined train, slithered over the desert-bed towards him, eyes like turquoise-shaded searchlights, shifting rocks out of its way with muscular arms.

Gone. Over.

The insight passed. He gasped reflexively for air.

"Atlantis will rise, Sunset Boulevard will fall," Cass Elliott was singing on a single that would be released in October. Like so many doomed visionaries in her generation, Mama Cass was tuned into the vibrations. Of course, she didn't know there really had been a sunken city off Santa Monica, as recently as 1942. Not Atlantis, but the Sister City. A battle had been fought there in a World War that was not in the official histories. A War that wasn't as over as its human victors liked to think.

He looked where the finger pointed.

The landscape would change. Scrub rather than sand, mountains rather than flats. More people, less quiet.

He took steps.

He was on a world-wide walkabout, buying things, picking up skills and scars, making deals wherever he sojourned, becoming what he would be. Already, he had many interests, many businesses. An empire would need his attention soon, and he would be its prisoner as much as its master. These few years, maybe only months, were his alone. He carried no money, no identification but a British passport in the name of a newborn dead in the blitz. He wore unscuffed purple suede boots, tight white thigh-fly britches with a black zig-zag across them, a white Nehru jacket, and silver-mirrored sunglasses. A white silk aviator scarf wrapped burnoose-style about his head, turbanning his longish hair and keeping the grit out of his mouth and nose.

Behind him, across America, across the world, he left a trail. He thought of it as dropping pebbles in pools. Ripples spread from each pebble, some hardly noticed yet but nascent whirlpools, some enormous splashes no one thought to connect with the passing Englishman.

It was a good time to be young, even for him. His signs were everywhere. Number One in the pop charts back home was "Fire," by The Crazy World of Arthur Brown. "I am the God of Hellfire," chanted Arthur. There were such Gods, he understood. He walked through the world, all along the watchtower, sprung from the songs—an Urban Spaceman, Quinn the Eskimo, this wheel on fire, melting away like ice in the sun, on white horses, in disguise with glasses.

In recent months, he'd seen *Hair* on Broadway and *2001: A Space Odyssey* at an Alabama Drive-In. He knew all about the Age of Aquarius and the Ultimate Trip. He'd sabotaged Abbie Hoffman's magic ring with a subtle counter-casting, ensuring that the Pentagon remained unlevitated. He knew exactly where he'd been when Martin Luther King was shot. Ditto, Andy Warhol, Robert Kennedy, and the VC summarily executed by Colonel Loan on the *Huntley-Brinkley Report*. He'd rapped with Panthers and Guardsmen, Birchers and Yippies. To his satisfaction, he'd sewn up the next three elections, and decided the music that children would listen to until the Eve of Destruction.

He'd eaten in a lot of McDonald's, cheerfully dropping cartons and bags like apple seeds. The Golden Arches were just showing up on every

Main Street, and he felt Ronald should be encouraged. He liked the little floods of McLitter that washed away from the clown's doorways, perfumed with the stench of their special sauce.

He kept walking.

Behind him, his footprints filled in. The pointing hand, so nearly human, sank under the sands, duty discharged.

At this stage of his career, the Devil put in the hours, wore down the shoe-leather, sweated out details. He was the start-up Mephisto, the journeyman tempter, the mysterious stranger passing through, the new gun in town. You didn't need to make an appointment and crawl as a supplicant; if needs be, Derek Leech came to you.

Happily.

Miles later and days away, he found a ship's anchor propped on a cairn of stones, iron-red with lichen-like rust, blades crusted with empty shells. An almost illegible plaque read *Sumatra Queen*.

Leech knew this was where he was needed.

It wasn't real wilderness, just pretend. In the hills close to Chatsworth, a town soon to be swallowed by Los Angeles, this was the Saturday matinee West. Poverty Row prairie, Monogram mountains. A brief location hike up from Gower Gulch, the longest-lasting game of Cowboys and Indians in the world had been played.

A red arch stood by the cairn, as if a cathedral had been smitten, leaving only its entrance standing. A hook in the arch might once have held a bell or a hangman's noose or a giant shoe.

He walked under it, eyes on the hook.

Wheelruts in sandy scrub showed the way. Horses had been along this route too, recently.

A smell tickled in his nose, triggering salivary glands. Leech hadn't had a Big Mac in days. He unwound the scarf from his head and knotted it around his neck. From beside the road, he picked a dungball, skin baked hard as a gob-stopper. He ate it like an apple. Inside, it was moist. He spat out strands of grass.

He felt the vibrations, before he heard the motors.

Several vehicles, engines exposed like sit-astride mowers, bumping over rough terrain on balloon tyres. Fuel emissions belching from mortar-like tubes. Girls yelping with a fairground Dodg'em thrill.

He stood still, waiting.

The first dune buggy appeared, leaping over an incline like a roaring cat, landing awkwardly, squirming in dirt as its wheels aligned, then heading towards him in a charge. A teenage girl in a denim halter-top drove, struggling with the wheel, blonde hair streaming, a bruise on her forehead. Standing like a tank commander in the front passenger seat, hands on the roll-bar, was an undersized, big-eared man with a middling crop of beard, long hair bound in a bandanna. He wore ragged jeans and a too-big combat jacket. On a rosary around his scraggy neck was strung an Iron Cross, the *Pour le Mérite* and a rhinestone-studded swastika. He signalled vainly with a set of binoculars (one lens broken), then kicked his chauffeuse to get her attention.

The buggy squiggled in the track and halted in front of Leech.

Another zoomed out of long grass, driven by an intense young man, passengered by three messy girls. A third was around somewhere, to judge from the noise and the gasoline smell.

Leech tossed aside his unfinished meal.

"You must be hungry, pilgrim," said the commander.

"Not now."

The commander flashed a grin, briefly showing sharp, bad teeth, hollowing his cheeks, emphasising his eyes. Leech recognised the wet gaze of a man who has spent time practising his stares. Long, hard jail years looking into a mirror, plumbing black depths.

"Welcome to Charlie Country," said his driver.

Leech met the man's look. Charlie's welcome.

Seconds—a minute?—passed. Neither had a weapon, but this was a gunfighters' eye-lock, a probing and a testing, will playfully thrown up against a wall, bouncing back with surprising ferocity.

Leech was almost amused by the Charlie's presumption. Despite his hippie aspect, he was ten years older than the kids—well into hard thirties, at once leathery and shifty, a convict confident the bulls can't hang a jailyard shivving at his cell-door, an arrested grown-up settling for status as an idol for children ignored by adults. The rest of his tribe looked to their *jefé*, awaiting orders.

Charlie Country. In Vietnam, that might have meant something.

In the end, something sparked. Charlie raised one hand, open, beside his face. He made a monocle of his thumb and forefinger, three other fingers splayed like a coxcomb.

In Britain, the gesture was associated with Patrick McGoohan's "Be seeing you" on *The Prisoner*. Leech returned the salute, completing it by closing his hand into a fist.

"What's that all about?" whined his driver.

Not taking his eyes off Leech, Charlie said, "Sign of the fish, Sadie."

The girl shrugged, no wiser.

"Before the crucifix became the pre-eminent symbol of Christianity, Jesus's early followers greeted each other with the sign of the fish," Leech told them. "His first disciples were net-folk, remember. 'I will make you fishers of men.' Originally, the Galilean came as a lakeside spirit. He could walk on water, turn water to wine. He had command over fish, multiplying them to feed the five thousand. The wounds in his side might have been gills."

"Like a professor he speaks," said the driver of the second buggy.

"Or Terence Stamp," said a girl. "Are you British?"

Leech conceded that he was.

"You're a long way from Carnaby Street, Mr. Fish."

As a matter of fact, Leech owned quite a bit of that thoroughfare. He did not volunteer the information.

"Is he The One Who Will...?" began Charlie's driver, cut off with a gesture.

"Maybe, maybe not. One sign is a start, but that's all it is. A man can easily make a sign."

Leech showed his open hands, like a magician before a trick.

"Let's take you to Old Lady Marsh," said Charlie. "She'll have a thing or two to say. You'll like her. She was in pictures, a long time ago. Sleeping partner in the Ranch. You might call her the Family's spiritual advisor."

"Marsh," said Leech. "Yes, that's the name. Thank you, Charles."

"Hop into Unit Number Two. Squeaky, hustle down to make room for the gent. You can get back to the bunkhouse on your own two legs. Do you good."

A sour-faced girl crawled off the buggy. Barefoot, she looked at the flint-studded scrub as if about to complain, then thought better of it.

"Are you waitin' on an engraved invitation, Mr. Fish?"

Leech climbed into the passenger's seat, displacing two girls who shoved themselves back, clinging to the overhead bar, fitting their legs in behind the seat, plopping bottoms on orange-painted metal fixtures. To judge from the squealing, the metal was hot as griddles.

"You are comfortable?" asked the kid in the driver's seat.

Leech nodded.

"Cool," he said, jamming the ignition. "I'm Constant. My accent, it is German."

The young man's blond hair was held by a beaded leather headband. Leech had a glimpse of an earnest schoolboy in East Berlin, poring over Karl May's books about Winnetou the Warrior and Old Shatterhand, vowing that he would be a blood brother to the Apache in the West of the Teuton Soul.

Constant did a tight turn, calculated to show off, and drove off the track, bumping onto an irregular slope, pitting gears against gravity. Charlie kicked Sadie the chauffeuse, who did her best to follow.

Leech looked back. Atop the slope, "Squeaky" stood forlorn, hair stringy, faded dress above her scabby knees.

"You will respect the way Charlie has this place ordered," said Constant. "He is the Cat That Has Got the Cream."

The buggies roared down through a culvert, overleaping obstacles. One of the girls thumped her nose against the roll-bar. Her blood spotted Leech's scarf. He took it off and pressed the spots to his tongue.

Images fizzed. Blood on a wall. Words in the blood.

HEALTER SKELTER.

He shook the images from his mind.

Emerging from the culvert, the buggies burst into a clearing and circled, scattering a knot of people who'd been conferring, raising a ruckus in a corral of horses which neighed in panic, spitting up dirt and dust.

Leech saw two men locked in a wrestling hold, the bloated quarter-century-on sequel to the Wolf Man pushed against a wooden fence by a filled-out remnant of Riff of the Jets. Riff wore biker denims and orange-lensed glasses. He had a chain wrapped around the neck of the sagging lycanthrope.

The buggies halted, engines droning down and sputtering.

A man in a cowboy hat angrily shouted "Cut, cut, cut!"

Another man, in a black shirt and eyeshade, insisted "No, no, no, Al, we can use it, keep shooting. We can work round it. Film is money."

Al, the director, swatted the insister with his hat.

"Here on the Ranch, they make the motion pictures," said Constant.

Leech had guessed as much. A posse of stuntmen had been chasing outlaws all over this country since the Silents. Every rock had been filmed so often that the stone soul was stripped away.

Hoppy and Gene and Rinty and Rex were gone. Trigger was stuffed and mounted. The lights had come up and the audience fled home to the goggle box. The only Westerns that got shot these days were skin-flicks in chaps or slo-mo massacres, another sign of impending apocalypse.

But Riff and the Wolf Man were still working. Just.

The film company looked at the Beach Buggy Korps, warily hostile. Leech realised this was the latest of a campaign of skirmishes.

"What's this all about, Charlie?" demanded the director. "We've told you to keep away from the set. Sam even goddamn paid you."

Al pulled the insister, Sam, into a grip and pointed his head at Charlie.

Charlie ignored the fuss, quite enjoying it.

A kid who'd been holding up a big hoop with white fabric stretched across it felt an ache in his arms and let the reflector sag. A European-looking man operating a big old Mickey Mouse-eared camera swivelled his lens across the scene, snatching footage.

Riff took a fat hand-rolled cigarette from his top pocket, and flipped a Zippo. He sucked in smoke, held it for a wine-bibber's moment of relish, and exhaled, then nodded his satisfaction to himself.

"Tana leaves, Junior?" said Riff, offering the joint to his wrestling partner.

The Wolf Man didn't need dope to be out of it.

Here he was, Junior: Lennie Talbot, Kharis the Caveman, Count Alucard—the Son of the Phantom. His baggy eyes were still looking for the rabbits, as he wondered what had happened to the 1940s. Where were Boris and Bela and Bud and Lou? While Joni Mitchell sang about getting back to the garden, Junior fumbled about sets like this, desperate for readmission to the Inner Sanctum.

"Who the Holy Hades is this clown?" Al thumbed at Leech.

Leech looked across the set at Junior. Bloated belly barely cinched by the single button of a stained blue shirt, grey ruff of whiskers, chili stains on his jeans, yak-hair clumps stuck to his cheeks and forehead, he was up well past the Late, Late Show.

The Wolf Man looked at Leech in terror.

Sometimes, dumb animals have very good instincts.

"This is Mr. Fish," Charlie told Al. "He's from England."

"Like the Beatles," said one of the girls.

Charlie thought about that. "Yeah," he said, "like the Beatles. Being for the benefit of Mr. Fish..."

Leech got out of the buggy.

Everyone was looking at him. The kerfuffle quieted, except for the turning of the camera.

Al noticed and made a cut-throat gesture. The cameraman stopped turning.

"Hell of a waste," spat the director.

In front of the ranch-house were three more dune buggies, out of commission. A sunburned boy, naked but for cut-off denims and a sombrero, worked on the vehicles. A couple more girls sat around, occasionally passing the boy the wrong spanner from a box of tools.

"When will you have Units Three, Four, and One combat-ready, Tex?"

Tex shrugged at Charlie.

"Be lucky to Frankenstein together one working bug from these heaps of shit, Chuck."

"Not good enough, my man. The storm's coming. We have to be ready."

"Then schlep down to Santa Monica and steal... *requisition*... some more goddamn rolling stock. Rip off an owner's manual, while you're at it. These configurations are a joke."

"I'll take it under advisement," said Charlie.

Tex gave his commander a salute.

Everyone looked at Leech, then at Charlie for the nod that meant the newcomer should be treated with respect. Chain of command was more rigid here than at Khe Sanh.

All the buggies were painted. At one time, they had been given elaborate psychedelic patterns; then, a policy decision decreed they be redone in sandy desert camouflage. But the first job had been done properly, while the second was botched—vibrant flowers, butterflies, and peace-signs shone through the thin diarrhoea-khaki topcoat.

The ranch-house was the basic derelict adobe and wood hacienda. One carelessly flicked roach and the place was an inferno. Round here, they must take pot-shots at safety inspectors.

On the porch was propped a giant fibreglass golliwog, a fat grinning racial caricature holding up a cone surmounted by a whipped swirl and a red ball cherry. Chocko the Ice Cream Clown had originally been fixed to one of the "requisitioned" buggies. Someone had written "PIG" in lipstick on Chocko's forehead. Someone else had holed his eyes and cheek with 2.2 rifle bullets. A hand-axe stuck out of his shoulder like a flung tomahawk.

"That's the Enemy, man," said Charlie. "Got to Know Your Enemy."

Leech looked at the fallen idol.

"You don't like clowns?"

Charlie nodded. Leech thought of his ally, Ronald.

"Chocko's coming, man," said Charlie. "We have to be in a state of eternal preparedness. Their world, the dress-up-and-play world, is over. No more movies, no more movie stars. It's just us, the Family. And Chocko. We're major players in the coming deluge. Helter Skelter, like in the song. It's been revealed to me. But you know all that."

Funnily enough, Leech did.

He had seen the seas again, the seas that would come from the sundered earth. The seventh flood. The last wave.

Charlie would welcome the waters.

He was undecided on the whole water thing. If pushed, he preferred the fire. And he sensed more interesting apocalypses in the offing, stirring in the scatter of McDonald's boxes and chewed-out bubblegum pop. Still, he saw himself as a public servant; it was down to others to make the choices. Whatever was wanted, he would do his best to deliver.

"Old Lady Marsh don't make motion pictures any more. No need. Picture Show's closed. Just some folk don't know it yet."

"Chuck offered to be in their movie," explained Tex. "Said he'd do one of those nude love scenes, man. No dice."

"That's not the way it is," said Charlie, suddenly defensive, furtive. "My thing is the *music*. I'm going to communicate through my album. Pass on my revelation. Kids groove on records more than movies."

Tex shrugged. Charlie needed him, so he had a certain license.

Within limits.

Charlie looked back, away from the house. The film company was turning over again. Riff was pretending to chain-whip Junior.

"Something's got to change," said Charlie.

"Helter skelter," said Leech.

Charlie's eyes shone.

"Yeah," he said, "you dig."

Inside the house, sections were roped off with crudely lettered PELIGROSO signs. Daylight seeped through ill-fitting boards over glassless windows. Everything was slightly damp and salty, as if there'd been rain days ago. The adobe seemed sodden, pulpy. Green moss grew on the floor. A plastic garden hose snaked through the house, pulsing, leading up the main staircase.

"The Old Lady likes to keep the waters flowing."

Charlie led Leech upstairs.

On the landing, a squat idol sat on an occasional table—a buddha with cephalopod mouth-parts.

"Know that fellow, Mr. Fish?"

"Dagon, God of the Philistines."

"Score one for the Kwiz Kid. Dagon. That's one of the names. Old Lady Marsh had this church, way back in the '40s. Esoteric Order of Dagon. Ever hear of it?"

Leech had.

"She wants me to take it up again, open storefront chapels on all the piers. Not my scene, man. No churches, not this time. I've got my own priorities. She thinks *infiltration*, but I know these are the times for catastrophe. But she's still a fighter. Janice Marsh. Remember her in *Nefertiti*?"

They came to a door, kept ajar by the hose.

Away from his Family, Charlie was different. The man never relaxed, but he dropped the Rasputin act, stuttered out thoughts as soon as they sprung to him, kept up a running commentary. He was less a Warrior of the Apocalypse than a Holocaust Hustler, working all the angles, sucking up to whoever might help him. Charlie needed followers, but was desperate also for sponsorship, a break.

Charlie opened the door.

"Miss Marsh," he said, deferential.

Large, round eyes gleamed inside the dark room.

Janice Marsh sat in a tin bathtub, tarpaulin tied around her wattled throat like a bib, a bulbous turban around her skull. From under the tarp came quiet splashing and slopping. The hose fed into the bath and an overspill pipe, patched together with hammered-out tin cans, led away to a hole in the wall, dribbling outside.

Only her flattish nose and lipless mouth showed, overshadowed by the fine-lashed eyes. In old age, she had smoothed rather than wrinkled. Her skin was a mottled, greenish colour.

"This cat's from England," said Charlie.

Leech noticed that Charlie hung back in the doorway, not entering the room. This woman made him nervous.

"We've been in the desert, Miss Marsh," said Charlie. "Sweeping Quadrant Twelve. Scoped out a promising cave, but it led nowhere. Sadie got her ass stuck in a hole, but we hauled her out. That chick's our mineshaft canary."

Janice Marsh nodded, chin-pouch inflating like a frog's.

"There's more desert," said Charlie. "We'll read the signs soon. It will be found. We can't be kept from it."

Leech walked into the dark and sat, unbidden, on a stool by the bathtub.

Janice Marsh looked at him. Sounds frothed through her mouth, rattling in slits that might have been gills.

Leech returned her greeting.

"You speak that jazz?" exclaimed Charlie. "Far out."

Leech and Janice Marsh talked. She was interesting, if given to rambles as her mind drifted out to sea. It was all about water. Here in the desert, close to the thirstiest city in America, the value of water was known. She told him what the Family were looking for, directed him to unroll some scrolls that were kept on a low-table under a fizzing desk-lamp. The charts were the original mappings of California, made by Fray Junipero Serra before there were enough human landmarks to get a European bearing.

Charlie shouldered close to Leech, and pulled a magic marker out of his top pocket.

The vellum was divided into numbered squares, thick modern lines blacked over the faded, precious sketch-marks. Several squares were shaded with diagonal lines. Charlie added diagonals to the square marked "12."

Leech winced.

"What's up, man?"

"Nothing," he told Charlie.

He knew what things were worth; that, if anything, was his special talent. But he knew such values were out of step with the times. He did not want to be thought a breadhead. Not until the 1980s, when he had an itchy feeling that it'd be mandatory. If there was to be a 1980s.

"This is the surface chart, you dig," said Charlie, rapping knuckles on the map. "We're about here, where I've marked the Ranch. There are other maps, showing what's underneath."

Charlie rolled the map, to disclose another. The top map had holes cut out, marking points of convergence. The lower chart was marked with interlinked balloon-shapes, some filled in with blue pigment that had become pale with age.

"Dig the holes, man. This shows the ways down below."

A third layer of map was almost all blue. Drawn in were fishy, squiddy shapes. And symbols Leech understood.

"And here's the prize. The Sea of California. Freshwater, deep under the desert. Primordial."

Janice Marsh burbled excitement.

"Home," she said, a recognisable English word.

"It's under us," said Charlie. "That's why we're out here. Looking. Before Chocko rises, the Family will have found the way down, got the old pumps working. Turn on the quake. With the flood, we'll win. It's the key to ending all this. It has properties. Some places—the cities, maybe, Chicago, Watts—it'll be fire that comes down. Here, it's the old, old way. It'll be water that comes up."

"You're building an Ark?"

"Uh uh, Arks are movie stuff. We're learning to *swim*. Going to be a part of the flood. You too, I think. We're going to drown Chocko. We're going to drown Hollywood. Call down the rains. Break the rock. When it's all over, there'll only be us. And maybe the Beach Boys. I'm tight with Dennis Wilson, man. He wants to produce my album. That's going to happen in the last days. My album will be a monster, like the *Double White*. Music will open everything up, knock everything down. Like at Jericho."

Leech saw that Charlie couldn't keep his thinking straight. He wanted an end to civilisation and a never-ending battle of Armageddon, but still thought he could fit in a career as a pop star.

Maybe.

This was Janice's game. She was the mother of this family.

"He came out of the desert," Charlie told the old woman. "You can see the signs on him. He's a dowser."

The big eyes turned to Leech.

"I've found things before," he admitted.

"Water?" she asked, splashing.

He shrugged. "On occasion."

Her slit mouth opened in a smile, showing rows of needle-sharp teeth.

"You're a hit, man," said Charlie. "You're in the Family."

Leech raised his hand. "That's an honour, Charles," he said, "but I can't accept. I provide services, for a fee to be negotiated, but I don't take permanent positions."

Charlie was puzzled for a moment, brows narrowed. Then he smiled. "If that's your scene, it's cool. But are you The One Who Will Open the Earth? Can you help us find the Subterranean Sea?"

Leech considered, and shook his head, "No. That's too deep for me."

Charlie made fists, bared teeth, instantly angry.

"But I know who can," soothed Leech.

The movie people were losing the light. As the sun sank, long shadows stretched on reddish scrub, rock-shapes twisted into ogres. The cinematographer shot furiously, gabbling in semi-Hungarian about "magic hour," while Sam and Al worried vocally that nothing would come out on the film.

Leech sat in a canvas folding chair and watched.

Three young actresses, dressed like Red Indians, were pushing Junior around, tormenting him by withholding a bottle of firewater. Meanwhile, the movie moon—a shining fabric disc—was rising full, just like the real moon up above the frame-line.

The actresses weren't very good. Beside Sadie and Squeaky and Ouisch and the others, the Acid Squaws of the Family, they lacked authentic drop-out savagery. They were Vegas refugees, tottering on high heels, checking their make-up in every reflective surface.

Junior wasn't acting any more.

"Go for the bottle," urged Al.

Junior made a bear-lunge, missed a girl who pulled a face as his sweat-smell cloud enveloped her, and fell to his knees. He looked up like a puppy with progeria, eager to be patted for his trick.

There was water in Junior's eyes. Full moons shone in them.

Leech looked up. Even he felt the tidal tug.

"I don't freakin' believe this," stage-whispered Charlie, in Leech's ear. "That cat's gone."

Leech pointed again at Junior.

"You've tried human methods, Charles. Logic and maps. You need to try other means. Animals always find water. The moon pulls at the sea. That man has surrendered to his animal. He knows the call of the moon. Even a man who is pure in heart…"

"That was just in the movies."

"Nothing was ever *just* in the movies. Understand this. Celluloid writes itself into the unconscious, of its makers as much as its consumers. Your revelations may come in music. His came in the cheap seats."

The Wolf Man howled happily, bottle in his hug. He took a swig and shook his greasy hair like a pelt.

The actresses edged away from him.

"Far out, man," said Charlie, doubtfully.

"Far out and deep down, Charles."

"That's a wrap for today," called Al.

"I could shoot twenty more minutes with this light," said the cameraman.

"You're nuts. This ain't art school in Budapest. Here in America, we shoot with light, not dark."

"I make it *fantastic*."

"We don't want fantastic. We want it on film so you can see it."

"Make a change from your last picture, then," sneered the cinematographer. He flung up his hands and walked away.

Al looked about as if he'd missed something.

"Who are you, mister?" he asked Leech. "Who are you *really*?"

"A student of human nature."

"Another weirdo, then."

He had a flash of the director's body, much older and shaggier, bent in half and shoved into a whirlpool bath, wet concrete sloshing over his face.

"Might I give you some free advice?" Leech asked. "Long-term advice. Be very careful when you're hiring odd-job men."

"Yup, a *weird* weirdo. The worst kind."

The director stalked off. Leech still felt eyes on him.

Sam, the producer, had stuck around the set. He did the negotiating. He also had a demented enthusiasm for the kind of pictures they made. Al would rather have been shooting on the studio lot with Barbra Streisand or William Holden. Sam liked anything that gave him a chance to hire forgotten names from the matinees he had loved as a kid.

"You're not with them? Charlie's Family?"

Leech said nothing.

"They're fruit-loops. Harmless, but a pain the keister. The hours we've lost putting up with these kids. You're not like that. Why are you here?"

"As they say in the Westerns, 'just passing through.'"

"You like Westerns? Nobody does much anymore, unless they're made in Spain by Italians. What's wrong with this picture? We'd love to be able to shoot only Westerns. Cowboys are a hell of a lot easier to deal with than Hells' Angels. Horses don't break down like bikes."

"Would you be interested in coming to an arrangement? The problems you've been having with the Family could be ended."

"What are you, their agent?"

"This isn't Danegeld, or a protection racket. This is a fair exchange of services."

"I pay you and your hippies don't fudge up any more scenes? I could just get a sheriff out here and run the whole crowd off, then we'd be back on schedule. I've come close to it more'n once."

"I'm not interested in money, for the moment. I would like to take an option on a day and a night of time from one of your contractees."

"Those girls are *actresses*, buddy, not whatever you might think they are. Each and every one of 'em is SAG."

"Not one of the actresses."

"Sheesh, I know you longhairs are into everything, but…"

"It's your werewolf I wish to subcontract."

"My what? Oh, Junior. He's finished on this picture."

"But he owes you two days."

"How the hell did you know that? He does. I was going to have Al shoot stuff with him we could use in something else. There's this *Blood* picture we need to finish. *Blood of Whatever*. It's had so many titles, I can't keep them in my head. *Ghastly Horror… Dracula Meets Frankenstein… Fiend with the Psychotropic Brain… Blood a-Go-Go….* At the moment, it's mostly home movies shot at a dolphinarium. It could use monster scenes."

"I would like to pick up the time. As I said, a day and a night."

"Have you ever done any acting? I ask because our vampire is gone. He's an accountant and it's tax season. In long shot, you could pass for him. We could give you a horror star name, get you on the cover of *Famous Monsters*. How about 'Zoltan Lukoff?' 'Mongo Carnadyne?' 'Dexter DuCaine?'"

"I don't think I have screen presence."

"But you can call off the bimbos in the buggies? Damp down all activities so we can finish our flick and head home?"

"That can be arranged."

"And Junior isn't going to get hurt? This isn't some Satanic sacrifice deal? Say, that's a great title. *Satan's Sacrifice*. Must register it. Maybe *Satan's Bloody Sacrifice*. Anything with blood in the title will gross an extra twenty percent. That's free advice you can take to the bank and cash."

"I simply want help in finding something. Your man can do that."

"Pal, Junior can't find his own pants in the morning even if he's slept in them. He's still got it on film, but half the time he doesn't know what year it is. And, frankly, he's better off that way. He still thinks he's in *Of Mice and Men*."

"If you remade that, would you call it *Of Mice and Bloody Men*?"

Sam laughed. "*Of Naked Mice and Bloody Men*."

"Do we have a deal?"

"I'll talk to Junior."

"Thank you."

After dark, the two camps were pitched. Charlie's Family were around the ranch-house, clustering on the porch for a meal prepared and served by the girls, which was not received enthusiastically. Constant formulated elaborate sentences of polite and constructive culinary criticism which made head chef Lynette Alice, a.k.a. Squeaky, glare as if she wanted to drown him in soup.

Leech had another future moment, seeing between the seconds. Drowned bodies hung, arms out like B-movie monsters, faces pale and shrivelled. Underwater zombies dragged weighted boots across the ocean floor, clothes flapping like torn flags. Finned priests called the faithful to prayer from the steps of sunken temples to Dagon and Cthulhu and the Fisherman Jesus.

Unnoticed, he spat out a stream of seawater which sank into the sand.

The Family scavenged their food, mostly by random shoplifting in markets, and were banned from all the places within an easy reach. Now they made do with whatever canned goods they had left over and, in some cases, food parcels picked up from the Chatsworth post office sent by suburban parents they despised but tapped all the time. Mom and Dad were a resource, Charlie said, like a seam of mineral in a rock, to be mined until it played out.

The situation was exacerbated by cooking smells wafting up from the film camp, down by the bunkhouse. The movie folk had a catering budget. Junior presided over a cauldron full of chili, his secret family recipe doled out to the cast and crew on all his movies. Leech gathered that some of Charlie's girls had exchanged blowjobs for bowls of that chili, which they then dutifully turned over to their lord and master in the hope that he'd let them lick out the crockery afterwards.

Everything was a matter of striking a deal. Service for payment.

Not hungry, he sat between the camps, considering the situation. He knew what Janice Marsh wanted, what Charlie wanted, what Al wanted, and what Sam wanted. He saw arrangements that might satisfy them all.

But he had his own interests to consider.

The more concrete the coming flood was in his mind, the less congenial an apocalypse it seemed. It was unsubtle, an upheaval that epitomised the saw about throwing out the baby with the bathwater. He envisioned more intriguing pathways through the future. He had already made an investment in this world, in the ways that it worked and played, and he was reluctant to abandon his own long-range plans to hop aboard a Technicolor spectacular starring a cast of thousands, scripted by Lovecraft, directed by DeMille, and produced by Mad Eyes Charlie and the Freakin' Family Band.

His favoured apocalypse was a tide of McLitter, a thousand channels of television noise, a complete scrambling of politics and entertainment, proud-to-be-a-breadhead buttons, bright packaging around tasteless and nutrition-free product, audiovisual media devoid of anything approaching meaning, bellies swelling and IQs atrophying. In his preferred world, as in the songs, people bowed and prayed to the neon god they made, worked for Matthew and Son, were dedicated followers of fashion, and did what Simon said.

He was in a tricky position. It was a limitation on his business that he could rarely set his own goals. In one way, he was like Sam's vampire: He couldn't go anywhere without an invitation. Somehow, he must further his own cause, while living up to the letter of his agreements.

Fair enough.

On his porch, Charlie unslung a guitar and began to sing, pouring revelations over a twelve-bar blues. Adoring faces looked up at him, red-fringed by the firelight.

From the movie camp came an answering wail.

Not coyotes, but stuntmen—led by the raucous Riff, whose singing had been dubbed in *West Side Story*—howling at the moon, whistling over emptied Jack Daniel's bottles, clanging tin plates together.

Charlie's girls joined in his chorus.

The film folk fired off blank rounds, and sang songs from the Westerns they'd been in. "Get Along Home, Cindy, Cindy." "Gunfight at O.K. Corrall." "The Code of the West."

Charlie dropped his acoustic, and plugged in an electric. The chords sounded the same, but the ampage somehow got into his reedy voice, which came across louder.

He sang sea shanties.

That put the film folk off for a while.

Charlie sang about mermaids and sunken treasures and the rising, rising waters.

He wasn't worse than many acts Leech had signed to his record label. If it weren't for this apocalypse jazz, he might have tried to make a deal with Charlie for his music. He'd kept back the fact that he had pull in the industry. Apart from other considerations, it'd have made Charlie suspicious. The man was naïve about many things, but he had a canny showbiz streak. He scorned all the trappings of a doomed civilisation, but bought *Daily Variety* and *Billboard* on the sly. You don't find Phil Spector wandering in the desert eating horse-turds. At least, not so far.

As Charlie sang, Leech looked up at the moon.

A shadow fell over him, and he smelled the Wolf Man.

"Is your name George?" asked the big man, eyes eager.

"If you need it to be."

"I only ask because it seems to me you could be a George. You got that Georgey look, if you know what I mean."

"Sit down, my friend. We should talk."

"Gee, uh, okay."

Junior sat cross-legged, arranging his knees around his comfortable belly. Leech struck a match, put it to a pile of twigs threaded with grass. Flame showed up Junior's nervous, expectant grin, etched shadows into his open face.

Leech didn't meet many Innocents. Yet here was one.

As Junior saw Leech's face in the light, his expression was shadowed. Leech remembered how terrified the actor had been when he first saw him.

"Why do I frighten you?" he asked, genuinely interested.

"Don't like to say," said Junior, thumb creeping towards his mouth. "Sounds dumb."

"I don't make judgements. That's not part of my purpose."

"I think you might be my Dad."

Leech laughed. He was rarely surprised by people. When it happened, he was always pleased.

"Not like that. Not like you and my Mom... you know. It's like my Dad's in you, somewhere."

"Do I look like him, Creighton?"

Junior accepted Leech's use of his true name. "I can't remember what he really looked like. He was the Man of a Thousand Faces. He didn't have a real face for home use. He'd not have been pleased with the way this turned out, George. He didn't want this for me. He'd have been real mad. And when he was mad, then he showed his vampire face..."

Junior bared his teeth, trying to do his father in *London After Midnight*.

"It's never too late to change."

Junior shook his head, clearing it. "Gosh, that's a nice thought, George. Sam says you want me to do you a favour. Sam's a good guy. He looks out for me. Always has a spot for me in his pictures. He says no one else can do justice to the role of Groton the Mad Zombie. If you're okay with Sam, you're okay with me. No matter about my Dad. He's dead a long time and I don't have to do what he says no more. That's the truth, George."

"Yes."

"So how can I help you?"

The Buggy Korps scrambled in the morning for the big mission. Only two vehicles were all-terrain-ready. Two three-person crews would suffice.

Given temporary command of Unit Number Two, Leech picked Constant as his driver. The German boy helped Junior into his padded seat, complimenting him on his performance as noble Chingachgook in a TV series of *The Last of the Mohicans* that had made it to East Germany in the 1950s.

This morning, Junior bubbled with enthusiasm, a big kid going to the zoo. He took a look at Chocko, who had recently been sloshed with red paint, and pantomimed cringing shock.

Leech knew the actor's father sometimes came home from work in clown make-up and terrified his young son.

The fear was still there.

Unit Number Two was scrambled before Charlie was out of his hammock.

They waited. Constant, sticking to a prearranged plan, shut down his face, covering a pettish irritation that others did not adhere to such a policy, especially others who were theoretically in a command position.

The Family Führer eventually rolled into the light, beard sticky as a glazed doughnut, scratching lazily. He grinned like a cornered cat and climbed up onto Unit Number One—actually, Unit Number Four with a hastily-repainted number, since the real Number One was a wreck. As crew, Charlie cut a couple of the girls out of the corral: the thin and pale Squeaky, who always looked like she'd just been slapped, and a younger, prettier, stranger creature called Ouisch. Other girls glowered sullen resentment and envy at the chosen ones. Ouisch tossed her long dark hair smugly and blew a gum-bubble in triumph. There was muttering of discontent.

If he had been Charlie, Leech would have taken the boy who could fix the motors, not the girls who gave the best blowjobs. But it wasn't his place to give advice.

Charlie was pleased with his mastery over his girls, as if it were difficult to mind-control American children. Leech thought that a weakness. Even as Charlie commanded the loyalty of the chicks, the few men in the Family grumbled. They got away with sniping resentment because their skills or contacts were needed. Of the group at the Ranch, only Constant had deal-making potential.

"Let's roll, Rat Patrol," decreed Charlie, waving.

The set-off was complicated by a squabble about protocol. Hitherto, in column outings—and two Units made a column—Charlie had to be in the lead vehicle. However, given that Junior was truffle-pig on this expedition, Unit Number One had to be in the rear, with Number Two out front.

Squeaky explained the rules, at length. Charlie shrugged, grinned, and looked ready to doze.

Leech was distracted by a glint from an upper window. A gush of dirty water came from a pipe. Janice Marsh's fish-face loomed in shadows, eyes eager. Stranded and flapping in this desert, no wonder she was thirsty.

Constant counterargued that this was a search operation, not a victory parade.

"We have rules or we're nothing, Kaptain Kraut," whined Squeaky.

It was easy to hear how she'd got her nickname.

"They should go first, Squeak," said Ouisch. "In case of mines. Or ambush. Charlie should keep back, safe."

"If we're going to change the rules, we should have a meeting."

Charlie punched Squeaky in the head. "Motion carried," he said.

Squeaky rubbed her nut, eyes crossed with anger. Charlie patted her, and she looked up at him, forcing adoration.

Constant turned the ignition—a screwdriver messily wired into the raped steering column—and the engine turned over, belching smoke.

Unit Number Two drove down the track, towards the arch.

Squeaky struggled to get Unit Number One moving.

"We would more efficient be if the others behind stayed, I think," said Constant.

Unit Number One came to life. There were cheers.

"Never mind, li'l buddy," said Junior. "Nice to have pretty girlies along on the trail."

"For some, it is nice."

The two-buggy column passed under the arch.

Junior's *feelings* took them up into the mountains. The buggies struggled with the gradient. These were horse-trails.

"This area, it has been searched thoroughly," said Constant.

"But I got a *powerful* feeling," said Junior.

Junior was eager to help. It had taken some convincing to make him believe in his powers of intuition, but now he had a firm faith in them. He realised he'd always had a supernatural ability to find things misplaced, like keys or watches. All his life, people had pointed it out.

Leech was confident. Junior was well cast as the One Who Will Open the Earth. It was in the prophecies.

Unit Number Two became wedged between rocks.

"This is as far as we can go in the buggy," said Constant.

"That's a real shame," said Junior, shaking his head, "'cause I've a rumbling in my guts that says we should be higher. What do you think, George? Should we keep on keeping on?"

Leech looked up. "If you hear the call."

"You know, George, I think I do. I really do. The call is calling."

"Then we go on."

Unit Number One appeared, and died. Steam hissed out of the radiator.

Charlie sent Ouisch over for a sit-rep.

Constant explained they would have to go on foot from now on.

"Some master driver you are, Schultzie," said the girl, giggling. "Charlie will have you punished for your failure. Severely."

Constant thought better of answering back.

Junior looked at the view, mopping the sweat off his forehead with a blue denim sleeve. Blotches of smog obscured much of the city spread out toward the grey-blue shine of the Pacific. Up here, the air was thin and at least clean.

"Looks like a train-set, George."

"The biggest a boy ever had," said Leech.

Constant had hiking boots and a backpack with rope, implements, and rations. He checked over his gear, professionally.

It had been Ouisch's job to bottle some water, but she'd got stoned last night and forgot. Junior had a hip-flask, but it wasn't full of water.

Leech could manage, but the others might suffer.

"If before we went into the high desert a choice had been presented of whether to go *with* water or *without*, I would have voted for 'with,'" said Constant. "But such a matter was not discussed."

Ouisch stuck her tongue out. She had tattooed a swastika on it with a blue ballpoint pen. It was streaky.

Squeaky found a Coca-Cola bottle rolling around in Unit Number One, an inch of soupy liquid in the bottom. She turned it over to Charlie, who drank it down in a satisfied draught. He made as if to toss the bottle off the mountain like a grenade, but Leech took it from him.

"What's the deal, Mr. Fish? No one'll care about littering when Helter Skelter comes down."

"This can be used. Constant, some string, please."

Constant sorted through his pack. He came up with twine and a Swiss army knife.

"Cool blade," said Charlie. "I'd like one like that."

Squeaky and Ouisch looked death at Constant until he handed the knife over. Charlie opened up all the implements, until the knife looked like a triggered booby-trap. He cleaned under his nails with the bradawl.

Leech snapped his fingers. Charlie gave the knife over.

Leech cut a length of twine and tied one end around the bottle's wasp-waist. He dangled it like a plum-bob. The bottle circled slowly.

Junior took the bottle, getting the idea instantly.

Leech closed the knife and held it out on his open palm. Constant resentfully made fists by his sides. Charlie took the tool, snickering to himself. He felt its balance for a moment, then pitched it off the mountainside. The Swiss Army Knife made a long arc into the air and plunged, hundreds and hundreds of feet, bounced off a rock, and fell further.

Long seconds later, the tumbling speck disappeared.

"Got to rid ourselves of the trappings, Kraut-Man."

Constant said nothing.

Junior had scrambled up the rocky incline, following the nose of the bottle. "Come on, guys," he called. "This is it. El Doradio. I can feel it in my bones. Don't stick around, slowcoaches."

Charlie was first to follow.

Squeaky, who had chosen to wear flip-flops rather than boots, volunteered to stay behind and guard the Units.

"Don't be a drag-hag, soldier," said Charlie. "Bring up the freakin' rear."

Leech kept pace.

From behind, yelps of pain came frequently.

Leech knew where to step, when to breathe, which rocks were solid enough to provide handholds and which would crumble or come away at a touch. Instinct told him how to hold his body so that gravity didn't tug him off the mountain. His inertia actually helped propel him upwards.

Charlie gave him a sideways look.

Though the man was thick-skinned and jail-tough, physical activity wasn't his favoured pursuit. He needed to make it seem as if he found the mountain path easy, but breathing the air up here was difficult for him. He had occasional coughing jags. Squeaky and Ouisch shouldered their sweet lord's weight and helped him, their own thin legs bending as he relaxed on their support, allowing himself to be lifted as if by angels.

Constant was careful, methodical, and made his way on his own.

But Junior was out ahead, following his bottle, scrambling between rocks and up nearly sheer inclines. He stopped, stood on a rocky outcrop, and looked down at them, then bellowed for the sheer joy of being alive and in the wilderness.

The sound carried out over the mountains and echoed.

"Charlie," he shouted, "how about one of them songs of yours?"

"Yes, that is an idea good," said Constant, every word barbed. "An inspiration is needed for our mission."

Charlie could barely speak, much less sing "The Happy Wanderer" in German.

Grimly, Squeaky and Ouisch harmonised a difficult version of "The Mickey Mouse Marching Song." Struggling with Charlie's dead weight, they found the will to carry on and even put some spit and vigour into the anthem.

Leech realised at once what Charlie had done.

The con had simply stolen the whole idea outright from Uncle Walt. He'd picked up these dreaming girls, children of postwar privilege raised in homes with buzzing refrigerators in the kitchen and finned automobiles in the garage, recruiting them a few years on from their first Mouseketeer phase, and electing himself Mickey.

Hey there ho there hi there…

When they chanted "Mickey Mouse… Mickey Mouse," Constant

even croaked "Donald Duck" on the offbeat.

Like Junior, Leech was overwhelmed with the sheer joy of the century.

He loved these children, dangerous as they were, destructive as they would be. They had such open, yearning hearts. They would find many things to fill their voids and Leech saw that he could be there for them in the future, up to 2001 and beyond, on the generation's ultimate trip.

Unless the rains came first.

"Hey, George," yelled Junior. "I dropped my bottle down a hole."

Everyone stopped and shut up.

Leech listened.

"Aww, what a shame," said Junior. "I lost my bottle."

Leech held up a hand for silence.

Charlie was puzzled, and the girls sat him down.

Long seconds later, deep inside the mountain, Leech heard a splash. No one else caught the noise.

"It's found," he announced.

Only Ouisch was small enough to pass through the hole. Constant rigged up a rope cradle and lowered her. She waved bye-bye as she scraped into the mountain's throat. Constant measured off the rope in cubits, unrolling loops from his forearm.

Junior sat on the rock, swigging from his flask.

Squeaky glared pantomime evil at him and he offered the flask to Charlie.

"That's your poison, man," he said.

"You should drop acid," said Squeaky. "So you can learn from the wisdom of the mountain."

Junior laughed, big belly-shaking chuckles.

"You're funnin' me, girl. Ain't nothing dumber than a mountain."

Leech didn't add to the debate.

Constant came to end of the rope. Ouisch dangled fifty feet inside the rock.

"It's dark," she shouted up. "And wet. There's water all around. Water with things in it. Icky."

"Have you ever considered the etymology of the term 'icky'?" asked Leech. "Do you suppose this primal, playroom expression of disgust could be related to the Latin prefix 'ichthy,' which translates literally as 'fishy'?"

"I was in a picture once, called *Manfish*," said Junior. "I got to be out on boats. I like boats."

"*Manfish*? Interesting name."

"It was the name of the boat in the movie. Not a monster, like that Black

Lagoon thing. Universal wouldn't have me in that. I did *The Alligator People*, though. Swamp stuff. Big stiff suitcase-skinned gator-man."

"Man-fish," said Charlie, trying to hop on the conversation train. "I get it. I see where you're coming from, where you're going. The Old Lady. What's she, a mermaid? An old mermaid?"

"You mean she really looks like that?" yelped Squeaky. "The one time I saw her I was tripping. Man, that's messed up! Charlie, I think I'm scared."

Charlie cuffed Squeaky around the head.

"Ow, that hurt."

"Learn from the pain, child. It's the only way."

"You shouldn't ought to hit ladies, Mr. Man," said Junior. "It's not like with guys. Brawlin' is part of being a guy. But with ladies, it's, you know, not polite. Wrong. Even when you've got a snoutful, you don't whop on a woman."

"It's for my own good," said Squeaky, defending her master.

"Gosh, little lady, are you sure?"

"It's the only way I'll learn." Squeaky picked up a rock and hit herself in the head with it, raising a bruise. "I love you, Charlie," she said, handing him the bloody rock.

He kissed the stain, and Squeaky smiled as if she'd won a gold star for her homework and been made head cheerleader on the same morning.

Ouisch popped her head up out of the hole like a pantomime chimneysweep. She had adorable dirt on her cheeks.

"There's a way down," she said. "It's narrow here, but opens out. I think it's a, whatchumacallit, passage. The rocks feel smooth. We'll have to enbiggen the hole if you're all to get through."

Constant looked at the problem. "This stone, that stone, that stone," he said, pointing out loose outcrops around the lip of the hole. "They will come away."

Charlie was about to make fun of the German boy, but held back. Like Leech, he sensed that the kid knew what he was talking about.

"I study engineering," Constant said. "I thought I might build houses."

"Have to tear down before you can build up," said Charlie.

Constant and Squeaky wrestled with rocks, wrenching them loose, working faults into cracks. Ouisch slipped into the hole, to be out of the way.

Charlie didn't turn a hand to the work. He was here in a supervisory capacity.

Eventually the stones were rolled away.

"Strange, that is," said Constant as sun shone into the hole. "Those could be steps."

There were indeed stairs in the hole.

Constant, of course, had brought a battery flashlight. He shone it into the hole. Ouisch sat on a wet step.

The stairs were old, prehuman.

Charlie tapped Squeaky, pushed her a little. She eased herself into the hole, plopping down next to Ouisch.

"You light the way," he told Constant. "The girls will scout ahead. Reconnaissance."

"Nothing down there but water," said Junior. "Been there a long time."

"Maybe no people. But big blind fish."

The Family crowd descended the stairs, their light swallowed by the hole.

Leech and Junior lingered topside.

Charlie looked up. "You comin' along, Mr. Fish?"

Leech nodded. "It's all right," he told Junior. "We'll be safe in the dark."

Inside the mountain, everything was cold and wet. Natural tunnels had been shaped by intelligent (if webbed) hands at some point. The roofs were too low even for the girls to walk comfortably, but scarred patches of rock showed where paths had been cut, and the floor was smoothed by use. Sewer-like runnel-gutters trickled with fresh water. Somehow, no one liked to drink the stuff—though the others must all have a desert thirst.

They started to find carved designs on the rocks. At first, childish wavy lines with stylised fish swimming.

Charlie was excited by the nearness of the sea.

They could hear it, roaring below. Junior felt the pull of the water.

Leech heard the voices in the roar.

Like a bloodhound, Junior led them through triune junctions, down forking stairways, past stalactite-speared cave-dwellings, deeper into the three-dimensional maze inside the mountain.

"We're going to free the waters," said Charlie. "Let the deluge wash down onto the city. This mountain is like a big dam. It can be blown."

The mountain was more like a stopper jammed onto a bottle. Charlie was right about pressure building up. Leech felt it in his inner ears, his eyes, his teeth. Squeaky had a nosebleed. The air was thick, wet with vapour. Marble-like balls of water gathered on the rock roof and fell on them, splattering on clothes like liquid bullets. In a sense, they were already underwater.

It would take more than dynamite to loose the flood; indeed, it would take more than physics. However, Charlie was not too far off the mark in imagining what could be done by loosening a few key rocks. There was the San Andreas fault to play with. Constant would know which rocks to take out of the puzzle. A little directed spiritual energy, some sacrifices, and the Coast of California could shear away like a slice of pie. Then the stopper would be off, and the seas would rise, waking up the gill-people, the mer-folk, the squidface fellows. A decisive turn and a world war would be lost, by the straights, the over-thirties, the cops and docs and pols, the Man. Charlie and Chocko could stage their last war games, and the sea-birds would cheer *tekeli-li tekeli-li…*

Leech saw it all, like a coming attraction. And he wasn't sure he wanted to pay to see that movie.

Maybe on a rerun triple feature with drastically reduced admission, slipped in between *Night of the Living Dead* and *Planet of the Apes*.

Seriously, *Hello Dolly!* spoke to him more on his level.

"The Earth is hollow," said Charlie. "The Nazis knew that."

Constant winced at mention of Nazis. Too many Gestapo jokes had made him sensitive.

"Inside, there are the big primal forces, water and fire. They're here for us, space kiddettes. For the Family. This is where the Helter Skelter comes down."

The tunnel opened up into a cathedral.

They were on an upper level of a tiered array of galleries and balconies. Natural rock and blocky construction all seemed to have melted like wax, encrusted with salty matter. Stalactites hung in spiky curtains, stalagmites raised like obscene columns.

Below, black waters glistened.

Constant played feeble torchlight over the interior of the vast space.

"Far out, man," said Ouisch.

"Beautiful," said Junior.

There was an echo, like the wind in a pipe organ.

Greens and browns mingled in curtains of icy rock, colours unseen for centuries.

"Here's your story," said Constant.

He pointed the torch at a wall covered in an intricate carving. A sequence of images—an *underground comic!*—showed the mountain opening up, the desert fractured by a jagged crack, a populated flood gushing forth, a city swept into the sea. There was a face on the mountain, grinning in triumph—Charlie, with a swastika on his forehead, his beard and hair tangled like seaweed.

"So, is that your happy ending?" Leech asked.

For once, Charlie was struck dumb. Until now he had been riffing, a yarning jailbird puffing up his crimes and exploits, spinning sci-fi stories and channelling nonsense from the void. To keep himself amused as he marked off the days of his sentence.

"Man," he said, "it's all true."

This face proved it.

"This is the future. Helter Skelter."

Looking closer at the mural, the city wasn't exactly Los Angeles, but an Aztec-Atlantean analogue. Among the drowning humans were fishier bipeds. There were step-pyramids and Studebaker dealerships, temples of sacrifice and motion picture studios.

"It's *one* future," said Leech. "A possible, maybe probable future."

"And you've brought me to it, man. I knew you were the real deal!"

The phrase came back in an echo, "real deal... real deal."

"The real deal? Very perceptive. This is where we make the real deal, Charles. This is where we take the money or open the box, this is make-your-mind-up-time."

Charlie's elation was cut with puzzlement.

"I've dropped that tab," announced Ouisch.

Junior looked around. "Where? Let's see if we can pick it up."

Charlie took Constant's torch and shone it at Leech.

"You don't blink."

"No."

Charlie stuck the torch under his chin, demon-masking his features. He tried to snarl like his million-year-old carved portrait.

"But I'm the Man, now. The Man of the Mountain."

"I don't dispute that."

"The Old Lady has told me how it works," said Charlie, pointing to his head. "You think I don't get it, but I do. We've been stashing ordinance. The kraut's a demolition expert. He'll see where to place the charges. Bring this place down and let the waters out. I know that's not enough. This is an imaginary mountain as much as it is a physical one. That's why they've been filming crappy Westerns all over it for so long. This is a place of stories. And it has to be opened in the mind, has to be cracked on another plane. I've been working on the rituals. My album, that's one. And the blood sacrifices, the offerings of the pigs."

"I can't wait to off my first pig," said Ouisch, cutely wrinkling her nose.

"I'm going to be so freakin' *famous*."

"Famous ain't all that," put in Junior. "You think bein' famous will make things work out right, but it doesn't at all. Screws you up more, if you ask me."

"I didn't, Mummy Man," spat Charlie. "You had your shot, dragged your leg through the tombs..."

Squeaky began to sing, softly.

"We shall over-whelm, we shall over-whe-e-elm, we shall overwhelm some day-ay-ay..."

Charlie laughed.

"It's the end of their world. No more goddamn movies. You know how much I hate the movies? The *lies* in the movies. Now, I get to wipe Hollywood off the map. Hell, I get to wipe the *map* off the map. I'll burn those old Spanish charts when we get back to the Ranch. No more call for them."

Constant was the only one paying attention to Leech. Smart boy.

"It'll be so *simple*," said Charlie. "So pure. All the pigs get offed. Me and Chocko do the last dance. I defeat the clowns, lay them down forever. Then we start all over. Get it right this time."

"Simple," said Leech. "Yes, that's the word."

"This happened before, right? With the Old Lady's people. The menfish. Then we came along, the menmen, and fouled it up again, played exactly the same tune. Not this time. This time, there's the Gospel According to Charlie."

"Hooray and Hallelujah," sang Ouisch, "you got it comin' to ya…"

The drip of water echoed enormously, like the ticking of a great clock.

"I do believe our interests part the ways here," said Leech. "You yearn for simplicity, like these children. You hate the movies, the storybooks, but you want cartoons, you want a big finish and a new episode next week. Wipe it all away and get back to the garden. It's easy because you don't have to think about it."

He hadn't lost Charlie, but he was scaring the man. Good.

"I like complexity," said Leech, relishing the echo. "I *love* it. There are so many more opportunities, so many more arrangements to be made. What *I* want is a rolling apocalypse, a transformation, a thousand victories a day, a spreading of interests, a permanent revolution. My natural habitat is civilisation. Your ultimate deluge might be amusing for a moment, but it'd pass. Even you'd get bored with children sitting around adoring you."

"You think?"

"I *know*, Charles."

Charlie looked at the faces of Ouisch and Squeaky, American girls, unquestioningly loyal, endlessly tiresome.

"No, Mr. Fish," he said, indicating the mural. "This is what I want. This is what I want to do."

"I brought you here. I showed you this."

"I know. You're part of the story too, aren't you? If the Mummy Man is the One Who Will Open the Earth, you're the Mysterious Guide."

"I'm not so mysterious."

"You're a part of this, you don't have a choice."

Charlie was excited but wheedling, persuasive but panicky. Having seen his preferred future, he was worried about losing it. Whenever the torch was away from the mural, he itched lest it should change in the dark.

"I promise you this, Charles, you will be famous."

Charlie thumped his chest. "Damn right. Good goddamn right!"

"But you might want to give this up. Write off this scripted Armageddon as just another fish story. You know, the one that got away. It was *this big*. I have other plans for the end of this century. And beyond. Have you ever noticed how it's only Gods who keep threatening to end the world? Father issues, if you ask me. Others, those of my party, promise things will continue as they are. Everyone gets what they deserve. You ain't seen nothin' yet because what you give is what you get."

Charlie shook his head. "I'm not there."

Squeaky and Ouisch were searching the mural, trying to find themselves in the crowded picture.

Charlie's eyes shone, ferocious.

"Our deal was to bring you here," said Leech, "to this sea. To this place of revelation. Our business is concluded. The service you requested has been done."

Junior raised a modest flipper, acknowledging his part.

"Yeah," said Charlie, distracted, flicking fingers at Junior, "muchas grassy-asses."

"You have recompensed our friend for his part in this expedition, by ensuring that his employers finish their shoot unimpeded. That deal is done and everyone is square. Now, let's talk about *getting out* of the mountain."

Charlie bit back a grin, surprised.

"What are you prepared to offer for that?"

"Don't be stupid, man," said Charlie. "We just go back on ourselves."

"Are you so confident? We took a great many turns and twists. Smooth rock and running water. We left no signs. Some of us might have a mind to sit by the sea for a spell, make some rods and go fishing."

"Good idea, George," said Junior. "Catch a marlin, I bet. Plenty good eating."

Charlie's eyes widened.

After a day or so, the torch batteries would die. He might wander blindly for months, *years*, down here, hopelessly lost, buried alive. Back at the Ranch, he'd not be missed much; Tex, or one of the others, maybe one of the girls, could be the new Head of the Family, and would perhaps do things better all round. The girls would be no use to him, in the end. Squeaky and Ouisch couldn't guide him out of this fish city, and he couldn't live off them for more than a few weeks. Charlie saw the story of the Lost Voyager as vividly as he had the Drowning of Los Angeles. It ended not with a huge face carved on a mountain and feared, but with forgotten bones, lying forever in wet darkness.

"I join you in fishing, I think," said Constant.

Charlie had lost Constant on the mountain. Later, Leech would formalise a deal with the boy. He had an ability to put things together or take them apart. Charlie had been depending on that. He should have taken the trouble to offer Constant something of equal value to retain his services.

"No, no, this can't be right."

"You show Charlie the way out, meanie," said Ouisch, shoving Junior.

"If you know what's good for you," said Squeaky.

"One word and you're out of here safe, Charles," said Leech. "But abandon the deluge. I want Los Angeles where it is. I want *civilisation* just where it is. I have plans, you dig?"

"You're scarin' me, man," said Charlie, nervy, strained, near tears.

Leech smiled. He knew he showed more teeth than seemed possible.

"Yes," he said, the last sound hissing in echo around the cavern. "I know."

Minutes passed. Junior hummed a happy tune, accompanied by musical echoes from the stalactites.

Leech looked at Charlie, outstaring his Satan glare, trumping his ace.

At last, in a tiny voice, Charlie said, "Take me home."

Leech was magnanimous. "But of course, Charles. Trust me, this way will suit you better. Pursue your interests, wage your war against the dream factory, and you will be remembered. Everyone will know your name."

"Yeah, man, whatever. Let's get going."

"Creighton," said Leech. "It's night up top. The moon is full. Do you think you can lead us to the moonlight?"

"Sure thing, George. I'm the Wolf Man, ahhh-*woooooo!*"

Janice Marsh had died while they were under the mountain. Her room stank and bad water sloshed on the carpets. The tarpaulin served as her shroud.

Leech hated to let her down, but she'd had too little to bring to the table. She had been a coelacanth, a living fossil.

Charlie announced that he was abandoning the search for the Subterranean Sea of California, that there were other paths to Helter Skelter. After all, was it not written that when you get to the bottom you start again at the top. He told his Family that his album would change the world when he got it together with Dennis, and he sang them a song about how the pigs would suffer.

Inside, Charlie was terrified. That would make him more dangerous.

But not as dangerous as Derek Leech.

Before he left the Ranch, in a requisitioned buggy with Constant at the wheel, Leech sat a while with Junior.

"You've contributed more than you know," he told Junior. "I don't often do this, but I feel you're owed. So, no deals, no contracts, just an offer. A no-strings offer. It will set things square between us. What do you want? What can I do for you?"

Leech had noticed how hoarse Junior's speech was, gruffer even than you'd expect after years of chili and booze. His father had died of throat cancer, a silent movie star bereft of his voice. The same poison was just touching the son, extending tiny filaments of death around his larynx. If asked, Leech could call them off, take away the disease.

Or he could fix up a big budget star vehicle at Metro, a Lifetime Achievement Academy Award, a final marriage to Ava Gardner, a top-ten record with the Monkees, a hit TV series...

Junior thought a while, then hugged Leech.

"You've already done it, George. You've already granted my wish. You call me by my name. By my Mom's name. Not by *his*, not by 'Junior.' They had to starve me into taking it. That's all I ever wanted. My own name."

It was so simple. Leech respected that; those who asked only for a little respect, a little place of their own—they should get what they deserve, as much as those who came greedily to the feast, hoping for all you can eat.

"Goodbye, Creighton," he said.

Leech walked away from a happy man.

Cold Snap

I

"Nice motor," said Richard Jeperson, casting an appreciative eye over Derek Leech's Rolls Royce ShadowShark.

"I could say the same of yours," responded Leech, gloved fingertips lightly polishing his red-eyed Spirit of Ecstasy. Richard's car was almost identical, though his bonnet ornament didn't have the inset rubies.

"I've kept the old girl in good nick," said Richard.

"Mine has a horn which plays the theme from *Jaws*," said Leech.

"Mine, I'm glad to say, doesn't."

That was the pleasantries over.

It was the longest, hottest, driest summer of the 1970s. Thanks to a strict hosepipe ban, lawns turned to desert. Neighbours informed on each other over suspiciously verdant patches. Bored regional television crews shot filler about eggs frying on dustbin lids and sunburn specialists earning consultancy fees in naturist colonies. If they'd been allowed anywhere near here, a considerably more unusual summer weather story was to be had. A news blackout was in effect, and discreet roadblocks limited traffic onto this stretch of the Somerset Levels.

The near-twin cars were parked in a lay-by, equidistant from the seemingly Mediterranean beaches of Burnham-on-Sea and Lyme Regis. While the nation sweltered in Bermuda shorts and flip-flops, Richard and Leech shivered in arctic survival gear. Richard wore layers of bearskin, furry knee-length boots with claw-toes, and a lime green balaclava surmounted by a scarlet Andean bobble hat with chinchilla earmuffs—plus the wraparound anti-glare visor recommended by Jean-Claude Killy. Leech wore a snow-white, fur-hooded parka and baggy leggings, ready to lead an Alpine covert assault troop. If not for his black Foster Grants, he could stand against a whitewashed wall and impersonate the Invisible Man.

Around them was a landscape from a malicious Christmas card. They stood in a Cold Spot. Technically, a patch of permafrost, four miles across. From the air, it looked like a rough circle of white stitched onto a brown quilt. Earth stood hard as iron, water like a stone... snow had fallen, snow had fallen, *snow on snow*. The epicentre was Sutton Mallet, a hamlet consisting of a few farmhouses, New Chapel (which replaced the old one in 1829), and the Derek Leech International weather research facility.

Leech professed innocence, but this was his fault. Most bad things were.

Bernard Levin said on *Late Night Line-Up* that Leech papers had turned Fleet Street into a Circle of Hell by boasting fewer words and more semi-naked girls than anything else on the newsstands. Charles Shaar Murray insisted in *IT* that the multi-media tycoon was revealed as the Devil Incarnate when he invented the "folk rock cantata" triple LP. The Diogenes Club had seen Derek Leech coming for a long time, and Richard knew exactly what he was dealing with.

Their wonderful cars could go no further, so they had to walk.

After several inconclusive, remote engagements, this was their first face-to-face (or visor-to-sunglasses) meeting. The Most Valued Member of the Diogenes Club and the Great Enchanter were expected to be the antagonists of the age, but the titles meant less than they had in the days of Mycroft Holmes, Charles Beauregard, and Edwin Winthrop or Leo Dare, Isidore Persano, and Colonel Zenf. Lately, both camps had other things to worry about.

From two official world wars, great nations had learned to conduct their vast duels without all-out armed conflict. Similarly, the Weird Wars of 1903 and 1932 had changed the shadow strategies of the Diogenes Club and its opponents. In the Worm War, there had almost been battle-lines. It had only been won when a significant number of Persano's allies and acolytes switched sides, appalled at the scope of the crime ("the murder of time and space") planned by the wriggling mastermind ("a worm unknown to science") the Great Enchanter kept in a match-box in his waistcoat pocket. The Wizard War, when Beauregard faced Zenf, was a more traditional game of good and evil, though nipped in the bud by stealth, leaving the Club to cope with the ab-human threat of the Deep Ones ("the Water War") and the mundane business of "licking Hitler." Now, in what secret historians were already calling the Winter War, no one knew who to fight.

So, strangely, this was a truce.

As a sensitive—a Talent, as the parapsychology bods had it—Richard was used to trusting his impressions of people and places. He knew in his water when things or folks were out of true. If he squinted, he saw their real faces. If he cocked an ear, he heard what they were thinking. Derek Leech seemed perfectly sincere, and elaborately blameless. No matter how furiously Richard blinked behind his visor, he saw no red horns, no forked beard, no extra mouths. Only a tightness in the man's jaw gave away the effort it took to present himself like this. Leech had to be mindful of a tendency to grind his teeth.

They had driven West—windows rolled down in the futile hope of a cool breeze—through parched, sunbaked countryside. Now, despite thermals and furs, they shivered. Richard saw Leech's breath frosting.

"Snow in July," said Leech. "Worse. Snow in *this* July."

"It's not snow, it's *rime*. Snow is frozen rain. Precipitation. Rime is frozen dew. The moisture in the air, in the ground."

"Don't be such an arse, Jeperson."

"As a newspaperman, you appreciate accuracy."

"As a newspaper *publisher*, I know elitist vocabulary alienates readers. If it looks like snow, tastes like snow, and gives you a white Christmas, then…"

Leech had devised *So What Do You Know?*, an ITV quiz show where prizes were awarded not for correct answers, but for matching whatever was decided—right or wrong—by the majority vote of a "randomly selected panel of ordinary Britons." Contestants had taken home fridge-freezers and fondue sets by identifying Sydney as the capital of Australia or categorising whales as fish. Richard could imagine what Bernard Levin and Charles Shaar Murray thought of that.

Richard opened the boot of his Rolls and hefted out a holdall which contained stout wicker snowshoes, extensible aluminium ski-poles, and packs of survival rations. Leech had similar equipment, though his boot-attachments were spiked black metal and his rucksack could have contained a jet propulsion unit.

"I'd have thought DLI could supply a Sno-Cat."

"Have you any idea how hard it is to come by one in July?"

"As it happens, yes."

They both laughed, bitterly. Fred Regent, one of the Club's best men, had spent most of yesterday learning that the few places in Great Britain which leased or sold snow-ploughs, caterpillar tractor bikes, or jet-skis had either sent their equipment out to be serviced, shut up shop for the summer, or gone out of business in despair at unending sunshine. Heather Wilding, Leech's Executive Assistant, had been on the same fruitless mission—she and Fred kept running into each other outside lock-ups with "come back in November" posted on them.

Beyond this point, the road to Sutton Mallet—a tricky proposition at the best of times—was impassable. The hamlet was just visible a mile off, black roofs stuck out of white drifts. The fields were usually low-lying, marshy, and divided by shallow ditches called rhynes. In the last months, the marsh had set like concrete. The rhynes had turned into stinking runnels, with the barest threads of mud where water usually ran. Now, almost overnight, everything was deep-frozen and heavily frosted. The sun still shone, making a thousand glints, twinkles, and refractions. But there was no heat.

Trees, already dead from Dutch elm disease or roots loosened from the dry dirt, had fallen under the weight of what only Richard wasn't calling snow, and lay like giant blackened corpses on field-sized shrouds. Telephone poles were down too. No word had been heard from Sutton

Mallet in two days. A hardy postman had tried to get through on his bicycle, but not come back. A farmer set off to milk his cows and had also been swallowed in the whiteness. A helicopter flew over, but the rotor blades slowed as heavy ice-sheaths grew on them. The pilot had barely made it back to Yeovilton Air Field.

Word had spread through "channels." Unnatural phenomena were Diogenes Club business, but Leech had to take an interest too—if only to prove that he wasn't behind the cold snap. Heather Wilding had made a call to Pall Mall, and officially requested the Club's assistance. That didn't happen often or—come to think of it—ever.

Leech looked across the white fields towards Sutton Mallet.

"So we walk," he said.

"It's safest to follow the ditches," advised Richard.

Neither bothered to lock their cars.

They clambered—as bulky and awkward as astronauts going EVA—over a stile to get into the field. The white carpet was virginal. As they tramped on, in the slight trough that marked the rime-filled rhyne, Richard kept looking sidewise at Leech. The man was breathing heavily inside his polar gear. Being incarnate involved certain frailties. But it would not do to underestimate a Great Enchanter.

Derek Leech had popped up apparently out of nowhere in 1961. A day after Colonel Zenf finally died in custody, he first appeared on the radar, making a freak run of successful long-shot bets at a dog track. Since then, he had made several interlocking empires. He was a close friend of Harold Wilson, Brian Epstein, Lord Leaves of Leng, Enoch Powell, Roman Polanski, Mary Millington, and Jimmy Saville. He was into *everything*—newspapers (the down-market tabloid *Daily Comet* and the reactionary broadsheet *Sunday Facet*), pop records, telly, a film studio, book publishing, frozen foods, football, road building, antidepressants, famine relief, contraception, cross-channel hovercraft, draught lager, touring opera productions, market research, low-cost fashions, educational playthings. He had poked his head out of a trapdoor on *Batman* and expected to be recognised by Adam West—"it's not the *Clock King*, Robin, it's the English *Pop King*, Derek Leech." He appeared in his own adverts, varying his catch-phrase—"if I didn't love it, I wouldn't..." eat it, drink it, watch it, groove it, use it, wear it, bare it, shop it, stop it, make it, take it, kiss it, miss it, phone it, own it. He employed "radical visionary architect" Constant Drache to create "ultramoderne workplace environments" for DLI premises and the ranks upon ranks of "affordable homes for hard-working families" cropping up at the edges of conurbations throughout the land. It was whispered there were private graveyards under many a "Derek Leech Close" or "Derek Leech Drive." Few had tangled with Derek Leech and managed better than a draw. Richard counted himself among the few, but also suspected their occasional path-crossings hadn't been serious.

They made fresh, ragged footprints across the empty fields. They were the only moving things in sight. It was quiet too. Richard saw birds frozen in mid-tweet on boughs, trapped in globules of ice. No smoke rose from the chimneys of Sutton Mallet. Of course, what with the heat wave, even the canniest country folk might have put off getting in a store of fuel for next winter.

"Refresh my memory," said Richard. "How many people are at your weather research station?"

"Five. The director, two junior meteorologists, one general dogsbody, and a public relations–security consultant.'

Richard had gone over what little the Club could dig up on them. Oddly, a DLI press release provided details of only *four* of the staff.

"Who's the director again?" he asked.

"We've kept that quiet, as you know," said Leech. "It's Professor Cleaver. Another Dick, which is to say a *Richard*."

"Might have been useful to be told that," said Richard, testily.

"I'm telling you now."

Professor Richard Cleaver, a former time-server at the Meteorological Office, had authored *The Coming Ice Age*, an alarmist paperback propounding the terrifying theory of World Cooling. According to Cleaver, natural thickening of the ozone layer in the high atmosphere would, if unchecked, lead to the expansion of the polar icecaps and a global climate much like the one currently obtaining in Sutton Mallet. Now, the man was in the middle of his own prediction, which was troubling. There were recorded cases of individuals who worried so much about things that they made them happen. The Professor could be such a Talent.

They huffed into Sutton Mallet, past the chapel, and went through a small copse. On the other side was the research station, a low-lying cinderblock building with temporary cabins attached. There were sentinels in the front yard.

"Are you in the habit of employing frivolous people, Mr. Leech?"

"Only in my frivolous endeavours. I take the weather very seriously."

"I thought as much. Then who made those snowmen?"

They emerged from the rhyne and stood on hard-packed ice over the gravel forecourt of the DLI weather research facility. Outside the main doors stood four classic snowmen: three spheres piled one upon another as legs, torso, and head, with twigs for arms, carrots for noses, and coals for eyes, buttons, and mouths. They were individualised by scarves and headgear—top hat, tam o'shanter, pith helmet, and two toy bumblebees on springs attached to an alice band.

Leech looked at the row. "Rime-men, surely?" he said, pointedly. "As a busybody, you appreciate accuracy."

There were no footprints around the snowmen. No scraped-bare patches or scooped-out drifts. As if they had been grown rather than made.

"A frosty welcoming committee?" suggested Leech.

Before anything happened, Richard *knew*. It was one of the annoyances of his sensitivity—premonitions which come just too late to do anything about.

Top Hat's headball shifted: It spat out a coal, which cracked against Richard's visor. He threw himself down, to avoid further missiles. Top Hat's head was packed with coals, which it could sick up and aim with deadly force.

Leech was as frozen in one spot as the snowmen weren't. This sort of thing happened to others, but not to *him*.

Pith Helmet, who had a cardboard handlebar moustache like Zebedee from *The Magic Roundabout*, rose on ice-column legs and stalked towards Leech, burly white arms sprouting to displace feeble sticks, wicked icicles extruding from powdery fists.

Tam and Bee-Alice circled round, making as if to trap Richard and Leech in the line of fire.

Richard got up, grabbed Leech's arm, and pulled him away from Pith Helmet. It was hard to run in polar gear, but they stumped past Tam and Bee-Alice before the circle closed, and legged it around the main building.

Another snowman loomed up in front of them. In a postman's cap, with a mail-bag slung over its shoulder. It was a larger and looser thing than the others, more hastily made, with no face coals or carrot. They barrelled into the shape, which came apart, and sprawled in a tangle on the cold, cold ground—Richard felt the bite of black ice through his gauntlets as the heel of his hand jammed against grit. Under him was a dead but loose-limbed postman, grey-blue in the face, crackly frost in his hair. He had been inside the snowman.

The others were marching around the corner. Were there people inside them too? Somehow, they were frowning—perhaps it was in the angle of their headgear, as if brows were narrowed—and malice burned cold in their eye-coals.

Leech was on his feet first, hauling Richard upright.

Snow crawled around the postman again, forming a thick carapace. The corpse stood like a puppet, dutifully taking up its bag and cap, insistent on retaining its identity.

They were trapped between the snowmen. The five walking, hat-topped heaps had them penned.

Richard was tense, expecting ice-daggers to rip through his furs and into his heart. Leech reached into his snowsuit as if searching for his wallet—in this situation, money wasn't going to be a help. A proper devil would have some hellfire about his person. Or at least a blowtorch. Leech—who had recorded a series of anti-smoking adverts—managed to produce a flip-top cigarette lighter. He made a flame, which didn't seem to phase the snowmen, and wheeled around, looking for the one to negotiate with. Leech was big on making deals.

"Try Top Hat," suggested Richard. "In cartoon terms, he's obviously the leader."

Leech held the flame near Top Hat's face. Water trickled, but froze again, giving Top Hat a tear-streaked, semitransparent appearance. A slack face showed inside the ice.

"Who's in there?" asked Leech. "Cleaver?"

Top Hat made no motion.

A door opened, and a small, elderly man leaned out of the research station. He wore a striped scarf and a blue knit cap.

"No, Mr. Leech," said Professor Richard Cleaver, "I'm in here. You lot, let them in, now. You've had your fun. For the moment."

The snowmen stood back, leaving a path to the back door. Cleaver beckoned, impatient.

"Do come on," he said. "It's fweezing out."

Richard looked at Leech and shrugged. The gesture was matched. They walked towards the back door.

The last snowman was Bee-Alice. As they passed, it reared up like a kid pretending to be a monster, and stuck out yard-long pseudopods of gleaming ice, barbed with jagged claws. Then it retracted its arms and silently chortled at the shivering humans.

"That one's a comedian," said Cleaver. "You have to watch out."

Leech squeezed past the Professor, into the building. Richard looked at the five snowmen, now immobile and innocent-seeming.

"Come on, whoever you are," urged Cleaver. "What are you waiting for? Chwistmas?"

Richard slipped off his sun-visor, then followed Leech.

II

"You in the van, wakey-wakey," shouted someone, who was also hammering on the rear doors. "The world needs saving…"

"Again?" mumbled Jamie Chambers, waking up with another heat-headache and no idea of the time. Blackout shields on the windows kept out the daylight. Living in gloom was part of the Shade Legacy. He didn't even need Dad's night-vision goggles—which were around here somewhere—to see well enough in the dark.

He sorted through stiff black t-shirts for the freshest, then lay on his back and stuck his legs in the air to wriggle into skinny jeans. Getting dressed in the back of the van without doing himself an injury was a challenge. Sharp metal flanges underlay the carpet of sleeping bags, and any number of dangerous items were haphazardly hung on hooks or stuffed into cardboard boxes. When Bongo Foxe, the drummer in Transhumance, miraculously gained a girlfriend, he'd tactfully kicked Jamie out of the squat in Portobello Road. The keys and codes to Dad's old lair inside Big Ben were around somewhere, but Jamie could never get used to the constant ticking. Mum hated that too. Between addresses, the Black Van was his best option.

"Ground Control to Major Shade," called the hammerer, insistent and bored at the same time. Must be a copper.

"Hang on a mo," said Jamie, "I'm not decent."

"Hear that, Ness?" said the hammerer to a (female?) colleague. "Shall I pop the lock and give you a cheap thrill?"

One of the few pluses of van living, supposedly, was that gits like this couldn't find you. Jamie guessed he was being rousted by gits who could find *anybody*. For the second time this week. He'd already listened to Leech's twist, Heather Wilding. This'd be the other shower, the Diogenes Club. One of the things Jamie agreed with his father about was that it made sense to stay out of either camp and make your own way in the night.

Even parked in eternal shadow under railway arches, the van was like a bread oven with central heating. The punishing summer continued. After seconds, his t-shirt was damp. Within minutes, it'd be soaked and dried. This last six weeks, he'd sweated off pounds. Vron was freaked by how much his skeleton was showing.

He ran fingers through his crispy shock of raven hair (natural), checked a shaving mirror for blackheads (absent), undid special locks the hammerer oughtn't have been able to pop, and threw open the doors.

A warrant card was held in his face. Frederick Regent, New Scotland Yard (Detached). He was in plainclothes—blue jeans, red fred perry (with crimson sweat-patches), short hair, surly look. He couldn't have been more like a pig if he'd been oinking and had a curly tail. The girlfriend was a surprise—a red-haired bird with a *Vogue* face and a *Men Only* figure. She wore tennis gear—white plimsolls, knee-socks, shorts cut to look like a skirt, bikini top, Cardin cardigan—with matching floppy hat, milk-blank sunglasses (could she see through those?), and white lipstick.

"I'm Fred, this is Vanessa," said the Detached man. "You are James Christopher Chambers?"

"Jamie," he said.

Vanessa nodded, taking in his preference. She was the sympathetic one. Fred went for brusque. It was an approach, if tired.

"Jamie," said Fred, "we understand you've come into a doctorate?"

"Don't use it," he said, shaking his head. "It was my old man's game."

"But you have the gear," said Vanessa. She reached into the van and took Dad's slouch hat off a hook. "This is a vintage 'Dr. Shade' item."

"Give that back," said Jamie, annoyed.

Vanessa handed it over meekly. He stroked the hat as if it were a kitten, and hung it up again. There was family history in the old titfer.

"At his age, he can't really be a doctor," said Fred. "Has there ever been an Intern Shade?"

"I'm not a student," he protested.

"No, you're one of those dropouts. Had a place at Manchester University, but left after a term. Couldn't hack the accents oop North?"

"The band was taking off. All our gigs are in London."

"Don't have to justify your life-choices to us, mate. Except one."

Fred wasn't being quite so jokey.

"I think you should listen," said Vanessa, close to his ear. "The world really does need saving."

Jamie knew as much from Heather Wilding. She'd been more businesslike than this pair, drenched in Charlie, cream suit almost invisibly damp under the arms, two blouse buttons deliberately left unfastened to show an armoured white lace foundation garment.

"The other lot offered a retainer," he said. "Enough for a new amp."

"We heard you'd been approached," said Vanessa. "And were reluctant. Very wise."

Wilding hinted that Transhumance might be signed to a Derek Leech label. They didn't only put out moaning hippie box sets and collected bubblegum hits.

"You won't need an amp in the ice age," said Fred. "They'll be burning pop groups to keep going for a few more days."

"Yeah, I'm already shivering," said Jamie, unpicking wet cotton from his breastbone. "Chills up my spine."

"All this heat is a sign of the cold, they say."

"You what?"

Fred cracked a laugh. "Trust us, there could be a cold spell coming."

"Roll on winter, mate."

"Careful what you wish for, Jamie," said Vanessa.

She found his Dad's goggles in a box of eight-track tapes, and slipped them over his head. He saw clearly through the old, tinted glass.

"Saddle up and ride, cowboy," she said. "We're putting together a posse. Just for this round-up. No long-term contract involved."

"Why do you need me?" he asked.

"We need *everybody*," said Fred, laying a palm on the van and wincing—it was like touching a griddle. "Especially you, shadow-boy. You've got a license to drive and your own transport. Besides standing on the front lines for democracy and decent grub, you can give some of your new comrades a lift to the front. And I don't mean Brighton."

Jamie didn't like the sound of this. "What?" he protested.

"Congratulations, Junior Shade. You've got a new backing group. Are you ready to rock and—indeed—roll?"

Jamie felt that a trap had snapped around him. He was going into the family business after all.

He was going to be a doctor.

III

Inside the research station, crystals crunched underfoot and granulated on every surface. White stalactites hung from door-frames and the ceiling. Windows were iced over and stunted pot-plants frostbitten solid. Even lightbulbs had petals of ice.

Powdery banks of frost (indoor rime? snow, even?) drifted against cabinets of computers. Trudged pathways of clear, deep footprints ran close to the walls, and they kept to them—leaving most of the soft, white, glistening carpet untouched. Richard saw that little trails had been blazed into the rooms, keeping mainly to the edges and corners with rare, nimbler tracks to desks or work-benches. The prints had been used over again, as if their maker (Professor Cleaver?) were leery of trampling virgin white and trod carefully on the paths he had made when the cold first set in.

The Professor led them through the cafeteria, where trestle tables and chairs were folded and stacked away to clear the greatest space possible. Here, someone had been playing—making snow-angels, by lying down on the thick frost and moving their arms to make wing-shapes. Richard admired the care that had been taken. The silhouettes—three of them, with different wings, as if writing something in semaphore—matched Cleaver's tubby frame, but Richard couldn't imagine why he had worked so hard on something so childish. Leech had said he didn't employ frivolous people.

If anything, it was colder indoors than out. Richard felt sharp little chest pains when he inhaled, as if he were flash-freezing his alveoli. His exposed face was numb. He worried that if he were to touch his moustache, half would snap off.

They were admitted to the main laboratory. A coffee percolator was frosted up, its jug full of frothy brown solid. On a shelf stood a goldfish bowl, ice bulging over the rim. A startled fish was trapped in the miniature arctic. Richard wondered if it were still alive—like those dinosaurs they found in the 1950s. Here, the floor had been walked over many times, turned to orange slush and frozen again, giving it a rough moon-surface texture. Evidently, this was where the Professor lived.

Richard idly fumbled open a ring-binder that lay on a desk, and pressed his mitten to brittle blue paper.

"Paws off," snapped Cleaver, snatching the file away and hugging it. "That's tip-top secwet."

"Not from me," insisted Leech, holding out his hand. "I sign the cheques, remember. You work for me."

If Derek Leech signed his own cheques, Richard would be surprised.

"My letter of wesignation is in the post," said Cleaver. He blinked furiously when he spoke, as if simultaneously translating in Morse. Rhotacism made him sound childish. How cruel was it to give a speech impediment a technical name sufferers couldn't properly pronounce? "I handed it to the postman personally. I think he twied to deliver it to you outside. Vewy dedicated, the Post Office. Not snow, nor hail, and so on and so forth."

Leech looked sternly at the babbling little man.

"In that case, you'd better hand over all your materials and leave this facility. Under the circumstances, the severance package will not be generous."

Cleaver wagged a shaking hand at his former employer, not looking him in the eye. His blinks and twitches shook his whole body. He was laughing.

"In my letter," he continued, "I explain fully that this facility has declared independence from your organisation. Indeed, fwom all Earthly authowity. There are pwecedents. I've also witten to the Pwime Minister and the Met Office."

Leech wasn't used to this sort of talk from minions. Normally, Richard would have relished the Great Enchanter's discomfort. But it wasn't clear where his own—or, indeed, anybody's—best interests were in Ice Station Sutton Mallet.

"Mr. Leech, I know," said Cleaver, "not that we've ever met. I imagine you thought you had more important things to be bothewing with than poor old Clever Dick Cleaver's weather wesearch. Jive music and porn and so forth. I hear you've started a holiday company. Fun in the sun and all that. Jolly good show. Soon you'll be able to open bobsled runs on the Costa Bwava. I'm not surprised you've shown your face now. I expected it and I'm glad you're here. You, I had planned for. No, the face I don't know... don't know at all... is *yours*."

Cleaver turned to Richard.

"Richard Jeperson," he introduced himself. "I'm from..."

"...the *Diogenes Club*!" said Cleaver, viciously. "Yes, yes, yes, of course. I see the gleam. The wighteous gleam. Know it of old. The insuffewability. Is that fwightful Miss Cathewina Kaye still alive?"

"Catriona," corrected Richard. "Yes."

Currently, Catriona Kaye was Acting Chairman of the Ruling Cabal of the Diogenes Club. She had not sought the position. After the death of Edwin Winthrop, her partner in many things, no one else had been qualified. Richard was not yet ready to leave active service, and had a nagging feeling he wouldn't be suited to the Ruling Cabal anyway. There was talk of reorganising—"modernising"—the Club, and some of their rivals in Whitehall were bleating about "accountability" and "payment by results." If it weren't arcanely self-financing, the Club would have been dissolved or absorbed long ago.

"If it weren't for Cathewina Kaye, and a disservice she did me many many years ago, I might have taken a diffewent path. You know about this, Mr. Jeperson?"

A penny, long-teetering at the lip of a precipice, dropped—in slow motion, setting memory mechanisms ticking with each turn.

"Richard Cleaver? Clever Dick. You called yourself Clever Dick. That's who you are!"

"That's who I was... until that w-woman came along. She hates people like me... like both of you, pwobably... she only likes people who are n-normal. People who can't *do* anything. You know what I mean. *Normal.*"

He drew out the word, with contempt. Richard remembered a time—at school, as a young man—when *he* might have given the word such a knife-twist. Like Dick Cleaver, he had manifested a Talent early. While Cleaver demonstrated excess brain capacity, Richard showed excess feeling. Insights did not always make him happy. Ironically, it was Catriona—not his father or Edwin Winthrop—who most helped him cope with his Talent, to connect with people rather than become estranged. Without her, he might be a stuttering, *r*-dropping maniac.

"It was never about who you were, Cleaver," said Richard, trying to be kind. "It was about what you did."

Fury boiled behind Cleaver's eyes.

"*I didn't do anything!* We were the Splendid Six, and she took us apart, one by one, working in secwet with your dwatted Diogenes Club. We were heroes... Blackfist, Lord Piltdown, the Blue Stweak... and sh-she made us *small*, twied to make us *normal*. I'm the last of us, you know. The Splendid *One*. The Bwightest Boy in the World. The others are all dead."

Cleaver was coming up to pensionable age, but he was as frozen inside as his goldfish—still eleven, and poisonous.

"If I suffered a speech impediment like yours, I'd avoid words like 'dratted,'" commented Leech. "All this ancient history is fascinating, I'm sure. I know who you used to be, Professor. I don't hire anyone without knowing everything about them first. But I don't see what it has to do with all this... this cold business."

A sly look crept into Cleaver's eye. An I-know-a-secret-you're-not-going-to-like look.

"I wather think I've pwoved my point, Mr. Leech. You've wead my book, *The Coming Ice Age*?"

"I had someone read it and summarise the findings for me," said Leech, offhandedly. "Very convincing, very alarming. It's why you were headhunted—at a salary three times what you got at the Met—to head my weather research program."

What exactly had Derek Leech been doing here? Scientific weather control? For reasons which were now all too plain, Richard did not like the notion of a Great Enchanter with command over the elements.

"I employ the best, and you were the best man for this job. What you did as a schoolboy was irrelevant. I didn't even care that you were mad."

Clever Dick Cleaver sputtered.

"Sorry to be blunt, pal, but you are. I can show you the psych reports. Your insanity should not have hindered your ability to fulfil your contract. Quite the contrary. Derek Leech International has a policy of easing the lot of the mentally ill by finding them suitable positions. We consider it our social service remit, repaying a community that has given us so much."

Richard knew all about that. Myra Lark, acknowledged leader in field of shaping minds to suit the requirements of government and industry, was on Leech's staff. Some jobs you really had to be mad to take. Dr. Lark's, for instance.

"Your book convinced me it could happen. World Cooling. And only drastic action can forestall the catastrophe. With the full resources of DLI at your disposal, I was expecting happier results. Not this... this big fridge."

Cleaver smiled again.

"If you'd actually wead my book, you wouldn't be so surprised. Tell him, Jeperson."

Leech looked at Richard, awaiting enlightenment.

"Professor Cleaver writes that an imminent ice age will lead to worldwide societal collapse and, in all probability, the extinction of the human race."

"Yes, and...?"

"He does *not* write that this would be a bad thing."

Realisation dawned in Leech's eyes. Cleaver grinned broadly, showing white dentures with odd, cheap blue settings.

Derek Leech had given his weather control project to someone who *wanted* winter to come and freeze everything solid. Isidore Persano and his worm would be proud.

"What about the snowmen?" Leech asked.

"I was wondewing when you'd get to them. The snowmen. Yes. I'm not alone in this. I have fwiends. One fwiend, mainly. One big fwiend. I call her the Cold. You can call her the End."

IV

He was supposed to park outside the Post Office Tower and wait for the other recruits. One of the group would have further instructions and, he was promised, petrol money. Jamie was off to the Winter War.

Now he'd (provisionally) taken the Queen's Shilling, he wondered whether the Diogenes Club just wanted him as a handy, unpaid chauffeur, ferrying cannon fodder about. Dad wouldn't have thought a lot of that. Still, Jamie only wanted to dip a toe in the waters. He was leery about the shadow life. The Shade Legacy hadn't always been happy, as Mum would tell him at the drop of a black fedora with razors in the brim. At the moment, he was more interested in Transhumance—especially if they could find a better, preferably celibate drummer... and a new bass player, a decent PA, and enough songs to bump up their set to an hour without reprises. Vron had been promising new lyrics for weeks, but said the bloody heat made it hard to get into the proper mood. Perhaps he should scrub Transhumance and look for a new band.

The GPO Tower, a needle bristling with dish-arrays, looked like a leftover design from *Stingray*. The revolving restaurant at the summit, opened by Wedgy Benn and Billy Butlin, stopped turning in 1971, after an explosion the public thought was down to the Angry Brigade. Jamie knew the truth. His father's last "exploit" before enforced retirement had been the final defeat of his long-time enemies, the Dynamite Boys. The Tower was taken over by the now-octogenarian Boys, who planned to use the transmitters to send a coded signal to activate the lizard stems of every human brain in the Greater London area and turn folks into enraged animals. Dad stopped them by setting off their own bombs.

Jamie found a parking space in the thin shadow of the tower, which shifted within minutes. Inside the van, stale air began to boil again. Even with the windows down, there was no relief.

"Gather, darkness," he muttered. He hadn't Dad's knack with shadows, but he could at least whip up some healthy gloom. The sky was cloudless, but a meagre cloud-shadow formed around the van. It was too much effort to maintain, and he let it go. In revenge, the sun got hotter.

"Jamie Chambers," said a girl.

He looked out at her. She was dressed for veldt or desert: leather open-toe sandals, fawn culottes, baggy safari jacket, utility belt with pouches, burnt orange sunglasses the size of saucers, leopard-pattern headscarf, Australian bush hat. In a summer when Zenith the Albino sported a nut-brown suntan, her exposed lower face, forearms, and calves were pale to the point of colourlessness. People always said Jamie—as instinctively nocturnal as his father—should get out in the sun more, but this girl made him look like an advert for Air Malta. He would have guessed she was about his own age.

"Call me Gené," she said. "I know your aunt Jenny. And your mother, a bit. We worked together a long time ago, when she was Kentish Glory."

Mum had stopped wearing a moth-mask and film-winged leotards decades before Jamie was born. Gené was much older than nineteen.

He got out of the van, and found he was several inches taller than her.

"I'm from the Diogenes Club," she said, holding up an envelope. "You're our ride to Somerset. I've got maps and money here. And the rest of the new bugs."

Three assorted types, all less noticeable than Gené, were loitering.

"Keith, Susan, and... Sewell, isn't it?"

A middle-aged, bald-headed man stepped forward and nodded. He wore an old, multi-stained overcoat, fingerless Albert Steptoe gloves, and a tightly wound woolly scarf as if he expected a sudden winter. His face was unlined, as if he rarely used it, but sticky marks around his mouth marked him as a sweet-addict. He held a paper bag, and was chain-chewing liquorice allsorts.

"Sewell Head," said Gené, tapping her temple. "He's one of the *clever* ones. And one of theirs. Derek Leech fetched him out of a sweetshop. Ask him anything, and he'll know."

"What's Transhumance?" asked Jamie.

"A form of vertical livestock rotation, practiced especially in Switzerland," said Sewell Head, popping a pink coconut wheel into his mouth. "Also a London-based popular music group which has never released a record or played to an audience of more than fifty people."

"Fifty is a record for some venues, pal."

"I told you he'd *know*," said Gené. "Does he look evil to you? Or is Hannah Arendt right about banality? He's behaved himself so far. No decapitated kittens. The others are undecideds, not ours, not theirs. Wavering."

"I'm not wavering," said the other girl, Susan. "I'm neutral."

She wore jeans and a purple t-shirt, and hid behind her long brown hair. She tanned like most other people and had pinkish sunburn scabs on her arms. Jamie wondered if he'd seen her before. She must be a year or two older than him, but gave off a studenty vibe.

"Susan Rodway," explained Gené. "You might remember her from a few years ago. She was on television, and there was a book about her. She was a spoon-bender. Until she stopped."

"It wore off," said the girl, shrugging.

"That's her story, and she's sticking to it. According to tests, she's off the ESP charts. Psychokinesis, pyrokinesis, psychometry, telepathy, levitation, clairvoyance, clairaudience. She has senses they don't even have Latin names for yet. Can hard-boil an egg with a nasty look."

Susan waved her hands comically, and nothing happened.

"She's pretending to be normal," said Gené. "Probably reading your mind right now."

Irritated, Susan snapped. "One mind I *can't* read, Gené, is yours. So we'll have to fall back on the fount of all factoids. Mr. Head... what can you tell us about Geneviève Dieudonné?"

Sewell Head paused in mid-chew, as if collecting a ledger from a shelf in his mental attic, took a deep breath, and began, "Born in 1416, in the Duchy of Burgundy, Geneviève Dieudonné is mentioned in..."

"That's quite enough of that," said Gené, shutting him off.

Jamie couldn't help noticing how sharp the woman's teeth were. Did she have the ghost of a French accent?

"I'm Keith Marion," said the kid in the group, smiling nervously. It didn't take ESP to see he was trying to smooth over an awkward moment. "Undecided."

He stuck out his hand, which Jamie shook. He had a plastic tag around his wrist. Even looking straight at Keith, Jamie couldn't fix a face in his mind. The tag was the only thing about him he could remember.

"We have Keith on day-release," said Gené, proudly. "He has a condition. It's named after him. Keith Marion Syndrome."

Jamie let go of the boy's hand.

"I don't mind being out," said Keith. "I was sitting around waiting for my O Level results. Or CSEs. Or call-up papers. Or..."

He shrugged, and shut up.

"We make decisions all the time, which send us on varying paths," said Gené. "Keith can *see* his other paths. The ones he might have taken. Apparently, it's like being haunted by ghosts of yourself. All those doppelgangers."

"If I concentrate, I can anchor myself here," said Keith. "Assuming this is the real here. It might not be. Other heres feel just as real. And they bleed through more than I'd like."

Sewell Head was interested for a moment, as if filing some fact nugget away for a future *Brain of Britain* quiz. Then he was chewing Bertie Bassett's liquorice cud again.

"He's seen two other entirely different lives for me," said Gené.

"I'm having enough trouble with just this one," commented Susan.

"So's everybody," said the pale girl. "That's why we've been called— the good, the bad, and the undecided."

She opened her envelope and gave Jamie a map.

"We're heading West. Keith knows the territory. He was born in Somerset."

Jamie opened the rear doors of the van. He had tidied up a bit, and distributed cushions to make the space marginally more comfortable.

Susan borrowed 50p from him and the foursome tossed to see who got to sit up front with the driver. Keith called "owl," then admitted to Gené his mind had slipped into a reality with different coins. Head droned statistics and probabilities but couldn't decide what to call, and lost to Susan by default. In the final, Gené called tails. The seven-edged coin spun surprisingly high—and slower than usual—then landed heads-up in Susan's palm.

"Should have known not to toss up with a telekinetic," said Gené, in good humour. "It's into the back of the van with the boys for me."

She clambered in and pulled the door shut. There was some kicking and complaining as they got sorted out.

Susan gave the coin back to Jamie. It was bent at a right-angle.

"Oops," she said, arching her thick eyebrows attractively.

"You said it wore off."

"It did. Mostly."

They got into the front of the van. Jamie gave Susan the map and appointed her navigator.

"She can do it with her eyes closed," said Gené, poking her head through between the high-backed front seats.

"Just follow the Roman road," said Keith.

Susan held the map up the wrong way, and chewed a strand of her hair. "I hate to break it to you, but I'm not that good at orienteering. I can tell you about the three people—no, four—who have owned this map since it was printed. Including some interesting details about Little Miss Burgundy. But I don't know if we're best off with the A303."

Gené took the map away and playfully swatted Susan with it.

"Mr. Head," she began, "what's the best route from the Post Office Tower, in London, to Alder, in Somerset?"

"Shortest or quickest?"

"Quickest."

Sewell Head swallowed an allsort and recited directions off the top of his head.

"I hope someone's writing this down."

"No need, Jamie," said Gené. "Tell him, Susan."

"It's called eidetic memory," said Susan. "Like photographic, but for sounds and the spoken word. I can replay what he said in snippets over the next few hours. I don't even need to understand what he means. Now, 'turn left into New Cavendish Street, and drive towards Marylebone High Street...'"

Relaying Sewell Head's directions, Susan imitated his monotone. She sounded like a machine.

"One day all cars will have gadgets that do this," said Keith.

Jamie doubted that, but started driving anyway.

V

An hour or so into Professor Cleaver's rhotacist monologue, Richard began tuning out. Was hypothermia setting in? Despite thermals and furs, he was freezing. His upper arms ached as if they'd been hit with hammers. His jaws hurt from clenching to prevent teeth-chattering. He no longer had feeling in his fingers and toes. Frozen exhalation made ice droplets in his moustache.

Cold didn't bother Clever Dick. He was one of those mad geniuses who never outgrew a need for an audience. Being clever didn't count unless the people he was cleverer than knew it. The Professor walked around the room, excited, impassioned, frankly barking. He touched ice-coated surfaces with bare hands Richard assumed were freezer-burned to nervelessness. He puffed out clouds of frost and delighted in tiny falls of indoor hail. He constantly fiddled with his specs—taking them off to scrape away the thin film of iced condensation with bitten-to-the-quick thumbnails, putting them back on until they misted up and froze over again. And he kept talking. Talking, talking, talking.

As a child, Dick Cleaver had been indulged—and listened to—far too often. He'd been an adventurer, in the company of immature grown-ups who didn't take the trouble to teach him how to be a real boy. When that career ended, it had been a mind-breaking shock for Clever Dick. Richard had read Catriona Kaye's notes on the Case of the Splendid Six. Her pity for the little boy was plain as purple ink, though she also loathed him. An addendum (initialled by Edwin Winthrop) wickedly noted that Clever Dick suffered such extreme adolescent acne that he become known as "Spotted Dick." Angry pockmarks still marred the Professor's chubby cheeks. As an adult, he had become a champion among bores and deliberately entered a profession which required talking at length about the most tedious (yet inescapable) subject in Great British conversation—the weather. Turned out nice again, eh what? Lovely weather for ducks. Bit nippy round the allotments. Cleaver's best-selling book was impossible to read to the end, which was why many took *The Coming Ice Age* for a warning. It was actually a threat, a plan of action, a promise. To Professor Cleaver, the grip of glaciation was a consummation devoutly to be wished.

Behind his glasses, Cleaver's eyes gleamed. He might as well have traced hearts on frozen glass with a fingertip. He was a man in love. Perhaps for the first time. A late, great, literally all-consuming love.

Derek Leech, who rarely made the mistake of explaining *his* evil plans at length, had missed the point when he funded Cleaver's research. That alarmed Richard—Leech might be many things, but he was not easily fooled. Cleaver came across as a ranting, immature idiot with a freak IQ, but had serious connections. If anything could trump a Great Enchanter, it was the Cold.

"The Cold was here first," continued Cleaver. "Before the dawn of man, she weigned over evewything. She was the planet's first evolved intelligence, a giant bwain consisting of a near-infinite number of ice cwystals. A gweat white blanket, sewene and undying. When the glaciers weceded, she went to her west. She hid in a place out of weach until now. Humanity is just a blip. She'd have come back eventually, even without me. She was not dead, but only sleeping."

"Lot of that about," said Leech. "King Arthur, Barbarossa, Great Cthulhu, the terra-cotta warriors, Gary Glitter. They'll all be back."

Cleaver sputtered with anger. He didn't like being interrupted when he was rhapsodising.

"You won't laugh when blood fweezes in your veins, Mr. Leech. When your eyes pop out on ice-stalks."

Leech flapped his arms and contorted his face in mock panic.

"How many apocalypses have come and gone and fizzled in this century, Jeperson?" Leech asked, airily. "Four? Five? Worm War, Wizard War, Water War, Weird War, World War… and that's not counting Princess Cuckoo of Faerie, Little Rosie Farrar as the Whore of Babylon, the Scotch Streak and the Go-Codes, the Seamouth Warp, *six* alien invasions counting two the Diogenes Club doesn't think I know about, two of my youthful indiscretions you don't think I know you know about, and the ongoing Duel of the Seven Stars."

"Don't the Water War, the Scotch Streak, and the Egyptian Stars count as alien invasions?" asked Richard. "I mean, *technically*, the Deep Ones are terrestrial, but your Great Squidhead Person is from *outer* outer space. And the other two bothers were down to unwelcome meteorites."

"You've a point. Make that *eight* alien invasions. The Water War was a local skirmish, though. Extra-dimensional, rather than extra-terrestrial…"

Cleaver hopped from one foot to the other. The little boy in him was furious that grown-ups were talking over his head. If he hadn't been chucked off his course in life—by Catriona, as he saw it—he might have been in on the Secret History. The Mystic Maharajah, oldest of the Splendid Six, had carried a spear (well, an athane) in the Worm War. Captain Rattray (Blackfist), another Splendid, emerged from disgrace to play a minor role in the Wizard War. Teenage Clever Dick was too busy squeezing pus-filled blemishes to get involved in that set-to. Child sleuths, like child actors, seldom grew up to be stars. Richard was named after Richard Riddle, the famous Boy Detective of the turn of the century (so was Cleaver, probably). Few knew what, if anything, happened to Riddle in later life.

"You won't listen, you won't listen!"

"Have you considered that the Cold might be extra-dimensional rather than antediluvian?" asked Leech, offhandedly. "Seems to me a bright young man of my acquaintance reported something similar in a continuum several path-forks away from our own. It cropped up there in 1963 or so, during the Big Freeze. Didn't do much harm."

"You can't say anything about her," insisted Cleaver, almost squeaking.

"Interesting that you see the Cold as a her," continued Leech. "Then again, I suppose women have been 'cold' to you all your life. You made a poor impression on Miss Kaye, from all accounts. And she's always been generous in her feelings."

Cleaver's face tried to burn. Blood rose in his blueing cheeks, forming purplish patches. He might break out again.

"I know what you're twying to do, you wotter!"

Leech laughed out loud. Richard couldn't help but join in.

"I'm a 'wotter,' am I? A wotten wetched wight woyal wascally wotter, perhaps?"

"You're twying to get me angwy!"

"Angwy? Are you succumbing to woawing wed wage?"

Cleaver couldn't help sounding like a toffee-nosed Elmer Fudd. It was cruel of Leech to taunt him Fourth Form fashion. Richard remembered bullies at his schools. With him, it had been his darker skin, his literal lack of background, the numbers tattooed on his wrist, his longer-than-regulation hair, his *eyelashes* for heaven's sake. He had learned early on to control his temper. If he didn't, people got hurt.

"You missed one off your list of apocalypses," said Cleaver, trying to be sly again. "Perfidious Albion. That was an extwa-dimensional thweat. An entire weality out to oblitewate the world. And we stopped it. In 1926! Not your Diogenes Club or those Undertaker fellows, but us! The Splendid Six! Clever Dick, yes. They first called me that to poke fun, but I pwoved it was a wightful name. I stood with the gwown-ups. Blackfist and Lord Piltdown and the Blue Stweak…"

"…and Aviatrix and the Mystic Maharajah," footnoted Richard.

"Should never have let girls and foreigners in," muttered Cleaver. "That's where the wot started."

"Chandra Nguyen Seth turned out to be Sid Ramsbottom, from Stepney," said Richard. "As British as corned-beef fritters and London fog. Used boot polish on his face for years. He might have been Mystic, but he was no Maharajah."

Cleaver didn't take this in—he was a ranter, not a listener. "Seth and the girl *helped*," he admitted. "The Splendids saved the day. Beat back the Knights of Perfidious Albion. Saved evewyone and evewything. Without us, you'd all be cwawling subjects of Queen Morgaine. I was given a medal, by the pwoper King. I was witten up in *Bwitish Pluck*, for months and months. I had an arch-nemesis. Wicked William, my own cousin. I bested the bounder time after time. Made him cwy and cwy and cwy. There was a Clever Dick Club, and ten thousand boys were members. No g-girls allowed! I was in the Lord Mayor's Show and invited to tea at the palace *twice*. I could have been in your wotten old wars. Won them, even. In half the time. Dark Ones, Deep Ones, Wet Ones, Weird Ones. I could have thwashed the lot of 'em and been home before bed-time. But you couldn't leave me alone, could you? No woom in the Gwown-Ups' Club for Clever Dick. Not for any of the Splendids. That w-w-woman had to bwing us down to her level."

"He means your club now," said Leech. "In some circumstances, I'd agree with him."

"You'd both have to climb a mountain to be on a level with Catriona Kaye."

"Touché," said Leech.

"You're both just twying to change the subject."

"Oh dearie me," said Leech. "Let's talk about the weather again, shall we? It's an endless topic of fascination. I was getting bored with writing heatwave headlines…"

Leech's *Daily Comet* had been censured for running the headline "Sweaty Betty" over a paparazzo shot of Queen Elizabeth II perspiring (in ladylike manner) at an official engagement.

"How do you think he's done it, Jeperson? Science or magic?"

"No such thing as magic," said Cleaver, quickly.

"Says the boy whose best friend used a *magic diamond* to become hard as nails. What was his name again, Captain…?"

"Wattway!" shouted the Professor, duped into a using a double-*r* name. When he wasn't angry, he spoke carefully, avoiding the letter *r* if possible. Sadly, Cleaver was angry most of the time. "Dennis Wattway! Blackfist!"

"Not a magic person, then?"

"The Fang of Night was imbued with an unknown form of wadioactivity. It altered Captain Wattway's physiology."

"I could pull a hat out of the air and a rabbit out of the hat, and you'd say I accessed a pocket universe."

"A tessewact, yes."

"There's no 'weasoning' with you. So, Jeperson, what do you think?"

Richard wondered whether he should follow Leech's tactic, getting the Professor more and more flustered in the hope of breaking him down and finding a way to roll back the Cold. It was all very well unless Clever Dick decided to stop trying to impress his visitors and just had the snowmen stick icicles through their heads.

"I assume the phenomenon is localised," said Richard. "Deep under the levels. There must have been a pocket of the Cold. Once it was all over the world, a giant organism—a symbiote, drawing nourishment from the rock, from what vegetation it let live. When the Great Ice Age ended, it shrank, shedding most of its bulk into the seas or ordinary ice, but somewhere—maybe in several spots around the world—it left parcels of itself."

"No, you're wong, wong, wong," said Cleaver, nastily.

"Is that a Chinese laundry?" said Leech. "Wong, Wong, and Wong."

"*Wwong*," insisted Cleaver. "Ewwoneous. Incowwect. Not wight."

He sputtered, frustrated not to find an *r*-free synonym for "wrong."

"The Cold didn't hide below the gwound, but beyond the spectwum of tempewature. Until I weached out for her."

"I see," continued Richard. "With the equipment generously supplied by your former employer, you made contact with the Cold. You woke up Sleeping Beauty… with what? A kiss. No, a signal. An alarm-call. No, you had instructions. What common language could you have? Music, Movement, and Mime? Doubtful. Mathematics? No, the Cold hasn't got that sort of a mind. A being on her scale has no use for any number other than 'one.'"

Richard looked about the room, at the thickening ice which coated everything, at the white dusting over the ice. Tiny, tiny jewels glittered in the powder. He made a leap—perhaps by himself, perhaps snatching from Cleaver's buzzing mind.

"Crystals," he mused. "'A near-infinite number,' you said. Each unique and distinctive. An endless alphabet of characters. Chinese cubed."

Cleaver clapped his hands, delighted.

"Yes, *snowflakes*! I can wead them. It cost a gweat deal of Mr. Leech's money to learn how. First, to wead them. Then to *make* them."

"Your bird must think you're a right mug," said Leech, sourly. "She must have seen you coming for a million years."

"Eighteen million years, at my best guess," said Cleaver, smugness crumpling. He didn't like it when his goddess was disrespected.

"How do you make snowflakes?" Richard asked. "I mean, snow is frozen rain…"

Cleaver was disgusted, as Richard knew he would be. "You don't know anything! Fwozen rain is *sleet*!"

Leech laughed bitterly as Richard was paid back for his pedantry.

"Snow forms when *clouds* are fwozen," said Cleaver, lecturing. "You need humidity *and* cold. It's vapour to ice, not water to ice. Synthetic snow cwystals have been made in vapour diffusion chambers since 1963. But no one else has got beyond dendwitic stars. *Janet and John* cwystallogwaphy! The colder you get inside the box, the more complex the cwystals—hollow plates, columns on plates, multiply capped columns, skeletal forms, isolated bullets, awwowhead twins, multiple cups. Then combinations of forms. I can sculpt them, shape them, *carve* them. *Finnegan's Wake* cwystallogwaphy! You need extwemes of tempewature, and a gweat deal of electwicity. We dwained the national gwid. There was a black-out, wemember?"

A week or so ago, a massive power-cut had paralysed an already sluggish nation. Officially, it was down to too many fans plugged in and fridge doors left open.

"You knew about that?" Richard asked Leech.

The Great Enchanter shrugged.

"He *authowised* it!" crowed the Professor, in triumph. "He had no idea what he was doing. None of the others did, either. Kellett and Bakhtinin. McKendwick. And certainly not your spy, Mr. Pouncey!"

Leech had listed the other staff: "two junior meteorologists, one general dogsbody, and a public relations–security consultant."

"McKendwick had an inkling. He knew I was welaying instwuctions. He made the Box—the vapour diffusion chamber—to my specifications. He kept asking why all the extwa conductors. Why the *designs*? But he cawwied out orders like a good little wesearch assistant."

Cleaver stood by an odd apparatus which Richard had taken for a generator. It consisted of a lot of blackened electrical coils, bright copper slashes showing through shredded rubber. There was a cracked Bakelite instrument panel, and—in the heart of the coils—a metal box the size of a cigarette packet, ripped open at one edge. It had exploded *outward*. The metal was covered with intricate, etched symbols. Line after line of branching, hexagonally symmetrical star-shapes. Representational snowflakes, but also symbols of power. Here, science shaded into magic. This was not only an experimental apparatus, but an incantation in copper-wire and steel-plate, a conjuring machine.

"It's burned out now," he said, slapping it, "but it did the twick. In the Box, I took the tempewature down to minus four hundwed and fifty-nine point seven thwee degwees Fahwenheit!"

Richard felt a chill wafting from the ice-slopes of Hell.

"We're supposed to be impressed?" said Leech.

"You can't get colder than *absolute zero*," said Richard. "That's minus four hundred and fifty-nine point *six seven* Fahrenheit."

"I have bwoken the Cold Bawwier," announced Cleaver, proudly.

"Not using physics, you haven't."

"So what was it, magic?"

Richard wasn't going to argue the point. There weren't instruments capable of measuring theoretically impossible temperatures, but Richard suspected the Professor wasn't making an idle boast. Within his Box, reality had broken down. Quantum mechanics gave up, packed its bags, and went to Marbella, and the supernatural house-sat for a while.

"It's where I found the Cold. Minus point zewo six. She was sleeping there. A basic hexagon. I almost missed her. Bweaking so-called absolute zewo was so much of an achievement. McKendwick saw her first. The little lab assistant took her for pwoof we had failed. There shouldn't *be* ordinawy cwystals at minus point zewo six. And she wasn't ordinawy. McKendwick found that out."

Richard assumed McKendrick was the snowman with the tam o'shanter. The others must be the rest of Cleaver's staff. Kellett, Bakhtinin, Pouncey. And whoever the postman was. What about the few other residents of Sutton Mallet? Frozen in their homes? Ready to join the snow army?

"Fwom a hexagon, she gwew, into a dendwitic star, with more stars on each bwanch. A hexagon squared. A hexagon cubed."

"Six to the power of six to the power of six?"

"That's wight, Mr. Leech. Amusing, eh what? Then, she became a *cluster* of cwystals. A snowflake. Then... whoosh. The Box burst. The power went out. But she was fwee. She came fwom beyond the zewo bawwier. A pinpoint speck. Woom tempewature plummeted. The walls iced over, and the fweeze spwead out of the building. She took the village in hours. She took McKendwick and the others. Soon, she'll be evewywhere."

"What about you?" asked Leech. "Will you be the Snow Queen's 'Pwime Minister?'"

"Oh no, I'm going to die. Just like you. When the Cold spweads, over the whole planet, I'll be happy to die with the west of the failed expewiment, humanity. It's quite inevitable. Hadn't you noticed... when you were coming here... hadn't you noticed she's gwowing? I think we'll be done in thwee months or so, give or take an afternoon."

Richard whistled.

"At least now we know the deadline," he told Leech, slipping the hypodermic out of his hairy sleeve.

Cleaver frowned, wondering if he should have given so much away. It was too late to consider the advisability of ranting.

Leech took hold of the Professor and slammed his forehead against the older man's, smashing his spectacles. A coconut shy crack resounded. Cleaver staggered, smearing his flowing moustache of blood.

"Yhou bwoke mhy nhose!"

Richard slid the needle into Cleaver's neck. He tensed and went limp.

"One down," said Leech. "One to go."

"Yes, but she's a big girl. What are the snowmen doing?"

Leech looked out of the window, and said "most have wandered off, but the postman's still there, behaving himself."

"While Cleaver's out, they shouldn't move," Richard said, unsure of himself. "Unless the Cold gets angry."

Richard plopped the Professor in a swivel chair and wheeled him into a corner, out of the way. Leech unslung his giant backpack and undid white canvas flaps to reveal a metal box studded with dials and switches like an old-time wireless receiver. He unwound an electrical cord and plugged it into a socket that wasn't iced over. His bulky gadget lit up and began to hum. He opened a hatch and pulled out a trimphone handset, then cranked a handle and asked for an operator.

"Who else would want a telephone you have to carry around?" asked Richard.

Leech gave a feral, humourless smile and muttered "wouldn't you like to know?" before getting through.

"This is DL 001," he said. "Yes, yes, Angela, it's Derek. I'd like to speak with Miss Catriona Kaye, at the Manor House, Alder."

Leech held the trimphone against his chest while he was connected.

"Let's see if Madam Chairman has gathered her Talents," he said.

Richard certainly hoped she had.

VI

They were on the road to Mangle Wurzel Country because some paranormal crisis was out of hand. Jamie had a fair idea what that meant.

Growing up as the son of the current Dr. Shade and the former Kentish Glory, it had taken several playground spats and uncomfortable parent–teacher meetings to realise that other kids (and grown-ups) didn't know these things happened regularly and—what's more—*really* didn't want to know. After getting kicked out of a third school, he learned to answer the question "what does your Daddy do?" with "he's a doctor" rather than "he fights diabolical masterminds." Since leaving home, he'd seen how surreally out-of-the-ordinary his childhood had been. No one ever said he was expected to take over his father's practice, but Dad taught him about the Shade Legacy: how to summon shadows and travel the night-paths, how to touch people inside with tendrils of velvet black, how to use the get-up and the gadgets. Jamie was the only pupil in his class who botched his mock O levels because he'd spent most of his revision time on the basics of flying an autogyro.

Jamie thought Mum was pleased he was using the darkness in the band rather than on the streets. He was carrying on the Shade line, but in a different way. His father could drop through a skylight and make terror blossom in a dozen wicked souls; Jamie could float onto a tiny stage in a pokey venue and fill a dark room with a deeper shadow that enveloped audiences and seeped into their hearts. When Jamie sang about long, dreadful nights, a certain type of teenager *knew* he was singing about them. Because of Transhumance, they knew—if only for the forty-five minutes of the set—that they weren't alone, that they had friends and lovers in the dark, that tiny pinpoints of starlight were worth striving for. They were kids who only liked purple lollipops because of the colour they stained their lips, wore swathes of black even in this baking summer, would drink vinegar and lie in a bath of ice cubes to be as pale as Gené, lit their squats with black candles bought in head shops, and read thick paperback novels "from the vampire's point of view." Teenagers like Vron—who, come to think of it, he was supposed to be seeing this evening. If the world survived the week, she'd make him pay for standing her up.

Gené had found Vron's dog-eared *Interview With the Vampire* under a cushion in the back of the van, and was performing dramatic passages. Read out with a trace of (sexy) French accent, it sounded sillier than it did when Vron quoted bits of Anne Rice's "philosophy" at him. Vron wrote Transhumance's lyrics, and everyone said—not to her face—the lyrics needed more work. Bongo said "you can't rhyme 'caverns of despair' with 'kicking o'er a chair' and expect folk not to laugh their kecks off." About the only thing the band could agree on was that they didn't want to be funny.

So what was he doing on the road? In a van with four weird strangers—weird, even by his standards.

Gatherings of disparate talents like this little lot were unusual. Fred had said they needed "*everybody*." Jamie wondered how far down the list the likes of Sewell Head came—though he knew enough not to underestimate anyone. According to Gené, the Diogenes Club were calling this particular brouhaha "the Winter War." That didn't sound so bad. After the last few months, a little winter in July would be welcome.

Beyond Yeovil, they came to a roadblock manned by squaddies who were turning other drivers away from a "military exercise" barrier. The van was waved out of the queue by an NCO and—with no explanation needed—the barrier lifted for them. A riot of envious hooting came from motorists who shut up as soon as a rifle or two was accidentally pointed in their direction. Even Gené kept mum once they were in bandit country—where they were the only moving thing.

As they drove along eerily empty roads, Susan continued to relay Head's directions. "Follow Tapmoor Road for two and a half miles, and turn *right*, drive half a mile, go through Sutton Mallet, then three miles on, to Alder—and we're there."

Jamie spotted the signpost, which was almost smothered by the lower branches of a dying tree, and took the Sutton Mallet turn-off. It should have been a shortcut to Alder, the village where they were supposed to rendezvous with the rest of the draftees in the Winter War. The van ploughed to a halt in a four-foot-deep snowdrift.

The temperature plunged—an oven became a fridge in seconds. Gooseflesh raised on Jamie's bare arms. Keith and Sewell Head wrapped themselves in sleeping bags. Susan's teeth chattered, interrupting her travel directions—which were academic anyway. The road was impassable.

Only Gené didn't instantly and obviously feel the cold.

Jamie shifted gears, and reversed. Wheels spun, making a hideous grinding noise for half a minute or so, then the van freed itself from the grip of ice and backed out of the drift. A few yards away, and the temperature climbed again. They were all shocked quiet for a moment, then started talking at once.

"Hush," said Gené, who was elected Head Girl, "look."

The cold front was advancing, visibly—a frozen river. Hedges, half-dead from lack of rain, were swallowed by swells of ice and snow.

They all got out of the van. It was as hot as it had been, though Jamie's skin didn't readjust. He still had gooseflesh.

"It'll be here soon and swallow us again," said Keith.

"At the current rate, in sixteen minutes forty-five seconds," said Sewell Head.

It wasn't just a glacier creeping down a country lane, it was an entire wave advancing across the countryside. Jamie had no doubt Head knew his sums—in just over a quarter of an hour, an arctic climate would reach the road, and sweep around the van, stranding them.

"We have to go ahead on foot," said Gené. "It's only a couple of miles down that lane."

"Three and a half," corrected Head.

"A walk in the park," said Gené.

"Thank you, Captain Scott," said Susan. "We're not exactly equipped."

"You were told to bring warm clothes."

"Naturally, I didn't believe it," said Susan. "We should have been shouted at."

Jamie hadn't been told. He'd take that up with Fred and Vanessa.

"Fifteen minutes," said Head, unconcerned.

"There's gear in the back of the van," said Jamie. "It'll have to do."

"I'm fine as I am," said Gené. "Happy in all weathers."

Jamie dug out one of his father's black greatcoats for Susan. It hung long on her, edges trailing on the ground. Head kept the sleeping bag wrapped around him, and looked even more like a tramp. He must be glad he came out with his scarf and gloves. Keith found a black opera cloak with red silk lining, and settled it around his shoulders.

"Careful with that, Keith," Jamie cautioned. "It was the Great

Edmondo's. There are hidden pockets. You might find a dead canary or two."

Jamie pulled on a ragged black-dyed pullover and gauntlets. He fetched out a holdall with some useful items from the Legacy, and—as an afterthought—slung the Shade goggles around his neck and put on one of his Dad's wide-brimmed black slouch hats.

"Natty," commented Gené. "It's the Return of Dr. Shade!"

"Sod off, Frenchy," he said, smiling.

"Burgundina, remember?"

The cold front was nearly at the mouth of the lane, crawling up around the signpost. He rolled up the van windows, and locked the doors.

Gené climbed onto the snowdrift, and stamped on the powder. It was packed enough to support her. Bare-legged and -armed, she still looked comfortable amid the frozen wastes. She held out a hand and helped haul Susan up beside her. Even in the coat, Susan began shivering. Her nose reddened. She hugged herself, sliding hands into loose sleeves like a mandarin.

"Come on up, lads, the water's l-lovely," she said.

Jamie, Keith, and Head managed, with helping hands and a certain amount of swearing, to clamber up beside the girls.

Ahead was a snowscape—thickly carpeted white, trees weighed down by ice, a few roofs poking up where cottages were trapped. Snow wasn't falling, but was whipped up from the ground by cold winds and swirled viciously. Jamie put on his goggles, protecting his eyes from the spits of snow. The flakes were like a million tiny fragments of ice shrapnel.

Gené pointed across the frozen moor, at a tower.

"That's Sutton Mallet chapel. And, see, beyond that, where the hill rises… that's Alder."

It ought to have been an hour's stroll. Very pleasant, if you liked walking in the country. Which Jamie didn't, much. Now, it seemed horribly like a Death March.

Susan, he noticed, stopped shivering and chattering. She was padding carefully across the powder, leaving deep footprints.

Gené applauded. "Now that's *thinking*," she said.

Jamie didn't know what she meant.

"She's a pyrokinetic, remember?" explained Gené. "That's not just setting fire to things with your mind. It's control over *temperature*. She's made her own cocoon of warmth, inside her coat. Look, she's steaming."

Susan turned, smiling wide. Hot fog rose from her shoulders, and snowflakes hissed when they got near her as if falling onto a griddle.

"Are my ears burning?" she asked.

"Never mind your ears," said Keith. "What about everything else?"

Susan's footprints were shallow puddles, which froze a few seconds after she had made them.

"I'm not a proper pyro," she said. "I don't set fires. I just have a thing with warmth. Saves on coins for the meter. Otherwise, it's useless—like wiggling your ears. It takes me an hour to boil enough water for a cup of tea, and by then I'm so fagged out I have to lie down and it's cold again when I wake up. That's the trouble with most of my so-called Talents. Party pieces, but little else. I mean, who needs a drawer full of bent spoons?"

"I think it's amazing," commented Keith. "Mind over matter. You could be on the telly. Or fight crime."

"I'll leave that to the professionals, like Jamie's Dad. You're not seeing me in a Union Jack bikini and one of those eye-masks which aren't really disguises."

"You'd be surprised how well those masks work," said Jamie. "When she was Kentish Glory, Mum wore this moth-wing domino. Even people she knew really well didn't clock it was her."

"I like a quiet life," said Susan. "So, enough about me being a freak. Gené, what's your secret?"

The blonde shrugged, teasing. "Diet and lots of sleep."

"Come on, slowcoaches," said Susan, who was getting the hang of it. "Last one there's a rotten…"

The snow collapsed under her and she sank waist-deep, coat-skirts spreading out around her.

"Shit," she said. "Pardon my Burgundian."

"Didn't Gené say you could levitate?" said Keith, going to help her.

"She's not the one who knows everything," said Susan. "That was only once, and I was six. I've put on weight since then."

Keith took her hands—"she's all warm!"—and hauled her out of her hole.

"Abracadabra," he said, flapping the cloak.

"It doesn't do to get overconfident," cautioned Gené.

Susan made a rude gesture behind the other girl's back.

Jamie felt something. Deeper than the cold. He looked around. The whirling blizzard was thickening. And something was different.

"Hey, gang," he said. "Who made the snowmen?"

VII

"I *know* the Cold is spreading," Catriona Kaye told Derek Leech. "It's here, in Alder. We're three miles from you. Now put Richard on, would you?"

In the Manor House, the telephone was on a stand near the front door. She had to leave her guests in the drawing room to take Leech's call. The hallway was still cluttered from Edwin's days as Lord of this

Manor: hats and umbrellas (and Charles Beauregard's old swordstick) in a hideous Victorian stand, coats on hooks (she liked to use Edwin's flying jacket—still smelling of tobacco and motor-oil—for gardening), framed playbills from the 1920s, shotguns (and less commonplace armaments) in a locked case. Since Edwin's death, she'd tidied away or passed on most of his things, but here she let his ghost linger. Upstairs, on the landing, his shadow was etched permanently into the floorboards. After a lifetime in service to the Diogenes Club, it was all he had for a grave. She supposed she should throw a carpet over it or something.

As she waited for Leech to pass the phone to Richard, Catriona caught sight of herself in the tall, thin art deco mirror from the Bloomsbury flat she had shared with Edwin. At a glance, she was the girl she recognised—she had the same silhouette as she had in her, and the century's, twenties. If she looked for more than a few seconds, she saw her bobbed hair was ash-grey, and even that was dyed. Her wrists and neck were unmistakably a seventy-six-year-old's. Once, certain Valued Members had been grumpily set against even admitting her to the building in Pall Mall, never mind putting her on the rolls. Now, she was practically all that was left of the Diogenes Club as Mycroft Holmes would have recognised it. Even in the Secret World, things were changing.

"Catriona," said Richard, tinny and distorted as if bounced off a relay station in the rings of Saturn. "How are you? Is the Cold…?"

"In the village? Yes. A bother? No. We've enough lively minds in the house to hold it back. Indeed, the cool is misleadingly pleasant. What little of the garden survived the heatwave has been killed by snow, though—which is really rather tiresome."

Richard succinctly explained the situation.

"'The planet's first evolved intelligence?'" she queried. "That has a familiar ring to it. I shall put the problem to our little Council of War."

"Watch out for snowmen."

"I shall take care to."

She hung up and had a moment's thought, ticking off her long string of black pearls as if they were rosary beads. The general assumption was that they had been dealing with an unnatural phenomenon, perhaps a bleed-through from some parallel wintery world. Now, it seemed there was an *entity* in the picture. Something to be coped with, accommodated, or eliminated.

The drawing room was crowded. Extra chairs had been brought in.

Constant Drache, the visionary architect, wanted news of Derek Leech. Catriona assured him that his patron was perfectly well. Drache wasn't a Talent, just a high-ranking minion. He was here with the watchful Dr. Lark, corralling the persons Leech had contributed to the Council and making mental notes on the others for use after the truce was ended. That showed a certain optimism, which Catriona found mildly cheering. She had told Richard's team not to call Leech's people "the villains," but the label was hard to avoid. Fred and Vanessa were still in London, liaising with the Minister.

Anthony Jago, wearing a dog-collar the Church of England said he was no longer entitled to, was Leech's prime specimen—an untapped Talent, reputed to be able to overwrite reality on a large scale. The former clergyman said he was looking for property in the West Country and had taken a covetous liking to the Manor House. The man had an understandable streak of self-regarding megalomania, and Lark was evidently trying to keep him unaware of the full extent of his abilities. Catriona would have been terrified of Jago if he weren't completely trumped by Ariadne ("just Ariadne"). The white-haired, utterly beautiful creature had made her way unbidden to the Club and offered her services in the present emergency. She was an Elder of the Kind. Even the Secret Files had almost nothing on them. The Elders hadn't taken an interest in anything in Geneviève Dieudonné's lifetime, though some of their young—the Kith—had occasionally been problematic.

Apart from Jago, none of Leech's soldiers were in the world-changing (or -threatening) class. The unnaturally thin, bald, haggard Nigel Karabatsos—along with his unnaturally small, plump, clinging wife—represented a pompous Neo-Satanic sect called the Thirteen. Typically, there weren't thirteen of them. Maureen Mountmain was heiress to a dynasty of Irish mystics who'd been skirmishing with the Club for over eighty years. Catriona would gladly not have seen the red-headed, big-hipped, big-busted Amazon in this house again (she'd been here when the shadows took Edwin). Maureen and Richard had one of those complicated young persons' things, which neither cared to talk of and—Catriona hoped—would not be resumed. There were enough "undercurrents" in this Council for several West End plays as it was. Jago and Maureen, comparatively youthful and obnoxiously vital, pumped out more pheromones than a beehive. They took an interest in each other which Dr. Lark did her best to frustrate by interposing her body. Leech obviously had separate plans for those two.

The mysterious Mr. Sewell Head, the other side's last recruit for the Winter War Effort, was out in a snowfield somewhere with Geneviève's party. Catriona suspected they'd have a hard time getting through. Fair enough. If this council failed, someone needed to be left alive to regroup and try a second wave. Geneviève had Young Dr. Shade and the interesting Rodway Girl with her—they had the potential to become Valued Talents, and the Cold Crisis should bring them on. Still, it didn't do to think too far ahead. In the long run, there's always an unhappy outcome—except, just possibly, for Ariadne.

Watching Jago and Maureen flex and flutter, attracting like magnets, Catriona worried that the Club's Talents were relics. Swami Anand Gitamo, formerly Harry Cutley, was only here for moral support. He had been Most Valued Member once, but had lately taken a more spiritual role. Still, it was good to see Harry again. His chanted mantras irritated Jago, a point in his favour. Paulette Michaelsmith had even more obviously been hauled out of retirement. She could only use her Talent (under the direction of others) when asleep and dreaming, and was permanently huddled in a bath-chair. Catriona noted that Dr. Lark wasn't too busy playing gooseberry to take an interest in poor, dozy Paulette. Dr. Cross, the old woman's minder, was instructed to ward the witch off if she made any sudden moves. Louise Magellan Teazle, one of Catriona's oldest friends, always brought the sunshine with her—a somewhat undervalued Talent this summer, though currently more useful than all Karabatsos's dark summonings or Jago's reality-warping. It was thanks to Louise that the Cold was shut out of the Manor House. She was an author of children's books, and a near neighbour. In her house out on the moor, she'd been first to notice a change in the weather.

While Catriona relayed what Leech and Richard had told her, Louise served high tea. Paulette woke up for fruitcake and was fully alert for whole minutes at a time.

"This Cold," Drache declared. "Can it be killed?"

"Anything can be killed," said Karabatsos.

"Yes, dear, *anything*," echoed his wife.

"We know very little about the creature," admitted Catriona. "The world's leading expert is Professor Cleaver, and his perspective is—shall we say—distorted."

"All life is sacred," said Anand Gitamo.

"Especially ours," said Maureen. "I'm a mum. I don't want my girl growing up to freeze in an apocalypse of ice and frost."

Catriona had a minor twinge of concern at the prospect of *more* Mountmains.

"How can all life be sacrosanct when some lifeforms are inimical, *hein*?" said Drache. "Snake and mongoose. Lion and gazelle. Humanity and the Cold."

"Tom and Jerry," said Paulette, out of nowhere.

"I did not say 'sacrosanct,'" pointed out Anand Gitamo.

"The Cold can die," said Ariadne. Everyone listened to her, even Jago. "But it should not be killed. It can kill you and live, as you would shrug off a virus. You can not kill it and expect to survive, as you can not murder the seas, the soil, or the great forests. The crime would be too great. You could not abide the consequences."

"But we do not matter?" asked Drache.

"I should miss you," admitted Ariadne, gently. "As you cannot do without the trees, who make the air breathable, the Kind cannot do without you, without your dreams. If the Cold spreads, we would outlive you—but eventually, starved, we would fade. The Cold has mind, but no memory. It would retain nothing of you."

"The world doesn't end in ice, but *fire*," said Jago. "This, I have seen."

"The Old Ones will return," said Karabatsos.

"Yes, dear, *Old*," echoed his wife.

It seemed to Catriona that everyone in this business expected a personal, tailor-made apocalypse. They enlisted in the Winter War out of jealousy—a pettish wish to forestall every other prophet's vision, to keep the stage clear for their own variety of Doom. The Cold was Professor Cleaver's End of the World, and the others wanted to shut him down. Derek Leech, at least, needed the planet to stay open for business—which was why Catriona had listened when he called a truce with the Diogenes Club.

The doorbell rang. Catriona would have hurried back to the hall, but David Cross gallantly went for her. Louise poured more tea.

It was not Geneviève and her party, but Mr. Zed, last of the Undertakers. He brought another old acquaintance from the Mausoleum, their collection of oddities (frankly, a prison).

Mr. Zed, eyes permanently hidden behind dark glasses, stood in the drawing room doorway. Everyone looked at him. The brim of his top hat and the shoulders of his black frock coat were lightly powdered with snow. Many of the Council—and not only those on Derek Leech's side of the room—might once have had cause to fear immurement in the Mausoleum, but the Undertaking was not what it had been. Mr. Zed politely took off his hat and stood aside.

Behind him was a little girl who could have stepped out of an illustration from one of Louise's earliest books. She had an Indian braid tied with a silver ribbon, and wore a neat pinafore with a kangaroo pouch pocket. She looked like Rose Farrar, who disappeared from a field in Sussex in 1872, "taken by the fairies." This creature had turned up on the same spot in 1925, and come close to delivering an apocalypse that might have suited Jago's Biblical tastes. At least she wasn't playing Harlot of Babylon any more.

"Good afternoon, Rose."

Catriona had not seen the girl-shaped creature since the Undertaking took her off. She still had a smooth, pale patch on her hand—where Rose had spat venom at her.

The creature curtseyed. When she looked up, she wore another face—Catriona's, as it had been fifty years ago. She used the face to smile, and aged rapidly—presenting Catriona with what she looked like now. Then, she laughed innocently and was Rose Farrar again.

The procedure was like a slap.

The thing that looked like Rose was on their side, for the moment. But, unlike everyone else in the room—good, bad, or undecided—she didn't come from *here*. If the Cold won, Rose wouldn't necessarily lose a home, or a life, or anything she put value on.

Catriona wasn't sure what Rose could contribute, even if she was of a mind to help. Ariadne, Louise, and, perhaps, the Rodway girl were Talents—they could alter reality through sheer willpower. Jago and Paulette were "effective dreamers"—they could alter reality on an even larger scale, but at the whim of their unconscious minds. Rose was a living mirror—she could only change *herself*, by plucking notions from the heads of anyone within reach. She resembled the original Rose because that's who the people who found her in Angel Field expected her to be. She had been kept captive all these years by confining her with people (wardens *and* convicts) who *believed* the Mausoleum to be an inescapable prison—which wasn't strictly true.

"What a dear little thing," said Ariadne. "Come here and have some of Miss Teazle's delicious cake."

Rose meekly trotted over to the Elder's side and presented her head to be stroked. Jago turned away from Maureen, and was fascinated. Until today, he hadn't known there were other Talents in the world. Paulette perked up again, momentarily—the most powerful dreamer on record, now in a room with at least two creatures who fed on dreams.

End of the World or not, Catriona wondered whether bringing all these big beasts together was entirely a bright idea.

"More tea, Cat," suggested Louise, who had just given a steaming cup to the Undertaker.

Catriona nodded.

VIII

Jamie wasn't surprised when the snowmen attacked. It wouldn't be a war if there weren't an enemy.

The frosties waited until the five had tramped a hundred difficult yards or so past them, committing to the path ahead and an uncertain footing. They were in Sutton Mallet. It wasn't much of a place. Two Rolls Royces were parked by the path, almost buried, icicles dripping from the bonnet ornaments. Nice machines. His Dad drove one like them.

"What's that thing called again?" he muttered, nodding at the dancers.

"The Spirit of Ecstasy," said Sewell Head. "Originally, the Spirit of

Speed. Designed by Charles Sykes for the Rolls-Royce Company in 1911. The model is Eleanor Velasco Thornton."

"Eleanor. That explains it. Dad always called the little figure 'Nellie in Her Nightie.' I used to think she had wings, but it's supposed to be her dress, streaming in the wind."

Everyone had fallen over more than once. It stopped being remotely funny. Each step was an uncertain adventure which only Gené was nimble enough to enjoy. Then, even she skidded on a frozen puddle and took a tumble into a drift.

She looked up, and saw the four snowy sentinels.

"What are you laughing at?" she shouted.

At that, the snowmen upped stumps and came in a rush. When they moved, they were localised, roughly human-shaped blizzards. They had no problem with their footing, and charged like touchy rhinos whose mothers had just been insulted by howler monkeys.

"There are people inside," yelled Keith. "I think they're dead."

"They better hope they're dead," said Gené, flipping herself upright and standing her ground, adopting a fighting stance.

The first and biggest of the frosties—who wore a top hat—barrelled towards the Burgundian girl, growing into a creature that seemed all shoulders. She met it with an ear-piercing "ki-*yaaa*" and a Bruce Lee-approved power-kick to the midriff. The topper fell off and the frosty stopped in its tracks, shedding great chunks of packed ice to reveal a well-dressed gent with a deeply cut throat and a slack mouth. He had bled out before freezing. The snow crawled back up around the corpse, cocooning it with white powder, building layers of icy muscle, growing icicle spines and teeth. It reached down with an extensible arm, picked up its hat, and set it back on its head at a jaunty angle. The coals of its mouth rearranged themselves into a fierce grin.

And the other three—who wore a tartan cap, a jungle hat, and two bugs on springs—caught up with their leader. They were swollen to the size of big bruisers.

Jamie looked down at his hands. His gauntlets were mittened with black clouds, containing violet electrical arcs. Out in the open, with snow all around and cold sunlight, there was too little shade. Night was far off. He cast darkstuff at the Scotch Snowman, who was nearest, and sheared away a couple of icicles. They instantly grew back.

He would have to do better.

Fred Astaire Snowman patted its healed-over tummy, and shot out a big fist which clenched around Gené's throat. Astaire lifted Gené off the ground. She kicked, but floundered with nothing to brace against. Jamie saw she had longer, sharper nails than normal—but any tears she made in the snow-hand were healed over instantly. She gurgled, unable to talk.

Comical Bugs Snowman and Jungle Explorer Snowman shifted, in opposite directions. They were forming a circle. A killing circle.

Astaire grew a yard-long javelin of solid ice from its shoulder, and snapped it off to make a stake. It pressed the ice-spear against Gené's ribs, ready to hoist her up like a victim of Frosty the Impaler.

Susan had her eyes shut, and radiated warmth—but not heat. Sewell Head was chattering about snowmen in fact and fiction, citing pagan precedents, Christmas cake decorations, and the Ronettes. Keith wrapped himself in his magician's cape, and rolled his eyes up so that only the whites showed. Jamie supposed he was having a fit.

Gené squeaked a scream out through her crushed throat. Scarlet blood showed on her safari jacket.

He tried to gather more darkness, from inside.

Suddenly, Keith's eyes snapped back—but they were different.

"Don't waste your energy, Shade," he said, in a commanding tone: "Use this."

From the depths of the cloak, Keith produced a thin, diamond-shaped, black object. It was Dennis Rattray's Fang of Night. Jamie had wondered where Dad had put it after taking it from Blackfist. Keith tossed the jewel to Jamie, who caught it and staggered back. The Fang was the size of a gob-stopper, but weighed as much as a cannonball. He held it in both hands. It was like sticking his fingers into a live electric socket.

"Sue," Keith said, "cover Shade's—Jamie's—back. Imagine a wall of heat, and concentrate. Swellhead, give me some dark refraction indices, considering available light, the Blackfist gem, and whatever these snow-things are. Today would be a help."

Astonished, Head scrawled sums in the snow with his forefinger.

"Gené, hang on," said Keith. Gené even tried to nod, though her face was screwed up in agony and spatters of her blood stained the snow under her kicking feet.

"Can you feel it, Shade?"

Jamie was seeing a different Keith Marion. And the jewel didn't seem so heavy once he'd worked out how to hold it. Rattray had tapped into its energy by making a fist around it, but Dad said that was what had killed him in the end. There were other ways of using the Fang of Night.

Head put his hand up, and pointed to a formula he had traced.

"Well played, Swellhead," said Keith, patting Head's bald bonce. "Shade, hold the Fang up to your forehead and focus. Aim for the hat!"

Behind him, Susan grunted, and he heard slushing, melting sounds.

"Ugh, disgusting," she said.

Jamie fought an urge to turn and find out what had happened.

"Concentrate, man," insisted Keith. "Gené can't hold out much longer."

Head began to give a figure in seconds, but Keith shut him up.

Jamie held the stone to his forehead. It seemed to fit into the V above his goggles. The dark matter was sucked in through the gauntlets, thrilling into his palms, surging through his veins and nerves, and gathered in his forebrain, giving him a sudden ice-cream migraine. Then, it was set free.

He saw a flash of dark purple. Astaire's top hat exploded in flames that burned black, and the snowman fell apart. Gené was dropped, and pulled out the ice-shard in her chest before she sprawled in the snow. She crabwalked away from the well-dressed, still-standing corpse that had been inside Astaire. Its knees kinked, and it pitched forward.

"Now, turn," ordered Keith. "The others."

Jamie wheeled about. Susan was on her knees, with her arms held out, fingers wide. Scotch Snowman and Explorer Snowman loomed over her, meltwater raining from their arms and chests and faces—the trapped corpses showing through. Susan was running out of charge, though. A slug of blood crawled out of her nose. Angry weals rose around her fingernails.

This time, it was like blinking. He zapped the tartan cap and the solar topee to fragments, and the snowmen were downed. Susan swooned, and Keith was there to catch her, wrapping her in his cloak, wiping away the blood, squeezing her fingers. She woke up, and he kissed her like someone who'd known her longer and better than a few hours.

"Excuse me," said Gené, "but I nearly had an icicle through my heart."

Keith looked at her and asked brusquely, "you all right?"

Gené eased her bloody jacket out of the way. Her scrape was already healing.

"Seem to be," she admitted.

"Good, now help Shade with the last of them. It's the most dangerous."

Gené saluted.

"Sue," whispered Keith.

"Do I know you?" she asked, frankly irritated. He let her go, and stood up, stiffly. In his cloak, he looked like the commander of a victorious Roman legion. Jamie didn't know where the kid had got it from.

Bugs had either legged it or melted into the ground.

Jamie had purple vision. It was like night-sight, but in the daytime. With the Fang of Night, he could think faster. He didn't feel the cold. He could take anyone, any day of the week. He could only imagine what he would sound like if he used this onstage.

Keith plucked the jewel from his grasp, holding it between thumb and forefinger as if it were radioactive, then magicked it away with a conjurer's flourish.

"You of all people should know to treat those things carefully," said Keith.

For an instant, Jamie wanted to batter the kid's face and take back the jewel. Then, he understood. Use it, but don't let it get its hooks in you. Dad had said that all the time.

"So, which Keith is this?" said Gené, tugging on the kid's wrist-tag. "What school do you go to?"

"School? There hasn't been any school since the Spiders came. Good job too. They don't teach you anything useful. You have to learn survival, and *resistance*, on the job."

This Keith had a firmer jaw, healed-over scars, and a steady, manly, confident gaze. People snapped in line when he spoke and threw themselves under trains if there was a tactical advantage in it.

"He told us about this before we met you," Gené explained. "Some other Keith lives on an Earth overrun by arachnoid aliens. He's a guerrilla leader. He also plays opening bat for Somerset and has three girlfriends. Opinion is split as to whether it's a viable alternate timeline or some sort of Dungeons and Dragons wish-fulfilment fantasy. At the moment, I don't really care."

She kissed Keith on the mouth. He took it as if it were his right, and then started struggling.

"What happened?" he asked, shaking free of Gené. "Who was here?"

Gené let the familiar—the original?—Keith go, and edged away from him. He still looked confused. The other Keith had been useful in a pinch, but Jamie couldn't say he missed him.

IX

Putting Professor Cleaver to sleep hadn't brought back the summer, but did shut him up—which was a relief.

Richard looked through the heavily frosted window. There was proper snow, now. Precipitation. It dropeth-ed like the gentle rain from Heaven, fluttering down picturesquely before being caught in erratic, spiralling winds and dashed hither and yon. The Cold's sphere of influence scraped the upper atmosphere, where it found clouds to freeze.

According to Catriona, the white blanket was gaining pace, spreading across the moors and fields. Soon, the perimeter of exclusion would be breached. So far, three villages had been evacuated on a flimsy cover story. When the Cold gripped fair-sized towns like Yeovil and Sedgwater, the domesticated feline would be well and truly liberated from the portable container.

Cleaver snorted in his sleep, honking through his broken nose. Not content with tying the Professor to a swivel chair, Leech had shoved a sock in his mouth and bound a scarf around his jaws. Richard loosened the gag, so he wouldn't asphyxiate on bri-nylon and his own false teeth.

Leech shot him a pitiful look. He was picking through Clever Dick's papers.

"The man couldn't maintain an orderly file if his soul depended on it," he said, in exasperation. "From now on, every scientist or researcher who works for me gets shadowed by two form-fillers and a pen-pusher. What's the use of results if you can't *find* them?"

"He wasn't working for you," said Richard.

"Oh yes he was," insisted Leech. "He drew his pay-packet and he signed his contract. Derek Leech International *owns* his results. If this Cold creature is real, then we own *her*. The *Comet* has exclusive rights to her story. I could put her in a zoo, hunt her for sport, license her image for t-shirts, or dissect her crystal by crystal to advance the progress of science and be entirely within my legal rights."

"Tell *her* that."

Leech turned a page and found something. "I just might," he said.

He tore out a sheaf of papers covered in neat little diagrams. Richard thought it might be some form of cipher, then recognised the hexagonal designs as snow crystals. Under each was a scrawl—mirror-written words, not in English.

"Backwards in Latin," mused Leech. "Paranoid little boffin, wouldn't you say? This is Cleaver's rosetta stone. Not many words, no subtleties, no syntax at all. But he received instructions. He made and used his Box. He broke the Zero Barrier, and violated the laws of physics."

"All because he could grow snowflakes?"

"Yes, and now I *own* the process. There might not be applications yet, but things get smaller. Transistorisation won't stop at the visible. Imagine: trademarked weather, logos on bacteria, microscopic art, micro-miniaturised assassins…"

"Let's ensure the future of mankind on the planet before you start pestering the patent office, shall we?"

Leech bit down, grinding his teeth hard. Richard thought something had snapped in his mouth.

"You should watch that," he advised.

Leech smiled, showing even, white, perfect gnashers. Richard suspected he had rows of them, eternally renewed—like a shark.

All rooms have ghosts. Acts and feelings and ideas all have residue, sometimes with a half-life of centuries. Richard took his gauntlets off and began to touch things, feeling for the most recent impressions. His fingertips were so numb that the cold shocks were welcome. His sensitivity was more attuned to living people than to dead objects, but he could usually read something if he focused. He scraped a brown stain on the wall, and had a hideous flash: Cleaver, with a knife, smiling; a red-haired man in a white coat, gouting from an open throat.

"What is it?" Leech asked.

Richard forced himself to disconnect from the murder. "The staff," he said. "I saw what happened before they were snowmen."

"Where are they, by the way?" asked Leech.

"Wandered off. Didn't seem to be the sorts to listen to reason. I doubt if you can negotiate with them."

The memory flashes floated in his mind, like neon afterimages. He blinked, and they began to dispel. Cleaver had made four sacrifices to the Cold. McKendrick, Kellett, Bakhtinin, Pouncey.

"Were the staff dead before or after they got snow-coated?" asked Leech.

"Does it matter?"

"If the Professor killed them to give the Cold raw material to make catspaws, they were just unused machines when she got them. If they were alive when the Cold wrapped them up, she might have interfaced with minds other than Clever Dick's."

Richard didn't approve of Leech's use of "interfaced" as a verb-form, but saw where he was going.

"He killed them first," he confirmed. Leech didn't ask him how he knew. "They aren't even zombies. The dead people are more like armatures. The only traces of personality they have..."

"The hats."

"...were imposed by Professor Cleaver. I think he was trying to be funny. He's not very good at humour. Few solipsists are."

Richard proceeded to the remains of the Box. The Cold had come through this doorway. He doubted it could be used to send her back, even if it were repaired. Banishing was never as easy as conjuring. Sometimes performing a ritual backwards worked, but not in a language with six planes of symmetry. You would always get hexagonal palindromes.

Pressing his palm to a frost patch on the surface of a work-bench, he felt the slight bite of the crystals, the pull on skin as he took his hand away. He didn't sense an entity, not even the life he would feel if he put his naked hand against the bark of a giant redwood. Yet the Cold was here.

"When the Cold broke through the Zero Barrier," said Leech, "the Professor's Box blew up. After that, he couldn't make his little tiny ice sculptures, but they still talked. She turned the others into snowmen, but spared him. How could he make her understand he was a sympathiser?"

Richard thought about that. "He persuaded the Cold he was her High Priest," he said. "And she let him live... for a while."

"Cleaver said the Cold was an intelligent form of life," said Leech. "He did *not* say she was *clever*. Imagine: You're utterly unique, near-omnipotent, and have endured millennia upon millennia. You wake up and the only person who talks to you—the only person you have *ever* talked to—is Clever Dick Cleaver. What does that give you?"

"A grossly distorted picture of the world?"

"Exactly. Perhaps it's time our Cold Lady heard another voice."

"Voices," said Richard, firmly.

"Yes, of course," said Leech, not meaning it.

Derek Leech was excited, fathoming possibilities, figuring out angles. Letting the Great Enchanter cut a separate deal with the Cold would be a terrible idea. He was entirely too good at negotiating contracts.

"Now," Leech thought out loud, "how did he talk with her?"

Richard remembered the snow angels. He wandered out of the laboratory. Not caring to maintain Cleaver's obsessive little paths, he waded through snow. It drifted over his ankles. From the cafeteria doorway, he looked again at the three angels. They had reminded him of semaphore signals.

"This is how," he said.

Leech had tagged along with him. He saw it at once too.

"See the feet," said Leech. "Not heel-marks, but toe-marks. When kids make snow angels, they lie on their backs. Cleaver lies on his front. You can see where his face fits, like a mould for a mask."

A muffled screech sounded. Back in the laboratory, the Professor was awake.

Richard stepped into the room and knelt by an angel, touching the negative impression of Cleaver's face. He felt nothing. If this had been the connection, it was dead now. The Cold had moved on.

He would have to try outside.

"Leech," he said, "get on your backpack blower and ring Catriona again. We have to tell her what we're doing, in case it doesn't work. No sense the next lot making the same mistakes..."

A chill rolled down the corridor.

The doorway was empty. Richard saw a white tangle on the floor. Leech's parka. And another further away. His leggings.

Richard's stomach turned over. He was feeling things *now*.

"Leech!" he shouted.

Only the Professor responded, rattling his chair and yelling around his gag.

Richard jogged down the corridor, past more of Leech's discarded arctic gear. He turned a corner. The main doors were open. One flapped in the blizzard.

He made it to the doors and took the full force of the wind in his face.

Leech—in a lightweight salmon suit—had walked a few yards away from the building. He stood in the middle of whirling snow, casually undoing his wide orange knit tie.

One of the snowmen was back. It was Bee-Alice, swollen to mammoth size, twelve or fourteen feet tall, body-bulbs bulging as if pregnant with a litter of snow-babies. Queen Bee-Alice stood over Leech like a Hollywood pagan idol, greedy for human sacrifice.

It should be a summer evening. Daylight lasting past ten o'clock. Plagues of midges and supper in the garden. A welcome cool after another punishingly blazing drought day. Any sunlight was blocked by the Cold, and premature gloom—not even honest night—had fallen.

Leech popped his cat's-eye cufflinks and began unbuttoning his chocolate-brown ruffle shirt. He exposed his almost-hairless chest, clenching his jaws firmly to keep from chattering. He wasn't quite human, but Richard had known that.

This was not going to happen on Richard's watch. Bad enough that the Cold's wake-up call had come from an embittered lunatic whose emotional age was arrested at eleven. If her next suitor were Derek Leech, the death by freezing of all life on Earth might seem a happier outcome.

Richard tried to stride towards Leech, but wind held him back. He forced himself, inch by inch, out into the open, struggling against pellets of ice to take the few crucial steps.

Queen Bee-Alice creaked, head turning like the world before the BBC-TV news. The novelty bumblebees bounced over her, a crown or a halo. She had giant, wrecking-ball fists. Sharon Kellett, junior meteorologist. Two years out of a polytechnic, with a boyfriend in the Navy and a plan to be national weathergirl on the television station Derek Leech wanted to start up. She was among the first casualties of the Winter War. Dead, but not yet fallen. Richard ached at the life lost.

Leech shucked his snug-at-the-crotch, flappy-at-the-ankles trousers. He wore mint-green Y-fronts with electric blue piping.

Richard got to the Great Enchanter and crooked an arm around his neck.

"I won't let you do this," he shouted in his ear.

"You don't understand, Jeperson," he shouted back. At this volume, attempted sincerity sounded just like whining. "*I have to*. For the greater good. I'm willing to sacrifice my—or anyone's—life to end this."

Richard was taken aback, then laughed.

"Nice try, Derek," he said. "But it won't wash."

"It won't, will it?" replied Leech, laughing too.

"Not on your nellie."

"I still have to go through with this, though. You understand, Jeperson? I *can't* pass up the opportunity!"

Leech twisted as if greased in Richard's grip, and shot a tight, knuckley fist into his stomach. Even through layers of protective gear, Richard felt the piledriver blow. He lost his hold on Leech and the Great Enchanter followed the sucker-punch with a solid right to the jaw, a kick to the knee, and another to the goolies. Richard went down, and took an extra kick—for luck—in his side.

"'You rearn now, Grasshopper,'" said Leech, fingers pulling the corners of his eyes, "'not to charrenge master of ancient and noble art of dirty fighting!'"

Leech couldn't help gloating. Stripped to his underpants, whipped by sleet, skin scaled by gooseflesh, his expression was a mask of ugly victory. His exultant grin showed at least a hundred and sixty-eight teeth. Was this the Great Enchanter's true face?

"Really think you can make a deal with the Cold?"

Leech wagged his finger. "You're not getting me like that, Grasshopper. I'm no Clever Dick. I'm not going to explain my wicked plan and give you a chance to get in the way. I'm just going to do what I'm going to do."

Richard had a lump in his fist, an ice-chunk embedded with frozen gravel. His eyes held Leech's gaze, but his hand was busy with the chunk, which he rolled in the snow.

"You didn't go to public school, did you, Derek?"

"No, why?"

"You might have missed a trick."

Richard sat up and, with practiced accuracy, threw the heavy-cored snowball at Leech's forehead. The collision made a satisfying sound. Richard's heart surged with immature glee and he recalled earlier victories: as an untried Third Form bowler, smashing the centre-stump and putting out the astonished Captain of the First Eleven; on an autumn playground, wielding a horse chestnut fresh from the branch to split the vinegar-hardened champion conker of the odious Weems-Deverell II.

A third eye of blood opened above Leech's raised brows. His regular eyes showed white and he collapsed, stunned. He lay, twitching, on the snow.

Queen Bee-Alice made no move. Richard hoped she was impartial.

Unable to leave even Derek Leech to freeze, Richard picked him up in a fireman's lift and tossed him inside the building—slamming the doors after him. He didn't know how much time he had before Leech's wits crept back.

He took off his furs. Cold bit, deeper with each layer removed. He went further than Leech, and eventually stood naked in the blizzard. Everything that could shrivel, turn blue, or catch frost did so. When the shivering stopped, when subzero (if not sub-*absolute zero*) wind-blast seemed slightly warm, he recognised the beginnings of hypothermia. There was no more pain, just a faint pricking all over his body. Snow packed his ears and deafened him. He was calm, light-headed. Flashes popped in his vision, as the cold did something to his optic nerves he didn't want to think about. He shut his eyes, not needing the distraction. There were still flashes, but easier to ignore.

He knelt before Queen Bee-Alice. Some feeling came from his shins as they sank into the snow—like mild acid, burning gently to the bone. His extremities were far distant countries, sending only the occasional report, always bad news. Cleaver had lain face down, but indoors—with no snowfall. Richard lay back, face up, flakes landing on his cheeks and forehead, knowing his whole body was gradually being covered by layer after layer. His hands were swollen and useless. With his arms he shovelled snow over himself. Snow didn't melt on his skin—any body warmth was gone. He fought the urge to sit up and struggle free, and he fought the disorienting effects that came with a lowering of the temperature of his brain. He was buried quickly, as the Cold made a special effort to clump around him, form a drift, smooth over the bump, swallow him.

As his body temperature lowered, he had to avoid surrendering to the sleep that presaged clinical death. His blood slowed, and his heartbeats became less and less frequent. He was using a meagre repertoire of yogic techniques, but couldn't be distracted by the business of keeping the meat machine running.

He opened up, physically, mentally, spiritually.

In the darkness, he was not alone.

Richard felt the Cold. It was hugely alive, and more alien than the few extraterrestrials he'd come across. Newly awake, it stretched out, irritated by moving things and tiny obstructions. It could barely distinguish between piles of stone and people. Both were against the nature it had known. It had an impulse to clean itself by covering these imperfections. It preferred people wrapped in snow, not moving by themselves. But was this its genuine preference, or something learned from Clever Dick Cleaver?

"Hello," shouted Richard, with his mind. "Permit me to introduce myself. I am Richard, and I speak for Mankind."

Snow pressed around his face, like ice-fingers on his eyes.

He *felt* tiny crystals forming inside his brain—not a killing flash-freeze, but the barest pinheads. The Cold was inside him.

"You are not Man."

It wasn't a voice. It wasn't even words. Just snowflake hexagons in the dark of his skull, accompanied by a whisper of arctic winds. But he understood. Meaning was imprinted directly into his brain.

To talk with the Cold, it had to become part of him. This was an interior monologue.

"I am Richard," he tried to reply. It was awkward. He was losing his sense of self, of the *concept* of Richard. "I am not Man." *Man* was what the Cold called Cleaver. :I am *another* Man."

To the Cold, the idea of "other" was still fresh, a shock which had come with its awakening. It had only just got used to Man/Cleaver. It was not yet ready for the independent existence of three billion more unique and individual intelligences. As Richard had guessed, it hadn't previously had use for numbers beyond One/Self. The corpse-cores of its snowmen weren't like Man/Cleaver. They were tools, empty of consciousness. Had Cleaver killed his staff because he knew more voices would confuse his ice mistress? Probably.

What would Leech have said to the Cold? He would try to make a deal, to his own best advantage. Richard couldn't even blame him. It was what he did. In this position, the Great Enchanter might become a senior partner, stifle the Cold's rudimentary mind and colonise it, use it. Leech/Cold would grip the world, in a different, ultimately crueller way. He wanted slaves, not corpses; a treadmill to the inferno, not peace and quiet.

What should Richard say?

"Please," he projected. "Please don't k--- us."

There were no snowflakes for "kill" or "death" or "dead." He shuffled through the tiny vocabulary, and tried again. "Please don't stop/cover/ freeze us."

The Cold's mind was changing: not in the sense of altering its intention, but of restructuring its internal architecture. So far, in millennia, it had only needed to make declarative statements, and—until the last few days—only to itself. It had been like a goldfish, memory wiped every few seconds, constantly reaffirming "this is me, this is my bowl, this is water, this is me, this is my bowl, this is water." Now, the Cold needed to keep track, to impose its will on *others*. It needed a more complicated thought process. It was on the point of inventing a crucial mode of address, of communication. It was about to ask its first *question*.

Richard had got his point over. The Cold now understood that its actions would lead to the ending of Man/Richard. It had a sense Man/ Richard was merely one among unimagined and unimaginable numbers of others. For it, "three" was already equivalent to a schoolboy's "gajillion-quajillion-infinitillion to the power of forever." The Cold understood Man/ Richard was asking to be allowed to continue. The life of others was in the Cold's gift.

"Please don't kill us," Richard repeated. There *was* a hexagram for "kill/end" now. "Please don't."

The Cold paused, and asked, "Why not?"

X

It was getting dark, which didn't bother Jamie. He lifted his goggles and saw in more detail. He also felt the cold less. Most of his teammates were more spooked as shadows spread, but Gené was another night-bird. You'd never know she'd come close to having a dirty great icicle shoved all the way through her chest. Perhaps she had a little of the Shade in her. She'd said she knew Auntie Jenny.

Regular Keith was bewildered about what had happened while he was away, and Susan was trying to fill him in. Sewell Head was quoting weather statistics since before records began. It was snowing even harder, and the slog to Alder wasn't going to be possible without losing one or more of the happy little band. Finding shelter was a high priority. They were in the lee of Sutton Mallet church—which was small, but had a tower. The place was securely chained.

"Can't you break these?" Jamie asked Gené.

"Normal chains, yes. Chapel chains, I have a bit of a mental block about. Try the spoon-bender."

Susan stepped up and laid hands on the metal. She frowned, and links began to buckle.

"Where's Head?" asked Keith.

Captain Cleverclogs wasn't with them. Jamie couldn't understand why anyone would wander off. Had the last snowman got him?

"Here are his tracks," said Gené.

"I can't see any," said Keith.

"Trust me."

Jamie saw them too. Sewell Head had gone into a thicket of trees, just beyond what passed for the centre of Sutton Mallet. There were buildings on the other side.

"I'll fetch him back," he said.

"We're not being that stupid, Jamie," said Susan, dropping mangled but unbroken chains. "You go, we all go. No sense splitting up and getting picked off one by one."

She had a point. He was thinking like Dad, who preferred to work alone.

Beyond the trees were ugly buildings. A concrete shed, temporary cabins.

"This is Derek Leech's weather research station," said Gené. "Almost certainly where all the trouble started."

Derek Leech was in the public eye as a smiling businessman, but Jamie's Dad called him "a human void." Jamie had thought Dad a bit cracked on the subject of Derek Leech—like everyone else's parents were cracked about long hair or short hair or the Common Market or some other bloody thing. He was coming round to think more of what his old man said.

"Shouldn't we stay away from here?" cautioned Keith. "Aren't we supposed to join up with folks more qualified than us?"

"You mean grown-ups?" asked Jamie.

"Well, yes."

"Poor old Swellhead'll be an ice lolly by the time you fetch a teacher."

Beside the building was a towering snowman. Bugs, grown to Kitten Kong proportions. The front doors were blown inward and jammed open by snowdrifts. It was a fair guess Head had gone inside. If he could get past the snow-giant, they had a good chance.

"Susan," he said. "Can you concentrate on the snowman? At the first sign of hassle, melt the big bastard."

The woman snapped off a salute. "Since you ask so nicely," she said, "I'll give it a whirl."

"Okay, gang," he said. "Let's go inside."

They sprinted from the thicket to the doors. Bugs didn't make a move, but Keith tripped and Gené had to help him up and drag him.

Inside the building, which was an ice-palace, the wind was less of a problem, and they were protected from the worst of the snow. Overhead lights buzzed and flickered, bothering Jamie's eyes. He slipped his goggles back on.

They found Sewell Head in a room which might have been a mess hall. He was acting as a valet, helping a man dress in arctic gear. Jamie recognised the bloke from the telly. He was the one who said "If I didn't love it, I wouldn't own it." He must love lots of things, because he owned a shedload of them.

"Hi," he said. "I'm Derek. You must be the new Doctor Shade."

Yes, Jamie realised. He must be.

Leech's smile jangled his shadow-senses. The dark in him was something more than night.

"I'm a big fan of your father's," said Leech. "I learned to read from tear-sheets of the newspaper strip they ran about his adventures. Ahh, 'the Whooping Horror,' 'the Piccadilly Gestapo.' How I longed for my own autogyro! I have a car just like Dr. Shade's. A ShadowShark."

Jamie remembered that there had been *two* Rollses in the snow. Whose was the other one?

"Leech," said Gené, acknowledging him.

"Geneviève Dieudonné," said Leech, cordially. "I thought you'd aged hundreds of years and died."

"I got better."

"Well done. Though live through the night before you pat yourself on the back too much. Where's the rest of the army? The heavy mob. Ariadne, Jago, Mrs. Michaelsmith, Little Rose? The Cold's already got Jeperson. We need to go all-out on the attack if we're to have a chance of stopping it."

"We're it, right now," said Jamie.

"You'll have to do, then."

Jamie boiled inside at that. He didn't even know the people Leech had listed. Whoever they might be, he doubted they'd have done as well against the snowmen.

"Who might you be, my dear?" Leech said to Susan.

"I might be Susan Rodway. Or Susan Ames. Mum got remarried, and I have a choice."

"I know exactly who you are," said Leech. "Shade, why didn't you say you had her? She's not Rose Farrar or an Elder of the Kind, but she's a bloody good start."

Susan began primping a bit at the attention. Jamie couldn't believe she'd let this hand-kissing creep smarm her up like that. He'd never understand birds.

"Now, Sewell," said Leech, addressing his instant orderly. "Get on the blower and tell Miss Kaye to pull her finger out. The telephone kit is in the laboratory down the hall. The room with the tied-up-and-gagged idiot in it. It's simple to use. You'll have the specs for it in your head somewhere."

Head meekly trotted out of the room. He was taking orders without question.

Leech looked over the four of them—Jamie, Gené, Susan, Keith.

"Susan," he said, "can you do something about the room temperature?"

Susan, bizarrely, seemed smitten. "I can *try*," she said, and shut her eyes.

A little warmth radiated from her. Some icicles started dripping. Jamie felt his face pricking, as feeling returned.

"Good girl," said Leech. "You, young fellow-me-lad. Any chance of getting some tea going?"

"Give it a try, sir," said Keith, hunting a kettle.

Jamie already resented Derek Leech. For a start, he had released all those triple LPs of moaning woodwind hippies which got played over and over in student common rooms. Even if he weren't the literal Devil, that alone made him a man not to be trusted. But he was magnetic in person, and Jamie felt a terrible tug—it would be easier to go along with Leech, to take orders, to not be responsible for the others. Dad could be like that too, but he always drummed it into Jamie that he should become his own man. Dad didn't even disapprove of him being in a band rather than joining the night-wars—though he realised he'd done that anyway, as well. If he was the new Dr. Shade, he was also a different Shade.

It was Leech's world too. If this big freeze was spreading, it was his interest to side with the angels. If everyone was dead, no one would make a deal with him. No one would buy his crappy music or read his raggy papers.

Jamie saw that Gené was sceptical of anything Leech-related, but Susan and Keith were sucked in. Keith had found his grown-up, his teacher. Susan had found something she needed too. Jamie had been revising his impression of her all day. Leech saw at once that she was the most useful Talent in their crowd. Jamie hadn't even noticed her at first, and he had been around Talents all his life. Susan Rodway was not only Shade-level or better in her abilities, but extremely good at keeping it to herself. She kept talking about the things she couldn't do, or making light of the things she could.

Leech had been briefly interested in Jamie, in *Dr. Shade*—but he had instantly passed over him, and latched onto Susan.

Jamie realised—with a tiny shock—that he was jealous. But of whom? Susan, for going to the head of the class? Or Leech, for getting the girl's attention? There wasn't time for this.

"What did you say about Richard Jeperson?" Gené asked Leech.

Jamie knew Jeperson was Fred and Vanessa's guv'nor at the Diogenes Club. He tied in with Gené too.

"Mad, definitely," said Leech, with just a hint of pleasure. "Dead, probably. The Cold took him—it's a thinking thing, not just bad weather— and he went outside, naked. He lay down and let himself be buried. I tried to stop him, but he fought like a tiger, knocked me out... gave me this."

Leech indicated a fresh wound on his forehead.

"Stone in a snowball," he said. "Playground trick."

Gené thought a few moments and said, "we've got to go out and find him. He might still be alive. He's not helpless. He's a Talent too. If he's buried, we can dig him up."

"I think that's a good idea," said Leech.

Anything Leech thought was a good idea was almost certainly good mostly or only for him. But Jamie couldn't see any alternative. That Fred would give him a right belting if he let Jeperson die.

"Okay, I'll go," he said. "Gené, Susan, stay here. Give Mr. Leech any help he needs..."

i.e.: keep a bloody eye on him! Gené, though worried for her friend, picked that up.

Leech was bland, mild, innocent.

"Keith," said Jamie, at last. "Find a shovel or something, and come with me."

Keith, infuriatingly, looked to Leech—who gave him the nod.

"Come on, find someone useful inside you. Let's get this rescue party on the road!"

Keith gulped and said "o-okay, Jamie."

XI

Derek Leech was on the telephone again. Really, the man had the most terrible manners. He had some minion bother Catriona, then brushed her aside because he wanted to talk with Maureen Mountmain, of all people. Catriona passed the receiver to the woman, who listened—to her master's voice?—and clucked. *Yes, Mr. Leech, no, Mr. Leech, three bags bloody full, Mr. Leech....* Catriona caught herself: This was no time to be a cranky old woman.

The Cold was getting into the Manor House, overwhelming Louise Teazle's bubble of summer. Frost grew on the insides of the windows. Sleet and snow rattled against the panes.

In the gloom of the gardens, drifts and banks shifted like beasts.

Catriona had pain in her joints, and was irritated. She could list other age-related aches and infirmities, exacerbated by the Cold.

Only Rose Farrar and Ariadne were immune. Rose skipped around the drawing room, exhaling white clouds. Ariadne stood by the fireplace— where the wood wouldn't light, and shivers of snow fell on tidy ashes— and smoked a cigarette in a long, elegant holder.

Paulette Michaelsmith shivered in her sleep, and Louise rearranged her day-blanket without any effect. Karabatsos and his wife huddled together. Mr. Zed was white. Swami Anand Gitamo chanted mantras, but his nose was blue. Lark and Cross, the white-coats, passed the china teapot between them, pressing their hands against the last of its warmth. Even Anthony Jago, who feared not the ice and fire of Hell, had his hands in his armpits. The house itself creaked more than usual.

"Richard?" exclaimed Maureen. "Are you sure?"

Catriona, who had been trying not to listen, had a spasm of concern. Maureen had blurted out the name in shock. She and Richard had...

Maureen hung up, cutting off Catriona's train of thought. The room looked to Maureen for a report.

"Derek needs us all," she said. "He needs us to hurt the Cold."

A lot of people talked at once, then shut up.

"Catriona," said Maureen, fists pressed together under her impressive bosom, "your man Richard Jeperson is lost."

"Lost?"

"Probably dead. I'm sorry, truly. Derek says he tried to reach the Cold, and it took him. It's a monster, and wants to kill us all. We have to hit it with all we've got, now. All our big guns, he says. Maybe it can't be killed, but can be hurt. Driven back to its hole."

A tear dribbled from Maureen's eye.

"Reverend Jago, Lady Elder, Rose… you're our biggest guns. Just tear into the Cold. Miss Teazle, work on Mrs. Michaelsmith—direct her. Think of the heatwave. Karabatsos, clear a circle and make a summoning. A fire elemental. The rest of you, pray. That's not a figure of speech. The only way we can beat this thing is with an enormous spiritual attack."

The news about Richard was a terrible blow. Catriona let Maureen go on with her "to arms" speech, trying to take it in. She was not a sensitive in the way any of these Talents were, but she was not a closed mind. And Maureen had said Richard was only *probably* dead.

Mr. and Mrs. Karabatsos were the first to act. They rolled aside a carpet and began chalking a circle on the living room floor.

"Excuse me," said Catriona. "Is this your house?"

Karabatsos glared at her, nastily triumphant. Catriona would not be looked at like that in her home.

"No need to bother with that," said Anand Gitamo.

"Summoning a fire elemental requires a circle, and a ritual," said Karabatsos. "Blood must be spilled and burned."

"Yes dear, *spilled* and *burned*," echoed his wife.

"In normal company, maybe," said the Swami, sounding more like plain old Harry Cutley. "But we've got extraordinary guests. We can take shortcuts. Now, you two sorcerers shut your eyes and think about your blessed fire elemental. Extra-hot and flaming from the Pits of Abaddon and Erebus and all that. Think hard, now think harder. Imagine more flames, more heat, more burning. Take your basic fire elemental, add the Japanese pikadon, the Norse Surtur, Graeco-Roman Haephaestus or Vulcan, the phoenix, the big bonfire at the end of *The Wicker Man*, that skyscraper from *The Towering Inferno*, the Great Fire of London in 1666, enough napalm to deforest the Republic of Vietnam and the eternal blue flame of the lost city of Kôr…"

Nigel Karabatsos and his wife shut their eyes and thought of fire.

"Rose dear," said Gitamo. "Peek into those tiny minds."

Rose Farrar caught fire and expanded. She grew into a nine-foot-tall column of living flame, with long limbs and a blazing skull-face. Though she was hard to look at and her radiant heat filled the room, she didn't burn the ceiling or the carpet. She was Fire.

"Reverend Jago," said Gitamo, "would you open the doors? Rose needs to go outside."

The man in the dog-collar was astonished by what the apparent little girl had become. Anthony Jago didn't know whether to bow down before a fiery angel of the Lord or cast out a demon from Hell. His already-peculiar belief system was horribly battered by this experience. Catriona feared no good would come of that.

But, if anything could hurt the Cold, it would be Fire Rose.

Louise Teazle reported that the snow outside was melting. Fire Rose was radiating, beyond the walls.

"No," said Ariadne, snapping her fingers. "I think not."

Fire Rose went out. Spent-match stink filled the room. The little girl, unburned and unburning, sat on the floor exactly as she had been. She was bewildered. No one had ever switched her off like a light before.

Jago was enraged. All the cups, saucers, and cutlery on the table near him and all the books on the shelves behind him leaped at once into the air, and hovered like projectiles about to be slung. Catriona had known he was a telekinetic, but this was off the scale. In any other drawing room, parapsychologists like Cross and Lark would be thinking of the book deals and the lecture tour—though, after Fire Rose, this little display scarcely made the needle tick. Jago's eyes smouldered.

Ariadne shook her head, and everything went neatly back to its place. Not a drop of tea spilled or a dust-jacket torn. Jago knit his brows, blood vessels pulsing, but not so much as a teaspoon responded.

Mr. Zed took out a gun, caught Ariadne's gaze, then pointed it at his own head. He stood still as a statue.

"If we're not going off half-cocked," said the Elder of the Kind, "let us review our plan of action. In dealing with the Cold, do we really want to do *what Derek Leech says*."

Exactly. Ariadne had said what Catriona felt.

"You can't win a Winter War with fire," she said. "Fire consumes, leaves only ashes."

"Then what?" said Maureen, frustrated, red-eyed. "If not Derek's plan, what? I'd really like to know, ladies. I'm freezing my tits off here."

"There there," said Catriona, touching Maureen's shoulder. "Have faith. He'll be all right."

Maureen didn't ask who she meant.

"He'll see us through," Catriona said.

Richard.

XII

On some other path in life, an expert outdoorsman Keith had loads of survival training in extreme weather conditions. Probably, Keith had to weed out a couple of dozen plonkers who didn't know how to tie their own shoelaces, but he'd found the useful life in seconds. Not a bad trick. While Jamie scanned for tracks or a human-shaped bump in the snow, Keith barked instructions—keep moving, breathe through your nose, turn your shoulder to the wind.

One good thing: In all this mucky weather, Richard Jeperson couldn't have gone far.

Any footprints were filled by new snow. The marks they had made coming from the thicket to the buildings were already gone. Jamie looked for dark traces, the shadows of shadows. It was Dad's game, and he wasn't expert in it yet—but he could usually see shadow-ghosts, if he caught them in time.

He found a discarded fur boot. And another.

A shaggy clump a little past the boots turned out not to be the missing man, but an abandoned coat. A fold of Day-Glo green poking up from the snow was a cast-off balaclava. Leech had said Jeperson went out naked. That was not true. Jeperson had gone outside, *then* taken his clothes off. Leech wouldn't have got that wrong unless he were deliberately lying. If Jeperson knocked Leech out and left him inside, Leech would not have known what Jeperson did next—but he had said Jeperson took his clothes off, went out, and lay down in the show. Had Leech attacked Jeperson, stripped him, and left him to freeze to death, cooking up a story to exonerate himself? Jamie should have checked at once—tried to replay the shadows in the building. He had an inkling it wouldn't have worked. There was something wrong with Leech's shadow.

He hoped Gené and Susan could take care of themselves. Derek Leech was dangerous.

They were near Bugs, the mammoth snowman. It had lost human shape and become a mountain. Novelty insects still bobbed on its summit like the Union Flag on top of Everest.

Jamie saw the shadow lying at the foot of Mount Bugs. A man, stretched out. Jeperson was under here.

He pointed to the spot and told Keith, "dig there, mate. *There*."

"Where?"

Keith didn't have the Shade-sight. Jamie knelt and began scooping snow away with gloved hands. Keith used a tray from the cafeteria as a spade, digging deep.

A face emerged, in a nest of long, frozen hair. Thin, blue, hollow-cheeked, jagged-moustached, and open-eyed.

"Hello," said Jeperson, smiling broadly. "You must be the new boys."

XIII

Suddenly, Richard felt the cold. Not the Cold—he was disconnected, now. The little crystals were out of his brain. He hoped he had given the Cold something to think about.

"Would you happen to have seen some clothes in your travels?" he asked the two young men. One wore a long dark greatcoat and goggles, the other a red-lined magician's cloak.

They dragged his fur coat along and tried to wrap him in it. What he could see of his skin was sky-blue.

"It's stopped snowing," he observed.

The wind was down too. And sun shone through, low in the West. It was late evening. Long shadows were red-edged.

The Cold was responding to his plea, drawing in its chill. It could live on in perpetuity as a submicroscopic speck inside a rock, or confine itself to the poles, or go back to the void below absolute zero. Without Cleaver telling it what it wanted, it had its own choices. Richard hoped he had persuaded the Cold that other life on Earth was entertaining enough to be put up with.

Now, he would probably die.

He hoped he had done the right thing. He was sorry he'd never found out who his real parents had been. He wished he'd spent more time with Barbara, but—obviously—he'd been busy lately. His personal life hadn't been a priority, and that was a regret. He could trust Fred and Vanessa to keep on, at least for a while. And, if these lads were anything to judge by, the Diogenes Club, or something like it, would continue to stand against Great Enchanters present and future, and all manner of other inexplicable threats to the public safety.

The boy in the goggles tried rubbing Richard's hands, but his friend— who knew something about hypothermia treatment—told him not to. Friction just damages more blood vessels. Gradual, all-round warmth was needed. Not that there was an easy supply around here.

He tried to think of quotable last words.

Some people came out of the building. Leech, and two women. One flew to him. Geneviève. Good for her. They'd not worked together much, but the old girl was a long-standing Valued Member.

"Richard, you won't die," she said.

"I think I'll need a second opinion," he muttered. "A less optimistic one."

"No, really," she insisted.

Leech hung back, shiftily. Richard expected no more. Geneviève pulled the other woman—a brown-haired girl who kept herself to herself—to help, and got her to press her hands on Richard's chest.

Warmth radiated from her touch.

"That's very… nice," he said. "Who are you?"

"This is Susan," said Geneviève. "She's a friend."

Richard had heard of her. Susan Rodway. She was on Catriona's list of possibles.

He felt as if he were sinking into a hot, perfumed bath. Feeling returned to his limbs. He heard hissing and tinkling, as snow and ice melted around them. A bubble of heat was forming. Susan took it slowly, not heating him too fast. His temperature came up like a diver hauled to the surface in stages to avoid the bends.

He tactfully rearranged a flap of fur to cover his loins. Susan's magic warmth had reached there, with an unshrivelling effect he rarely cared to share on such brief acquaintance.

"What did you do?" asked Geneviève. "Are we saved?"

Richard tried to shrug. "I did what I could. I think the Cold is getting a sense of who we are, what we're about, and why we shouldn't just be killed out of hand. Who knows what something like that can really feel, think, or do? You have to call off the blitzkrieg, though. Any smiting with fire and sword is liable to undo the work of diplomacy and land us back in the big fridge."

Leech was expressionless. Richard wondered how things would be if he'd had his way.

Geneviève looked back and said, "make the call, Derek."

He made no move. Geneviève stood. Leech nodded, once, and walked back to the building.

"I see you've met Dr. Shade and Conjurer Keith," said Geneviève. "They've done all right too."

Susan took her hands away. Richard regretted it, but knew her touch couldn't last. Everyone looked at the huge, liquefying snow-giant as he stood up and got dressed as best he could. Sharon Kellett would be inside that glacier. The others would be strewn around the fields.

This patch of Somerset would be better-irrigated than the rest of Britain—for a few days.

"Who else turned up for the ice age?" Richard asked.

"There's a knowledgeable little fellow you don't need to meet just now," said Geneviève. "He didn't even waver, like some folks. Went straight to Leech. He's inside the weather station. At the Manor House, Catriona has a whole tea-party. Old friends and new. Including a strong contingent from the Other Side."

"I can imagine."

"Maureen Mountmain's here," she said, pointedly.

Richard was glad to be warned of that potential complication. Geneviève let the point stick with a needling glance.

"It was a ritual," said Richard, knowing how weak the excuse was.

"It was still…" she mouthed the word "sex."

Richard knew he was being ribbed. Now they were less doomed, they could start squabbling, gossiping, and teasing again.

Leech came back.

"We're invited to supper at the Manor House," he said. "It's only nine o'clock, would you believe it? You'll have to make my excuses, I'm afraid. I have to get back to London. Things to do, people to buy. Give my best to Miss Kaye. Oh, Cleaver's dead. Choked on his false teeth. Pity."

The blotch on his forehead was already gone. Leech recovered quickly.

"See you soon," he said, and walked away.

Richard knew an autopsy wouldn't show anything conclusive. Professor Cleaver would be listed as another incidental casualty.

"I feel much warmer now he's gone," said Geneviève. "Didn't he say something about supper?"

XIV

Most of the company had scurried back to their holes. Catriona was relieved to have them out of the house.

She sat in her drawing room. Paulette Michaelsmith was upstairs, tucked up and dreaming safely. Louise Teazle had walked home to the Hollow, her house on the moor. Geneviève was outside in the garden, with the young people. She was the last of the old ladies.

Ariadne had taken Rose with her. Mr. Zed, round weal on his temple, didn't even complain. The Undertakers were a spent force, but even in their prime they couldn't have stood against an Elder of the Kind. Rose would be safe with Ariadne, and—more to the point—the world would be safe from her. Catriona assumed that Ariadne could pack Rose off to where she came from, just as—eighty years ago—Charles Beauregard sent Princess Cuckoo home. However, the Elder might choose to raise the creature who usually looked like a little girl as her own. At this stage of her life, Catriona doubted she'd live to find out. Charles wasn't here. Edwin wasn't here. At times, Catriona wondered if she were really here. She knew more ghosts than living people, and regretted the rasher statements made about spirits of the unquiet dead in books she had published in her long-ago youth. Occasionally, she welcomed the odd clanking chain or floating bedsheet.

Maureen Mountmain, clearly torn, had wanted to stay and see Richard—she babbled a bit about having something to tell him—but Leech had ordered her to rally a party—Mr. and Mrs. Karabatsos, Myra Lark, Jago—and leave. Jago, well on the way to replacing Rose as Catriona's idea of the most frightening person on the planet, took a last look around the Manor House, as if thinking of moving in, and slid off into the evening with Maureen's group. They wouldn't be able to keep him for long. Jago had his own plans. Leech had picked up Sewell Head, too—though Catriona had looked over his file, and concluded it would take a lot to lure him out of his sweet shop and away from his books of quiz questions.

On the plus side, the Club had tentative gains. Susan Rodway and

Jamie Chambers—the new Dr. Shade!—were hardly clubbable in the old-fashioned sense, but Mycroft Holmes had founded the Diogenes Club as a club for the unclubbable. Even Keith Marion, in a reasonable percentage of his might-have-been selves, was inclined to the good—though finding a place for him was even more of a challenge. Geneviève reported that the Chambers Boy showed his father's dark spark, tempered with a little more sympathy than habitually displayed by Jonathan Chambers. Derek Leech must want to sign up Dr. Shade. The Shades wavered, leaning towards one side or the other according to circumstance or their various personalities. The boy could not be forced or wooed too strongly, for fear of driving him to the bad. Leech would not give up on such a potent Talent. There might even be a percentage in letting Jamie get close to Leech, putting the lad in the other camp for a while. Susan was reluctant to become a laboratory rat for David Cross or Myra Lark, but was too prodigious to let slip. Without her warm hands, Richard would not have lived through this cold spell. Susan needed help coping with her Talent, and had taken Catriona's card. If Jamie could be a counter for Leech, Susan was possibly their best hope of matching Jago. It chilled Catriona that she could even consider sending a girl barely in her twenties up against an Effective Talent like Anthony Jago, but no one else was left to make the decisions.

She was thinking like Edwin now, or even Mycroft. The Diogenes Club, or whatever stood in its stead, had to play a long game. She had been a girl younger than Susan or Jamie when this started for her. The rector's daughter, not the lady of the manor. At eighteen, with Edwin away at the front, she had been escorted by Charles to Mycroft's funeral. That had been a changing of the guard. Some of the famous names and faces of generations before her own seemed like dinosaurs and relics in her eyes. Even Mycroft's famous brother was a bright-eyed old gaffer with a beaky nose, fingers bandaged from bee-stings and yellow teeth from decades of three-pipe problems. Richard Riddle had been there, with his uncle and aunt. In his RFC uniform and jaunty eye-patch, the former boy detective was impossibly glamorous to her. She had a better idea than most where he had flown to in 1934, and still expected him to turn up again, with his chums Vi and Ernie.

Charles had pointed out Inspector Henry Mist, Thomas Carnacki, Sir Henry Merrivale, Winston Churchill, General Hector Tarr, John Silence, Sir Michael Calme, Mansfield Smith-Cumming, Margery Device, the Keeper of the Ravens, and others. Now, Catriona knew Geneviève had been there too, spying through blue lenses from the edge of the crowd—Mycroft's most *secret* secret agent and, contrary to the public record, the first Lady Member of the Diogenes Club. After all the fuss, Catriona turned out not to be the first of her sex to be admitted to the Inner Rooms—though she was the first woman to chair the Ruling Cabal.

It had been a busy sixty years. Angel Down, Irene Dobson, the Murder Mandarin, the Seven Stars, the last flight of the Demon Ace, Spring-Heel'd Jack, Dien Ch'ing, the Splendid Six, Weezie's Hauntings, the Rat Among the Ravens, the Crazy Gang, Parsifal le Gallois, the Water War, Adolf Hitler, Swastika Girl, the Malvern Mystery, the Scotch Streak, the Trouble with Titan, Castle De'ath, the Drache Development, Paulette's dream, the Soho Golem, the Ghoul Crisis, the Missing Mythwrhn, and so many others. And now the Cold. There was more to come, she knew. Richard Jeperson's work wasn't done. Her work wasn't done. The Secret Files of the Diogenes Club remained open.

She felt a whisper against her cheek.

XV

The garden was Disneyfied: white pools of melting ice, nightbirds singing. Light spilled onto the lawns from the upstairs windows of the Manor House. Glints reflected in dwindling icicles. Jamie saw activity streaks in the shadows. With the Cold drawn in, the land was healing.

No one had to worry about World Cooling any more.

Richard Jeperson, the Man from the Diogenes Club, tried to explain what he had done. It boiled down to getting the attention of a vast, unknowable creature and asking it very nicely not to wipe out all life-forms which needed a temperature above freezing to survive. Jamie realised how lucky they had been. Only someone who could ask *very* politely and tactfully would have got a result. A few bumps the other way, along one of Keith's paths, and it could have been Derek Leech under the snow...

Leech had left Jamie his card, and he hadn't thrown it away.

Many of the people drawn to the Winter War had melted away like the ice. Some were sleeping over in the house. Jamie's van was parked next to Richard's ShadowShark in the drive.

He sat on a white filigree lawn-chair, drinking black coffee from an electric pot. The hostess, an elderly lady who had not joined them outside, provided a pretty fair scratch supper for the survivors and their hangers-on. Now, there were wafer-thin mints. Gené was in a lawn-swing, drinking something red and steaming which wasn't tomato soup. Richard, still glowing with whatever Susan had fed into him, smoked a fat, hand-rolled cigarette that wasn't a joint but wasn't tobacco either. Considering what he'd done, Jamie reckoned he could demand that the Archbishop of Canterbury and the Prime Minister hand-deliver an ounce of Jamaican, the Crown Jewels, and Princess Margaret dressed up in a St. Trinian's uniform to his room within the next half-hour and expect an answer of "right away, sir."

"How was your first day on the job?" Gené asked him.

"Job?"

"Your Dad called it a practice. Being Dr. Shade."

"Not sure about the handle. I thought I'd just go with 'Shade' for a bit. 'Jamie Shade,' maybe? I'd use it for the band, but it sounds too much like Slade."

"I quite like Slade," said Richard.

"You would," said Jamie. "What a year, eh?"

"It has had its meteorological anomalies."

"No, I mean the charts. Telly Savalas, Real Thing, The Brotherhood of Man, ABBA, the Wurzels, J.J. Barrie, Demis Roussos… 'Brand New Combine Harvester,' 'Save Your Kisses for Me,' bloody 'No Charge'…. It has to be the low-point in music since forever. It's like some great evil entity was sucking the guts out of our sounds. Some *other* great evil entity. You can't blame Leech for all of it. Even he wouldn't touch the Wurzels. Something's got to change. Maybe I'll stick with the band, leave monsters and magic to other folk. Kids are fed up, you know. They want to hear something new. And you lot are getting on."

"Do you feel 'long in the tooth', Geneviève?" Richard asked.

Gené bared teeth which Jamie could have sworn were longer than they had been earlier.

"It's not about how old you are," said Susan, who had been quietly sipping a drink with fruit in it. "It's about what you do."

"Here's to that," said Richard, clinking his glass to hers.

Keith was sitting quietly, not letting on which of his selves was home. The primary Keith had reluctantly given Jamie back the Great Edmondo's cloak and its hidden tricks. He had asked if Dr. Shade needed an assistant, and started shuttling through selves when Jamie told him he really needed a new drummer. Now, despite what he'd said, he wasn't sure. Being Dr. Shade meant something, and came with a lot of baggage. He half-thought Vron was only with him because of who his Dad was. These people kept calling him "Junior Shade," "Young Dr. Shade," or "the New Dr. Shade." Perhaps he should take them seriously. He was already a veteran of the Winter War, if something over inside two days counted as a war.

Like Dad, he wasn't much of a joiner. He couldn't see himself putting a tie on to get into some fusty old club. But he played well with others. How randomly had his vanload of raw recruits been assembled? Even Sewell Head, now lost to Leech, had come in handy. Maybe, he'd found his new band. Susan, Gené, and Keith all had Talents. Perhaps the old hippie with the ringlets and the 'tache could take the odd guest guitar solo. One thing was for certain, they wouldn't sign with a Derek Leech label.

In the house, the lights went off, and the garden was dark. Jamie didn't mind the dark. From now on, he owned it.

"Catriona's gone to bed," said Richard.

Gené, another night person, stretched out on the grass, as if sunning herself in shadows.

"Some of us never sleep," she said. "Someone has to watch out for the world. Or we might lose it."

"We're not going to let that happen," said Richard.

NOTES

Al Adamson. Adamson and Sam Sherman were a director–producer team responsible for, among others, *Satan's Sadists* (with Russ Tamblyn), *Blood of Dracula's Castle*, *Five Bloody Graves*, and *Dracula vs. Frankenstein* (with Lon Chaney Jr. as Groton the Mad Zombie). Tamblyn and Chaney Jr. both appeared in *The Female Bunch* (1969), which was shot on the Spahn Ranch, then home to the Manson Family. In 1995, Adamson was murdered by an odd-job man named Fred Fulford, who buried his body under concrete in a jacuzzi. Sherman is rereleasing all their old films on DVD with commentary tracks.

the Angel of Mons. The rumoured appearance of angels above the British lines during the battle of Mons in 1914. It seems the legend arises from Arthur Machen's short story "The Bowmen," in which spectral longbowmen from Henry V's era help out their descendants against another foreign foe. The tale escaped its creator and circulated in many variant versions, with warrior angels, phantom cavalrymen, and St. George smiting the Hun.

apple-scrumpers. Children who steal apples from farmers' trees, or—with a certain assumption that it's a less serious offence—from the ground underneath farmers' trees. Opinions vary as to whether it's a harmless, healthy, mildly amusic aspect of a country childhood or the first step on a road that leads to the gallows.

ash-can. Dustbin

Barbara. Professor Barbara Corri. See: "The Serial Murders" in *The Man From the Diogenes Club*.

the bee's roller-skates. Colloq: pretty darned impressive.

Wedgy Benn. Anthony Wedgwood Benn, Lord Stansgate—who gave up his title and spent decades trying to get the media to call him Tony Benn. A minister in the Wilson government of the 1960s, later a left-wing gadfly.

blower. Colloq: telephone.

Boney was a warrior way-aye-aye. The first line of a sea-chanty, which exists in almost as many versions as "Louie Louie." The first verse usually goes: "Boney was a warrior way-aye-aye/A warrior, a terrier, John Fran-Swah!"

Brain of Britain. A radio quiz program. It's still running.

Laird Brunette. See: *Farewell, My Lovely*, by Raymond Chandler.

Billy Butlin. The founder of Butlins Holiday Camps.

century of centuries. In cricket, a century means scoring a hundred runs. If you do that a hundred times, you've scored a century of centuries.

charabanc. A kind of open-topped omnibus, much used for holiday excursions, works outings, and the like in early 20th Century Britain. The name comes from the French *char-à-bancs* (carriage with benches).

cipher. The key-word for the R.R.D.A. cipher is 'dinosaur'

the Cobb. The distinctive stone harbour wall of Lyme Regis. It's the setting for an important scene in John Fowles's novel *The French Lieutenant's Woman*, and can be seen in the film.

the Common Market. Forerunner of the European Union.

Crystal Palace Park. The dinosaur statues were sculpted by Benjamin Waterhouse Hawkins, with advice from the palaeontologist Sir Richard Owen. They were commissioned in 1851 and gradually completed over the next fifty years—only the Crystal Palace Company's decision to cut funding in 1895 ended the project. Now of more historical than scientific interest, they are still there in South London, renovated in 2002, and well worth a visit.

Harry Cutley. See: "The Man Who Got Off the Ghost Train" in *The Man From the Diogenes Club*.

Leo Dare, Isidore Persano, Colonel Zenf. Stories for which the world is not ready, but see "A Drug on the Market" for Dare and "Sorcerer Conjurer Wizard Witch" for Persano and Zenf.

dead cert. A dead certainty. Often, a horse-racing expression.

"Derek Leech had popped up apparently out of nowhere in 1961." In the first chapter of *The Quorum*, actually.

Zuleika Dobson. Title character of a 1911 novel by Max Beerbohm.

Ivan Dragomiloff. See: *The Assassination Bureau, Ltd.*, by Jack London (completed by Robert L. Fish). The film, with Oliver Reed as Dragomiloff, is fun, but the book is much better.

Duel of the Seven Stars. See: *Seven Stars*.

dustbin. Ash-can.

eggplant. Here's a rare note for British readers: aubergine.

Brian Epstein. The Beatles' manager.

The Esoteric Order of Dagon. See: "The Shadow Over Innsmouth," by H.P. Lovecraft.

florin. A two-shilling coin. In modern British money, ten pence.

fred perry. A type of shirt, named after a tennis player.

Girls' Paper. Properly, *Girls' Own Paper*, sister publication to the better-known *Boys' Own Paper*.

Gary Glitter. UK pop performer, prominent in the early 1970s "glam rock" trend with hits like "Rock and Roll, Parts 1 and 2" and "I'm the Leader of the Gang (I Am)." In 2005, he was convicted of child sexual abuse in Vietnam. In current rhyming slang, "the Gary" means "rectum" (Gary Glitter = shitter).

Gosse. Philip Henry Gosse (1810–88), author of *Omphalos: An Attempt to Untie the Geological Knot* (1857). Best known now thanks to his son Edmond Gosse's memoir *Father and Son* (1907).

Gower Gulch. The intersection of Sunset Blvd. and Gower Street in Hollywood, so named because out-of-work cowboys would gather there, hoping to land jobs in the many Westerns made in the nearby studios. Derek Leech is very happy that today, a mall which calls itself Gower Gulch stands on the site.

the Great Edmondo. Robert Edmond Stone; see "Sorcerer Conjurer Wizard Witch." Edmondo was the Conjurer.

the Great Game. The phrase was first used by Arthur Conolly, referring to the diplomatic and espionage stratagems and counterstratagems of the British and Russian Empires in Central Asia in the late 19th Century. It was popularised by Rudyard Kipling in *Kim*, which—incidentally—was my mother's favourite novel.

Frank Harris. Irish-born editor, author of the scandalous *My Life and Loves* (1922–27).

Dr. Martin Hesselius. See: *In a Glass Darkly*, by J. Sheridan LeFanu.

the Hindu Kush. A mountain range in Afghanistan.

Home Rule. The movement for Irish self-government.

"If you wake at midnight, and hear a horse's feet…" "A Smuggler's Song" by Rudyard Kipling.

IT. The *International Times*, an "underground" paper published from 1966.

Janet and John. The UK equivalent of Dick and Jane—much better brought-up, they wouldn't dream of running after Spot but would walk politely after the dog.

Jubilee. Queen Victoria's Golden Jubilee, celebrating 50 years on the throne, was in 1887. Her Diamond Jubilee came ten years later.

Jutland. The Battle of Jutland, largest naval engagement of WWI.

Nigel and Joanne Karabatsos. See: "Mother Hen."

Jean-Claude Killy. French ski champion.

Kingstead Cemetery. Last resting place of Lucy Westenra, Mycroft Holmes, and George Oldrid Bunning. See: "Egyptian Avenue," in *The Man From the Diogenes Club*.

Kitten Kong. A well-remembered 1971 episode of the BBC-TV series *The Goodies* features a giant cat which climbs the Post Office Tower.

"Knocked 'Em in the Old Kent Road." Music hall ditty, written and popularised by Albert Chevalier. Shirley Temple sings it (hideously) in *A Little Princess* (1939).

Late Night Line-Up. A BBC-TV show that ran on BBC2 from 1964 to 1972. Its original remit was to publicise other programs on the then-new channel, but this expanded to cover many cultural, political, and media topics.

Bernard Levin. Journalist, author, and broadcaster—a very familiar TV pundit in the 1960s and '70s.

a long-case clock. A grandfather clock.

Lord Leaves of Leng. See "Soho Golem" in *The Man From the Diogenes Club.*

the Lord Lieutenant. Commander of a county militia, and historically the sovereign's local representative—with varying powers and authorities.

Lobby Ludd. These circulation-building newspaper stunts were a phenomenon of the 1920s and '30s. Strictly, I'm fudging chronology—the first of these, the *Westminster Gazette*'s Lobby Lud, appeared a few years after this scene, in 1927. That's why the extra "d."

"maiden tributes of modern Babylon." The phrase was used by the Pall Mall Gazette in an exposé of Victorian child prostitution.

malarkey. Hijinx, impertinence, horseplay.

Manfish (1956), directed by W. Lee Wilder. It's a loose adaptation of Edgar Allan Poe's "The Gold Bug."

Maple White Land. See: *The Lost World,* by Sir Arthur Conan Doyle.

the Married Women's Property Act. Passed 1907, a key piece of legislation in the Edwardian emancipation of women—it meant that husbands could no longer dispose of their wives' property without their permission.

MCC. The Marylebone Cricket Club, the original governing body of cricket in England and throughout the world. Originally, the MCC organised the English national cricket side. They held out against allowing women to become members well after the Diogenes Club did.

Sir Henry Merrivale. A.k.a. H.M. John Dickson Carr, Sir Henry's biographer (and Arthur Conan Doyle's), mentions his membership in the Diogenes Club.

Paulette Michaelsmith. See: "End of the Pier Show" in *The Man From the Diogenes Club*.

Mary Millington. The leading British porn star of the 1970s. She appeared in films (*Come Play With Me*, *The Playbirds*), stag reels, and many magazine and newspaper spreads. She claimed to have had a one-night stand with Harold Wilson, and committed suicide at the age of 33 in 1979.

Mr. Huggins and Mr. Young. A brand of coffee, favoured by hard-boiled private eyes as a substitute for soft-boiled eggs at breakfast.

Charles Shaar Murray. Journalist, who specialised in pop music. He was at *IT* between spells at *Oz* and the *NME*. He wrote the introduction to *In Dreams*, an original anthology I edited with Paul J. McAuley.

new bugs. School slang—new pupils, rookies, fresh fish.

O Levels. CSEs. Exams taken in the 1970s by UK schoolchildren at about sixteen.

the Oval. Kennington Oval, a cricket ground in South London.

parlour. A reception room, so called because people used it mostly for talking.

pasty-stall. Cornish pasties, traditionally a balanced lunch for tin-miners: meat, potatoes, and vegetables cooked in a pastry parcel. Mostly horrible if bought from supermarkets, but a culinary delight if homemade. You used to be able to get excellent pasties from waterfront stalls and pubs in Lyme Regis.

Pentonville. HM Prison, Pentonville.

perambulators. Baby carriages.

Isidore Persano. See Leo Dare.

the Post Office Tower. Now the BT Tower.

the Pour le Mérite. A German medal, better known (at least thanks to the book and film) as the Blue Max.

Enoch Powell. Far-right politician of the 1960s and '70s, who left the Conservatives to join the Ulster Unionists. A controversial figure (to put it mildly), he famously espoused anti-immigration and repatriation policies (as expressed in his racially inflammatory "rivers of blood" speech). Arthur Wise's novel *Who Killed Enoch Powell?* (1972) imagines his assassination.

prang. WWI flying slang: crash.

read the riot act. To lay down the law. The expression comes from a law passed by the British parliament in 1714 against riotous assemblies—when an official read out a proclamation that a given crowd should disperse, the malcontents had twenty minutes to go away before the authorities used force to break them up.

rooking. Colloq: deceiving, conning.

the Royal Vic. The Royal Victoria Military Hospital, Netley. A famous building in its day, demolished in 1966. See: *Spike Island: The Memory of a Military Hospital*, by Philip Hoare.

Neville St. Clair. See "The Man With the Twisted Lip," by Arthur Conan Doyle.

St. Trinian's. A notorious girls' school, first seen in cartoons by Ronald Searle, then a series of films starting with *The Belles of St. Trinian's* (1954).

sarky. Sarcastic.

Jimmy Saville. Disc jockey and TV personality, host of the long-running *Jim'll Fix It*, and known in the 1970s for creepy road safety adverts ("clunk-click, every trup") in which he smarmed over children who'd been horribly mangled in car accidents.

the Scotch Streak and the Go-Codes. See: "The Man Who Got Off the Ghost Train" in *The Man From the Diogenes Club*.

the Seamouth Warp. See: "End of the Pier Show" in *The Man From the Diogenes Club*.

Sam Sherman. See Al Adamson.

Dr. Silence. See: *John Silence, Physician Extraordinary*, by Algernon Blackwood.

Dame Ethel Smyth. British composer and a leading suffragette.

the snug. A small bar-room, separate from the larger "public" bar of a pub.

some scandal which was never spoken of in the village. See: *Jago.*

spend a penny. Use a public convenience—they once had coin-operated stalls.

Albert Steptoe. The "dirty old man" played by Wilfrid Brambell in the BBC-TV sitcom *Steptoe and Son* (1962–75). A *considerably* more unpleasant character than the equivalent played by Redd Foxx in the US remake *Sanford and Son.*

take the money or open the box… make-your-mind-up-time. Catch-phrases on UK TV quiz shows.

a Tiller girl. The Tiller Girls were a troupe of dancers, founded in 1886 by the choreographer John Tiller. Many troupes around the world used the name and the distinctive high-kicks. Tiller also choreographed the original New York Rockettes.

Titfer. Cockney rhyming slang: tit fer tat = hat.

"To Be Specific, It's Our Pacific," "So Long Momma, I'm Off to Yokahama," "We're Gonna Slap the Jap Right Off the Map," "When Those Little Yellow Bellies Meet the Cohens and the Kellys." I didn't make any of these up.

Tripella Liplik Pik. The sea-ghost is actually pronouncing this properly—it's "The Three Little Pigs" in Pidgin English. The other two books, for the record, are *Alice in Wonderland* and the *Tales of Edgar Allan Poe.*

tweeny. An "in-between maid," so called because she was expected to work downstairs, assisting the cook, and upstairs, assisting the parlour-maid.

Zanuck. Darryl F. Zanuck, head of 20th Century-Fox.

Zebedee from The Magic Roundabout. A moustachioed puppet on a spring, who featured in a truly bizarre children's program. Originally made in

France, *The Magic Roundabout* became a popular and cult success in the UK thanks to overdubbed narration by Eric Thompson (Emma's Dad). It displaces about as much cultural water in Britain as *Rocky and Bullwinkle* in the US. There was a horrible CGI revival movie.

Colonel Zenf. See Leo Dare.

Zenith the Albino. Anthony Zenith, dilettante master criminal, most active in the 1920s and '30s, repeatedly clashing with the detective Sexton Blake. See: *Zenith the Albino* (1936), by Anthony Skene. Reported killed in the blitz, but we'll take the word of a Dr. Shade over hearsay...

Who's Who

ARIADNE. Ariadne, Elder of the Kind, has occasionally lived a relatively ordinary life, for instance as the wife of a schoolmaster at Dulwich College at the turn of the century, and as a costume designer in Hollywood ("gowns by Ariadne") in the 1940s. The Kind, a race apart from humanity, mostly keep themselves to themselves, but there have been a few notable troublemakers. See: *Bad Dreams*.

CHARLES BEAUREGARD. Among the first Valued Members recruited by Mycroft Holmes (q.v.), Charles Beauregard succeeded his mentor as Chairman of the Ruling Cabal upon Mycroft's death in 1918. He politely declined six knighthoods. For his activities in another timeline, see: the *Anno Dracula* cycle, *Anno Dracula*, *The Bloody Red Baron: Anno Dracula 1918* and *Dracula Cha Cha Cha* (a.k.a. *Judgment of Tears: Anno Dracula 1959*).

JENNIFER CHAMBERS. The sister of the original Dr. Shade. In the 1920s and '30s, Dr. Chambers had many unusual adventurers on the books of her Harley Street practice. See: "Sorcerer Conjurer Wizard Witch."

THE COLD. For its existence in another universe, see *Doctor Who: Time and Relative*.

DR. DAVID CROSS. A parapsychologist, associated with both the Institute of Psi Technology and the Diogenes Club. He worked with both Susan Rodway and Keith Marion. After the death of Adam Onions, he was appointed director of IPSIT and discontinued the remote viewing program which provided overwhelming evidence that Saddam Hussein had weapons of mass destruction. See: *Jago*.

REBECCA D'ARBANVILLIERS. In later life, Rebecca was a famously nervous socialite. She married the visionary ladies' wear tycoon Benjamin Blandford Holmes, who she met in the waiting room of the prominent (and presumably pseudonymous) alienist "Sigmund von Doppelganger"; she was being treated for an acute terror of rabbits and he sought a cure for compulsive self-abuse. On his deathbed, Rebecca's father ceded his title to Gonville Tregellis-d'Aulney, a distant cousin, so she never did become Lady D'Arbanvilliers. Rebecca's sisters Arrabella ("Bella") and Gwendollyn ("Dolly") grew up to marry the abacus and tally-stick tycoon

Bartholomew Cleaver (remembered as the inventor of the "end-user license") and the decadent poet D'Arcy Guillaume, respectively. Rebecca's nephews Richard Cleaver ("Clever Dick") and William Guillaume ("Wicked William") inherited her speech impediment. Guinevere Guillaume ("Gee-Gee"), William's twin sister, evaded this family curse and became an artists' model, notorious for her affairs with Fantômas, Pablo Picasso, Colonel Sebastian Moran, and Barbara Stanwyck. Guinevere was the first woman to dance the Charleston on the wing of a monoplane. Rebecca's granddaughter Theresa worked as a striptease artiste under the name "Tiger Sharkey" and starred in the underground classic stag film *Sixth Form Girls in Chains* before marrying a Conservative Member of Parliament (see: "Soho Golem"). Theresa's niece Andrea was the breakout star of the "reality TV" program *It's a Madhouse!* (see: "Going to Series"). Andrea survived well into the third series of *Celebrity Madhouse*—but became a national pariah when she stabbed a glove-puppet worn by a popular children's entertainer.

GENEVIÈVE DIEUDONNÉ. A long-lived adventuress. For her lives and loves in other timelines, see *Anno Dracula, Dracula Cha Cha Cha,* "Castle in the Desert," and "The Other Side of Midnight" for another involvement with the Diogenes Club, and the books collected in Jack Yeovil's *The Vampire Genevieve* for a further-flung reality. For more of the Geneviève featured in "The Big Fish" and "Cold Snap," see "Sorcerer Conjurer Wizard Witch" and *Seven Stars*. Little-known fact: Krzystztof Kieslowski tried to persuade her to star in ~~Trois~~ *Quatre Couleurs: Ultra-Violette*.

THE DIOGENES CLUB. Sir Arthur Conan Doyle introduced the Diogenes Club in "The Greek Interpreter," along with its most prominent member, Mycroft Holmes. Later, in "The Bruce-Partington Plans," we learn that not only does brother Mycroft work for the British government but, under certain circumstances, he *is* the British government. The notion that the Diogenes Club is the ancestor of Ian Fleming's Universal Export, a covert front for British Intelligence, was first made by Billy Wilder and I.A.L. Diamond in *The Private Life of Sherlock Holmes*. The timeline of *The Secret Files of the Diogenes Club* and *The Man From the Diogenes Club* is shared by "Sorcerer Conjurer Wizard Witch" and *Seven Stars*. Separate alternate timeline versions feature in the *Anno Dracula* cycle and "The Man on the Clapham Omnibus."

CONSTANT DRACHE. East German-born visionary architect, and probable diabolist. His buildings win awards, but are notoriously uncomfortable to live and work in. See: "Organ Donors," "Going to Series." Also, an alternate timeline equivalent of the villain of Jack Yeovil's *Drachenfels*.

THE GUMSHOE. The narrator of "The Big Fish" returns in "The Trouble With Barrymore," an episode of *Seven Stars*. An *Anno Dracula* universe version of the character appears in the story "Castle in the Desert." If he isn't Raymond Chandler's Philip Marlowe, then he has a lot in common— including a wife, an office, and that problem with frequently getting hit on the head—with him.

ANTHONY JAGO. The Reverend Anthony John Jago, a unique Talent, is the major character in *Jago*. An ancestor, John Jago, features in *Anno Dracula*. Much of his eventual belief system comes from the Victorian Reverend Henry James Prince, though his paranormal abilites have much in common with the novelist John Morlar (see: *The Medusa Touch*, by Peter Van Greenaway).

RICHARD JEPERSON. The Most Valued Member of the Diogenes Club in the 1970s. See the stories collected in *The Man From the Diogenes Club* and *Seven Stars*. Alternate timeline versions appear in "Who Dares Wins: Anno Dracula 1980" and "The Man on the Clapham Omnibus."

CATRIONA KAYE. Catriona first appeared in my play *My One Little Murder Can't Do Any Harm* (1981). She also pops up in *Jago* (which features the Mystery of Swastika Girl), *The Bloody Red Baron: Anno Dracula 1918*, "The Pierce-Arrow Stalled, and...," *Seven Stars*, and "Sorcerer Conjurer Wizard Witch."

KENTISH GLORY. An adventuress of the 1930s, who took her name from a variety of moth. See "Sorcerer Conjurer Wizard Witch." She briefly teamed with Dr. Shade, and later married him. Played by Valerie Hobson in *Dr. Shade's Phantom Taxi Mystery* (1936). Not to be confused with Penny Stamp, Dr. Shade's *other* assistant.

SEWELL HEAD. This psychic prodigy is the focal character of "Swellhead" in *The Man From the Diogenes Club*. An alternate timeline version appears in "Pitbull Brittan."

DR. MYRA LARK. A psychologist more interested in the *uses* of insane people than their cures. See: "You Don't Have to Be Mad…" in *The Man From the Diogenes Club* and "Going to Series."

DEREK LEECH. The controversial multimedia tycoon appears most prominently in in "The Original Dr. Shade," "SQPR," "Organ Donors," "Where the Bodies Are Buried 3: Black and White and Red All Over," "Going to Series," and *The Quorum*. At his most diabolical, he is the narrator of *Life's Lottery*.

KEITH MARION. The mixed-up fellow appears in *Life's Lottery*. One of his many, many selves features in "The Intervention."

INSPECTOR HENRY MIST. The canny Victorian policeman first tangled with "publicist" Billy Quinn in "A Drug on the Market." Head of Scotland Yard's Bureau of Queer Complaints from 1892 to 1911.

MAUREEN MOUNTMAIN. Descendant of the Mountmain family, a dynasty of Irish black magicians active over several centuries. She was the mother of Mimsy, the daughter Richard Jeperson didn't know about until 2006. See: *Seven Stars*.

KATE REED. Katharine Reed was originally going to be a character in *Dracula*, but Bram Stoker never managed to include her. To make up for that, she is prominent in the *Anno Dracula* cycle. For more of the Kate of "The Gypsies in the Wood," see "The Mummy's Heart" in *Seven Stars*.

FREDERICK REGENT. A London policeman, seconded to work with the Diogenes Club in "The End of the Pier Show." By the time of "Swellhead," he had risen to the rank of Chief Inspector—despite marrying a stripper.

SUSAN RODWAY a.k.a. SUSAN AMES. After demonstrating various paranormal abilities in her early teens, Susan became a minor celebrity and the subject of a trashy paperback biography *The Mind Beyond*. After being caught in an apparent hoax, she retreated from the public eye. See: *Jago*.

DR. SHADE. For various incarnations of this character (or holders of this title), see: "The Original Dr. Shade" and *The Quorum*. It seems many equivalent figures have operated over the years. Jonathan Chambers and his son James both worked as Dr. Shade. Christine Chambers—Jonathan's granddaughter, James's niece—current bearer of the Shade Legacy, calls herself Lady Shade.

LOUISE MAGELLAN TEAZLE. Author of popular children's books: *Weezie and the Gloomy Ghost, The Haunting of Chasemoor Grange School*, etc. Once caused a minor controversy by referring to the works of Enid Blyton as "utter piffle" on a BBC Radio broadcast. A long-time associate of Catriona Kaye, she lived in the Hollow, Sutton Mallet—purportedly, the most haunted house in Britain. The Louise Magellan Teazle Appreciation Society Web-site is at http://www.johnnyalucard.com/ghost.html.

VANESSA. No last name known. Latterly, Mrs. Alexander Coates. Richard Jeperson's closest associate, well-remembered by everybody who ever met her. See *The Man From the Diogenes Club*. Rumour has it that Mrs. Coates is the current Chair of the Ruling Cabal—though the Diogenes Club supposedly closed its doors for the last time in 1984, shortly after the reelection of Margaret Thatcher.

THE UNDERTAKING. More is revealed about these mystery men, "the undertakers in smoked glasses," in "Sorcerer Conjurer Wizard Witch." Officially, out of business. Then again, officially, they were never in business. They maintained the Mausoleum, a museum-cum-prison on Egdon Heath.

HEATHER WILDING. Derek Leech's executive assistant appears in "The Serial Murders" (in *The Man From the Diogenes Club*) and "Going to Series." Along with her twin sister Priscilla, she's in *The Quorum* too. She was manager of the Free Martha Stewart campaign fund.

EDWIN WINTHROP. WWI veteran-cum-manipulative-psychic investigator Edwin Winthrop first appeared, with his girlfriend Catriona Kaye (q.v.), in the play *My One Little Murder Can't Do Any Harm* (1981), in which he was played by me and exposed a villain by feigning his own death during a séance. He is a leading character in *The Bloody Red Baron: Anno Dracula 1918*, and shows up also in *Jago*, Jack Yeovil's *Demon Download*, *Seven Stars* (an account of his death can be found in the episode "The Biafran Bank Manager"), and "Sorcerer Conjurer Wizard Witch." Little-known fact: He finally shot down Hans von Hellhund, the Demon Ace, in a dogfight over Molesey Reservoir in 1938.

ABOUT THE AUTHOR

Kim Newman is a novelist, critic and broadcaster. His fiction includes *The Night Mayor*, *Bad Dreams*, *Jago*, the *Anno Dracula* novels and stories, *The Quorum*, *The Original Dr Shade and Other Stories*, *Famous Monsters*, *Seven Stars*, *Unforgivable Stories*, *Dead Travel Fast*, *Life's Lottery*, *Back in the USSA* (with Eugene Byrne), *Where the Bodies Are Buried*, *Doctor Who: Time and Relative* and *The Man From the Diogenes Club* under his own name and *The Vampire Genevieve* and *Orgy of the Blood Parasites* as Jack Yeovil. His non-fiction books include *Nightmare Movies*, *Ghastly Beyond Belief* (with Neil Gaiman), *Horror: 100 Best Books* (with Stephen Jones), *Wild West Movies*, *The BFI Companion to Horror*, *Millennium Movies* and BFI Classics studies of *Cat People* and *Doctor Who*. He is a contributing editor to *Sight & Sound* and *Empire* magazines and has written and broadcast widely on a range of topics, scripting radio documentaries about Val Lewton and role-playing games and TV programs about movie heroes and Sherlock Holmes. His short story "Week Woman" was adapted for the TV series *The Hunger* and he has directed and written a tiny short film *Missing Girl* (http://www.johnnyalucard.com/missinggirl.html). He has won the Bram Stoker Award, the International Horror Critics Award, the British Science Fiction Award and the British Fantasy Award but doesn't like to boast about them. He was born in Brixton (London), grew up in the West Country, went to University near Brighton and now lives in Islington (London). His official web-site, "Dr. Shade's Laboratory" can be found at www.johnnyalucard.com.